Stella Chaplin lives in London.
This is her first novel.

Cashier: JANET

```
                                      £
*MATTHEWS,FOR,BETTER,
CHAPLIN,LIP KISSES            5.99
*A4 POLYPRO N'BK BLUE         4.99
                              3.49

3 BAL DUE                    14.47

CASH                         20.00
CHANGE                        5.53

2878  004  27 4416 13:55 17SEP01
```

Lip Kisses

Stella Chaplin

ORION

Copyright © Stella Chaplin 2001

The right of Stella Chaplin to be identified as the author of
this work has been asserted by her in accordance with
the Copyright, Designs and Patents Act 1988.

First published in Great Britain in 2001 by
Orion
An imprint of Orion Books Ltd
Orion House, 5 Upper St Martin's Lane, London WC2H 9EA

ISBN 0 752845985

A CIP catalogue record for this book is available
from the British Library

Typeset at The Spartan Press Ltd
Lymington, Hants
Printed by Clays Ltd, St Ives plc

one

'Elke!'

'Elke!'

'Over here, Elke!'

'Give us a smile, darlin'!'

'This way, Elke!'

When I was at school and people asked me what I wanted to do when I grew up, standing on an aluminium ladder shouting at supermodels wasn't exactly top of my list.

'Can you lean forward, Elke?'

'Oi, Elke! Show us yer tits!'

Tonight it's a book launch. Another freak of nature with legs like flagpoles is sharing her diet secrets (actually her ghost-writer's diet secrets because a regime of cocaine, Ecstasy and sticking your fingers down your throat wouldn't get the nutritionist's seal of approval and be serialised in the *Daily Mail*) and I'm up on my ladder in Harrods with my camera ready, waiting for her to pout in my general direction.

I don't shout. I'm a girl. Girls don't shout 'Show us yer tits!' at other girls. It's just not polite. I know that sooner or later Elke will look my way and when she does, I'll take my snap, fold up my ladder, bike the negs over to the paper in time for tomorrow's edition and go home. That's me, there in the second row. The one with the purple trousers.

It's weird how life turns out. I can still remember the day I got my first camera for my fourteenth birthday and suddenly everything just clicked. If you see what I mean. This isn't what

I thought I'd end up doing, but it pays the mortgage: book launches; press shows; film premieres. People arriving, people leaving. Girls in tiny bikinis holding enormous cardboard cheques as proof that you could win a million pounds if you buy *The Ledger* every day this week. Daytime TV stars pretending to be digging their garden (with plants supplied by the stylist). Soap stars pretending to be redecorating their living rooms (with paint, wallpaper, furniture and usually the entire house supplied by the stylist). Children's TV presenters showing us what they've bought at the supermarket. Earth-shattering stuff. Look out, Kate Adie.

The flash guns stop for a few moments while the publicist, a thin, blonde, fluttery woman who looks terrified of the Finnish Amazon she's supposed to be in charge of, anxiously rearranges the pile of books by Elke's side. A man with a black pointed goatee swishes in to blot some more powder on Elke's tiny little nose (or quite possibly in it) and the gang of snappers surrounding her jostle for position again with their stepladders.

This ladder thing always makes me laugh. I suppose once upon a time a photographer – probably a short photographer like me – had the bright idea that if he stood on a ladder he'd be able to see over all the other photographers' heads. But of course what happened was that everybody else cottoned on to this and got ladders of their own. So now we're all back where we started from, except we have to carry a stupid aluminium stepladder with us wherever we go. Like we didn't have enough to carry as it was.

On the other side of the scrum I suddenly notice another photographer I haven't seen before. A young guy. Maybe my age-ish. Not one of the drunken old scroats you usually get at these dos. He's wearing a fawn Carhartt jacket and Diesel jeans and he's got floppy dark brown hair just flicking over his collar. I'm a sucker for long hair. Not too long, you under-stand. I mean, not Spinal Tap or anything. Grungy but clean. The kind of hair I'd have if I was a guy.

He's looking at me and I glance back. Just for a second. Just long enough to make a Connection.

You know about the Connection, don't you? Of course you do.

It was a long time before I understood what the Connection was. I spend most of my life looking at people – that's my job – but the Connection is a one-in-a-million occurrence. Actually, I haven't really calculated the odds. I'm just guessing here. The Connection is when you look at a guy and he looks at you and, in a nanosecond, or even less, a micro-nano-second, some kind of an electrical current flows between you like a magnetic force. And you know and he knows beyond a shadow of a doubt that you will make love. Maybe not that night. Maybe not tomorrow. But one day. It's an agreement. A secret. A promise. A law of physics. It's the most exciting thing in the world. And it's better than sex, because it's all still to come.

Elke tosses me a bored smile and I snap away. She flicks back her new chestnut hair, points her cheekbones towards the light and bends her knee half an inch to reveal several yards of creamy white thigh through the slit in her Dolce & Gabbana sheath dress. Ta very much. That's me done.

The publicist calls time in a nervous little voice and Elke gets hustled away by the Armani army – four brutes in suits who can't quite believe their luck. I take one last snap of her checking out her reflection in the brass wall fittings and start to pack up my things. The paper will probably never use it anyway. A supermodel on her own? Not kissing anybody? Not crying? Not pregnant? Not accidentally revealing her cellulite? Where's the story in that? Oh, well.

I run downstairs to where the bike's waiting, hand over my roll of film, then run back to collect my things, hoping nobody has stolen my camera.

At least it pays better than the local paper where I started out. I got a job there straight out of college until they were swallowed up by another bigger paper and most of us were made redundant. So I touted my portfolio around the nationals until *The Ledger* took me on. They weren't my first choice, or even my fifth choice, but it was a job and it would tide me over until something better came along. Four years later, I'm still there.

Waiters are already hovering with trays of champagne. Perhaps just one glass, then. It's only seven o'clock. Debbie, the reporter I'm working with, comes trotting over on her three-inch heels. She's a little bruiser from Bermondsey, cunningly disguised as a lady-who-lunches. Or, in Debbie's case, a lady-what-lunches. Actually, a lady-what-lurches would be nearer the mark.

'Wotcha get, doll?'

'The usual. Supermodel looking hungry and pissed off. Have you done your interview yet?'

'Nah. That's where I'm going now. She's doing them all at 'er hotel. All I want to ask her about is 'er alcoholic dad and 'er implants. Did they look like they was leakin' to you?'

'Er, no. But I don't think you can actually see them leaking.'

Debbie looks confused. 'Can't you? Well where does it go then?'

'I think it – you know – sort of leaks inside your body.'

Debbie stares at me like I'm mad. 'That's disgusting!' she barks and totters off after Elke. Sometimes I wonder about Debbie. Doesn't she ever read the papers?

I help myself to a glass of champagne. 'Oh, thank you so much,' I beam at the waiter. There's something about press launches that always makes me come over all Audrey Hepburn. Just to make it perfectly clear that even though a low-life tabloid may pay my wages, they haven't bought my soul.

I sip my champagne, confident that the waiter has managed to read the subliminal message I have just sent him and will now be running back into the kitchen to pass on the word to all his waiter chums.

4

'Zey are all scum, I tell you. Scum! But ze beautiful girl in ze purple trousers – ah, she ecz a real lady!'

Huddles of liggers have already formed around the book displays. Packs of hackettes in their uniform of black suits, scoffing spring rolls and leaving wet-glass rings on the piles of Elke's books on the tables around them. I look around for a familiar face. Who are all these people? Where do they all come from? I must do, on average, six of these jobs every week and I never speak to any of this lot but they all seem to know each other. Was there some giant lig five years ago when all the hacks in London were herded into Wembley Arena and formally introduced to one another? I must have been away that day.

The guy with the long hair and the Carhartt jacket suddenly appears at my side. Well, what a surprise.

'Where'd you get the champagne?' he says.

'Oh, they were around here a minute ago,' I say breezily, looking for a waiter. 'Would you like some of mine?'

Without hesitating, he takes a long sip from my glass and then hands it back to me. 'Where are you from?'

'*The Ledger*. Lindy Usher.' I sip my champagne casually. I've only known him two seconds and already we're sharing germs. That's what the Connection does, you see – cuts through all that boring preamble and gets right down to business.

'Nick Weber. The *Standard*.'

'I've seen your by-line.' One pro to another. He's got fantastic green eyes. 'I haven't seen you around before,' I tell him.

'No. I normally just do the political circuit, but the diary guy's wife is having a baby.'

'Oh, I see.' What would he be? Six foot two? Six foot three? I hadn't realised when he was up his ladder just how tall he was. I don't know what it is about tall men. If you rewind the video of my life, it's littered with tall men. Not big, just tall. I'm only five foot four and I'm so impressed by anyone clever enough to grow above six foot, it's quite pathetic. As though they've got there by sheer brilliance. As though short men just haven't tried hard enough. When I remember all the times my heart has been broken by a guy who's six foot three, I get a stiff neck just thinking about it.

One of the waiters refills my glass and gives Nick a glass of his own.

'Cheers,' we say. Clink.

He's telling me about the conference he covered earlier in the day, how he reckons he might have the front page tomorrow. How he's been at the *Standard* for years but they've just put him on staff. He's really working hard to impress them. You don't say. Fascinating. How old is he anyway? He could be twenty-seven – he's got that rumpled little boy look about him.

He's standing very close to me. His hand is resting on the wall just to the side of my head. Probably went to public school. Very clean fingernails. Talks quite posh. Not that posh: a nice, deep voice. He could be thirty-two – he sounds like a grown-up.

Somehow I seem to have finished my second glass of champagne in five seconds. Oh look, there's the waiter. 'Thank you so much.'

I tell Nick how I photographed Charlie Dimmock that morning. He leans closer. Laughs in all the right places, picks up a stray piece of cotton off my jacket and lightly brushes it away. For the millionth time I wish I worked on a glossy magazine and not some scurrilous daily rag. He probably goes out with girls called Arabella.

'Is this your last job tonight?' I ask. Just asking.

'Yeah, I'm done for the day. I'll probably just go straight home after this. Get something to eat.' Lots of eye contact.

'Me too.' Did I shave my legs this morning? Damn. I can't remember.

'Do you need a lift anywhere?'

I think of my car in the car park just around the corner.

'That would be really kind of you,' I say. 'I got a lift here with the writer, but she's already left.'

I can always pick up my car tomorrow on the way into work. It'll probably only cost me . . . oh, £30 for overnight parking in Knightsbridge. No more than £50 anyway.

'More champagne, madam?'

'Why not!' Not so much Audrey Hepburn now. More like Audrey Roberts in *Corrie*. 'Could you be an absolute darling and send over the man with the little prawns?'

'Certainly, madam.'

'I'm starving, aren't you?'

'Starving,' Nick agrees. He takes a tempura prawn off the tray and hands it to me so that our fingers touch just for a moment.

'Perhaps another glass of champagne before we go?' he says.

'Great idea.' When the waiter goes past Nick grabs the bottle and we don't leave until it's empty. I tell him I've got to shoot Barbara Windsor's new waxwork at Madame Tussaud's in the morning and he seems to find this hilarious. He's doing William Hague and for some reason we both find this even funnier.

'What if they cast William Hague as Phil Mitchell?' he says, and I have to hold on to his arm because I'm laughing so much.

An hour later, as we stagger through Harrods' bedding department on our way to the back exit, it becomes apparent that my legs have decided to function independently of each other and are now heading in separate directions. This makes carrying an aluminium ladder and a heavy camera bag rather problematic.

I have a glimpse of the far-off future. Nick and I make love and we have a child – a beautiful curly-haired doll with her father's fabulous green eyes and floppy brown hair. 'Mummy, Mummy,' she asks me one day, 'where did I come from?' And I tell her truthfully, 'Harrods, darling.'

'What's so funny?' says Nick.

'Nothing,' I giggle stupidly. 'Private joke.'

We hit the fresh air and Nick props me up against the side of the building so I won't fall over. 'You shouldn't drive,' I tell him. 'You're in no state.'

He puts his thumb against my lips telling me to be quiet. 'Shh,' he whispers and his eyes meet mine. I don't look away. Leaning closer. Closer. 'Shh.'

Then he's kissing me. Delicious, warm kisses tasting of champagne and Marlboro Lights. Or am I kissing him? A mingling of lips and tongues. I can't tell where his mouth ends and mine begins. His eyelashes softly brush my cheek. Nick's fingers interlace with mine, stroking my hand slowly, one finger at a time, sealing our agreement. I'm putty in his hands. Intoxicated. I'll follow this kiss anywhere. I can feel the imprint of every brick against my back as his body presses against me, pushing me harder against the wall. My hand under his jacket. The heat of his back through his shirt. I'm on a magic carpet flying far away from the Knightsbridge smog to a place where nothing else exists except this kiss. Until the blast of a taxi horn behind me and I'm jolted back to sober reality.

'I'm sorry. I'm sorry, I can't do this,' I blurt out. 'I've just remembered. I'm married.'

two

I lay in bed and tried not to move. There was a very large lead ball rolling around in my skull but if I kept my head very still I could almost stop it from banging against my eyes. Perhaps if I held my breath the pain would go away.

'Would you like a cup of tea?'

I couldn't shake my head. Too painful. I wagged my finger to say no. That hurt too. Andrew sat down on the bed looking very concerned. His eyebrows actually go up in the middle when he's concerned, just like they do in cartoons.

'Oh, poor bunny.'

'I think it's food poisoning,' I croaked. 'I had a prawn last night. I thought it smelt funny.' Nothing wrong with my lying reflexes then. All in perfect working order.

'Do you want me to phone work for you?'

'Would you? Speak to Geoff on the picture desk. Tell him I'll be in after lunch. Tell him he'll have to get Peter to do the Madame Tussaud's job.'

'Do you want me to call the doctor?'

'No, I'll be fine. I just have to lie very, very still.'

'OK. I'll call you later. Love you, bunny.'

'I love you too.'

He kissed me gently on the forehead – ouch – and tiptoed downstairs.

That's Andrew. My husband. Isn't he fantastic? We've been married almost three years. That's three years compared to ten years of dating and being at the mercy of the Connection. Bugger the bloody Connection. I didn't know it would still happen after I got married. Nobody ever told me that. Now what was I supposed to do? Thank God I had come to my senses in time. Nick had been shocked, as you would be, but actually very gentlemanly about it. Flagging down a taxi. Saying he hoped I'd be all right. Me trying to get the ladder into the taxi sideways.

Oh God, I'm going to end up like one of those mad women who walk up and down the Kilburn High Road wearing shoes made of string and newspapers and shouting at shop windows.

With me and Andrew it's weird, because the Connection didn't come into it when we met. That's how I knew our relationship was based on real love and not just lust or electricity or laser beams or phases of the moon, or whatever irresistible force of nature powers the Connection. With me and Andrew it happened gradually. It wasn't such an instant attraction. Well, not on my part anyway.

We met on a skiing holiday in Austria six years ago and we were staying in the same chalet. There were twelve of us altogether. There was Jill, my best friend since Sixth Form, and her boyfriend Simon, plus Simon's sister Iris who's a trainee solicitor, and a bunch of Iris's mates who all skied like maniacs. Andrew's an accountant so as far as I was concerned we had nothing in common. Plus he's only five foot nine so he kind of swooped in under my radar.

I had just broken up with Justin (six foot three, floppy black hair) and was still enjoying moping about and wallowing in self-pity. I'd been seeing Justin for almost five months (something of a record for me) before I got the 'I'm not ready for a relationship right now' speech which, in this particular case, translated as: 'My ex-girlfriend who I forgot to tell you about gets back from Australia tomorrow.'

Anyway, Andrew trailed around me for days before I even noticed he was doing it. At breakfast in the chalet somehow he'd always be at my end of the table. Whenever I went to catch the ski lift, he'd suddenly appear in line, ready to take the seat beside me. Jill and I were learning to snowboard and instead of hitting the mogul runs and going off-piste with the other lads Andrew announced that he wanted to learn to snowboard too – even though he'd just bought a brand new pair of wildly expensive ski-boots.

There were only two bathrooms in the chalet and every evening Andrew would saunter across the living room to have his shower, bare-chested with a towel around his waist so I'd get the full benefit of his chunky little physique. Every night in the bar down the road, there he was, with a conveniently empty bar-stool beside him waiting for me.

Walking back to the chalet one night, he even held my hand but I just assumed this was so neither of us would slip on the icy footpath. I didn't read the signs. I didn't want to read the signs. He just wasn't my type.

Then, on the last day, Jill and I decided we'd collected enough bruises between us to last a lifetime. Nobody had warned us that when you fall over snowboarding it's like being shot out of a cannon and we'd both fallen over about thirty times a day. So we rented skis for the day and went off with the rest of the group thinking we'd be in for a nice relaxing time. Of course, they'd been skiing all week and Jill and I hadn't been on skis for two years. Coming down a red run, the others were way ahead of us and I was making pathetic snowplough turns that covered every inch of snow available. I vaguely remembered an instructor telling me once that whenever you're scared, the best thing to do is just lean down the hill. I didn't want to be left up there on my own so I overdid it, hit a patch of ice and slid 100 yards down the mountain on my face with my skis trailing behind me. Lindy Usher: Human Toboggan. But a funny thing happened as I was sliding. I realised that the thought upper-most in my mind, well, after 'I hope there isn't a cliff at the bottom of this mountain' was 'I hope Andrew's watching this'.

I don't know what made me think he'd be impressed by what I have to admit was a truly spectacular wipe-out, but he was. When I stopped sliding and cleaned the snow out of my goggles, he was there helping me to my feet and laughing so hard he almost split his salopettes.

That night we made a snowman, just the two of us, and as we tumbled down together into the snow he kissed me. It was freezing but not as cool as I was. I let him kiss me once, then smacked a snowball down on top of his head – ha! – and ran back inside. He was staying an extra week, but the next morning I let him get up at five a.m. for the honour of helping me carry my suitcase downstairs to the bus. I didn't even kiss him goodbye. He wasn't my type.

I didn't tell Jill he'd kissed me. I didn't want her to think my standards had slipped so low after Justin that I went around snogging accountants. But at the airport while we were waiting for our flight to be called, two of his mates, Russell and Greg, asked me if I planned to see Andrew when I got back to London.

'No, I don't think so,' I said airily. 'It's just a holiday romance.'

'You know Andrew's crazy about you, don't you?' said Greg. 'He's very sincere. He's not messing about. You really ought to give him a chance. Nice guys like Andrew don't grown on trees.'

That's when I remembered how I'd sent Andrew out into the blizzard one night to buy a backgammon set from the supermarket down the road when I was bored and fancied a game. I remembered how he'd volunteered to keep me company back down the mountain the day my bindings broke, missing half a day of his own boarding in the process. I thought of his hopeful, hurt little face as the bus had driven off that morning. And then I thought about all the shitty bastards I'd been out with in my life. No wonder I thought Andrew wasn't my type. He was a nice guy! I'd never met one of those before!

All the way home on the plane, I was kicking myself. What had I done? Was it too late? Would he ever forgive me?

The next day, Sunday, I spent the whole day pacing up and down my flat in a state of high anxiety until it was seven-thirty Austrian time and I knew they'd all be gathering in the bar before dinner. Then I phoned the chalet, hoping the telephone number on the back of the complimentary postcard was actually correct.

Adam, one of the ski-reps, answered the phone.

'Can I speak to Andrew please?'

'Oh, hi. Is that you, Lindy?'

I was gobsmacked. If they'd asked, I was going to pretend to be Andrew's sister but everyone else obviously had us pegged as an item – even before I knew it myself.

On our first date, instead of taking me out to a trendy restaurant, he cooked me dinner at his place in Maida Vale: roast poussin, mangetout and baby sweetcorn. He even made gravy. When I arrived he was still making the chocolate mousse for dessert. I took a photo of him holding up the Magimix because I'd never seen a man make chocolate mousse before.

I was momentarily gripped by panic. What if he was gay?

But after dinner he did a pretty good impersonation of a heterosexual – twice, in fact. I was prepared to over-look the fact that he insisted on loading the dishwasher first.

'Do you think he's good looking?' I asked Jill, showing her the Magimix photos.

'Not good looking, exactly.'

'But he's not bad looking.'

'Oh no, he's not bad looking.'

'He has nice eyes, don't you think?'

'Oh, terrific eyes. Brown eyes are nice. Very romantic. Does he make you laugh?'

'His clothes do.'

'So you can buy him new clothes.'

'You're right.'

'What's he like in, um, you know?'

'Oh, really quite good actually.'

'Well, it's always good at first, isn't it?' said Jill. 'Three times a night, backwards, sideways, on the fridge. Doesn't last though, does it?'

'Doesn't it?' I hadn't actually been out with anyone long enough for that to wear off. I looked at the photos again thoughtfully.

'So would you say he's attractive?' I asked again.

'How much did you say he earned?'

'Forty grand.'

'Trust me,' said Jill. 'He's gorgeous.'

I couldn't get over the novelty of going out with a man who actually adored me. It was amazing. Why hadn't I thought of it before? It didn't seem to matter to Andrew what I did or what I looked like; as far as he was concerned, I was his perfect little bunny-bun.

I remember coming home from the gym one day and telling him about a woman I'd seen in the changing room.

'She had an amazing figure when she had her clothes on,' I said, 'but then when I saw her coming out of the shower, she turned out to have really bad cellulite.'

'What's cellulite?' Andrew wanted to know. I couldn't understand how anyone could live in the same world as women's magazines and still not know what cellulite was but I explained it to him anyway.

'You know – it's that lumpy, bumpy fat stuff women get on their thighs.'

He looked at me absolutely panic-stricken. 'Oh, but you won't get that will you, bunny?' he wailed.

I stared at him in utter amazement. He must have seen me naked at least four hundred times by this point and yet somehow my ripple-effect thighs had completely escaped his attention.

'No, darling, of course I won't,' I assured him, thanking the Lord for short-sighted men.

Well, I had to marry him after that, didn't I? After we'd been going out for two years, he whisked me away to a hotel in the country, produced an engagement ring and went down on one knee and everything. I was crying. He was crying. We were so happy.

My parents adored Andrew too. Especially when I told them that when he was made a partner, as he surely would be in maybe five or six years' time, I'd be able to pack up my aluminium stepladder for good and move to the country and breed horses. Perhaps even get a couple of goats.

So what on earth was I thinking, about to throw all that away just because of that old eyes-meeting-across-a-crowded-room bollocks? Good grief, I'd nearly committed adultery! That's right up there with murder and thou shalt not covet thy neighbour's ass.

I could hear him pottering happily about downstairs, clattering teacups – he's such a cheerful little thing. That's what I loved about him. He'd got a really high-pressured job but nothing seemed to wind him up or get him down. I'd seen him cross but I'd never seen him really lose his temper like the people I worked with, who'd scream at the top of their lungs all day long if somebody so much as borrowed their stapler. I wondered what he'd say if he found out I'd kissed another man last night. A total stranger I'd picked up at a photo call. I wondered if he'd lose his temper then. Or just screw up his eyebrows some more and offer to make me another cup of tea.

I was the worst wife in the world. How could I have let myself get into that situation last night? Just because I'd drunk an entire bottle of champagne was no excuse for snogging the first bloke who came along. What was I – a student?

God, he was gorgeous though.

No! No! I'm not going to think that.

When he touched me it was like I was on fire . . .

What are you doing?

He was like an animal.

Will you shut up!

I knew it from the moment I looked at him.

Stop it, stop it, stop it!

And so did he.

Remember your wedding vows – to keep yourself truly and only and all that.

I hope he didn't think I was fat.

Andrew doesn't deserve this.

Such a good kisser – mmmmmh.

You've got to stop thinking about him.

Mmmmmmmmh.

Think about Andrew.

Andrew doesn't kiss me like that.

That's not what I meant.

It's nothing like that with Andrew.

Andrew is your husband.

I wish Andrew had floppy hair.

Floppy hair is no basis for a marriage.

Andrew is so polite in bed.

You can't expect fireworks all the time.

With Andrew it's more like 'Would you like your orgasm now, bunny?'

Now you're just exaggerating.

Andrew doesn't taste of champagne and cigarettes.

You'd kill him if he smoked. You hate smoking.

He wouldn't kiss me up against a wall in the middle of Knightsbridge like Nick.

You've had men like Nick. They've broken your heart every time.

But he's so tall!

Will you listen to reason? You're married, so get a grip on

yourself before I kick you out of bed and you land on your stupid drunken head.

'I'm never going to drink again,' I vowed.

three

'Yes! Yes! Yes! Yes! YES!!!'

You could hear Elaine right across the office even though her office door was firmly closed.

'Yes! Yes! Yes!' She was banging the desk now with both hands. Slap! Slap! Slap! The door opened and Geoff the picture editor slunk out sheepishly, clutching four packets of transparencies, and came back to sit opposite me.

'She liked the gardening photos, then?' I said.

'Loved them,' said Geoff.

That was one thing you had to say about Elaine. She was very enthusiastic about her job. And bonkers of course. Completely hat-stand but extremely enthusiastic. Nothing – and I mean nothing – gave her more pleasure than a big juicy piece of gossip she could splash all over the front page.

If it was true, then so much the better.

I remembered when I'd come for the interview for the job, Geoff had flicked through my portfolio and asked me how I'd feel about working for Elaine Lewis. I'd sat there in my best suit choosing my words carefully.

'Well, I think she's an inspiration to women in this profession,' I began. 'She's shown what's possible through hard work, intelligence and determination and I understand that she's also increased the paper's year-on-year circulation by three per cent.'

Geoff snorted. 'She's a cunt. Bear that in mind at all times. Watch your back and don't let her fuck you over.'

*

Her office opened suddenly and Elaine swung around the doorway like a lap dancer around a fireman's pole. All eyeliner and cleavage in a red Chanel suit. 'Where's my splash?' she was screeching. She had a voice that would scrape paint off a battleship. 'Which of you lazy bastards has got my splash?'

The entire office kept their heads down, riveted to their computer screens, furiously clicking their mouses to simulate frantic productivity, trying desperately not to make eye contact with crazy Elaine. But, like a hyena stalking her prey in the African bush, she instinctively smelt out the weakest among us.

'Tony!' she barked at the showbiz editor who had failed to make a single story stand up in over three weeks. 'What've you got for me?'

'Yes, I'm still chasing that drug thing with Ryan from BoysRUs.' Tony tried to sound dynamic, but you could hear his voice actually shaking. 'Apparently he used to deal pot, er marijuana, uh, cannabis, when he was at school. I'm, uh, waiting for his ex-flatmate to call me back.' Tap-dancing madly. Improvising. He'd been waiting for the flatmate to call him back for over a month. I could see Tony praying that Elaine wouldn't walk around to his desk and see that the only thing on his computer screen was his CV which he was continually updating and embellishing.

Elaine's eyes narrowed. She looked spectacularly unimpressed. Fortunately for Tony she had the attention span of a five year old and she'd already forgotten all about him and was marching off to the loo.

I sipped my soluble Disprin and flicked through the Celebrity Diary to see who was coming into town. I'd staggered into work around midday feeling very guilty and full of apologies about a gynaecologist's appointment that had completely slipped my mind.

I knew Geoff didn't believe a word of it but I also knew he was so terrified I might say the words 'smear test' that he'd rather die than cross-examine me.

'Oh my gosh,' I gasped. 'Natalie's coming over!'

'Natalie who?' Geoff wanted to know.

'Natalie Brown. She's from *Don't Call Us*. It's on Channel 4.'

'Nobody watches Channel 4,' said Geoff mildly.

Normally, I would have put Geoff right on this point and explained that *Don't Call Us* was one of the top-rating sitcoms in America and that Natalie Brown was now a huge star. But instead I said, 'You're right. Nobody watches Channel 4. I heard they're taking the show off the air soon anyway.'

What I didn't tell Geoff was that I knew Natalie Brown. That she'd been my best friend at school before she'd gone to drama college and then to LA looking for fame and fortune. It had taken her a long time, but she'd actually done it. But I knew that if Elaine got wind of the fact that I knew a real live TV star, I would be expected to ring Natalie and ask her to share with *The Ledger* full details of how she'd lost her virginity, her pain over the break-up of her first marriage, her heartbreak over her inability to have children as well as her New Year's resolutions, her favourite diet tips and the contents of her garbage bin. Elaine had a thing about celebrity garbage bins which I'd never quite understood. Either way, my life would be made hell and so would Natalie's. Even though Natalie and I hadn't spoken to each other in over ten years, I wouldn't wish Elaine on my worst enemy. I casually folded up the diary page and hid it in my bag so no one else would find it.

I heard Elaine stomping back through the office and realised with horror that she was looking straight at me. Had she read my mind?

'Lindy, get yer ass in my office. Debbie, you too.'

What had I done? Everyone looked at me and Debbie with a mixture of pity and gloating: sorry for us but really, really glad it wasn't them who'd been called in.

Debbie and I sat down on Elaine's white leather sofa and

wondered what was coming. Were we being fired or promoted? There was no telling with Elaine.

'Whaddya know about Nigel Napier?' she demanded.

'Not much,' I admitted. Nigel Napier was a daytime television presenter whose latest show *That's My Dog!* was generally regarded as a bit of a comedown for a former newsreader. Even if he was going bald. 'What's he done?'

'Nothing – yet!' Elaine leaned forward, revealing more of her Wonderbra-ed cleavage than I cared to see. 'But I had a dream about him last night.'

'Really?' Something told me I didn't like the way this was going.

'You have ever such good dreams, Elaine.' Debbie was such a crawler.

'I dreamt that Nigel Napier topped himself,' announced Elaine dramatically. 'Whaddya think of that?'

Apparently this wasn't a rhetorical question because she was waiting for an answer.

'That's very – unusual,' was the best I could come up with.

'Hung himself,' she continued. 'Couldn't stand all the crap any more. Decided to end it all. So I want you two to go and sit outside his house and wait.'

She fixed Debbie and me with her beady stare waiting for our reaction. Neither of us said anything.

'Uh – wait for what?' I said finally.

'For him to do it!' Elaine banged the desk. 'And when he does, you'll be there. Ready!'

This was it. Elaine had finally gone completely mad. Perhaps I should dial 999.

'Do you want us to talk to the neighbours?' said Debbie, flipping open her notebook. 'Perhaps there's been some sign?'

'No. No!' Elaine banged the desk again. 'No! No! No! I don't want any other bugger getting a whiff of this story. Wait till he hangs himself, then ask the neighbours. And the wife. Has he got kids?'

'I think he's got two daughters,' I said hesitantly, remembering a photo I'd taken a while ago of them arriving at a Disney premiere.

'Brilliant. Little girls. Crying. Daddy's gone. Lots of sad photos. Love it. Well, what are you waiting for? Get out of here.'

We let ourselves out of the office but before we could get back to our desks, Elaine swung her head around the door again and bellowed, 'And don't come back till he's dead!'

Slam!

'What was all that about?' said Geoff.

I liked Geoff. He'd been in newspapers forever. They bored him silly. Whatever stunts Elaine pulled were water off a duck's back to Geoff. He'd been to Afghanistan. Nothing frightened him. He used to be news editor – a very big cheese in Fleet Street – but six years ago Elaine's third husband, who bore a passing resemblance to Adolf Hitler, had walked out on her and she'd decided she didn't want what she described as 'any more fuckers with moustaches' working on her paper. So she demoted Geoff and his moustache to picture editor in the hope that he'd get angry and resign. With twenty years service, he was too expensive to sack.

But Geoff didn't care. Geoff had never taken a photo in his life apart from holiday snaps of the missus in Tenerife, but if Elaine wanted to make him picture editor that was her look out. Geoff didn't give a toss. Particularly since the paper had to pay him the same money he'd been getting before. And the funny thing was, he turned out to be a really quite good picture editor. He might not know one end of a camera from the other, but he didn't deliberately choose the one shot on your roll that was out of focus or had a plant sticking out the top of somebody's head so that he could complain loudly about what untalented no-hopers he was forced to work with. And just to really piss Elaine off, he grew a beard as well. Geoff was my mate.

I groaned, put my head on my desk and buried it under my arms. 'She had a dream last night that Nigel Napier committed suicide and she thinks that means it's actually going to happen. She wants me and Debbie to go and cover the story. I think I'm supposed to get a photo of him dangling from the noose.'

'So, you go up there, stay in an expensive hotel, go shopping, get your hair done and your legs waxed or whatever it is you girls do, put all your restaurant meals on expenses, take a few snaps of the outside of his house to say you were there and then, in a couple of days, when Nostradamus's ugly sister has forgotten all about it, you come home again. And don't forget to take off a couple of days in lieu for all the overnights.'

'But it's such a waste of time,' I moaned.

'Of course it is,' said Geoff. 'I hope you weren't under the impression that anything we do here actually matters.'

By the time Debbie had finished the story she was working on, and we'd both gone home to get our overnight bags, it was already five o'clock as we hit the M1. Nothing like driving out of London in rush hour on a Friday night to lift your spirits. Debbie decided that we'd go straight to the hotel tonight, then check out Nigel Napier first thing in the morning. I felt really mean this time deserting Andrew. Every time I closed my eyes I remembered that kiss and then my guilty conscience would search for a way to make it up to my poor husband. I couldn't shake off the feeling that somehow he must know what I'd done. That anything that affected me so strongly must somehow be picked up by his radar. So maybe it was just as well if I kept out of his way for a bit.

I took out my mobile to call him for the third time that day. 'Hi, babe.'

'Hi, bunny. How are you feeling now?'

'Oh, much, much better.'

'Are you there yet?'

'No, we're sitting in a tailback on the M6. I just rang to tell you how much I miss you.'

'I miss you too. When do you think you'll be back?'

'I don't know. Not long, I hope. Are you getting a pizza tonight?'

'How did you know?'

'Oh, you know. Just a wild guess.' I couldn't think of anything else to say. 'Well, have a nice evening. Don't be too lonely.'

'I won't.'

'Love you.'

'I love you too.'

I hung up feeling a little bit better – but not much.

'Debbie?' I asked. 'How long have you and Ian been married?'

'Ten years next May.'

'You're kidding! I had no idea you'd been together that long.'

'Well, we was living togevver for four years before that.'

'Fourteen years!'

' 'E's comin' up tomorrer night to keep me company.'

'Really?' I was shocked. Ian was a building contractor with a fistful of gold signet rings. I'd met him a couple of times but he hadn't made much of an impression on me through his cloud of cigar smoke. He didn't seem the romantic type at all.

'We've never been apart for more than one night in all that time,' said Debbie. 'Ian can't go without nookie any longer than that and neither can I.' She laughed, a really raucous dirty laugh. I laughed too, just to be polite, but I was thinking, bloody hell. I tried to remember the last time Andrew and I had had nookie. Was it last week? No – because he'd stayed up late watching a video, and then we'd got a curry and we didn't feel like it. Then we were both working late.

What about the week before? My mind was blank. Now I remembered, it was the night we'd gone out for Jill's birthday, back in June.

'What's the date today, Debbie?'

She looked at her Rolex. 'The seventh of July.'

Jesus – we hadn't done it in over four weeks. And I hadn't even noticed.

four

Nigel Napier lived in a huge, graceful house in Alderley Edge in Cheshire. Electric gates, two Mercedes in the driveway and a magnolia tree in the front garden. For a washed-up newsreader he wasn't doing badly. Debbie drove past very slowly, squinting to see through the iron railings and her DKNY sunglasses.

'D'yer reckon he's in?'

'I don't care. We should just turn around and go home. This is ridiculous.'

'Wossamatta wiv ya?'

'What's the matter with me? What's the matter with you? You don't think Elaine really has prophetic dreams, do you? And even if she did, don't you think there's something just a little odd about hanging around the house of a complete stranger waiting for him to kill himself? What are you going to do if we drive back past Nigel Napier's house and see him dangling from that magnolia tree? Are you just going to wait until he stops kicking, then line up all his family and get them to sign exclusive contracts, or are you going to go and save his life?' I was getting myself in a bit of a state. I couldn't believe I was having this conversation.

'Yeah, it's a bit of a moral wossaname, innit?'

'No, it's not a moral whatsaname. It's an open-and-shut case. This is sick. End of story. I can't believe you're so desperate to see your name in the paper that you can't see that.'

We'd driven around the block and were about to turn back into Nigel Napier's road.

'Look, we're just going to park the car, watch the house, and wait and see what happens. That's all.' Debbie was talking to me very calmly and gently like I was a kid throwing a temper tantrum in Sainsbury's. Fobbing me off with a packet of Smarties.

'Fine. Whatever,' I told her. 'And when he's found dead and the police ask the neighbours if they've seen anyone suspicious hanging around lately, they'll say, "Yeah there've been two strange women sitting outside his house in a red Golf for the past week."'

Debbie pulled in across the road from his house, turned off the engine and stared at the front door as though she was willing it to open with the power of her mind. The curtains in the house next door twitched.

'I'm going to phone Elaine,' said Debbie, whipping out her mobile phone.

'You do that.' I opened the copy of *Hello!* magazine lying on the back seat and started to read. I was having no part of this. Listening to Debbie whispering to Elaine you'd think we were secret agents sneaking behind enemy lines. Which, in a way, I suppose we were.

'Yeah, we're outside the house now . . . There's two cars parked in the driveway, but no sign of the target.'

The target? Where on earth had she got that from?

'No other papers are here.'

What a surprise, considering nothing had happened. Or was likely to.

'We've still got it exclusive. So far. Obviously, if any other papers turn up, we'll deal with that when it happens. Don't worry, Elaine, we'll keep you fully posted.'

Ten minutes later I'd looked at all the pictures in *Hello!* and was bored. There was an old copy of the *Standard* on the back seat and I picked it up carefully, turning the pages nervously as though Nick himself were going to leap out at me. When I saw his by-line underneath one of the photographs, I was too alarmed to look at it. I just gave a kind of squeak and shoved it in my bag.

'Can I borrow this for later?' I asked Debbie.

She just shrugged.

There was a huge pile of glossy magazines back there too; it was where Debbie got all her feature ideas from. I spotted a moody black and white photo of Brad Pitt on the cover of something called *The Hoop* – a new one on me.

'I haven't seen this before,' I said, holding it up to Debbie.

'It's brand new. I got an advance copy.'

'American?'

'Nah, English, I think.'

I flicked through pages filled with the usual mix of movie stars, beauty and fashion. There was a swimsuit spread shot on top of a volcano in Bali – the models looked like aliens on the surface of a dead planet with spumes of yellow sulphur rising up behind them. I checked the photo credit to see who'd taken them and felt a twinge of guilt when I recognised the name of a guy I'd been at college with. He'd been in the year below me and his work hadn't been that great, but now he was doing fashion spreads for *The Hoop* and I was stalking imaginary suicides because my editor had lost her mind. What was wrong with this picture?

I remembered swapping work stories with Nick the other night and how embarrassed I'd been by the dim-witted jobs I'd been sent out on. I wished I'd been able to say casually, 'Oh, yeah, I've just come back from photographing swimwear on a volcano in Bali' or 'I'm off to do an underwater series swimming with penguins in the Galapagos Islands'. Instead of 'I took a photograph of the inside of Vanessa Feltz's bathroom cabinet'.

Debbie switched on her portable tape recorder and started dictating her story. 'Nothing in the quiet, tree-lined avenue gave any sign of the enormous tragedy that was about to befall its best-known and best-loved resident,' she began.

'Former newsreader and TV presenter Nigel Napier called this street home. He lived here in his six bedroom, two-million-pound mansion with his wife and children – get their names – for x years – have to find out how many. Theirs was said by many to be one of the happiest marriages in show business and their his-and-hers Mercedes with matching numberplates – NAP 1ER and NAP 2ER – were proof of their devotion. His garden, with its landscaped lawns and colourful flowerbeds, was one of his great passions, along with fly-fishing and golf. Check this later. He had planted the wisteria tree himself . . .'

'It's a magnolia,' I interrupted, wondering why I bothered.

'Napier's blossoming career had sadly nose-dived in the early nineties following allegations of sexual harassment by a colleague . . .'

Here it comes, I thought.

'. . . shapely blonde production assistant Tania Vickery, now a hostess on *Dial M For Money*. Tania accused the randy reporter of grabbing her breasts and saying he'd like to give her a bong. He resigned instantly rather than put his family through the ordeal of an industrial tribunal. As Tania's career skyrocketed, Nigel spent almost a decade out of the limelight and devoted himself tirelessly to charity work. But last year, he bounced back with a new daytime show *That's My Dog!* in which a celebrity panel try to match pooches with their human owners.

' "There's life in the old dog yet!" he famously promised at the time.

'So with everything to live for, why, neighbours were asking yesterday, why, oh why, did Nigel Napier decide to take his own life, so suddenly and so publicly, hanging himself from his beloved wisteria tree?

'It'll be a drag if he takes an overdose, 'cos I'll have to cut all the stuff about the tree,' she concluded, switching off her tape recorder.

Debbie could do it with her eyes shut but I didn't get this

tabloid stuff at all. Every day when I picked up the paper, I was constantly amazed by the guff it contained. I couldn't understand any of it. Who read this stuff?

Oh sure, we did fashion too, but you could forget about volcanoes. Our fashion pages were just a flimsy excuse to run a double page spread of top-heavy tarts in red nylon bras from a catalogue. If anyone bought me underwear like that I think I'd cry. Elaine's motives were even more transparent than the knickers. Sex was Elaine's answer to everything. No wonder the paper was nicknamed *The Lecher*. We only covered news if it involved pop stars, TV stars or sex. Preferably a pop star having sex with a TV star. If a nuclear warhead were heading in our direction, we'd still have to find the Spice Girls angle: 'Posh shows us what she'll be wearing for the nuclear winter', Or: 'Three minute warning? There's still time to go out with a bang. Scary's top ten tips for passion in a flash!'

'Look, there's somebody coming out of the house!' Debbie yelped. 'It's him!'

Nigel Napier himself was striding across the manicured lawn. He was a tall, extremely well-groomed man in his late fifties, wearing a navy-blue Adidas tracksuit and carrying a Head sports bag.

Debbie and I ducked down and hid on the front seat.

'What's he doing?' she hissed.

'I don't know. I can't see.' I whispered back.

'What shall we do?'

'I don't know. Why are we whispering?'

We heard the sound of a car starting and then the electronic gates swinging open as he drove out. Debbie leapt up in her seat and turned on the ignition.

'You're not going to follow him, are you?' I was almost pleading.

'Of course I am.' She was loving it. Debbie Gibb – Ace Girl Reporter. She loved all this cloak-and-dagger shit.

'Oh, God,' I groaned, sitting up.

She pulled out slowly and followed his dark grey Mercedes

at what was supposed to be a safe distance, Debbie with one hand on the wheel and the other clutching her tape recorder.

'Only the day before his tragic suicide, Nigel had left his home as usual at 11:47 a.m. to visit his local gym,' she intoned. 'As he pushed his body to the limit, no one could have guessed the turmoil racing through his mind. Take a photo of him driving,' she ordered.

'I can't,' I lied. 'He's going too fast. It would be all blurry.'

Fortunately Debbie knew as much about photography as she did about trees. I felt sick. I had never quite realised until now how much I despised this job. We followed him sedately through the traffic until, after about three miles, he turned into the car park of an extremely smart-looking health club.

'What shall we do?' whispered Debbie. 'It'll look suspicious if we drive straight in after him.' She parked opposite the club where we had a clear view of him getting out of his Mercedes and striding towards the entrance.

'Take his picture now! Take it now!' she squealed.

'I've just got to put a new film in the camera,' I told her, opening a canister and loading it as slowly as I could.

'Hurry up, hurry up!'

'I think the motor drive is jammed.'

'He's going in, he's going in! Oh, no, you've missed him!'

'Ohhhh no! Damn.'

'Right, we're going in!' Debbie started up her engine again and pulled into the car park. 'Come on,' she said. 'We're going to get fit.'

Day membership cost us £15 each. Then there were two swimming costumes, two T-shirts, two pairs of shorts, two pairs of socks and two pairs of trainers. A total of £309.90 to chalk up on expenses. The woman in the club shop must have thought she'd won the lottery.

I'd left my cameras in the car because, as I'd explained to Debbie, there was no way I could photograph Nigel Napier here without attracting attention. So I relaxed. I wasn't working. I was just working out. Not hurting anybody. If I saw Nigel Napier I would simply look the other way. I was rather pleased with the Lycra T-shirt I'd bought too. Perhaps this wasn't going to be so bad.

We padded down the long corridor towards the gym, trying to look as though we'd been coming here for years. All the gym equipment was contained in one long room with the weights at one end and the running machines, bikes and rowing machines down the other.

'There he is,' hissed Debbie. Nigel Napier was doing bench presses at the end of the gym under the supervision of a young black guy with a high-pitched laugh and arms like sides of beef. Nigel's face was contorted with pain as he squeezed the last drop of strength from his muscles.

'Fifteen!' he gasped.

'Why go to all that bother if you're just going to kill yourself?' whispered Debbie, as we hopped onto a couple of exercise bikes.

Being a Saturday morning the gym was packed with men and women huffing and puffing and sweating all over the place. They must have recognised Nigel too, but they were very cool and made a point of not catching his eye.

Nigel's personal trainer kept him far too busy to notice Debbie staring at him intently and memorising his entire workout to include in her story. I left her on the exercise bikes – she didn't want to budge because it gave her an uninterrupted view of the whole gym. Meanwhile, I sweated out my guilt on the weight machines and the treadmill. It wouldn't hurt to work on my thighs, just in case I ran into Nick again. Oh, no! Where had that thought come from?

Nigel Napier was on another treadmill further along the row, chatting to his trainer. I could see his reflection in the mirror, tilting his head this way and that as he ran, absent-mindedly checking out his bald spot. He was breathless and his sweaty T-shirt clung to his chest, but he wasn't going to give up. He said something to his trainer that made him laugh:

'Hee hee hee!' He certainly didn't look depressed. He was a man on a mission.

Debbie, on the other hand, was a picture of misery. Her legs had virtually stopped moving on the pedals over twenty minutes ago.

'How are you doing?' I asked her when I'd run enough.

'This seat is killing my bum,' she moaned.

When Nigel Napier's treadmill automatically slowed to a halt, he went over to the mats to stretch. His trainer pressed down his knees, leaned on his back, pushed each thigh into his bum. It must be nice, I thought, to be rich enough to pay someone to stretch you. Then, workout over, Nigel picked up his towel and walked out.

'Thank Christ!' said Debbie, hobbling after him. 'We'd better not have a shower in case we lose him. You go wait in the car park in case he comes out and I'll stay here and see what he does. He might be going for a swim.'

I sat in the car and twenty minutes later I looked up from my magazine to see Nigel Napier walking to his car with Debbie limping just a few paces behind.

Oh dear, the chase was on again.

She hoisted herself painfully into the driver's seat and we were off. But instead of heading back to his house, he got on the motorway to Manchester.

'Perhaps he's going to do some shopping,' said Debbie.

'Maybe.'

Debbie hung back as much as she could so as not to arouse suspicion. Surely he must have noticed her car by now? But either Nigel Napier didn't use his mirrors as often as he should, or perhaps he had other things on his mind, because he didn't seem to notice, not even when he turned into a smart residential street. When Debbie saw him indicate that he was going to turn into a driveway, she hung back at the end of the road for a couple of minutes.

'Well, he's not going shopping,' she said.

As we drove past, I saw his Mercedes parked in front of a

house even larger and grander than his own. He was already waiting on the doorstep and a blonde woman opened the door. She kissed him passionately, then they walked inside, closing the door behind them. I had to hand it to Debbie – her timing was pretty impressive. Debbie said just two words but she said them very loudly. 'TANIA VICKERY!' She was already grabbing her mobile phone to call Elaine at home. 'Elaine, you're not going to believe it. It's even bigger than you thought. Nigel Napier is alive and well and shagging Tania Vickery!'

I could hear Elaine screaming with delight all the way from her Hampstead mansion.

'Well, it certainly looks like they've patched up their differences,' shrieked Debbie. 'It looks like she's the one harassing him now.' More cackling. 'Yeah, so first she ruins his career, now she's going to wreck his marriage! It's brilliant. Unbelievable. Don't worry, Elaine. We're not leaving until we've got a picture of them together. Even if we have to stay here all night.'

And after a few hours, that looked like exactly what we would be doing. I was still wearing my sweaty shorts and T-shirt from the gym and we were both hungry and needed a bath, but Debbie wasn't going to budge. Not while she was sitting on the threshold of the showbiz scoop of her career. Not even when it got dark and Nigel Napier and Tania Vickery showed no sign of leaving the house. Ever.

Debbie amused herself by doodling front pages headlines for her story: DIAL M FOR MARRIAGE-WRECKER – WORLD EXCLUSIVE BY DEBBIE GIBB.

I had to admit it was pretty strange. Tania Vickery was only my age and Nigel was almost old enough to be her father. She'd been a nobody when she accused Nigel of sexual harassment – just a production assistant in the news department – but all the publicity surrounding the scandal had made her a big star. There were photos of her in the papers every day for a week. *The Ledger* had put her in a tight low-cut red dress and she'd crouched on the floor on all fours with the camera staring down her cleavage as she'd poured out her heart about the agony of being treated like a piece of meat by Nigel Napier. As she licked her lips and pressed her breasts closer together she'd revealed that she was having trouble sleeping and was on anti-depressants. 'Poor Tania,' said the television executives as they fell over each other in their rush to sign her up.

But I was wracked with guilt knowing that I was expected to get photographic evidence of Nigel and Tania's affair. What if one of the photographers last night had got it into his head to take a photo of me kissing Nick? Luckily for me I'm not on TV so a photo like that wouldn't count as news – but it certainly would have been news to Andrew if he'd seen it. It didn't bear thinking about.

'Listen, Debbie, I'm not sure about this,' I said. 'I don't think we should be here.'

Debbie was reapplying her olive green eye-shadow for the fifth time. 'Why?' she said. 'Would we get a better shot from the other side of the road?'

'No. I mean, I don't think we should be stalking them like this. It's an invasion of their privacy.'

'Oh, give it a rest – you're not going to give me the Princess Di speech again, are you? This could be the biggest story I've had this year. Don't you want to see your name on the front page?'

'Not really.'

'You're mad. It's the biggest buzz I know. It's better than sex. Whenever Ian wants to try anything really kinky, we get in the mood by going through my scrapbook.'

'I don't think I wanted to know that, Debbie.'

'You ought to try it sometime, you don't know what you're missing.'

'But what right do we have to ruin people's lives like this?'

'What are you talking about? That's our job.'

*

35

In the end, it was thanks to her husband Ian that I managed to get away. He'd been phoning Debbie every hour wanting to know when she was coming back and at one a.m. with the house in darkness, Debbie finally gave in and we went back to the hotel.

'We'll meet downstairs at six in the morning,' she ordered. 'I don't want to risk missing him coming out.'

I nodded. I was exhausted from a day of doing nothing and went up to bed wondering how much longer I could avoid actually taking a photo of poor Nigel Napier.

I was just collecting my gear together in the morning when the phone rang. I thought it was Debbie complaining that I was two seconds late but it turned out to be Geoff.

'Why are you calling so early?' I asked him. 'It's the middle of the night.'

'Well, you can thank Debbie for that. I've just had her giving me earache. She says you're not co-operating. Is that right?'

'No.' I could feel myself blushing.

'She said you wouldn't take the photos she wanted.'

'My flash didn't go off,' I lied. 'I had to change the battery pack.'

'Well, never mind. I'm too tired to argue. Peter's meeting Debbie up there this morning. He'll take over. You get yourself back to London. You can do Neil Morrissey's dustbin.'

'I don't think I can do that, Geoff.'

'It's OK. It's not till Monday. You can get the train back.'

'No, Geoff, you don't understand. I quit.'

five

'Life is too short,' I told Jill. 'I know I've done the right thing.'

So why was I panicking? Why was I gripped by the certain fear that I'd never work again? That no one would ever employ me. That I'd cracked up completely. That the combination of Nick and Nigel and Tania Vickery had somehow tipped me over the edge.

'I think it's brilliant,' said Jill. 'Good on you.'

'Really? You don't think I'm crazy?'

'No – you hated it there. You've done nothing but moan about it the whole time. I'm glad you've quit. Maybe you'll shut up about it now.'

I loved Jill. She always said exactly the right thing. She had a fantastic job in PR for a shoe company which she absolutely adored and was terrifyingly good at. But really, I think she missed her calling and should have been a counsellor.

'Do you want another glass of wine?' she was saying now.

See what I mean? Absolutely the right thing to say. If I sat in Jill's kitchen for the rest of the evening, I wouldn't have to think about the fact that I was now technically unemployed.

I'd given a month's notice, but because I was still owed three weeks' holiday, I'd been able to leave after just one week.

'So what do you want to do now?' Jill asked.

'I don't know. All I've ever done is photography.'

'Well, what about one of the proper papers – like the *Evening Standard*. You always read that.'

'Oh, I couldn't work there,' I said. 'I don't think they'd be interested in somebody from *The Ledger*.'

Don't think applying for a job at the *Standard* hadn't occurred to me. Bumping casually into Nick: 'Oh, hi, fancy seeing you here.' Too weird. Impossible. But Jill didn't know about Nick, of course. That was something else that changed after you got married, I realised.

When we were single, Jill and I knew every cough and spit of each other's love lives. No weekend was complete until Jill and I had got on the phone and analysed the life out of it. Where did you go? Who else went, was it just the two of you? What did you wear? What was he wearing? Did you stay at his place or your place? Huh. Typical. What did he say about that? What did you say? Then what? You're kidding! What does that mean? What time did he say he'd call? And so on and so on.

But Jill and Simon had two kids now and since Andrew and I got married there wasn't much point to those phone calls any more. I kind of missed them. But I couldn't tell Jill about Nick any more than I could tell Andrew. She may have been my best friend, but it wasn't fair to land her with a secret like that. It was too big a responsibility. And suppose she told Simon? He'd tell Andrew as surely as night follows day because men have no concept of the word 'secret'.

'What about a magazine?' suggested Jill. 'There's thousands of magazines, one of them's bound to give you a job.'

'Oh, thanks very much for the vote of confidence,' I laughed.

'You know what I mean.'

'Yeah, I know. In fact, I saw this new magazine last week that I really liked the look of.' I'd been carrying Debbie's copy of *The Hoop* in the bottom of my camera bag all week and, without even giving it any conscious thought, the little seed it had planted in my brain had been germinating quietly on its own over the last few days. I fished it out of my bag and showed it to Jill. 'What do you think?'

'Oh, I've seen this,' she said. 'Somebody at work had it. It's got a really mad fashion section.'

'The only trouble,' I said, 'is that I don't know anyone there. I'm a bit nervous about just ringing them up out of the blue.'

'Well, you didn't know anyone at *The Ledger* when you went there, did you?' she pointed out.

'True.'

But that hadn't been so scary. There was something about glossy magazines that frightened the life out of me. *The Ledger*'s standards were so low, there was nothing I felt I had to live up to. In fact, they didn't measure up to my standards, so I was on pretty safe ground. But somewhere like *The Hoop*? My hair was all wrong, my clothes were all wrong, I didn't go to the right parties. My lifestyle wasn't glossy. It was positively matt. And what was I supposed to show them? Four years at *The Ledger* had left me with a portfolio that *The Hoop* wouldn't use as a doorstop.

'Perhaps I should aim for something not so grand,' I said. 'One of the magazines my mum reads or something like that. Like *Take a Break* or *Gardeners' World*.'

'Have you seen *Take a Break* lately?' said Jill. 'It's all neighbours attacking each other with bread knives and shagging their daughters' boyfriends. It makes *The Ledger* look like *Vanity Fair*. You'd hate it there. You know you're a good photographer. You should have the guts to go for what you really want. You said it yourself, life's too short.'

I've said it before, but I'll say it again. I love Jill.

'By the way,' I said, changing the subject. 'You'll never guess who's coming to London.'

'Who?'

'Natalie.'

Jill's eyes widened and her jaw dropped open. 'Natalie Brown? *The* Natalie Brown?'

I nodded.

'Blimey. Are you going to see her, do you think?'

I made a sort of Phhh noise through my lips. 'I doubt it. We weren't speaking to each other before she was famous, so she's not very likely to beat a path to my door now that she's one of the highest paid women in TV.'

'Natalie Brown,' said Jill again. 'Well, I'd certainly like to see her. She borrowed my Pet Shop Boys LP and never gave it back.'

'She borrowed a lot of things and never gave them back,' I reminded her.

I spent Saturday cleaning the flat, shopping and preparing a three-course meal for that evening. Russell, Andrew's best friend, was coming to dinner with his fiancée, Robin. I looked forward to an evening filled with witty conversation and light-hearted banter amongst friends. I looked forward to that with all my heart – and wondered when I was ever likely to have one.

Having dinner with Russell and Robin was an ordeal, a ritual that had become so predictable I lost the will to live just thinking about it.

Russell and Robin and Andrew had met at university – sorry, Cambridge, they never referred to it as just university – and they'd all shared a house together. Robin and Russell had been engaged for about twelve years but so far showed no signs of actually getting married. They didn't like to rush into things. Robin researched community programmes for the BBC and Russell was on his third Internet start-up company. I couldn't remember if this was the one that provided expert medical advice or the one that sold dog food in bulk. I never liked to ask him exactly what he did because then he might tell me and I'd be forced to listen to his pompous, grating voice.

Russell was an arrogant pain in the arse and the world's leading authority on absolutely everything. If you mentioned that you'd seen a hole in the ground, Russell would be able to tell you precisely what kind of dirt was in it. Andrew just took all of Russell's crackpot theories in his stride, while I had to physically restrain myself from talking to Russell at all because the temptation to throw the gravy-boat at his head was, at times, almost overwhelming.

Robin, on the other hand, was so shy that making conversation with her was like pulling teeth. Every time we saw Russell and Robin, which was roughly every six weeks, I'd have to write down a list of subjects beforehand that she might possibly be persuaded to talk about. I'd jot down the name of every film I'd seen, every TV programme, every book I'd read, every restaurant I'd read a review of, every natural disaster or plane crash. If Sainsbury's stocked a new kind of lettuce it was cause for celebration because I could ask Robin if she'd tried it. I was that desperate. This week I planned to discuss: who's cooler, Anna Kournikova or Venus Williams? Flip-flops, suitable footwear for the office or what? And Cherie Blair – superwoman.

Andrew came and grabbed me around the waist while I was cleaning my teeth.

'Don't do that,' I spluttered. 'You'll make me get toothpaste all over my shirt.'

'I thought you liked me cuddling you.'

'Not while I'm cleaning my teeth. And do we have to listen to widdly guitar music again?'

'This is Yngwie Malmsteen!' he said in a shocked voice, as though I'd just tripped up his granny.

'Well, can't you listen to him when I'm not home?'

'What would you like to listen to, then?'

'Oh, I don't know. Anything released in the last five years would be nice.'

Andrew's taste in music was a constant source of arguments between us. His CD collection was so bizarre and middle-aged it was like being married to someone's dad. Since we'd met, he'd been through a discordant jazz phase, a mournful country and western phase, and now he'd discovered heavy metal guitarists with names even more unlikely than their hairstyles.

I did my best but his musical education was sorely lacking, probably because the only music he ever listened to on the radio was the theme tune from *The Archers*. The whole Brit-pop thing had passed him by. And as for dance music, forget about it. I would have loved to go clubbing, but the idea of going to a club with Andrew was just ridiculous. Andrew had the kind of face – and shoes – that bouncers just loved to humiliate. The words 'Sorry, mate, you're not coming in here dressed like that' might have been written with him in mind. Once, before we got married, I'd met him at a gig at the Brixton Academy and he'd turned up straight from work in his light grey suit and pink tie.

'What's the matter? Why aren't we going in?' he'd asked, as I hustled him back to the tube station.

And what would be the point of going clubbing with Andrew anyway? When Jill and I used to go out together, there was always the thrill of never knowing what might happen or who you might meet. Dancing with your husband didn't have quite the same air of excitement about it.

'I suppose you want to listen to M&M,' Andrew grumbled.

'It's not M&M. It's Eminem.'

'That's what I said, isn't it?'

'Yeah, but it's the way you said it.'

I needed a drink. A glass of Australian Shiraz – already opened to let it breathe – would do nicely. 'And we're really going to have to do something about this kitchen!' I shouted.

When I'd left my lovely little flat and moved in with Andrew it had been a temporary measure, I thought, until we bought somewhere else together. Somewhere with a garden. Four years later his anaglypta wallpaper and beige-and-brown kitchen tiles with a wheatsheaf motif were really starting to get on my nerves. The doorbell rang and I drained my glass in one gulp. Poured myself another. I was going to need it.

'Is there something wrong, Robin?' I asked, as we sipped our home-made roast tomato soup. It was the last time I would ever try one of Delia's recipes. Thank goodness we were having Jamie Oliver for a main course and Nigella for dessert. I'd spent all afternoon blanching tomatoes, skinning tomatoes, halving tomatoes, roasting tomatoes (with an individual leaf of basil on each one), pureeing tomatoes and chopping basil. It had taken five hours and it looked and tasted exactly like the stuff you can buy in cartons for £1.20. Only not quite so good.

'I'm sorry – it's just that I had tomato soup for lunch,' Robin whispered. 'But I'm sure it's delicious.'

'You need to use real Mediterranean tomatoes,' said Russell. 'Hot-house tomatoes ripen too quickly to have any sort of flavour.'

'That's true,' said Andrew. 'Remember those tomatoes we had in Portugal last year?'

'These are organic,' I said brightly. 'I believe they're Spanish. Would you like anything else, Robin?'

'No, I'm fine.'

Robin was a strange fish. On paper, she was actually very pretty. Tall, pale, skinny, with interesting black hair and blue eyes. On paper, she was Winona Ryder. But then you got a good look at her and noticed there was something a little disturbing about the way all her features were squashed too closely together – like she'd got her head stuck in the lift doors when they were closing.

'So, Robin, what about Cherie Blair, then?' I said. 'Amazing, isn't she?'

'What? Just because she's got a baby?' snorted Russell. 'Where's the skill in that? Now that you're not working, I suppose you're going to start getting broody too.'

'Actually, I am working,' I told him, clutching my soup spoon tightly. 'I've just gone freelance. I'm going to be working for lots of different magazines.'

'You're wasting your time. There's no point being in any sort of business unless it's on the Internet,' said Russell.

'Really?' I said. 'That's a very interesting theory.'

'It's not a theory. In five years' time, there won't be any books or newspapers or magazines – it'll all be on computer.'

'Oh, really? And what are people going to read on the bus on their way to work?'

'They won't go to work. Work will come to them. Everybody will tele-commute.'

'You don't say.'

'It's inevitable. Name me one job that can't be done better by doing it online.

'Air hostess.'

'Don't be stupid.

'Footballer.'

'That's hardly a job.'

'They get paid more than you do.'

'Not for long.'

'Brain surgeon.'

'There now, you see, all those people could be replaced by robots.'

'I wish somebody would replace you with a robot,' I muttered.

'What about it, bunny,' said Andrew, changing the subject. 'Shall we have a baby?'

'Er, not right now, I haven't finished my soup.' I didn't really feel like discussing it in front of Robin and Russell.

'No – but seriously,' he persisted. 'Wouldn't you like to have a little baby?'

'I don't think I'm ready for children just yet and I don't think you are either.'

'Well, babies don't have to change your life,' said Andrew.

'Are you serious?' I spluttered. 'Look at Jill. She can't even leave the house to buy a pint of milk without getting two kids dressed first. And besides, we can't think about children while we're living here. I don't want wet nappies hanging all over the radiators. We need a tumble drier. And a garden.'

'You don't need a garden for a tumble drier.'

'I meant for the children to play in.'

'You should move to Kent,' said Russell. Russell and Robin lived in Kent which was the most compelling argument I could think of not to go there.

'Besides,' I said, ignoring Russell. 'I know what would happen. You say you want kids, but I'd be the one who'd get lumbered with all the work looking after them.'

'I'd help.'

'Oh, yeah, sure you would. You mean like the way you help with Billy? You feed him maybe once a month and act like a big hero. But cats have to be fed twice a day – every day. If it was left up to you to look after a baby it'd starve to death in a week.'

'Well, Billy is your cat,' said Andrew.

'What about the window boxes, then? They're yours, aren't they, and you never water them.'

'But they look OK to me. They're not dead. Everyone always says how nice they look.'

'That's because I water them every day during the summer and feed them with seaweed fertiliser. You know that watering can in the bathroom? Didn't you ever wonder what that was for?'

'But you don't do anything around the house – you're the untidiest person I know.'

'Oh, so you do it all, do you?' I laughed. 'OK. I'll give you ten quid if you can tell me what colour the Hoover is.'

'Don't be silly.'

'Ten quid.'

'It's mauve.'

'Wrong!'

'Yes it is, it's dark red – that's mauve isn't it?'

'No, that's maroon. Mauve is more purple. You don't even know the names of colours.'

'So? I know what colour I meant.'

'Well, I'm glad to see that degree from Cambridge hasn't gone to waste.'

'Why are we talking about the Hoover? I thought we were talking about whether to have a baby.'

'OK, I tell you what. If you feed Billy twice a day for one week, I'll think about having a baby. That's one week. Not eighteen years until he grows up and leaves home, like a real baby would, just one week. Robin – you're a witness.'

Robin just blushed.

'I don't know what you're making such a fuss about,' said Andrew.

'Of course, in a few years' time, babies will be unnecessary,' said Russell. 'Life expectancy will be approximately 175 years. There'll be no need for humans to reproduce at all.'

175 years! I wasn't sure I'd make it through the evening.

I knew that Andrew would sit up for hours with Russell and Robin after dinner, drinking and playing backgammon, but I excused myself on the grounds of a headache and went up to bed early. The three of them had been friends for so long, I didn't need to play the domestic goddess; they'd manage just fine without me.

'Thank you for a lovely meal,' whispered Robin.

'You're welcome,' I told her, pointedly ignoring Russell and Andrew as I went upstairs with a mug of hot chocolate. We were supposed to be going on a long weekend break with Russell and Robin to Italy next month. I'd booked it for just me and Andrew ages ago for my birthday but then he'd had the brilliant idea of inviting those two as well.

'It'll be more fun in a group,' he'd insisted – the only instance I can ever recall of Robin and Russell's names and the word 'fun' occurring in the same conversation, except preceded by the words 'they're' and 'no'. I didn't even want to think about how I was supposed to put up with those two for four days. It made my head hurt just to think about it.

It was still early so I sat in bed, sipping grumpily on my hot chocolate and flicking through my cuttings file. It made me feel more and more dejected. There was hardly anything here I could show *The Hoop* that was going to impress them. A few celebrity portraits that I wasn't completely ashamed of, but nobody really famous. Not Brad Pitt famous. Unless you count Carol Vorderman. Some make-up shots. All the best photos were actually things I'd done at college. Nothing that was going to set the world on fire. I was kidding myself that I even had a hope.

I remembered the copy of the *Standard* I'd borrowed from Debbie and decided to have a proper look at the photo of Nick's I'd seen in there. How good was he anyway? The paper had been lying in the pile by my bed for over a week until I plucked up the courage to actually open it.

There it was – street kids begging in Brazil. My heart did a little backflip to see his name in print – Photograph: Nick Weber – but I told myself not to be so silly. What was he doing going to South America anyway? *The Ledger* used to kick up a fuss over my travel expenses if I went to South London. I looked at the photo pretending to be critical. Hmmm. Perfectly exposed *and* politically correct. Bastard. *Xavier would kill for a pair of football boots* said the caption.

And what did I have to match that? An Easter Egg tasting for *The Ledger* using Jill's little daughter Holly as one of the models. I looked at my picture of Holly and I looked at Nick's photo of the Brazilian beggars and I swear that a light bulb actually went on above my head.

I almost fell out of bed in my rush to phone Jill. It was only ten o'clock. She'd still be up.

'Jill, Jill – I have to ask you a huge favour. I need to borrow Holly and a suitcase full of shoe samples. Are you free next Sunday?'

When Andrew came upstairs hours later I scooted over as far as I could onto my side of the bed and pretended to be asleep.

'Bunny?' he wheedled. 'You're not still cross, are you?'

'I'm not cross,' I said.

'Shall we try and have a baby?'

'Oh, God, you're drunk, aren't you?'

'No,' he giggled and promptly farted.

'Oh, darling!' I wailed, trying not to breathe in.

'Sorry! Sorry!' he giggled again, and flapped the duvet.

'Well, don't make it go all over the room! That's disgusting!'

Billy came and jumped on the bed and started making a nest by my feet. There was lots of purring and dribbling going on. How many twelve-year-old boys still come and sleep with their mum every night, I wondered. Maybe for once Russell was right – who needs babies anyway?

six

'Wow. These are fantastic. Have you got these in a six?' I asked Jill, holding up a pair of satin embroidered mules.

'Mine!' snapped Holly rather ferociously, snatching them from me. She was already wearing a size nine diamanté sandal on one foot and a kitten-heeled lilac suede slipper on the other. The world's youngest fashion victim. I guess that's what comes of having a mum in shoe PR.

'It was nice of Geoff to let you use the studio,' said Jill, 'considering you don't even work here any more.'

'Well, in theory, I'm still working out my notice for another two weeks. Anyway, nobody ever uses this place on a Sunday.'

I'd set up the lights, organised some gold chairs and rolled out a pink backdrop which met with Holly's approval. She was only three, but she was more demanding than any model I'd ever worked with. Jill had brought all of Holly's favourite clothes and handbags and her paint box. We started off with Holly modelling the satin mules. Her tiny feet didn't even touch the sides as she stomped around the studio squealing with excitement. I very quickly abandoned any hope of telling Holly what to do or where to stand. We just gave her the shoes and let her get on with it. She was a natural.

'OK, now put the blue ones on,' said Jill.

Holly planted her mules firmly on the floor, stuck her little hands on her hips, pulled her bossiest face and told her mum firmly, 'No!'

What a great picture!

'God,' I laughed. 'What's she going to be like when she's eighteen?'

'She'll probably be running my company,' groaned Jill. 'I hope she doesn't sack me.'

Jill and I drank endless cups of tea and laughed our heads off all afternoon as Holly totally took command of the photo session, changing her outfits to suit the shoes, selecting just the right tiny handbag. It was one big dressing up game for her and she was loving every minute of it. So was I. I couldn't remember the last time I'd taken photos just for fun, or of somebody so enthusiastic about having their picture taken. Even before I got the transparencies back from the lab, I knew they were going to be fantastic.

The deputy editor of *The Hoop* had a jet-black crew cut and a silver stud in the cleft of her chin. She said 'Hey' instead of 'Hi' and her name was Atlanta Parrish.

I'd bought a snakeskin dress from Mango just for this meeting. One look at Atlanta's black combat trousers, Nike trainers, the Celtic tattoo encircling her skinny white bicep and the tiny camouflage T-shirt short enough to show off her belly-button ring told me I'd got it wrong again.

'Mmm. Mmm. Mmm.' She flipped over the pages of my portfolio, not really looking at any of it. Her forehead was propped up by two fingers of her right hand, a cigarette burning away between them.

She paused for a moment at one of my photos of Holly holding up a silver strappy sandal and a pink mule covered in beads and pleading to the camera, 'Which one?'.

'That's cool,' she said, but she said it accusingly as though being cool were highly suspect. She flipped back a few pages to look at the rest of the Holly photos and made a sort of 'Huh' noise that was as close as she was going to get to a laugh and scribbled something down on a Post-it note.

But before I could even say thank you or tell her about Holly, she'd flipped right to the back of the book, slapped it shut again and handed it back to me. She blew out of her bottom lip so that her spiky fringe flew up.

'There's some interesting stuff in there, but it's not really us,' she said in a self-satisfied drawl. '*The Hoop* is far more cutting edge than that.' She had a no-nonsense northern accent and I figured she was about twenty-four.

It was just as I'd thought. I was getting the bum's rush. Any second now, Lara Croft here was going to tell me I was too old and too un-hip for *The Hoop*. They probably had some sort of employment policy that said they only hired people with body piercings.

'Well,' I started to explain, 'until now, I've been working on daily papers. It's a very different market – that's why I want to change direction.'

For a tiny second I felt strangely protective of *The Ledger*. It might be crap but it sold more copies in one day than *The Hoop* would sell in a month. So where did she get off being so uppity with me?

Atlanta didn't give any sign that she'd actually heard me, and just ploughed on. 'Our fashion pages aren't just about the clothes – they're about capturing the zeitgeist, a way of being. The same with our celebrities. We're not interested in ordinary photos – we want to create a visual portfolio that reveals a side of the subject no one has ever seen before. Like an X-ray of their psyche. You need to be able to forge a special relationship with the kind of names we're looking for. Hervé was on set with Brad Pitt for three weeks before he shot a single frame. It's about trust. Being able to capture the dichotomy between the public façade and the private persona. I suppose what I'm trying to say is, my cleaning lady has got a Nikon, but I'm not going to send her out on assignments for *The Hoop* because for the kind of photos we're looking for it boils down to not what you know, but who you know.'

'I know Natalie Brown.' The words were out of my mouth before I even knew I was going to say them.

'Natalie Brown?' Despite herself, Atlanta sounded interested. 'Know her how exactly?'

'We've been best friends since we were five.'

'Really?' She opened my portfolio again and began studying the Holly photos intently.

'We used to have baths together.' Damn, why had I said that? 'She's going to be in the UK next month to shoot some episodes of *Don't Call Us* over here. She called me just last night to let me know when she'll be arriving. It was great to hear from her. She hasn't changed a bit.'

'We-ll,' said Atlanta. 'If you could get us someone like Natalie Brown, we might be interested in her for the cover. We were trying to get her for our launch issue but, as you know, she's notoriously publicity shy.'

'I'll ask her for you if you like,' I said sweetly. 'I know she'd have no problem at all with me photographing her and I'll put in a good word for you and all that. But the thing is, she might want to go with another magazine – someone a little bigger.' I didn't add 'You stuck-up art-school bitch', much as I would have loved to. I thought I'd made my point.

Atlanta shoved her business card in my hand and jotted her home number on the back. 'Call me as soon as you know,' she said. All smiles now.

'I will. And if you're not in, perhaps I can leave a message with your cleaning lady.'

'Ah ha ha ha,' trilled Atlanta.

'Ha ha ha,' I agreed.

Well, I won that round, I thought to myself smugly as I descended in their lift. It was one of those glass bubbles without a lift shaft so I could see the whole building as it slithered down. A different magazine on every floor; a whole new world of possibilities and I had just cracked it – brilliantly.

'Visual portfolio!' I sniffed to myself. 'Just a poncy name for a bunch of photos.' But before the lift doors bing-bonged open at the ground floor, I felt a sinking feeling of another kind.

Why had I pretended Natalie and I were still best mates just to stop that stupid girl from lording it over me? Natalie hadn't called me to say when she was arriving. Natalie and I hadn't spoken since Sixth Form. Not since they day she'd stolen my boyfriend and I'd lost them both.

seven

Natalie had been a star ever since I'd known her. On my first day of school I'd seen her in her little blue uniform, kissing goodbye to her mother. When I picture the scene now, I can see her mum wearing a sea-green shantung dress that clung to her hips and showed off her long, slender calves and smoking a cigarette in a long tortoiseshell holder. But I must have added this image later because no mum would dress like that to drop her kids off for school. Not even Natalie's mum, who used to be a model. But the aura of glamour clung to Natalie even then. Maybe it was the way she held her back just a little bit straighter than all the other girls (ballet lessons, from age three) or maybe it was the silver hair slide that held her glossy brown hair back from her face, or her serious blue eyes under perfectly shaped brows that looked out at the scary grown-up world with an unshakeable confidence. But whatever it was, I was fascinated by her and ran to get the seat in the desk beside her before anyone else could.

She was an only child, her daddy didn't live with her, she had a grey rabbit called Flash and she was going to be a ballerina when she grew up.

Natalie thought it was very funny to jab me with her sharpened pencil, but when she found out I wouldn't scream, she got bored and stabbed one of the other children instead. After that, we never fought. I sailed along happily in Natalie's wake. Let her make the decisions about what games we should play, which children we should be friends with, which ones we should bully or merely snub. I hoped a little of her magic would rub off on me. When I learned to write, one of the first sentences I ever wrote was 'My best friend is Natalie Brown' underneath a picture of Natalie with a blue triangle body and dripping in jewels.

It was Natalie who named me Lindy, announcing that Linda was too common and that if I was going to be her friend I would have to have a name that nobody else had. For a couple of weeks I was Linderella, but I grew out of that pretty quickly. We learned to ride our bikes together in Natalie's garden. Read her ballet books together. We measured every single part of each other's bodies with her mum's tape measure and solemnly recorded all the numbers in a ruled-up exercise book. We each vowed that if our little finger ever measured more than half an inch around we would go on a diet immediately. We were only seven and this statistic seemed as vital to us as any other.

We got mumps together. Laughed at the same TV shows. Spent two terms talking nothing but pig-Latin which infuriated everybody else and made us helpless with laughter and superiority. Practised kissing on each other's arms and gave each other marks out of ten like in ice-skating. We shop-lifted nail varnish from Boots together. Begged our mums to send us to the same school so we wouldn't be split up. Every now and then Natalie would have a day off school to do some modelling. There were posters of her in the supermarket smiling as she was about to bite into an apple – some ad campaign she'd done for healthy eating. She was in *Just 17* once, modelling a gingham boob tube.

Natalie was the first girl in our class to get a bra of course. While the rest of her stayed magically reed-thin, her chest became a source of fascination for every boy in school. But Natalie didn't seem as interested in boys as the rest of us. Maybe it was because she knew they'd always be there for the taking, and that it wouldn't require any effort on her part to grab whoever she liked. While the rest of us agonised over diets and hairstyles and make-up and clothes to make boys

55

notice us and like us, Natalie did precisely nothing and drove them all crazy.

At home we'd watch her video of *Cabaret* over and over again. We knew all the words and every dance step. We'd drag her mum's kitchen chairs upstairs and recreate the KitKat Club in Natalie's bedroom.

By the time she was fourteen she'd decided she didn't want to be a ballerina any more. She was going to be a movie star and started going to drama classes two nights a week after school. She announced this with the same authority that she said or did everything else. When she told our geography teacher that she didn't need to know about igneous rock formations because she was going to be a movie star, he didn't even argue. Like everyone else, Mr Naylor was a tiny bit in love with Natalie. Whenever she spoke to him he blushed.

I went to drama classes with her for a couple of months, but I was so shy they were like torture. When we all had to stand in a circle and sing, I'd stare at the floor so I wouldn't catch anyone else's eye. The high point, supposedly, of every lesson was an improvisation exercise and the teacher would pick pairs of us at random to stand up in the middle of the class and pretend to be arguing with a parent about what time we had to come home. Or we'd have to be two old-age pensioners talking about the younger generation. Watching everyone else stand up and do their bit, my heart would beat loudly with panic and I could feel my face burning, praying I wouldn't be called that week. Whenever it was my turn, I'd stand up and my mouth would be so dry I could barely speak. My lips and gums would be fused together. I'd gabble anything I could think of, desperate to get it over with so I could sit down again. Then I'd watch Natalie doing her bit and think to myself that she wasn't really so fantastic.

'Kids today, they've got no respect! They play their loud music and kick footballs into my flowerbeds and they never say they're sorry . . .' It was clichéd, childish stuff but Natalie didn't seem to notice. She stood up there speaking confidently in her flat north-London tones as though she was reciting Shakespeare at the National. A complete stranger to self-doubt.

Natalie went out with a lot of boys from the drama school. If they were lucky, they'd last a month or two before she got tired of them. Usually, they'd have a friend for me and I never thought it odd or unusual if my 'date' spent the whole time competing with his mate for Natalie's attention and completely ignoring me. It just seemed somehow like the natural order of things. I was as hungry for Natalie's attention as they were.

And now she was coming back to London. Would she do me this one favour, for old time's sake? Would she even remember who I was?

eight

To: j.zweig@artisticlicense.com

Dear Jonathan
I am writing to request a photo session with your client, Natalie
Brown, for *The Hoop*.

. As you may be aware, *The Hoop* is a new British monthly magazine
for the 18–35 market. I will also post you a copy of the launch issue
for your information. If Natalie is interested in appearing in *The Hoop*
to promote the next series of *Don't Call Us*, I can almost certainly
guarantee her the front cover.

I would like to add that I am a very old friend of Natalie's and . . .

**And what? If we're such old friends, why haven't I got her
phone number?**

 Delete that.

As I am an old school friend of Natalie's, I am sure that she would . . .

**What? Like to gloat about how she's a big star just like she
always said she would be? Like to explain why she stole my
boyfriend? Like to try and steal my husband for an encore?**

Would you also please pass on my best wishes to Natalie? We were
best friends at school in London, but we have, unfortunately, lost
touch. I would love to see her again.

That would have to do. At least it was the truth. And I added

my phone number, just in case Jonathan Zweig decided to say yes.

I pressed SEND NOW and my computer replied with the Dalek-farting noise that said my poorly worded begging letter was now zipping across the Atlantic to the computer belonging to Jonathan Zweig, Natalie's agent.

No point ringing the show's press office here. They'd simply pretend to be running my request past Natalie's agent but in reality they'd probably just do nothing. Publicists are even more afraid of agents than the press are. Journalists and photographers have got nothing to lose, so what's the harm in asking?

I made a special trip to the Fed Ex office in town so the magazine would get to the States quickly. I had just a few days left before my notice period was up and I was starting to get very anxious. Even though Andrew earned enough for both of us – more than enough – I couldn't stand the idea of him supporting me.

When we were at school, Natalie and I had vowed we would always cling to our independence. We'd never let men rule our lives, we said. We could quote Germaine Greer to anyone who was interested, and frequently did. Weird, then to think that it was a boy who'd come between us.

When I started going out with Richard, I was so proud of myself, you'd have thought I'd split the atom, discovered a cure for cancer and won Wimbledon. Richard and his mates turned up on their bikes one day while I was playing hockey after school. Being goalie, all I had to do was stand out there in my shin pads and padded over-shoes, trying to keep warm and waiting for the ball to come my way. I'd cheer for the other team and hope they'd attack the goal just so I'd have something to do.

Richard and co. camped out behind the goal and spent the rest of the match making 'hilarious' jokes about my shin pads. I wanted the ground to open up and swallow me because I'd had a crush on Richard ever since the first day at Sixth Form College when I'd spotted him hanging out on the library steps, but I'd never had the guts to talk to him. He was doing all maths and science subjects so our paths never crossed except in the corridor between lessons. He had blond hair and blue eyes and was, in my opinion anyway, the best-looking boy in school. And already six foot – the start of my lifelong weakness for tall men.

As I lumbered after the ball, I was bright red with embarrassment, knowing that I must look like the Incredible Hulk. When I let two goals in, Richard and his mates cheered at my hopelessness. Hockey hecklers. Just my luck. Natalie didn't play any sports because she said she didn't want to get ugly muscles. Why hadn't I listened to her?

But after the game, Richard and his mates were still hanging around, waiting to tease me some more after I'd had a shower and changed. Richard sat behind me on the bus going home even though I found out later he lived in the other direction. He insulted me all the way to my front door, telling me I was the worst hockey player he'd ever seen and that I looked like a pregnant elephant. But he was laughing as he said it.

A couple of days later he phoned and asked me to go see *Die Hard* with him. I couldn't believe my luck to have landed this Adonis. At seventeen years old, a good-looking boyfriend seemed like my life's greatest achievement. For eighteen months, life was pretty damn terrific. I was in love.

Richard knew I was a virgin and he said he was too, so he didn't put any pressure on me to have sex with him although we did everything else. His family were very strict Catholics. I loved the fact that he obviously respected me so much. Not like other boys I'd been out with, who expected a shag on the second date because they'd already paid for the condoms.

'You're crazy not to sleep with him,' Natalie said. 'He'll only go looking for it somewhere else.'

I knew Richard wasn't like that, but I really wanted him to

be the one and I read all my back issues of *Cosmopolitan* to make sure I did it right. It happened one Sunday afternoon when his parents were out. We did it in Richard's bedroom and I made him take down the crucifix that his mother had hung over the bed. I thought it would hurt – Natalie had done it loads of times and she told me the first time always hurt – but it didn't, not at all. I've forgotten the actual sex part but there are two things I still remember. I remember the way Richard stroked the inside of my arms so lightly that I wasn't sure if he was touching me at all. And once, when I opened my eyes, Richard had his eyes open too and he was smiling at me and I remember thinking that I'd never been happier in my whole life than I was at that moment.

When I told Natalie that Richard and I had finally done it, she was full of congratulations as though I'd joined an exclusive club. It was the start of a brand new chapter for me and I wondered why I'd waited so long.

But then, just as suddenly, everything stopped being wonderful.

The very next Saturday night, Richard and I had our first argument. One of Richard's friends was driving us to a party in his dad's car and his driving was so bad that I made him stop the car and let me out. I said I'd rather go on the bus than end up smashing into a tree. Two older boys at our school had been killed in a car accident the year before and we'd all been really shocked by it. I expected Richard to come with me but he told me not to be so silly and stayed in the car.

I was so angry with him that I didn't go to the party at all and walked all the way home. As soon as I got back, I rang Natalie and told her all about it and she agreed that I'd done absolutely the right thing. I knew she would, because we agreed about everything. Natalie was going to the party so I asked her to tell Richard I was sorry and that I'd forgive him if he'd say he was sorry too. I had a miserable night at home on my own but at least I knew I could trust Natalie to sort it all out.

I expected Richard to call me the next morning and apologise. And I expected Natalie to phone and tell me everything Richard had said. When she didn't call, I rang her house after lunch and her mum told me she'd gone out. That was weird – Natalie and I had spent every weekend together since we were five.

So I rang Jill to find out what had happened at the party. Jill and I were friends then, but I'd only known her since she started college, so she wasn't my best friend. Not yet. At first she was really vague. Oh, the party was nothing special, all the usual people there, too many people squashed into three tiny rooms, warm beer in paper cups. Tina Berriman threw up on the stairs.

'And what about Richard?' I said.

Jill didn't want to tell me. I had to practically force it out of her. She'd gone to get her jacket to go home and found them – Richard and Natalie, snogging on a pile of coats in the upstairs bedroom.

The next day at school neither of them would talk to me or even look at me. It was as if I was the one who'd done something wrong. When I passed Richard or Natalie in the corridor, they looked straight ahead as though I didn't even exist. I felt as if the whole world had gone mad. I told myself it was all a terrible mistake. Natalie and Richard must be playing some kind of a joke on me. I sat crying in the toilets for most of the afternoon.

I waited for Natalie at the gate after school so she couldn't avoid me. She was with another girl called Alice. There was no sign of Richard, thank goodness.

'What's going on?' I pleaded with her. 'Why aren't you talking to me? What have I done?' I was crying with hurt and frustration and fear that Natalie didn't want to be my friend any more.

Natalie just looked down at me with those uncompromising blue eyes. She was suddenly three inches taller than me. When had she got so tall, I wondered.

'Look. I'm going out with Richard now. And if you have a problem with that, it's probably best if we stop being friends.'

I was so shocked, I couldn't think straight. 'Fine,' I said. 'I never want to talk to you again anyway. I hope you two'll be very happy together.'

And I had to run off because I was crying so much. I thought I loved Richard. I thought I hated Natalie.

I made a few half-hearted attempts to talk to Richard again, but he blanked me completely at school and it was too humiliating to run after him. Eventually, after a week of this, his mum bullied him to come to the phone when I called.

'Does this mean we've broken up then?' I said.

'I guess so,' he said. And that was that. At least that made it official.

There were two months before our exams and I swear neither of them spoke a word to me after that. We avoided each other as much as we could and if we passed in the corridor we never made eye contact. God knows how I got through my exams. Those months are a red-eyed blur of crying and cramming.

'Don't worry, you'll get over him in time,' said Mum. 'There's plenty more fish in the sea.'

'He's not worth crying over,' said Jill. 'You're better off without him.'

I wrote a long letter pouring out all my feelings, saying how much I wanted us to be friends again.

'Don't be silly,' said Jill. 'Don't put anything in writing. You'll just regret it. All men are bastards. Forget about Richard.'

'It's not *to* Richard,' I told her. 'It's to Natalie.'

Getting dumped by Richard was nothing compared to being dumped by Natalie. I'd only known Richard eighteen months or so but I'd known Natalie practically my whole life. We'd done everything together since we were five. We were more like sisters than best friends. Every afternoon as soon as we got home from school, we'd be straight on the phone to each other for two hours to catch up on any gossip we might have missed. I couldn't go shopping without having Natalie along to tell me what I looked like from the back. I couldn't enjoy a TV programme until I'd rehashed it all with Natalie afterwards.

There was an ache in my heart for Richard, but there was a hole in my life where Natalie used to be. I couldn't understand why she'd suddenly turned on me like that. It was unbearable. If she wanted Richard that badly she could have him, I wrote. Just please let us be friends again.

I don't know if she even read my letter. She didn't make any sign that she had. I hadn't spoken to her since.

I didn't expect to hear anything from Jonathan Zweig for days, but two days later when I checked my e-mail I found a message waiting for me from him. I was too nervous to read it at first. Don't get your hopes up, I told myself. It's probably just a standard rejection letter. It's probably just a computer-generated reply saying that they've received my e-mail and that it's being dealt with. It's probably saying Natalie isn't coming to London after all. It's probably saying the show's been cancelled and that she's retiring from show business. Having prepared myself for the worst case scenario, I thought I'd be immune to disappointment. I was wrong.

Thank you for your correspondence. Unfortunately, Natalie Brown is unable to grant your request for a photo session at this time.

I read it a couple of times just to torture myself. Well. That was that. It wasn't really a surprise. It had been so long.

Loads of times I'd picked up the phone to call Natalie. But I'd always chickened out. I wrote her a long letter saying how sorry I was, but I never sent it. After A-Levels, Natalie went straight to drama school as she had always told us she would;

not RADA as she'd hoped, but Guildhall, her mum told me, and after a few months, she moved into a flat with some other students closer into town. Richard went to Leeds to do some kind of computer degree. I thought they'd break up for sure, but against the odds, they managed to keep their long-distance romance going.

One Christmas I saw Natalie and Richard together in the supermarket and I hid by the Pick'n'Mix, surprised at how much it still hurt to see them together.

One day, it must have been about three years later because I'd finished college by then, I bumped into Natalie's mum in the High Street looking like a Bond Girl and she told me Natalie and Richard had got married and had gone to live in California. Richard had got a job in Silicon Valley and Natalie was going to launch her career in Hollywood. It was all so neat it made me sick. Natalie had landed on her feet again with absolutely zero effort on her part. She hadn't even invited me to the wedding.

For years after that, nobody heard much of Natalie. Her mum told me she'd got an agent. Then she had a small part in a movie, but it was so small you couldn't even see her. There were a couple of tiny parts on TV – nothing that was seen in the UK. A couple of commercials. A pilot for a comedy series that never got made. Then three years ago came *Don't Call Us*, a sitcom about four wannabe actors sharing an apartment. There was a dumb one, a gay one, a nice one and Natalie was cast as the English one. Quite a stretch, wouldn't you say? Wannabe English actress living in LA playing wannabe English actress living in LA.

When the show came on TV in Britain, I watched every episode with a sick fascination. Natalie was a star. She had a new feathery haircut and they made her talk in a really fake Sloaney accent so that the Americans would get the point that she was meant to be English but it was Natalie all right.

And Richard? Well, that marriage was over. I read an article in an American magazine a while ago that said Natalie had got engaged again to an architect called Max Ogilvy. She looked glorious, positively glowing. Television's golden girl. Why on earth would she want to see me again?

nine

Next morning as I passed the news-stand on my way to the tube, Nigel Napier's name leapt out at me from the front page of *The Ledger*. No story – just a teaser.

What's Nigel Napier so dog-gone angry about? Pages 4 and 5.

So they'd got him had they?

Yes. But not in the way I expected. I turned to page four to see Debbie Gibb's photo by-line staring back at me. That serious, concerned expression that says, 'It saddens me enormously to have to break this terrible news to you, my dear readers. But anyway . . .'

And there was Nigel. And Mrs Nigel. On the beach in Florida with their kids and the headline: THAT'S MY DOG! Mrs Nigel had committed the ultimate tabloid sin of wearing a bikini whilst overweight – and boy, was she paying the price.

The paper had even gone to the trouble of circling the three rolls of fat on her stomach, for the benefit of any slow-witted readers (the majority of our circulation incidentally). The art department had really gone to town. They didn't usually put that sort of creative effort into their layouts. All during the war in the Balkans, the paper hadn't run a single map to show where the Balkans actually were because nobody could be arsed.

But this was different. This was a fat bird. Time to pull out all the stops.

In a little box in the corner, our health editor had weighed in with her two-cents worth to warn of the dangers of obesity. Mrs Nigel was apparently running the risk of heart disease, osteoporosis, several types of cancer and an early, unpleasant porky death.

But she wasn't even fat! I fumed. For a woman of forty-eight, she was in pretty good shape. She had great legs too, but the paper hadn't circled those. If I looked as good in a bikini as she did when I was forty-eight, I wouldn't have much cause for complaint.

On page five there was a photo of Nigel lunging angrily towards the camera. Oh dear, he'd beaten up Peter, the photographer. Well, the paper wouldn't let him get away with that. Even if they didn't press charges for assault, Elaine, our beloved Führer, probably had a team of crack reporters at his house in Cheshire going through his garbage bins at that very minute. And they'd be feeling very self-righteous about it, too, because now they were going to bring down an angry and violent man and make this world a better place in which to live.

Debbie would be practically bursting an artery over her scoop – not to mention her free holiday in Florida. I was well out of this one.

Andrew and I were reading in bed a few nights later when the phone rang.

'Is that Lindy?' I couldn't quite place the voice.

'Yeah. Who's that?'

'It's me. Natalie.'

Even though I'd been thinking about her so much lately, for a couple of seconds, I couldn't think for the life of me who Natalie was. Then it hit me and I screamed. 'Oh, my God! How are you?'

'I'm fine, I'm wonderful. How are you?'

'Good. I'm good. Where are you calling from?'

'I'm at work – in LA. What time is it there?'

'It's ten-thirty at night. What time is it where you are?'

'It's half past two in the afternoon.'

I could hear us saying these totally banal things to one another. I guess neither of us wanted to bring up the fact that we weren't supposed to be speaking to each other.

'How did you get my number?' I asked.

'It was on your e-mail, remember?'

'Oh, right. But I never expected to hear from you,' I said. 'Your agent said you didn't want to do it.'

'Oh, that's his entire job, saying no to people. He doesn't even bother to ask me whether I want to do things any more, because I've told him to say no to absolutely everything. But I happened to call him the day after he got your letter – because of all the hotels and things he's got to fix up for us on this trip – and he said that someone had written to him claiming to be an old friend of mine. It's frightening, the people who've been coming out of the woodwork these last few years. You wouldn't believe it. Somebody sold the *National Enquirer* one of my old school reports! Can you believe it?'

'Really! What, did they break into your mum's house and steal it? Is she OK?'

'Erm. No, nobody broke in.'

'Well, what happened? How did they get hold of it? Do you think it was one of the teachers?'

'Look – it's really not important. Just forget about it. Gosh. I can't believe I'm actually talking to you after all this time. I didn't think you'd ever want to talk to me again.' Her words came tumbling out in a big jumble; her voice sounded much posher than I remembered and just ever so slightly American-ised.

'Don't be silly. All that was ages ago. We were just kids. Life goes on.' Now that the words were out of my mouth, I realised that I really didn't care that much any more. I'd thought about Richard a lot over the years, obviously. I guess it's true what they say that you never forget your first love and sometimes I'd wonder how things would have turned out between us if Natalie hadn't stuck her oar in. I'd get out my old photo albums and look at the three photos I had of him and wonder where Richard was and how he was doing. But it was curiosity more than anything. It didn't hurt. I mean – I was eighteen years old then. Who marries the guy they went out with when they were eighteen? Apart from Natalie, that is.

When I heard that he and Natalie had split up, I'd even thought of phoning him, but International Directory Enquiries didn't have a listing and I wasn't sure where he was living. I should have rung his parents and asked them, but they'd moved and gone ex-directory. It seemed a little pathetic anyway, chasing after a guy who'd dumped you.

'So, how is Richard?' I said. There – I'd said his name and the world hadn't come to an end.

'It's a long story. A *very* long story. But I promise I'll tell you all about it. We get into London on Friday and we're staying at the Metropolitan on Park Lane.'

'Ooh, get you!'

'I know,' she said. 'It's not fair. I really wanted to stay at The Sanderson. So you'll have to let me take you to lunch somewhere madly expensive.'

'You're on. By the way, Jill says she wants her Pet Shop Boys album back.'

Natalie screamed with laughter. 'Do you two still see each other, then?'

'Uh huh. She's my best mate. She's got two kids now. Holly and Matthew.'

'Oh really?' Natalie sounded a little taken aback, as though she expected Jill and me to still be studying for our A-levels. 'Well, do you think she'd settle for a CD? I don't think you can buy LPs any more.'

'I'm sure she'd be delighted.'

'Look, I'm going to have to go now, because we're in the middle of rehearsals. It's utter madness here. But I'll call you as soon as we get to London and I know exactly what we're going to be doing. It's all a bit up in the air at the moment.'

'That's great. I can't wait to see you.'

'Me too. I'm so excited now.'

'I'm really glad you rang.'

'So we're friends again, then?' She sounded very unsure of herself suddenly, as though she expected me to turn on her at any minute.

'Of course we are.'

After I hung up, I sat on my bed with that sort of buzzy feeling you get after running upstairs. All the blood was racing around my body very fast.

'Who were you talking to?' asked Andrew.

'It was Natalie. She was calling from LA. I think we're going to be friends again.'

'Natalie Brown called you! That's amazing! Can I meet her? She's a major babe!' Andrew had been so impressed when he found out I'd gone to school with Natalie. I know he bragged to all the blokes at work about it, making it sound like Natalie was popping over to our house every five minutes to borrow my underwear.

'You probably will meet her. We're meeting up for lunch next week when she gets to London.'

I didn't have any qualms about Andrew lusting after Natalie. Half the men in Britain were in love with her so why should Andrew be any different? It wouldn't do him any good anyway. Natalie was so far out of his league it was almost funny. If he'd been at our school, he would have been top of her list of kids to stab with her sharp little pencils.

I realised that Natalie hadn't asked me about my life – hadn't asked if I was married or anything like that. But there was plenty of time to fill her in on what I'd been doing for the last eleven years. Come to think of it, she hadn't actually said whether or not she was going to let me photograph her either. Well, we'd talk about it when she got to London. For now, I was just so excited at the thought of seeing her again. Too excited to sleep.

I dragged down my old photo albums from the top of the

wardrobe. There were pages and pages of me and Natalie posing together in photo booths, sucking in our cheeks and looking cool. There was one of us on holiday in Norfolk standing on the beach in our bikinis.

'Wow! Is that her?' said Andrew.

'You've seen these,' I told him. 'I must have shown them to you before.'

'Yeah – but I wasn't paying attention then. Let me see.'

It was freezing that day, I remembered. What on earth were we thinking about? There was a man in the background walking his dog and wearing a quilted anorak. I'd never noticed him before. Was that really us in those photos? It was so long ago, it was like looking at two other people. There was another photo I'd forgotten about. A tiny colour snap of me and Natalie – we must have been about eight years old – at some kid's birthday party. We're lining up for some kind of race and there's a look on my face of pure determination, as though nothing and nobody was going to stand in my way. What had happened to that little girl? Where had she gone?

'Who's this?' said Andrew, pointing to a photo of me at a party with one arm thrown around the waist of a boy with blond hair. We're laughing with our mouths wide open at some long-forgotten joke. He's looking over my head at something out of shot and I'm lunging straight into the camera. The flash has made my eyes go red.

'That's Richard,' I say. 'A guy we were at school with. Natalie's ex-husband.'

It doesn't hurt when I say it now. How easily it's all been filed away. P for Past. P for Painless. It doesn't hurt a bit.

ten

We'd arranged to meet at The Ivy at one. I got there at ten past on purpose and still Natalie wasn't there. The waitress eyed me disbelievingly when I told her I was meeting Natalie Brown and led me to a table in the corner. I ordered a gin and slimline tonic and counted the coloured diamonds in the stained glass windows to give myself something to do until Natalie arrived.

My scalp still hurt from the vigorous blow-drying it had received that morning. The thought of seeing Natalie again had thrown me into a major panic. Apart from my new Mango dress which I was wearing today, nothing else in my wardrobe was suitable for lunch with a major TV star. Natalie probably spent more on manicures in a month than I spent on clothes in an entire year. And my hair was all wrong. I'd worn it scraped back in a pony tail for so long, I couldn't even remember what the style was supposed to be any more. And as for the colour – well, what colour? I couldn't meet Natalie with mousey brown hair. I wanted her to think I was on top of the world. I didn't want her to think I'd gone to pieces just because she wasn't my friend any more. Of course, what I really wanted was major reconstructive plastic surgery – just a little light liposuction and a couple of cheekbones – but there was no time for that. I'd booked into the hair-dresser's for a cut and colour that morning. My new, flicky-up auburn bob had cost a fortune and I'd been suckered into buying a bottle of their special hair serum as well on the way out. Blowing so much money when I didn't even have a job felt wonderfully exciting. As I walked through the West End to the restaurant, admiring my reflection in every shop window I passed, I spotted a pair of silver Nikes just like Atlanta's and went into the sports shop and put them on my credit card without a second thought. See how well I'm doing, Natalie? I can buy shoes without even looking at the price tag. When I signed the slip and saw that I'd just spent £130 on trainers I nearly fainted.

I'd never been to The Ivy before and was thrilled to spot Martine McCutcheon tucking into shepherd's pie. And was that Jamie Theakston over by the window? I noticed people pausing mid-conversation and looking surreptitiously towards the door. It was Natalie.

The man from the *Daily Express* reached out and touched her on the arm as she passed his table.

'So nice to see you again,' he purred but I'd have put money on the fact that he'd never met her before in his life.

'Have you been waiting ages?' she asked.

As I sprung to my feet, I had just a second to take in the sheen of her dark brown hair, the sparkle in her blue eyes, the elegance of her tailored chocolate-brown trouser suit. I felt tears spring unexpectedly to my eyes as I threw my arms around her.

'Oh God, you're so little!' I exclaimed. I could count the ribs on her back through her fine knitwear. 'There's nothing left of you!'

'I can't believe it's really you!' People were turning to watch as we hugged each other, squeezing for all we were worth. The whisper level went up a notch. Meanwhile, Natalie and I kept staring at each other, trying to take in the passing years.

'How long have you been a red-head?' she asked.

'Oh, ages. Years,' I fibbed. It was actually more like an hour. 'How long have you been so skinny?'

'Ever since I got to LA. I've been on a permanent diet for ten years.'

'You look so much smaller than you do on TV. Sorry, that's a stupid thing to say, isn't it? But you look fantastic.'

'So do you. You look really well. Really glowing.'

'It must be all that fresh London air I've been getting.'

'So. Wow. Here we are. I can't believe it.'

'Me neither. How long are you going to be in town for?'

'Not long. Our last shooting day is the end of August. I'm not sure how long we'll stay in town after that. We might go to Spain to visit Mummy. Max hasn't met her yet.'

'What's your mum doing in Spain?'

'She's married again. They've been there about six years.'

There was a second's silence that threatened to become awkward until Natalie said, 'I think we should get a bottle of champagne, don't you?'

'I think we deserve it,' I agreed.

She ordered a bottle of Laurent-Perrier which arrived in a silver bucket.

'What shall we drink to?' she asked.

'To us. To old friends.'

'And new beginnings.'

'Oh dear, now I'm going to cry again.'

Only after I had a couple of glasses of Laurent-Perrier safely tucked away and we had finally managed to concentrate on the menu long enough to order, did I feel it safe to bring up the topic that had kept us apart all these years.

'So,' I said. 'I was sorry to hear about you and Richard breaking up.'

'You don't mean that, do you?' She held a tiny forkful of Belgian endive salad poised in mid-air.

'No!' I laughed. And Natalie laughed too. That's when I knew everything was going to be OK. I remembered how I'd felt that day when we'd first sat together at school, hoping a bit of her glamour would rub off on me. And now here I was at The Ivy drinking champagne.

'So, what happened?' I asked her. 'I'm dying to know.'

'You mean you don't know?'

'Well, I know you got divorced and that you're engaged to someone else now – I read that in the papers, but that's it. I don't know any of the gory details. So come on, tell me. You owe me that much at least.'

I took another sip of champagne in excited anticipation. Natalie had drunk just half a glass and then moved on to hot water and lemon. Detoxing, she said.

She put down her fork and clasped her hands in front of her, suddenly serious. There was the finest line just above the left corner of her mouth. That was new.

'You must have thought I was such a bitch.'

'Hey.' I waved my hand. 'Ancient history and all that.'

'But you don't know how hard it was for me.'

'Hard?' Of everybody in the world I'd ever known, Natalie was the one person for whom life had been softer than a feather pillow.

'The pressure of knowing I had it in me to be somebody. Knowing I'd been given this talent and this – face – and I couldn't just waste it. You have no idea what that's like.'

'No. I don't.'

'And I was so jealous of you—'

'What?' I couldn't believe what I was hearing. 'You were jealous of *me*? That's the daftest thing I've ever heard of. What was it you were jealous of, exactly? Was it the chubby knees?'

'Because you were able to just be ordinary,' she continued. 'Your mother didn't stop you from eating chocolate and crisps and everything else that had so much as a gram of fat or sugar in it. She didn't weigh you every morning to make sure you hadn't gained an ounce. You didn't have to do ballet classes since you were three years old with a sadistic teacher who threatened to cut off your toes if we didn't point them properly. You didn't get dragged out of school to audition for stupid commercials for chicken nuggets that I wasn't allowed to eat anyway. You weren't treated like some empty-headed

76

china doll that had to be wrapped up in cotton wool in case she broke a fingernail. You were allowed to look scruffy once in a while.'

'Oh yeah, and didn't I make the most of that?' I laughed.

She was whispering now so that the four women at the next table couldn't hear what she was saying. 'And all the time I was really scared. Thinking, well, what if I'm not special after all? Then what? Because all my life I'd just been able to waltz in and get whatever I wanted. I thought it was just me. And then, when I started doing those drama classes, there were all these other dreadful kids who'd been brought up to think they were special too. And believe me, most of them weren't. Well, we couldn't all be right. We couldn't all be the best. Does that make any sense to you?'

'Kind of. But you never said any of this. I had no idea. You always seemed so confident.'

'Did I? And then when you started going out with Richard – you were so happy. I'd never stayed interested in a boy for more than a few weeks. They were always so boring, fawning over me like puppies. And it didn't matter who it was, Mummy would always say they weren't good enough for me. They were all too suburban, as though it was my fault we lived in the suburbs. She'd show me photos of all the men she'd gone out with before I was born – awful Hoorays and lead guitarists and cheesy Italian counts – and she'd say, "This is the sort of man you want to wait for. Don't bother with all these silly boys!" But I was only a kid. Who did she expect me to go out with? Bill Wyman? And then you started going out with Richard, who was the best-looking boy in the whole school.'

'Oh, did you think so?' I was suddenly really cheered up by this thought. Not that it mattered now of course.

'Absolutely. Mummy thought so too. And you know she has such good taste. And I was furious that he was going out with you and not me. The whole time you were together it bugged the hell out of me. I know this is a really terrible thing

to say and it might sound really bitchy but I kept thinking –
why on earth does he like her better than me?'

You're right, I thought. It does sound really bitchy but I was
used to Natalie speaking her mind. If you think she's bad
now, you should have heard her when she was twelve. I'd
waited too long and missed Natalie too much to suddenly
start getting offended.

'Anyway,' I said, 'carry on.'

'Well, do you remember the week I went up for that
cleanser commercial?'

'Er, vaguely,' I said, not remembering it at all.

'Don't be silly, of course you do. It was going to be
enormous. And then I didn't get it and I wanted to die. It
was so unfair. And there you were with Richard, not a care in
the world.'

'No – just A-Levels and wondering what I was going to do
with the rest of my life.'

'Exactly. And you just kept going on and on about how
happy you were because you'd finally discovered sex and I
guess I just snapped. So that night, when he was at the party
on his own, I just decided to grab him for myself. And in the
end, it turned out to be very easy. I didn't have to try too
hard.'

'I can imagine,' I whispered. God, did I really need to hear
all this? All the old sick feelings of jealousy and betrayal came
flooding back when I thought of that night and pictured them
together. Somehow, the thought of them kissing on a pile of
coats was more painful than the fact that they'd actually got
married. I know that doesn't make any sense, but there you
are. I took a sip of champagne.

'So,' she said, 'I had to choose – you or Richard. And I
chose Richard.'

'So what you're saying is, we haven't spoken in ten years
just because you didn't get a cleanser commercial.'

'Look, it wasn't just any commercial. It was going to be on
TV for a whole year. And I didn't expect it to last with me and

Richard anyway. He was going off to university in Leeds, and I thought that would be the end of it and you and I could be friends again.'

'So how come you ended up marrying him?'

'Well, after about three months I decided I ought to sleep with him and I planned this really special evening because I wanted it to be perfect. But he wasn't interested. He actually refused to have sex with me. He said he wasn't like that. He said he respected me too much and all this other bullshit that didn't make any sense either. I can't even remember half of it now.

'Anyway, it drove me crazy. I became obsessed with him. Instead of breaking up with him, I'd schlep all the way up to Leeds at least once a month to see him. He'd always introduce me to people as his girlfriend and I'd stay with him and we'd sleep in the same bed but he simply wouldn't do it to me. I was giving him blow jobs till I was blue in the face – literally – because somehow in his grand scheme of things that didn't count, but as for anything else forget it. And this went on for three years. Can you believe it? Three years.

'Meanwhile, back in London I must have shagged half the drama school but the only guy I really wanted was Richard. And you know, he said he loved me all the time. He said I was the most beautiful woman he'd ever met and that he didn't deserve me, but he was turning me into a basket case.' She paused to stare pointedly at the women on the next table who were desperately trying to ear-wig on the whole conversation.

'Do you mind?' she said and moved her chair right into the corner. I dragged my chair over too as she lowered her voice even more. 'I thought it was a religious thing, you know, on account of him being Catholic. So I kept trying to get him drunk.so I could seduce him. But it was useless. Just my luck to meet the only student in the whole country who'd have two pints and say, "That's my lot." Maybe three if he was really pushing the boat out. And he wouldn't even smoke a joint because he said it just makes you lazy and stupid.

'So the first time I ever slept with him was actually right after his finals. Everyone was knocking back tequila slammers and, for the first time in his life, Richard got absolutely hammered. Hallelujah! I thought. So I threw him into a taxi, took him back to his flat and basically just leapt on him.

'Well, it was unbelievable. Once he got started there was no stopping him. He was like a man possessed. It was fantastic. And that seemed to do the trick, because for about a month after that everything was completely normal between us. Sex and everything. Then, just a little while after that, he heard that he'd got a job with this research and development place in California and asked me to marry him and go with him.

'I was way too young to get married, but I couldn't bear the thought of him being so far away. It was bad enough when he'd just been in Leeds.'

'And of course it must have been really exciting for you,' I pointed out. 'The thought of going to California – Hollywood and all that.'

'Oh, that never even occurred to me,' she said. 'I didn't want to leave Mummy all on her own and leave my home, but I didn't want to be apart from Richard either. It was a terrible decision to have to make. I was *torn*.' She sipped her hot water. 'Of course, it did work out quite well, I suppose. Richard had a work visa all arranged for him and I was eventually able to apply for a Green Card on the strength of that. You would have loved the wedding. I wish you'd been there.'

'Where was it?' I said, thinking that I would rather have poked my eyes out with a stick.

'Just a very small ceremony at Chelsea Register Office and we didn't even have a honeymoon because two weeks later we flew out to the States.'

'How exciting.'

'No. Not really. As soon as we got there, everything changed almost immediately. It was like he suddenly turned into a different person.'

'Really? How d'you mean?'

'He'd come home at three in the morning, saying he'd been working late and not even trying to make it sound believable. I thought it must be another woman – maybe somebody he worked with.

'I thought I was cracking up. We'd only been married two months and I'd made love to him precisely twice in all that time – both times on the night of the wedding. Now here I was in a strange country all on my own, stuck out in San Jose which I expected to be really groovy like the Burt Bacharach song, but it turned out to be a giant industrial estate, right in the middle of California and absolutely miles from LA. If I'd bothered to look in an atlas before I got on the plane, I would have known that, but I was too busy organising my wedding.

'Meanwhile I didn't have a job and I didn't know a soul apart from Richard and he was treating me like I was a piece of luggage he'd brought with him and then decided he didn't really need any more.'

'Gosh. That doesn't make any sense,' I said.

'Then one night he just didn't come home at all. I was going out of my mind with worry. I phoned the police but they practically just laughed at me. They just said call again in the morning if he doesn't show up.

'The first thing the next day I rang his office to see if they'd heard from him and he picked up the phone himself. He didn't even say he was sorry. He was so cold. I remember his words exactly. He said he'd made a terrible mistake, and at first I didn't know what he meant. I thought he meant he'd made a terrible mistake last night and got lost, or he'd done something awful at work and pressed the wrong button on his computer or something. So I said, "What do you mean? Is there something I can do to help?" '

'And he said, "Getting married. We should never have got married. It's all been a big mistake." I couldn't believe what I was hearing. And when he came home that night he told me the whole story.'

I waited for her to go on. But apparently she had finished.

'Well,' I prompted. 'What did he say? What was the whole story?'

'Oh God, you really don't know, do you? I suppose I always thought that somehow the word would have got back to you.'

I shook my head blankly.

'Richard's gay,' she said.

'No! He can't be gay. That's impossible!'

'Last time I spoke to him he was living in San Francisco with a fifty-five-year-old history professor called Gregory.'

'Oh. My. God.' I didn't know what else to say. Being dumped for your beautiful best friend was one thing. Being dumped for a bloke called Gregory was another kettle of fish entirely. 'Gay.' I repeated the word again but it didn't sound any more believable. I sat there in silence for a few seconds unable to think of anything else to say. 'What does he look like now?' I said at last. It was a stupid thing to say under the circumstances but I'd always wondered.

Natalie hooted. 'Ha! Well, he lost his hair very quickly. You know what blonds are like. D'you remember, he had a receding hairline while he was still at school. By the time he'd left university there wasn't much of it left at all. After he came out he shaved the rest of it off and grew a moustache and turned into a total clone almost overnight. I was grateful that he did though because it made it easier for me to get over him. I didn't fancy him at all after that.'

'So what did you do when Richard told you he was gay?'

'It was a complete nightmare. I can't imagine now how I got through it. I just didn't know how to deal with it at all. I thought it must be something to do with me not being attractive enough. I nagged him to tell me all the horrible details – I was torturing myself but I just had to know. And at first he was a real coward about it. At first he said he'd never actually had sex with a man – he was just attracted to men. But I could just tell that was bullshit. I mean, I wanted to believe it but I thought about everything that had happened over the last four years and it just didn't add up.

'Then eventually he confessed that he'd had sex with a man once – somebody he'd met in Leeds. But I kept on and on badgering him until finally the whole thing came out, so to speak. Remember that strange guy George Fisher at college?'

'Yeah.'

'Well, he was the first, apparently.'

'But that must have been while I was going out with him.' I couldn't believe what I was hearing.

'No, babe. It was actually *before* you started going out with him.'

'Oh, Christ. It was George who was driving the car that night we had that fight.'

'Was it? Well, that would explain a lot, wouldn't it? Then when he got to Leeds it was shag city apparently. But he didn't want any of his family to find out, so he was always Mr Straight when he came back down to London. That's where I came in so handy. A nice pretty girlfriend to parade in front of his parents. And then, of course, once I'd got the truth out of him, I had this major, major panic attack thinking that I might have AIDS.'

'Oh, Natalie – I'm sorry. You poor, poor thing!'

'We'd only had sex maybe a dozen times in all those years – can you believe that? But still, I was out of my mind with worry. I went and had an AIDS test and it was the most humiliating experience in my whole life. The nurse at the clinic treated me like I was some degenerate junkie. I was too ashamed to tell her my husband was actually a shirt-lifter. I was dying to ask her if you could get it from blow jobs but I didn't have the guts.'

'But you're OK?' I asked.

'I had to wait a whole week for the results. It was like torture. I was so convinced that I was going to die and that God was punishing me for stealing Richard from you.'

'Oh, Natalie. I wish I'd known. I can't bear to think of you going through all that on your own. I wish I'd called you. I wanted to call you. I'm really, really sorry.'

She reached out and grabbed both my hands. 'Can you ever forgive me?' she whispered.

'Hey, forget about it,' I told her. I'd been all ready to be jealous of Natalie all over again for stealing Richard and for having a wonderful TV star life just handed to her on a plate but now I realised that she must have suffered every bit as much as I had. Even more. Poor Natalie! How could I be angry with her?

'It sounds like you did me a favour,' I told her.

'Yes, maybe I did,' she said, sounding rather pleased with this thought. 'Anyway, the test came back negative, but they said that if I thought I'd put myself at risk, I should go back for another test in six months' time, because it can take that long for anything to show up. I went backwards and forwards to that bloody clinic every six months for the next four years. Just to be really, really sure. Well, you can imagine what that did for my sanity.'

I nodded sympathetically.

'Anyway, there was no point Richard and I living together any more but neither of us wanted to get a divorce. It wasn't like he was planning to get married again or anything and besides he was still terrified of his parents finding out.'

'But that's ridiculous!' I interrupted. 'Who cares whether he's gay or not in this day and age? Apart from you and me – obviously. I mean, people don't still worry about stuff like that, do they?'

'Apparently his parents do. They're not exactly *Guardian* readers. And I think he was absolutely terrified of his father. He said his mum would probably have been OK about it, but that would have made his father even angrier and he couldn't bear the thought of them fighting about him. Whatever. In any case, it suited me to keep my mouth shut because as long as we were still married, I could hang on to my Green Card. I believe it's what's called a lavender marriage,' she sniffed.

'Except usually the groom has the courtesy to let the bride know beforehand that she's just a front.

'And he said he'd support me financially until I could get on my feet. He was already earning a fortune straight out of university playing with his computers and he could well afford it. So I moved to LA and rented an apartment in West Hollywood which isn't as glamorous as it sounds and I hammered on every door I could find until I got myself an agent. Waiting to find out if I was HIV positive made me realise that life was too short and that if I was going to make a success of my career I'd better get my skates on.'

'That's exactly what I've been telling myself,' I told her.

'Anyway, that's why I never do any interviews any more. I promised Richard that as long as his parents are still alive I'd never tell anyone the real reason why we'd split up. The only other person who knows is Max – and you. And you've got to promise me you won't breathe a word of it to anyone.'

'Sure. I promise.'

'Oh, good. I know I can trust you. You always keep your promises, don't you?'

'So you never do interviews at all?' I said. I could feel my big break at *The Hoop* slipping away.

'When I first got the series I did a bit of press because I was so excited to think that it was finally happening for me and that I was going to be famous.'

'That must have been amazing,' I said.

'But you know, I always knew that I was going to make it. I just knew it. Ever since I was very young. I knew that I had what it takes to be a great actress.'

'Really?'

'Yeah. I don't want to sound big-headed but say there was a camera in this restaurant now, secretly filming everybody.'

'Yeah?'

'Well, it would be more interesting for people to look at me and what I was doing, than it would be to look at anyone else. Do you know what I mean? It's just this quality I have.'

'Wow,' I said. 'That's really quite something.'

'And when it finally happened and the press wanted to talk to me I was so naïve, I thought they'd just want to talk about the TV show and maybe the fact I was English, but they kept on and on about who's your husband? And why didn't you and your first husband have any children? Just to shut them up I told them I couldn't have kids because of a medical condition – and that actually worked quite well because it got me a lot of sympathy. Much better than telling them, "I don't have kids because my gay husband would never have sex with me", don't you think?'

'I wish you'd told me all this,' I said. 'You must have been going through hell. Why didn't you ever call me?'

'I wanted to, all the time. I must have picked up the phone a million times. But I was afraid to. I thought you'd never forgive me for what I'd done. And then when I found out about Richard, I was so embarrassed, as though it was my fault he was gay. It was complicated.' She reached in her bag for a tissue. I thought she was going to cry but she just dabbed around her lips.

'Oh, come here,' I said. I leaned across the table and hugged her with tears in my eyes. 'I'm so glad to have you back.'

'Me too,' she said. 'You've got your sleeve in your sticky toffee pudding.'

'I don't care,' I laughed. I didn't care about anything. 'I can't believe we let a stupid boy come between us.'

'But what about you?' said Natalie. 'Here's me rabbitting on and you haven't told me anything about you.' She picked up my hand and did a quick inventory. 'Engagement ring. Wedding ring. Who is he? Anyone I know?'

'No, his name's Andrew. He's an accountant. I met him up a mountain in Austria and we've been married three years. That's it, really.' It all sounded so indescribably dull compared to Natalie's adventures.

'And how's married life?'

'Oh, you know,' I shrugged. 'The same as living-together life. Only now I've got nicer saucepans.'

'Any kids?'

'No – just a cat.' It was strange to realise how little we knew about each other any more.

'But you've kept your own name.'

'We always promised each other we would, didn't we?' I reminded her. 'Actually to tell the truth, I had to keep my own name. Otherwise I'd be Linda Pinder.'

'Speaking of husbands,' said Natalie, 'here comes my gorgeous man now.' She half stood up and waved and I looked over my shoulder as a tall man in a blue sports jacket and jeans walked over to our table, waving lots of shopping bags. He leaned over and gave her an enormous, noisy kiss. Mmmwah!

'Your timing's perfect,' she told him. 'Now you can eat my dessert. Pull up a chair.' A waiter had already glided over as if on silent casters, moving furniture to make way for the new arrival. 'Max, this is Lindy – my oldest friend in the whole world. Lindy, this is Max.'

'Hi,' I said.

'Oh, *hi*!' he said. He sounded so enthusiastic you would have thought that I was his oldest friend in the whole world too. He stuck out his hand and kissed me on the cheek at the same time, so that I was momentarily overwhelmed by all the activity. 'Natalie's told me all about you. She's been so excited about seeing you again. I've been quite jealous!'

'Really?'

He sat down and immediately started sorting through the shopping bags, looking for something.

'I've had the most fabulous morning!' he said. 'I've been up in the London Eye! And I walked across the Millennium Bridge! You should have come, darling!'

Everything he said seemed to end in an exclamation mark.

'I've seen London, remember?' Natalie smiled fondly. 'I don't need to walk across some smelly river.'

'I thought the Bridge was still closed,' I said. Max just laughed and tapped the side of his nose and Natalie smirked as if to say, well maybe it's closed to the likes of you . . . and I felt rather silly.

'And I found the best street!' said Max. 'Sloane Street. Do you know it?' he asked me.

'Yeah,' I laughed. 'It's pretty famous.'

'Look, honey, I bought you a present,' he said and handed Natalie a Prada carrier bag. She opened the box inside and unfolded the tissue paper to reveal a shirt made of light blue gauzy fabric.

'Oh, baby!' She flung her arms around his neck and kissed him. 'That's so sweet! It's divine!'

'I hope they renew your contract on this show, darling, because I've spent all your money this morning.' He laughed very loudly, absolutely delighted with his excellent shopping, his beautiful girlfriend, his fabulous life and his tasty pudding. 'This toffee pudding is to die for!' he announced loudly to a passing waiter. A very happy man indeed.

He told us a very dirty joke that the taxi driver had told him involving a nun and a breathalyser and Natalie and I were in fits.

'This is The Ivy, darling,' she laughed. 'I don't think they're used to that kind of language here.'

I'd been almost as nervous of meeting Max as I had been of seeing Natalie again. All I knew about him was that he was an award-winning architect and I'd expected a rather dry, dusty sort of man, serious and bookish and frighteningly intelligent. I hadn't expected Mr Life and Soul of the Party.

I was surprised though to see that Natalie's fiancé wasn't the most handsome man in the world. He wasn't as good looking as Richard had been, but then I expect Richard had turned Natalie off pretty boys for life. Max wore tortoise-shell rimmed glasses and his dark brown hair was going a bit thin on top. I wondered what Natalie saw in him.

'How did you two meet?' I asked him.

'Well, she hired me to re-design her apartment,' he began.

'I didn't hire him,' Natalie interrupted, rolling her eyes affectionately. 'I couldn't afford him! This was just after I'd got the show and I was flat broke. I was introduced to him at a party and when he said he was an architect, I just happened to mention that my kitchen ceiling was leaking. So he said he'd come and take a look at it. Which didn't make any sense, you know? Because this guy designs glass skyscrapers. He builds suspension bridges, for crying out loud! He's not an odd-job man.'

Max took up the tale. 'So I went over to her apartment and when I saw the squalor the poor girl was living in, I said I'd have to make some major changes.'

'It wasn't squalor, darling. You always have to exaggerate.' She turned back to me. 'It was a really lovely Spanish-style place near Venice Beach. So anyway, he turned up a week later with all these plans he'd drawn up and –' she started giggling '– he'd gotten rid of all the rooms. There was just a bathroom and a bedroom which was like eighty feet long with a thirty-foot-high ceiling. And I thought it was some kind of mistake. Maybe I wasn't reading the plans properly. So I said to him, "What's happened to the kitchen and the living room?"'

Max raised an eyebrow. 'And I told her that after I married her she wasn't going to have much time for cooking or watching TV.'

'He was outrageous,' laughed Natalie. 'I probably shouldn't say this but Max has got the highest sex drive of any man I've ever known. He's a minimalist in every department except one.'

Natalie and I both started laughing our heads off at this.

'I'm sorry, darling,' he said, patting her arm. 'Would you like to say that a bit louder? I think there were a couple of people in the theatre across the street who might have missed it.'

'It's all right, sweetie. You know I'm not complaining.'

'I should hope not.'

'When are you two getting married?' I asked. 'Have you set the date yet?'

'We keep trying,' sighed Natalie, 'but it's been impossible. I can't take time off while we're filming and Max keeps having to fly to Tokyo or Singapore or some place. Every time we set a date something comes up, doesn't it, honey? I'm hoping next summer now. You'll have to come.'

'And what about you?' asked Max, turning to me. 'Natalie says you're a photographer. Are you going to photograph her for your magazine?'

I didn't know what to say. We hadn't got around to discussing that yet. 'Well, I was hoping to,' I said. 'But it's up to Natalie, really.'

'Is that your camera?' Max asked, noticing my bag under the table. 'Can I have a look?'

'Sure.'

He started fiddling with all the dials and buttons in the way that men always do. It's a gadget thing.

'Go sit over there,' he said, 'and I'll take a photo of the two of you.'

I got up and went and crouched next to Natalie. She put her arm around me and we instinctively pressed our heads together – just like we always used to do in our endless photo-booth sessions.

'Everybody say PRADA!' said Max.

'PRADA!' we chorused as Max clicked away.

'So what about the photos for the magazine?' I asked her. 'Have you had a chance to think about it?'

'Why not?' she said. 'Provided they don't want an interview as well. Because I don't talk to journalists, full stop.' She gave me a meaningful look. 'But you can definitely do photos if you promise – promise – to let me have a look at them and get rid of any I absolutely hate.'

'Yeah, try not to make her look too ugly,' said Max. 'She can look like a real car-chaser, you know, if you don't get the lighting just right. You should see her in the morning sometimes! It's like waking up with Herman Munster's mother!'

'Max! Quit it!' Natalie started smacking him with a fork. 'If you don't stop it, I'm going to lock you in the hotel room for the next three weeks and you won't be allowed out.'

I didn't think I'd ever seen her so happy.

I got a lift back to the hotel with them in Natalie's chauffeur-driven white BMW.

'So what are you actually filming while you're here?' I said. 'I completely forgot to ask you.'

'Well, Vicki – that's my character – has just landed a part in a West End show which is being directed by the guy she used to go out with. He broke her heart by marrying another woman and that's the reason why she left London in the first place. Now she's come back and she's trying to impress him with what a big star she is, which is a huge lie. And what she doesn't know is that her friends – the rest of the cast, that is – have secretly booked flights out to London to come and see her in the play. She's told them she's playing the lead and it's actually only a really tiny part. She has one line. And of course she's still secretly in love with this English guy who's still married and it all gets complicated. You don't know in the end if she's going to stay in London and have an affair with him, or go home.'

'Look at that,' said Max, waving at Hyde Park. 'Right in the middle of the city you've got all this fabulous space. I can't get over it. Every time I come to London, it surprises me all over again.'

'Do you come over here a lot?' I asked.

'Maybe a dozen times altogether. London, Birmingham, Manchester, Cardiff, Edinburgh, Liverpool. But I've got this book on the top hundred churches in Britain so I'm going to try and see a few of those on this trip. Take a break from new buildings.

'I know the oldest church in Britain,' I told him. Andrew had proposed to me there.

'Really? Is it near here?'

'No, bad luck.' I laughed. 'It's miles away. In Somerset. Well, Exmoor actually.'

'Exmoor? I love words with an x in them.' Max's eyes lit up wickedly behind his glasses. 'Does that mean it's X-rated?'

'I don't think so.' I laughed again. 'It's wild – but not that wild. But it's near the sea.'

'Would you be able to show me? Would you have time?'

'Actually, I'm not working at the moment. I've just gone freelance and I'm kind of taking a bit of a break until I figure out exactly what it is I'm going to do next. I'd love to take you. But it's a very long way. About a four-hour drive.'

Max was flipping through his diary. 'I've got meetings tomorrow. How about Thursday?' he said. 'That's Natalie's first filming day.'

'OK.'

'Vince will drive you, won't you Vince?' said Natalie, leaning forward to the driver. 'You can drive me to the set then come back and take them.'

The chauffeur nodded his head. 'It would be my pleasure, Miss,' he said. But I could see him rolling his eyes and thinking, Somerset! Fuck me.

'Is eight too early for you?' said Max.

'No, we'll have to get an early start if you're going to go there and back in one day. I'll meet you here at the hotel.'

We were already outside the Metropolitan. Pedestrians walking by turned their heads to stare as Natalie got out of the car but none of them dared approach her.

'We're in Suite 910,' said Natalie, ignoring all the attention. 'It's booked under Max's name. Ogilvy.'

'OK, Mrs Ogilvy.'

'Do you want to come up to the room now and have a drink?' she asked.

'No. Thanks. I'll leave you guys to it. It's been wonderful to see you again.'

Natalie and I hugged and kissed each other. 'I'll call you and let you know when I'm free to do those photos,' she promised. 'But we'll get together again before that anyway. You must come on set.'

Then Max hugged me.

'It's been really nice to meet you,' I told him. 'I'll see you Thursday morning.'

The doorman in his Donna Karan livery stepped forward on cue to give a helpful push to the huge revolving doors for them and Mr Ogilvy and his future bride swept inside with all their shopping bags, Max magically finding a free hand to slip around Natalie's tiny hips and guide her to the lifts.

As soon as I got home I phoned Atlanta at *The Hoop*.

'Hey, babe,' she drawled in her fake American whine. 'I was going to call you. How's it going?'

'I had lunch with Natalie and her fiancé today and she says she's up for doing a photo session.'

'Brilliant!' The surprise in Atlanta's voice was unmistakable. Ha-bloody-ha, I thought to myself. And you thought I was bluffing. Actually, I had been bluffing, but Atlanta need never know that.

'Is her fella here too?' she was saying. 'He's even bigger than she is!'

'Really?' Now it was my turn to be surprised. Architecture was a total mystery to me.

'Oh, Christ, yeah. She's going out with Max Ogilvy, right? He's only the coolest architect in America. He's *so* absolutely *The Hoop*. Can you do him as well? It might be handy to have some photos of him on file.'

'Sure. I'm taking him sight-seeing next week as a matter of fact. But there's only one problem. Natalie won't do an interview. She absolutely doesn't do interviews.'

'Shit! Shit, shit, shit!' Atlanta went quiet and I was

convinced the whole thing was done for. Now that I thought about it, there was obviously no point doing the photos at all if there were no words to go with it. Even I could see that.

'Well, do the photos anyway. Butter her up. Maybe she'll change her mind.'

'I don't think that's very likely.'

'Do colour for the cover. That'll have to be a studio shot. But we only pay on publication, so if she doesn't cough up with an interview you'll have to meet the costs yourself. Is that OK?'

It didn't sound very OK at all, but what choice did I have?

Andrew brought home a mountain of paper work that night and took over the dining table with his lap-top and files while I tidied up the flat. So much junk, so little space. Andrew kept promising we'd move to a bigger flat with a garden, but he kept saying it wasn't the right time. So in the meantime, while we waited for the property market to go up or down – I was never sure which one he was waiting for – I gathered up all of Andrew's socks and boxer shorts that had been hung out on the radiators to dry.

It took me about half an hour every week to pair up all of Andrew's socks. I was the Cilla Black of socks. He always liked to put on a fresh pair when he came home from work, which meant each week there were twenty-eight socks searching for partners. They were a mixture of black and dark grey and navy blue and every pair was just slightly different, so I'd have to hold each one up to the light and measure the ribbing around the top to find its mate. And always somehow, at the end of every week, there'd be four or five socks left on the shelf that had mysteriously got split up from their sock husband or wife and were destined to spend the rest of their lives alone in the sock singles bar on top of the dressing table.

'You know,' I said to Andrew when I went to start dinner, 'I'm thinking of chucking all your socks out and starting again; just going to Marks and Spencer and buying you twenty pairs of identical black socks. I waste far too much time trying to match these stupid things up.'

'But if they were all identical, wouldn't that just make it impossible to tell which ones were a pair?' he asked.

'If they were all identical, it wouldn't matter,' I explained patiently. 'By the way, Jill's invited us around for supper. She said to ask which is better for you – Friday or Saturday?'

'Yeah, that's OK.'

'No, which day? You have to choose.'

'What?'

'Friday or Saturday?'

'Oh, Saturday. Sorry. I didn't understand the question.'

'Yeah, it was a tough one, wasn't it? I'll have to write it down and send it into Chris Tarrant.'

'Look, I'm concentrating on this – I'm trying to work.'

'No you're not. You're playing *Doom*. I can hear the monsters grunting from upstairs.'

'I needed a little break.'

'I hope you keep the sound turned down when you play that at work,' I told him.

Honestly, it's like living with a little kid sometimes.

eleven

The cheery Australian doorman looked me up and down as though he was considering whether it was worth getting repetitive strain injury pushing the revolving door for a nobody like me. Honestly, couldn't he tell how much these trainers had cost?

'Could you put me through to Mr Ogilvy's room, please?' I asked the girl on the desk who had blonde hair and perfectly shaped eyebrows. 'Suite 910.'

I leaned over to smell one of the flowers in the hugely exotic display and a big cloud of yellow pollen fell out and landed on the beautifully polished wooden counter.

'I'm sorry. There's no answer from his room.'

'Oh.' I looked at my watch. It was only a few minutes past eight. 'Can you try again, please? Perhaps he's in the shower.' I gave the pollen a little shove with my arm, trying to spread it around a bit.

The girl dialled the room again, and I heard it faintly ring and ring. I felt a bit panicky. He wouldn't have just gone without me, would he? How could he? He didn't even know where he was going.

When I felt a hand on my elbow, I jumped. I thought it was the Flower Police.

'Hey, Red!' It was Max.

'Oh, hi!'

He kissed me on the cheek. 'I'm just having breakfast. I thought I'd better come and find you. Have you eaten yet?'

'Just a cup of coffee,' I said.

'Well, come and join me.' As we got into the lift he explained, 'We get charged for two breakfasts but Natalie always leaves at the crack of dawn, so you might as well eat hers. You can be my wife for the day,' he said playfully.

He had a cosy corner booth in the breakfast room on the first floor. His book of churches and *The Pevsner Guide to the Architecture of Somerset* were sitting on the table beside him along with a very thick catalogue for toilets. No sooner had I sat down than a waiter appeared at my shoulder with a jug in each hand.

'Tea or coffee, Madam?'

'Coffee, please.'

'Would you care for some breakfast?'

'Could I have some scrambled eggs, please, and mushrooms?'

'Certainly, Madam.'

'Would you like a croissant, darling?' asked Max, more for the waiter's benefit than mine. He handed me the basket.

'Thank you, darling,' I said, trying not to laugh. 'You know, I'm sure everybody in this hotel must know that you're with Natalie,' I whispered, when the waiter had gone. 'I don't think you're fooling anybody.'

'Maybe I have two women,' teased Max. 'Maybe I have a whole bunch of women upstairs in my suitcase.'

'Would they be the special inflatable kind?' I enquired.

'Oh, you've met them then,' said Max. While he ate his breakfast he flicked through the toilet catalogue, shaking his head from time to time and tutting.

'What's the matter?' I asked him.

'It's no good,' he sighed. 'They don't have it. They Just Don't Have It.' He shut the catalogue contemptuously and pushed it away.

Maybe now was a good time to ask. 'Look,' I said, '*The Hoop* – that's the magazine I'm working for – said they'd really like me to photograph you as well. They're very keen on architects. Would you mind if I took a few snaps today? I've brought my camera, but if that's not cool, just say so.'

'Oh, I love having my photo taken. Take one of me now!' He stuck the bowls of two silver spoons in his eyes so that the handles stuck out like Elton John's glasses.

When we'd finished breakfast, Max called Vince and asked him to bring the car around – a white BMW with leather upholstery. A girl could get used to this, I decided. Driving out of London, Vince put on Simon Mayo's Mystery Years on Radio One and Max sang along loudly and confidently to pop songs he was hearing for the first time. '. . . now the trucks don't work, they just make you worse . . .'

It was funny and awful all at once.

'. . . Hope I mow! Before I die! . . .'

'Do you know any of the words?' I asked him in mock despair.

'Not really.'

'Or the tunes? Do you know any of the tunes?'

'Not yet – but think how great I'll be by the time I leave.' Everything with Max was a big joke. He was like the naughtiest boy in school who never got into trouble because the teachers secretly thought he was cute. He made up a game called 'Name That Movie' where you had to do something to the other person that suggested a film.

He clamped his hand over my face and spread out his fingers. 'Name That Movie! Name That Movie!' he said as I struggled to breathe.

'*Alien*!' I laughed. 'That was too easy. My turn.' I grabbed hold of his shoe and pulled his leg up in the air.

'Oooh, I don't know. I don't know. *The Godfather*!' he guessed.

'Don't be ridiculous!'

'*Blade Runner*!'

'Guess again!' I was laughing so much I could hardly get the words out.

'*Jaws*!'

'You're not even trying!'

'*My Left Foot*!' he shouted finally.

'Oh, well done!'

'OK. I've got one.' He grabbed my foot, pulled off my shoe and sock and held my bare foot in the air.

'We've just done that. It's *My Left Foot*,' I said.

'Wrong!'

'I don't know. I've got no idea. *American Psycho*. I give up.'

'*Tootsie*,' he said. 'That's one point to me.'

'Very good.'

And so the M4 whizzed by with Max and me giggling like a couple of kids in the back seat and Vince tutting occasionally and shaking his head at our stupidity. We turned off the M5 at Taunton and I started checking the road atlas. Halfway to Minehead I told Vince to turn off and take one of the B-roads that led onto Exmoor.

'I'm not entirely sure of the way,' I said, checking the map, 'but as long as we head for Simonsbath we should be OK.'

We drove down narrow lanes with no signposts, past thatched cottages and high hedges and Max stared out of the window in awe.

'This is amazing,' he said.

'We haven't got to the best bit yet,' I said. 'Vince, I think we need to go left here, then if we go right we should pick up the main road.'

We wound around for a minute or two and then the road opened up cutting straight through the middle of Exmoor.

'Oh, wow,' said Max. 'Stop the car.'

He was out of the car in an instant, gazing around him at the landscape. 'Unbelievable,' he said.

I took a big lungful of fresh Exmoor air. The sun was shining on us, the blue sky was decorated with a few white wisps of clouds for interest. The green and purple of the heather stretched out endlessly before us. This was pretty special.

'Can we walk from here?' Max asked.

'That depends where you want to walk to. The moor is enormous.'

'Well, could we walk up that hill?'

'We can try.'

'Are you coming with us, Vince?'

'No, I'll get out and stretch my legs a bit, but I'm not much of a walker,' said Vince, glad to see the back of us. 'I'll stay here with the car, Sir, if you don't mind. I'll park it just a bit further down the road by that gate so it's out of the way.'

Max and I had already set off across the fields. The heather was up around our knees, but we could see a dirt track a little further on and headed for that.

'This is wonderful,' said Max. 'Do you come here a lot?'

'Not as much as I'd like to. I'd love to move out of London and live here, but there's not much to do here in the way of work.'

'This is where I'd live if I lived in England,' Max agreed.

We carried on walking until we reached the crest of the hill and sat down on a rock to drink it all in, feeling pretty smug with ourselves for being clever enough to come here. It was like bunking off school.

There were no other people in sight; just a few sheep way off in the distance. Some kind of bird – a hawk, we announced confidently – circled high overhead. It was so quiet and still we might have been the only two people alive on the face of the earth.

Heaven.

'So now that I've got you all on your own,' said Max, 'you can tell me all of Natalie's secrets. Was she really ugly at school, with glasses and lots of spots?'

'I wish!' I laughed. 'She was exactly like she is now. I don't think I ever saw Natalie get a spot in her whole life. She'd pretend to sometimes just so she'd be one of the gang, but she didn't fool any of us. She did have braces on her teeth for about a year but they looked kind of cool on her, though.'

'I bet you two fought over boys the whole time.' From the teasing way he said it, I could tell that Natalie had never told him the whole Richard saga. Well, there was no point bringing it up now.

'Once or twice,' I smiled. 'But it was no contest really. Everyone was in love with Natalie. She could always get anyone she wanted without even trying. But we were just kids then, it wasn't like these were serious relationships.'

'And what about you? Could you get anyone you wanted?'

I was saved from having to answer that one by the sound of hoof beats – two riders cantering up the hill behind us. We jumped up and got off the path to let them trot past.

'Thank you!' they called, with a wave of their hands, then turned the corner and cantered on.

'Thank you for bringing me here. I never imagined anywhere like this existed,' Max said. 'This is definitely going to be the highlight of my trip.'

'My pleasure,' I assured him. It had been such a brilliant idea coming here and Max was terrific company. I was so happy that Natalie and I were friends again. And that would mean Max and I would be friends too, so it was great to have this chance to get to know each other.

I took out my camera and photographed him surrounded by the wilderness – black and white to bring out the contrasts in the landscape. He wasn't shy about having his photo taken at all. He stared straight into my camera lens as though he were the one taking a photo of me.

'So. Is there someplace around here we can get some lunch?' he said at last.

'I know just the place,' I told him and we walked back down the path to where Vince was snoozing in the car.

I took them to a little pub in Exford and ordered fish, chips and peas for us all, a Coke for Vince and I asked Max to order me half a lager, then fell about laughing, listening to him try to get his American accent around haff a larger.

'I must call Natalie and tell her I'm eating fish and chips on

Exmoor,' said Max. He took out his mobile phone and pressed a few buttons but nothing happened.

'Is that an American phone?' I asked him.

'No, it's an English one. The production company rented them for us while we're here, but it's not working.'

'I don't think you can get a signal out here,' I said. 'We're in the middle of nowhere.'

'Oh, well,' he said. 'Perhaps I can send her a postcard.'

We sat out in the sunshine by the river eating our lunch, Max picking all the batter off his fish and giving it to the sparrows who landed on our table and stared at us without a smidgen of shame.

'Come on, little birdies,' he cooed at them. 'Deep-fried flour. Yum yum. Let's see you take off after eating that.'

I flicked through the architectural guide book Max had brought with him.

'What sort of buildings do you design?' I asked him. I realised I had no idea.

He took out a pen and made a few rough sketches on the back of a napkin. 'This was a shopping centre I did in Stuttgart with a revolving restaurant on the top . . . This was an art gallery I designed in Florida – it looks a bit like a rocket . . . and this one . . . is an office building in Vancouver.'

I looked at his drawings of tall, thrusting buildings with cone-shaped domes and couldn't help smiling. 'They're all a bit – phallic, don't you think?' I ventured.

'The one in Vancouver had these two circular car parks next to it,' he said. He grabbed back the napkin and added a couple of crude, round details on either side of the sky-scraper.

'Oh, now I recognise your work,' I teased. 'You're the guy who does all those drawings on the back of toilet doors. I had no idea you were so famous.'

'I wanted to clad the car parks in fun-fur but it turned out it wasn't cost-effective,' he explained.

'That's a real pity,' I told him. 'I'd love to see you build that.'

'I've won prizes for my erections,' he informed me proudly.

'I don't doubt it for a minute,' I laughed. He was completely outrageous, but you had to love him.

After lunch, we drove into Winsford just a couple of miles away so Max could look at the church.

'That doorway could be Norman, but I'm pretty sure the chancel is thirteenth century,' I announced casually as we walked up the path. I'd had a peek in his book while he was in the toilet. 'I think you'll find the rest of it is Perpendicular.' I had no idea what any of this meant but I liked the sound of the words.

I tagged along with Max as he inspected the Jacobean pulpit and the circular Norman font, then we wandered out into the churchyard to look at the gravestones. Normally graveyards give me the creeps but this one was set on a sunny hill and the graveyard had a wonderful view overlooking the valley.

'This is where I want to be buried when I die,' said Max. 'Somehow it wouldn't be so gloomy being dead with a view like this.'

'If you say so,' I said.

'So now are you going to show me my church?'

'Follow me,' I told him.

We got back in the car and drove to Porlock Weir, where I amazed Max with my navigational skills by leading the way to a tiny path behind the pub that headed up the hill.

'It's about an hour's walk there and an hour's walk back. Are you sure you're up for it?'

What a silly question. Max was up for anything.

We passed a couple of hikers on the way, but mostly we had the path to ourselves, our feet crunching on the fallen leaves as we walked steadily uphill. Max told me the story of how he'd got into architecture. He'd originally wanted to be a cartoonist but when he was still at school he'd won a prize for a building design that he'd entered as a joke. He'd meant it to be a launching pad for the first colony on Mars, but it's now a cinema complex in New Jersey.

I slid on some leaves and Max shot out a hand to catch me. 'Careful!'

He kept a hold on my hand to steady me on the walk back down and we swung our arms and talked in loud jokey voices.

As soon as the ground levelled out, I said, 'Thanks, I'll be fine now' and dropped his hand, hoping I wouldn't seem rude.

Culbone Church is only thirty-five feet long and it's the smallest and the oldest church in Britain, sitting in total seclusion by the side of a stream. I felt a bit guilty bringing Max here. Andrew and I had discovered it on the second anniversary of us going out. Andrew had booked a big country hotel as a surprise. It had been our secret.

But, hey, it was in Max's book. It's not like we owned it or anything.

'This is amazing,' said Max, stepping inside the tiny building where people had knelt and prayed for more than six hundred years.

'It's like a fairy church, isn't it?' I said.

I photographed Max examining every tiny medieval detail, peering over the gravestones outside where generations of the same family rested in peace. Then, for my grand finale, I took him to a little shed on the other side of the stream where hikers could get cups of tea and biscuits. You filled the urn yourself and there was an honour-box for donations: 10p for a tea-bag, 15p for a biscuit. Max left a £10 note.

'This is definitely the highlight of my trip,' said Max again. 'I can't thank you enough.'

We sat drinking our tea in silence, watching the stream, perfectly at peace with the world. Could anything on earth be more perfect than this?

'So what about you? What were you like at school?' I asked.

'Oh I was the fat kid with glasses who always got sand kicked in his face.'

I laughed. 'Yeah, right. The world's first six-foot weakling.'

'Six foot two, actually. I was this weedy nerdy little kid, always reading comics and science-fiction books. Blowing stuff up. I was the only kid in Florida without a tan because I never went outside. If someone threw a football at me I think I would have fainted. I used to wish my parents would move to Alaska so people would quit telling me to go outside and play.'

'That's so sad.'

'Yeah, isn't it?' he giggled. 'I was one tragic kid.'

'So what happened?'

'My dad died when I was seventeen. He was shaving one morning and just fell down dead from a heart attack.'

'Oh. I'm so sorry.'

'And that completely freaked me out. My dad was like me, you know? Hated sports, a real couch potato kind of guy. The most exercise he ever got was moving the gear stick from Park to Drive. He was only fifty-four and I was real scared that what had happened to him would happen to me, so I joined a gym and started working out big time. Swimming, running. I even entered the New York marathon.'

'That's fantastic.'

'I said entered the marathon. I never actually ran the thing because about a month before I twisted my foot. That's how I met my first wife – she was a physiotherapist.'

'Oh.' I was a little shocked. 'I didn't know you'd been married before.'

He laughed. 'I've been married twice before. It took me a couple of practice runs I guess but I'll get it right this time.'

'What do you mean?'

'Well, I always meant to be faithful, but I guess I was just making up for lost time. If I'd known that all I had to do to score with girls was get a six-pack, I would have done it when

I was eleven. I couldn't get over it. I was like a kid in a candy store. But I guess the women I married didn't appreciate that too much. I think they would have preferred that I kept my pants on when they weren't around.'

'Mmm, women are funny like that,' I agreed. 'Do you have any kids?'

'Three. All girls. Ella, Olivia and Cassandra. But I don't get to see them much these days.'

He stared off across the moor and neither of us said anything for a while. 'I guess we'd better be getting back,' he said at last.

In the car back home, I dozed most of the way until we got to Chiswick. It had been dark for hours.

It had been an absolutely perfect day. I can't remember the last time I'd laughed so much and I was a little sad that it was over and I was going back to dull old reality. Max was still asleep with his mouth slightly open, his glasses a tiny bit crooked. What was it about him? I wondered. He looked so ordinary and yet he was going to marry one of the most fanciable women on TV.

When we got to Hammersmith, Max opened his eyes.

'Nearly home,' I said. 'It's been a wonderful day.'

'The very best. We should do it again.'

'That would be great,' I agreed. 'They have a pretty good moor in Yorkshire too.'

'Vince will drive you home,' he said. 'Is it easier if we drop you off first?'

I wasn't sure which way would be quicker, but for reasons I couldn't quite put a name to, I realised I didn't want Andrew to see me with Max or, more to the point, I didn't want Max to see Andrew, so I said, no, we'd go to the hotel first.

As we pulled up outside the Metropolitan, Max kissed me goodbye on the cheek. 'Thanks for a great day,' he said.

'My pleasure,' I assured him, gathering up my things.

'Hey, do you want to be on TV?' he asked out of the blue.

'How d'you mean?'

'They're shooting this café scene next week and I told Natalie I'd be an extra. She's always complaining that she never sees me when she's working, but these things are *sooo* boring. Why don't you come too and keep me company? I did it once before and I kept falling asleep.'

'I'd love to. I've never watched them making a TV show before. Do you think it will be OK? I don't want to be in the way.'

'You'll be doing them a favour. I'll ring the casting girl right now and tell her you're coming.' He got out his mobile phone immediately, and one of the call sheets he had in his inside pocket, to look up the telephone number. 'She's got her voicemail on,' he said, after a couple of seconds. 'Hi, Ruth. This is Max Ogilvy. I'm just calling to let you know that I've found you another extra for Monday. Her name's Lindy and I want her to sit at my table. Don't tell Natalie though, because she'll only get jealous.' He rang off. 'There. All fixed.'

'You know, you shouldn't go around saying things like that because somebody might take you seriously one day,' I scolded him.

'You'll have to be there at seven-thirty in the morning. They're shooting at a café near Ladbroke Grove. I can't remember the name of the street.'

'Ladbroke Grove is really near me,' I told him.

'Is it really? Well, then, why don't I get Vince to come by your house and we can pick you up in the morning? Is that OK with you Vince?'

'Not a problem,' said Vince, who was filling in his overtime form.

I scribbled down my address and gave it to Vince. 'If you're sure it's not a problem,' I said.

'Not at that time of morning. There'll be nothing on the roads,' said Vince.

'Oh, great. Don't come down the Harrow Road because there's roadworks. Thanks a lot.'

I was babbling. I was going to be on TV. I was going to see Natalie and Max again. I wasn't sure which I was looking forward to most.

twelve

Our Sunday night routine was fairly well established: an early movie and then a meal; usually a curry, usually the same restaurant, usually the bill came to £34. I'm not saying we were stuck in a rut or anything, but I did sometimes wonder what other people did on a Sunday night.

It was Andrew's week to choose and he wanted to see *Gone In 60 Seconds*, which was fine by me. At least it wasn't in Polish. Andrew thought there was something mind-improving about any film with sub-titles, even though I had pointed out to him that if you lived in Poland, *Mission Impossible* would have sub-titles. He said I was a philistine which was probably true. But he was also the one who liked films with lots of exploding helicopters in them. And car chases, which was all this one had going for it. Still, I came out ready for a nice chicken korma.

Andrew had been very taken with my new haircut, although a bit startled to discover that he was suddenly married to a redhead. I'd really have to make a bit of an effort with the old blow-drying, though. I was a bit disappointed to discover that the flicky-up bits didn't just happen on their own. They had to be beaten into submission. Still, no point going through all that palaver just to go to the pictures with Andrew.

As always, Andrew stopped to have a look in all three estate agents' windows between the cinema and the restaurant. He wasn't looking for anywhere to buy, he just liked to keep tabs on how much his place was worth.

'Look, this one's identical to ours in not such a good street and it's £195,000! I'm rich! That's £120,000 more than I paid for mine. Ours.'

'But you're only rich if you sell your flat and go live in a cardboard box,' I pointed out. 'Everything else has gone up £120,000 as well.'

But Andrew just shook his head and gave me one of his patronising smiles as if the whole concept was far too complicated for me to grasp. Well, I wasn't the one who'd paid fifteen grand over the odds for a poky one-bedroom flat in the wrong end of Maida Vale.

Andrew and I liked this particular Indian restaurant because it was always busy – there's nothing worse than sitting in an empty restaurant – but you could always get a table without having to book. We'd been coming here at least twice a month for the last five years and we ordered practically the same things every time: Garlic Chicken, Chicken Korma, Sag Prawn, Tarka Dhal, a Peshwari Naan, an Onion Bhaji, Pilau Rice and two Tiger beers. You'd think all the waiters would shout out 'Andrew!' or 'Lindy!' when we walked in like they do in *Cheers* but none of them ever recognised us and we never recognised a single one of them. I used to wonder if every person who walked in this restaurant was only visiting London for a two-week holiday and went straight back home to India as soon as they'd brought us our free mint chocolates. Perhaps we could bring Max and Natalie here, I thought. I wondered if Max liked Indian food.

'Natalie and I wanted to be ballet dancers when we were little,' I said. 'Would you like it if I was a ballet dancer?'

'No, I love you just the way you are,' Andrew smiled. 'You could wear one of those little skirts though.'

It was automatic. Andrew told me he loved me a hundred times a day.

'Why do you love me?' I asked. Half a pint of Tiger beer on an empty stomach and I was already a bit drunk.

'What do you mean?'

'I mean, what is it about me that made you want to spend the rest of your life with me?'

'That's a funny question.'

'No, it's not. What is it about me that you like?'

'Well, I don't know – it's just you.'

'Oh, go on, name one thing.'

'Well, it's everything.'

I was starting to get impatient. 'Look,' I said. 'This shouldn't be a difficult question. Do you want me to tell you what I love about you?'

'OK.'

'Well, I love your eyes. I love the way that you're always so cheerful. I love the way that you always buy a copy of the *Big Issue*, even if you've already got it. I love that you cried in *Toy Story 2*. And I love the fact that you tell me you love me fifty times a day. See – it's easy.'

'You left out that I'm very sexy,' he said helpfully.

'Don't push your luck,' I teased him. At least I hoped he'd take it for teasing. 'So go on then. What is it that you love about me?'

He thought a while. 'Well. You make me laugh.'

'Thank you. What else?'

'And.' He thought a while longer. 'And it's good that you don't take very long getting ready.'

I could feel my face setting into a rigid mask. 'And that's why you married me, is it?' I asked. 'So you wouldn't have to hang around too long at the church while I put on my lipstick?'

'Oh, don't get cross with me. I told you I was no good at this.'

'No, Andrew, I'm serious. When you met me, what made you want to go out with me in the first place?'

'Well – it was timing, wasn't it?'

'How d'you mean? Timing?'

'Well – you weren't going out with anyone. And I wasn't

going out with anyone. And I guess I was ready to have a relationship.'

'So what you're saying is, I could have been anyone.'

'That's not what I meant.'

'No, but it's what you said. You're saying you would have married the first girl who came along. It was only pure chance that it happened to be me.'

'Yes – but it was you.'

'But it could just as easily have been Jill?'

'No-o. Because she was going out with Simon.'

'And I'm supposed to be grateful for that, am I?'

'What do you want me to say? You know I love you.'

'Yes, but it would be nice if you could think of a single reason why.'

'Well, the way you're acting now I don't think I can. All I wanted to do was come out and have a nice dinner and you've managed to turn it into an argument.' Andrew got the bill and we drove home in a foul, grumpy silence. Officially not speaking to each other, which is really difficult when you live in the same flat and can't avoid each other. That's the trouble with being married. You can't just storm off home to your place. You still have to share the same bathroom, and spit out your toothpaste into the same basin.

When Andrew came to bed I just snorted and turned off the light then pretended to go to sleep. I was right and he was wrong. But I wasn't even sure what the question was any more.

thirteen

I couldn't sleep anyway. Knowing I had to be up at six, I woke up at three, convinced that I must have slept through the alarm, and then I couldn't get back to sleep. I tossed and turned, willing myself to relax, counting backwards from a hundred like they make you do when you have an anaesthetic. I must have eventually dozed off again at about one minute to six because it seemed like no sooner had I closed my eyes than the alarm clock was ringing.

I leapt out of bed feeling like death – only excited. It must be because I'm going to be on TV, I thought. It was still dark and I crept to the bathroom without turning on the lights so I wouldn't wake up Andrew. I closed my eyes on the loo, marvelling that Natalie could do this every day.

While the kettle was boiling, I had a shower, feeling more alive by the minute. I'd only allowed myself thirty minutes to get ready – Max was coming to pick me up at seven – but I'd laid all my clothes out the night before: a tiny olive green T-shirt, my black silk cargo pants from Warehouse and my new silver Nike trainers. If I wore them every day for the next two years they would practically be a bargain.

My basic one-minute make-up: Touché Eclat concealer to hide the dark rings under my eyes, Boots tinted moisturiser, Body Shop waterproof mascara and brown kohl pencil, and Clinique Barely There lipstick. It would have to do. The show was only watched in maybe a dozen or so countries, after all – how many people would that be? Twenty million? Fifty million? Now I was getting nervous. What was I letting myself in for?

It was already quarter to. I gulped the rest of my coffee and kissed Andrew goodbye, feeling guilt at our argument.

'I'm sorry for being so silly, darling,' I told him.

'Bye, bunny,' he murmured without opening his eyes. 'Have a good day. Don't wake me up' and rolled back onto his tummy.

I went downstairs and let myself out the front door quietly. I sat on the wall and waited for Max. It was already light. London was very quiet and still. I should get up at six o'clock every morning, I told myself. This is fantastic. Perhaps I should quit photography and become a milkman.

I felt a tingle of nerves as I saw Vince's white BMW turn the corner. I hoped I hadn't made them late, bringing them out of their way like this. They must think I was an awful nuisance. Why didn't I just say I'd drive myself? But as they pulled up, Max leaned over in the back seat to open the door for me with a huge smile on his face. His eyes were sparkling behind his specs, bright eyed and bushy-tailed.

'Good morning!' he boomed and planted a kiss on my cheek that was like an intravenous shot of pure adrenalin. 'And how are we this morning?'

'Terrific!' I said, feeling instantly better but slightly embarrassed. I wasn't used to being kissed so early in the morning. 'It was a bit of a struggle getting up but I feel great now. Where's Natalie?' I knew she would be on set already, but I suddenly had this weird compulsion to say her name out loud. It was like I was trying to prove something – but I wasn't sure what.

'She left half an hour before me. She'll be in make-up forever. These are great houses.'

I watched him staring out the window, craning his neck, not wanting to miss a thing. His enthusiasm was adorable. I loved the way he got such a kick out of the tiniest thing.

We turned into Ladbroke Grove and Vince turned left at a yellow and black sign marked 'Unit Base' pointing down a side street and into a church car park filled with caravans and an old blue double-decker bus.

Dozens of people were standing around a trestle table eating scrambled eggs or Fruit 'n' Fibre and drinking coffee out of polystyrene cups. The day hadn't even started and already they looked bored. Occasionally a walkie-talkie crackled.

'Breakfast?' said Max, getting out of the car. He wandered over to the catering truck and put a couple of croissants and a banana on a paper plate. 'I'm going to see how Natalie's doing,' he said. 'Are you coming to say hello?'

'No – I'll just grab a coffee,' I said. 'Say hi for me.'

He skipped over to one of the caravans with a sign on the window saying 'Vicki Fox' – the name of Natalie's character. I poured myself a cup of coffee from the urn and stood in the car park drinking it in what I hoped was a nonchalant manner. Everybody else ignored me. A tall bald man was selling fleecy jackets from the boot of his car. 'Only fifteen quid,' I could hear him telling one of the crew. 'You know how much something like that would fetch in the shops?'

I wished Max would hurry back.

A sulky-looking blonde girl with an earpiece and a walkie-talkie sidled over. 'Are you Max's friend?' she asked.

'No! I'm a friend of Natalie's. We were at school together.' I could feel myself going bright red.

'No. I mean, are you the extra he's brought with him?' If she'd sounded any less interested she would have been asleep.

'Oh. Yes. I am.'

'Can you sign this, then, please?' She handed me a sheet of paper – some kind of contract or release agreement – and I scribbled my name without even reading it. I could be donating a kidney to Steven Spielberg for all I knew. She kept the top copy and handed the bottom sheet back to me. 'You need to go into wardrobe now and let them have a look at you.'

'Sure. Where's that?'

'Right there,' she said, pointing. 'The trailer with the sign saying wardrobe.'

'Oh right. OK. Thanks very much. My name's Lindy, by the way.' But she had already walked away to talk to somebody else. Just then I saw Max coming out of Natalie's trailer. Thank God.

'How's Natalie doing?' I asked.

'She's not there,' he said. 'She must have already gone to the location. But the TV was on and I got wrapped up in *The Big Breakfast*.'

Meanwhile, I'd been standing outside on my own. 'We have to go to wardrobe anyway now,' I told him.

In the wardrobe trailer a middle-aged woman, sweltering in a tweed overcoat, was having her Polaroid taken.

'Hi, Max,' said a boy with a shaved head and a pair of scissors on a ribbon around his neck. 'Are you inside the café? I think you'll be OK in what you're wearing. We're not really dressing the background.'

'Oh, rats,' said Max. 'I wanted to go as a pirate.'

'Maybe you'd better have a hat so nobody recognises you.'

I was slightly surprised. Was Max that famous? He handed Max a light grey Kangol sunhat. 'Try that on.'

'What do you think?' Max asked me. 'Do I look like Puff Daddy?'

'You look like Puff Daddy's daddy,' I told him.

'What about Lindy?' said Max. 'She's in the same scene.'

Scissor Boy looked me up and down. I noticed we were wearing identical trainers. 'You'll do,' he said dismissively. 'You're not on my list anyway.'

'If anyone's looking for me, tell them I'm hangin' with my homies,' Max told Scissor Boy as we left. 'Do you know what that means?' he asked me.

'I have no idea,' I told him.

'No, me neither.'

In the make-up caravan, a boy and a girl wearing head-to-toe black leather and tall Mohicans were sitting in the two chairs having black lipstick applied.

'Hello, Max,' said one of the make-up girls. She looked

Spanish or Italian with a light olive complexion, a long mane of jet black curls, dramatic eyes and full lips. She wore figure-hugging black Lycra bootleg trousers that showed off her dancer's legs. 'I saw your name on the list. Are you coming to work with us today?'

'Isabella! You're looking very sexy this morning,' he said, and kissed her on the cheek. 'Hi, Yvonne,' he said to the other make-up lady – a rather dumpy woman with bad skin – and kissed her too.

See, I told myself. He kisses everyone. It doesn't mean anything.

'This is Lindy,' he told them. 'She's going to be my date today.'

Isabella raised her eyebrows knowingly.

'Hi,' I smiled, giving a little wave. 'I'm an old friend of Natalie's. Don't pay any attention to him.'

'You're OK. You can go now,' Isabella told the boy with the orange Mohican. Then turning back to me and Max she said, 'Who wants to go first?'

'You go, Max,' I told him. For some reason, I didn't like the idea of this Latin babe touching Max's face but I told myself not to be so silly. What difference did it make to me one way or the other?

Max sat down and closed his eyes as Isabella tucked some tissues around his collar. She dipped a sponge in some brown foundation and started dabbing it over his face. He had a blissful expression on his face. I forced myself to watch and smiled indulgently to show how cool I was. The way you do at a party when you suddenly realise you don't know a soul there.

'OK,' said Yvonne, as the girl punk got up to leave. 'Your turn. Lindy, is it?' I sat down, trying not to stare at Max and Isabella's reflection in the mirror in front of me. It was fairly impossible. I had to close my eyes.

'Do you already have make-up on?' Yvonne was asking.

'Just tinted moisturiser.'

'Well, I won't take that off, I'll just darken it up a bit so you don't look too washed out.' She dabbed away with her sponge. 'Your skin's very dry. You should really think about changing your moisturiser,' she said.

'Yes, I will,' I promised, wishing that Max wasn't listening to all of this. She dusted me with powder and then I felt her dotting shadow on my eyelids. 'Open your eyes,' she said and I saw a mascara wand coming towards me. 'Do you want me to tidy up your eyebrows too?'

What was wrong with my eyebrows? I wondered. 'No, thanks, they're fine,' I assured her. I suppose I should have been grateful she didn't offer to squeeze my spots while she was at it.

'Now what?' I asked Max as we emerged with our new brown faces.

'Now,' he said, 'we take the minibus to the location. Or we could walk. It's just around the corner.'

So we walked. I knew the café where they were going to be filming very well. It used to be one of my favourite greasy spoons but it had been given a chi-chi makeover by the *Don't Call Us* team. It used to be a caff – now it was definitely a café, with checked curtains at the window and an accent on the é. I remembered the walls being the colour of nicotine; suddenly they were lilac and acid green. There were already dozens of people at work erecting lights outside the window and laying track for the camera. Inside they were rearranging all the tables and chairs, hanging paintings on the walls, sweeping the floor and putting orange gerberas into blue glass vases. In the house across the road two little kids were hanging out of the upstairs window, watching all the activity and shouting out a running commentary to someone in another room.

'When Natalie and I used to go to Portobello on Saturdays we'd come here for jam roly-poly,' I told Max.

'Jam roly-poly!' he laughed. 'What's that?'

'Well, it's jam – and, I think, suet.' Just the thought of it made me feel fat.

'I don't even know what that is, but I think it would be illegal in Los Angeles,' said Max.

We wandered back to the café and saw Natalie walking through the scene with a man in scruffy shorts and a Cats T-shirt. I guessed he was the director. Natalie was wearing very tight Earl jeans and an orange paisley halterneck. Her hair was wrapped in a chiffon scarf covering a headful of jumbo rollers. Max knocked on the window to attract her attention. Natalie turned around and her face lit up to see him. He pressed his open lips on the window and gave her a big sloppy comedy kiss through the glass – tongue and all. She rolled her eyes and laughed, held up her fingers to us and mouthed, 'Five minutes.'

Max pulled away making a face. 'Eeew. That window didn't taste so good.'

A minion came running out with a J-cloth and some Windowlene to clear the slobber mark off the glass. She glared at Max who didn't seem to notice because he was happily playing with his new hat. After a couple of minutes Natalie came running out and hugged me and kissed Max. While they were in a clinch, I stepped a couple of paces away from them, to give them a bit of space. See how considerate I am? Totally cool.

'Love the hair,' Max told her, patting her curlers. 'You should wear it like this more often. Do these things spin around?'

'Thanks for coming, you guys,' she said. 'I really need to see some friendly faces this morning. Dan's having one of his I Hate Everything days. He hates the location. He hates the lighting. I think he even hates me today – and Dan loves me!'

'We're bored,' Max whined, stroking her arm.

Natalie ignored him. 'I hope you're going to behave yourself today. Last time he came on set he spent the whole day shouting out helpful suggestions,' she told me. 'You'll have to keep him in line, Lindy. Don't be afraid to hit him if you have to.'

'I won't,' I promised. I felt a bit like an interloper being with Natalie and Max together. It felt like I was having to make a special effort just to behave normally. Making my voice seem brighter. Why was that?

Natalie went off to make-up and Max went with her so I went and sat on the bus with the other extras who were drinking coffee and talking about *EastEnders*. The woman in the tweed overcoat was one of the market regulars apparently. They all looked at me suspiciously because I wasn't one of them. After three quarters of an hour another girl wearing a headset and carrying a walkie-talkie came over to round us up. 'Who are you?' she asked me.

'I'm meant to be in the café, I think.'

'OK. They're ready for you in there now.'

Where was Max? I looked up and down the street but there was no sign of him. Should I wait?

As soon as I entered the café, the bossy girl with the walkie-talkie grabbed me. 'Right. You sit over there with the woman in the blue shirt,' she ordered, pointing at one of the tables.

My heart sank. I didn't want to sit here all day with this woman. I wanted to sit with Max. I was surprised how disappointed I felt.

They did a run-through with Natalie's stand-in walking into the restaurant, pausing and then bumping into a waiter.

'What are we supposed to do?' I whispered to the woman in the blue shirt.

She tutted. 'Look like you're talking to me,' she said. 'Move your lips but don't make a sound. Mime it.'

'OK, STAND BY FOR REHEARSAL. QUIET EVERYWHERE!'

'HERE WE GO THEN! REHEARSING! AND ACTION!'

'Rhubarb, rhubarb, rhubarb,' Blue Shirt Woman mimed and nodded her head slightly as though she was explaining the theory of relativity to me.

'Rhubarb, rhubarb, rhubarb,' I mimed back without any enthusiasm.

'AND CUT!' shouted Jerry, the assistant director.

The café door opened and Max walked in.

'Oh, have you started already?' he asked, looking around and not the slightest bit phased. 'Have I missed anything?' He looked over at me but the girl with the headset was leading him over to a table on the other side of the room where a man was sitting reading a newspaper. He sat down obediently as they set up for another rehearsal. He was so far away, I wouldn't even be able to talk to him. This wasn't going to be much fun. The camera rolled back into its starting position and tracked back out again, following Natalie's stand-in as she walked into the café. I didn't look at Max. I pretended I was having a great time.

'Rhubarb, rhubarb,' I mumbled, feeling a weird empty, dizzy feeling in the pit of my stomach. But then, when Jerry yelled 'Cut!' again, I heard Max's voice pipe up.

'You know what, Dan? Why don't I go sit over there by the window and that other lady can come and sit here? That way we'll look more like couples, don't you think?'

'It doesn't make any difference to me, Max,' sighed Dan rather tetchily. 'Whatever makes you happy.'

Max was already on his feet and shooing Blue Shirt Woman out of her seat and over to the man with the newspaper.

'That's better,' said Max, as he sat down opposite me. I felt inordinately happy and mischievous as though we'd got away with something really naughty.

'So,' I said, trying to sound professional. 'What's this scene all about anyway?'

'Well! Vicki's come here to meet Toby – the theatre director – the one who broke her heart. So she wants to show him that she's completely over him and has absolutely no feelings left for him whatsoever. Here – you can read the whole thing if you like.' He handed me a couple of pages of photocopied script from his jeans pocket.

12 INT. CAFÉ – LONDON – DAY

Vicki enters the café and surveys the room. She sees Toby sitting on the other side of the café with his back to the door. He hasn't seen her. She's nervous but lifts her chin in the air, takes a deep breath and walks over to his table swinging her purse in a confident manner. Before she reaches him she collides with an Italian waiter and her purse sends two cups of espresso flying all over her shirt.

'Where it says purse, that means handbag, right?' I asked Max. He nodded. Americans! Why can't they call things by their proper names?

> ITALIAN WAITER
> Mamma Mia! Why you no looka where-a you goin?

> VICKI
> Oh, I'm so, so sorry!

Vicki starts trying to wipe down the Waiter and then realises that her own T-shirt is covered in black coffee. She is about to turn and flee from the restaurant when Toby, hearing the commotion, turns and waves. Vicki clutches her purse in front of her to hide the stain, waves back, smiles and points towards the ladies' restroom.

CUT TO

13 INT. LADIES' REST-ROOM IN CAFÉ – DAY

Vicki catches sight of her reflection in the mirror and reacts with horror at the sight of her wet and filthy T-shirt. The camera sees only her back and her face reflected in the mirror.

> VICKI
> Oh no! It's completely see-through!
> Now he's going to think I'm hot
> for him!

She tries flattening her nipples with the palm of her hand.

> VICKI
> Lie down, boys! Lie down, damn you!

Vicki is torn between cleaning her T-shirt and drying it out. A real dilemma. She spots a hot-air hand dryer on the wall so she wets a couple of paper towels and starts dabbing at the stain. She needs more water so she tries to wet the towels a bit more. The tap is really stiff and then it comes on in a torrent, squirting water up all over her T-shirt. It's a disaster.

> VICKI
> Oh my God! Oh my God!

Vicki leans back and sticks her chest under the hot air hand dryer and it starts humming away, doing its stuff. She breathes a sigh of relief. But after three seconds it stops. Vicki waves her chest under the dryer again. Nothing. She tries again, more frantically this time.

> VICKI
> Ohh!

An expensively dressed woman enters the restroom and looks at her curiously. Vicki pretends to be dancing. When the woman goes into a stall, Vicki waves her hands under the dryer. She bangs the dryer. Looks for a switch to turn it on. Nothing. Finally she tries the paper-towel dispenser – it's empty. She's just used the last of the paper towels to wash her T-shirt. She's dirty, completely soaked and will have to face Toby in a see-through wet T-shirt. In desperation, she knocks on the stall door.

> VICKI
> Miss? Excuse me?

> EXPENSIVELY DRESSED WOMAN
> (from behind closed door)
> What do you want?

VICKI

I've had a bit of an accident. I don't suppose you
would sell me your blouse?

Vicki opens her purse and counts her money.

VICKI (CONTD)

I've got £22 and some change. I'll give you all of
it.

EXPENSIVELY DRESSED WOMAN
(from behind closed door)
Laughter

VICKI

Please? I'm desperate!

EXPENSIVELY DRESSED WOMAN
(from behind closed door)
£22 for a Versace T-shirt? This isn't Oxfam,
love.

VICKI

Oh!

Clutching her purse across her chest, Vicki checks her
reflection one last time, then opens the door to return to the
café.

14 INT. CAFÉ – LONDON – CONTINUOUS
Vicki walks over to Toby's table, still hiding her chest with
her purse. He stands to greet her.

TOBY

Vicki! How wonderful to see you!

Toby hugs her. She's still holding the purse in front of her.

VICKI

Hi! Toby!

Here, let me take your purse.

VICKI

No!

They tussle over the purse. Toby wins but as he takes it from her, Vicki grabs a menu from a Passing Waiter and holds that in front of her chest as she sits down, looking at Toby over the top of the menu.

VICKI

Gosh. It all looks so good!

TOBY

You look terrific!

VICKI

Oh, no. Not really.

WAITER

Can I take your order?

TOBY

Yes, I'll have the risotto please. Vicki?

VICKI

Uh – I'd like a little more time looking at the menu.

WAITER

Certainly, signorina.

FADE TO

SAME SCENE – 15 MINUTES LATER

Toby and the Waiter are looking fed up. Vicki doesn't want to give up the menu.

VICKI

(stalling for time)
And the fish cakes? Do you know exactly what kind of fish there is in those?

WAITER

Eeza salmon, signorina

VICKI

Would that be that Scottish salmon or Canadian salmon?

WAITER

(wearily)
I will have to go and check, signorina.

The Waiter is about to leave when Vicki suddenly spots another diner being served spare ribs which come with a large bib.

VICKI

Oooh! Oooh! I'll have the ribs please. And the fishcakes.

WAITER

You want the ribs and the fishcakes?

VICKI

Uh huh! I'm starving!

The Waiter tries to take Vicki's menu, but she won't let go.

VICKI

No! I'll need this for dessert!

They wrestle over the menu, but Vicki hangs on. The Waiter sighs and leaves.

TOBY

You know, I'm really sorry about the way we broke up.

VICKI

(too casually)

Hey, forget it! I got over you like that (she snaps her fingers).

TOBY

(slightly taken aback)

Oh. Well, I'm really glad you're OK about it. You left in such a hurry. I'm glad things are going so well for you.

VICKI

(lying through her teeth to impress Toby)

Oh yeah, my career's going great. LA's a ball – working with all the big stars – Woody Allen, Robert de Niro, Quentin Tarantino, Laurence Olivier—

TOBY

But he's dead.

VICKI

Oh, yeah. Of course. He's dead *now*.

FADE TO

SAME SCENE 30 MINUTES LATER

Vicki is wearing a large ribs bib that says 'I'm A Big Baby' and finishing the last of her fishcakes. The plate of spare ribs sits untouched in front of her.

VICKI

That was delicious!

WAITER

May I take your plate, signorina?

VICKI

Oh, thank you.

There was something wrong with the ribs, signorina?

No. It's just that I don't eat red meat.

The Waiter leaves, very confused.

I put down the script pages just then as a man arrived to put
two cups of coffee on our table and a basket of ciabatta. I
went to take a sip of coffee but Max grabbed my hand to stop
me.

'Don't ever drink anything they give you on set. It's
probably just shoe polish and water.'

'It smells like real coffee,' I told him.

'Can we drink this?' he called over to the prop man. 'Will it
kill us?'

'You're OK, that's Starbucks,' the propman replied.

'See,' I teased him.

Max called him over again. 'Excuse me, I don't suppose you
have any jam roly-poly? My friend here is British – she's a bit
worried that she hasn't had her suet intake for the day.'

I laughed too loudly and the prop man looked at him like he
was a lunatic. He gave him a very fixed smile as if to say, 'I'm
rushed off my feet here trying to dress this fucking set single-
handed. Gimme a break.'

'Gosh,' I said. 'I've just figured out who it is you remind me
of. Austin Powers! I think it's the glasses. Did you see those
movies?'

'No, I didn't and, for God's sake, don't say that to Natalie,'
he warned. 'She's got a little Liz Hurley doll at home with pins
stuck in it.'

When Natalie arrived looking glossy and radiant, I decided
that Toby, the theatre-directing ex, would probably take one
look at her and break a leg in his hurry to ditch his wife. She

waved at me and all the other extras gave me a very dirty look.

'Who the hell are you?' they were thinking.

'OK. SHOOTING NEXT TIME! FINAL CHECKS!' Jerry yelled and there was a last-minute flurry of activity as tablecloths were straightened, shiny noses were powdered, hair was flicked, the waiter's espressos appeared and copies of the *Sun* and the *Guardian* crossword that the other extras were reading were whisked out of sight. I sat up a bit straighter and felt a tiny flurry of excitement and nerves.

'You've got a bit of chocolate on your mouth,' said Max. He'd forgotten to wear his hat.

'Oh, have I?' But before I could check, he'd stretched out a finger, wiped my lip and popped his finger in his mouth to lick it clean.

'All gone,' he said helpfully.

'Oh. Thanks.' I tried to sound as casual as I could, as if it were the most normal thing in the world for my best friend's lover to be cleaning my lips for me. Had Natalie seen that? No, she was standing by the door talking to the director. Act normal. Act normal. Be calm.

'QUIET EVERYWHERE PLEASE! STAND BY TO SHOOT!'

'AND TURN OVER!'

'SOUND AT SPEED!'

'MARK IT!'

'87 TAKE 1!'

'AND ... ACTION BACKGROUND! ... ACTION WAITER! ... AND ACTION!'

The two punks stomped past the window – hey look, everybody, we're in swinging London! – followed a second later by Tweed Overcoat Woman. Then the door opened and Natalie walked in, lifted her chin, took a deep breath, swung her handbag and walked into the centre of the café, straight into the path of the waiter carrying his tray of espressos.

'AND CUT!'

'AND WE'RE GOING AGAIN, PLEASE!'

'Is that it?' I whispered to Max. The whole thing had taken maybe nine seconds.

'They'll have to do it a couple more times until they get it right,' he explained.

'They do know, don't they, that there haven't been punks like that in London for about twenty years?'

'Hey, we're Americans. Humour us.'

'FIRST POSITIONS EVERYBODY, PLEASE!'

'NATALIE, CAN YOU HOLD IT AT THE DOOR FOR JUST A BEAT LONGER?'

The assistant director appeared at our table. Oh no, I thought, they're going to split us up!

'Max, can you lose the glasses? Dan's a bit worried that people will recognise you.'

'Sure – as long as I don't have to read any fine print.' He whipped off his specs and put them in the inside pocket of his jacket. 'Everything's all blurry,' he announced happily. As he looked at me with his clear blue eyes, I was glad he couldn't see my reaction. Hoped he wouldn't notice the loud thud as my jaw hit the table. It was like watching Clark Kent turn into Superman. It was 'Why, Miss Jones, you're beautiful'. It was frog becomes prince. Without his glasses, this guy was gorgeous. Who knew? I stared at him in total surprise.

'TURNOVER!'

'SOUND AT SPEED!'

'MARK IT!'

'87 TAKE 2!'

'ACTION BACKGROUND! . . . ACTION, JOHN! . . . AND ACTION!''

As Natalie did her walk across the café, I mouthed, 'Rhubarb, rhubarb, rhubarb' at Max, all the time thinking, 'You're gorgeous, gorgeous, gorgeous.' What was I thinking of saying he reminded me of Austin Powers? How could I not have noticed this amazing resemblance to Kevin Costner. Or was it Bruce Willis?

He mouthed something back at me but I couldn't make out what it was. Something . . . best?

'What did you say?' I mouthed at Max on take 3. I studied his lips carefully to make out his reply.

'I said – you have great breasts,' he mouthed at me.

'CUT!' shouted Jerry just in time as I spat out my coffee all over the table.

'CHECKING THE GATE!'

'Sorry, it must have gone down the wrong way,' I told the prop man who came running over to clean the table. 'You shouldn't say things like that,' I scolded Max, trying to sound cross rather than flattered.

'Hey, I'm just acting!' he said innocently. 'We're a couple on their first date – or maybe their second date – and my character is a terrible flirt.'

'Where did you read that?' I laughed.

'It says so in the script, didn't you see it? And you're playing this girl with great breasts.'

'IF THE GATE'S GOOD, WE'RE AROUND ON NATALIE.'

'Hi, guys, how's it going over here?' Natalie came over to say hello. I hoped she hadn't heard that particular bit of dialogue. They were moving the lights to shoot the bit where she gets covered in coffee.

'You were marvellous, darling,' gushed Max, stroking her hand. 'That was some of the best walking into a restaurant I've ever seen.'

'It's not too boring for you, is it, Lindy?' she asked me.

'No. No. Not a bit – it's really interesting.' I sounded so guilty. 'I was reading the script. I love the bit with the hot-air dryer.'

'We're not doing that here. We'll do that in the studio back in LA. They're trying to get Joanna Lumley.'

'Oh, right.'

'GOOD GATE!'

'Well, gotta go. Have to get coffee thrown at me.'

'Good luck!'

'Break a leg, darling,' called Max after her.

It took them ninety minutes, five white T-shirts and twenty cups of espresso to get the spilt coffee scene on film. Each take was over in a couple of seconds, just long enough for Max to totally flummox me.

'Is that a Wonderbra you're wearing?' he asked.

'Max – cut it out. You're embarrassing me.'

'Why?' he asked innocently. 'We're only acting.'

'ACTION!'

'Is your underwear a matching set?'

'Max, please!' My face felt like it was on fire.

'Is it silk or lace?'

'Honestly, just stop that, or I'll tell Natalie.' I was trying my hardest not to let on that I was secretly loving every minute of it. Max was treating it all like a huge game. When the cameras stopped rolling, he'd put on his glasses and revert back to normal innocent chit-chat, about his work, about their home in LA, about things he wanted to do while he was in London, and pretend nothing had happened. Mild-mannered Clark Kent. But as soon as they shouted ACTION! off would come the glasses and Superman would hit me another one.

'Does it tear easily?'

It was strange to think that if anybody else had asked me those same questions I would have probably hit them. I guess if you don't fancy someone it's sexual harassment – if you fancy them like mad, it's foreplay.

'Are your nipples innies or outies?' He had his back to the cameras so nobody else would ever be able to read his lips. All they'd ever see was my wide-eyed reaction – a mixture of exquisite embarrassment and guilty pleasure. By the time they'd finished the morning's shoot, there was absolutely no need for debate about whether my nipples were innies or outies.

'THANK YOU, EVERYBODY. THAT'S LUNCH. WE'RE BACK HERE AT ONE FORTY-FIVE!'

Natalie came whizzing over in her grubby T-shirt to grab

Max. The actor who played Toby was with her. 'Lindy, do you know Sean Reynolds?' she asked me.

No, of course I don't know Sean Reynolds, I thought. 'Hi,' I said, sticking out my hand.

'Lindy's my oldest friend in the whole world,' Natalie told him.

'Are you an actress too?' asked Sean as we piled into Natalie's limo which would drive us around the block back to unit base.

'No, I'm a photographer.' Pathetically, I couldn't think of a single other thing to say by way of small talk. I was too distracted watching Max and Natalie. Now that Natalie was back, Max's attention was entirely focused on her. It was as though I had suddenly ceased to exist. I fixed my face in a permanent smile to make it look as though I was completely at peace with the world. What right did I have to be jealous of Natalie? She and Max were an item. End of story.

I wasn't prepared for the enormous crowd of fans waiting behind the crash barrier at the end of the street. The screams when Natalie came out were deafening.

'Oh, God,' she said. 'It's started again. It's been unbearable the last couple of days because I'm the only one of the cast on set. I have to do it all myself.'

As if on cue, a red-faced girl with a huge quiff of blonde hair appeared at her side clutching a sheaf of publicity photos.

Natalie took them from her without a word of thanks, just a sigh, then marched over to the mob with a wave and her TV star smile. The cheer was enormous. She spent five minutes signing photos and chucking them into the crowd. Then she turned and walked back to us, so the crowd couldn't see her rolling her eyes in disgust.

'Is is like this all the time?' I asked.

'Every fucking day of my life,' she moaned. 'You have no idea what ass-holes these people are.'

*

There were no empty tables on the lunch-bus so Natalie made a big fuss about making two of the sparks move downstairs so I could sit with her and Max and Sean. Half of me just wanted to fade away into the background and disappear for ever. I was only a couple of miles from home and these Americans were on my turf, but I felt like an intruder – on set, in the show, in Natalie's life, on the lunch-bus, in London generally. They were talking about a cop show Sean was about to start, a British version of *Miami Vice* but without the pastel suits and set in Liverpool.

'I'm playing a young detective who's been to university, so he gets up everyone else's noses,' Sean was saying. 'He was supposed to get murdered in episode four but my agent's made them re-write it. Now I'm only going to be seriously wounded.'

'How's Andrew?' Natalie asked me.

'Oh, he's fine. Working hard,' I said.

'I'm dying to meet him. Tell him to stop working so hard so we can all get together one evening.'

'Sure. That would be great,' I said casually.

Max looked at me very strangely across the table but didn't say a word. He didn't have to. I knew exactly what he was thinking.

Before we went back to the location I excused myself to go to the loo, which everybody insisted on calling the Honey-wagon, and sat with my head in my hands wondering what the hell was going on.

Previously on *Don't Call Us*: I'm an extra in one of the top-rating shows in the world. My best friend, who stole my gay boyfriend, is the star. My best friend's fiancé is flirting with me big-time right under her nose. And the whole thing is being recorded for a world-wide television audience. Yes, that just about summed it up. I wondered what the etiquette guides would have to say about this particular social situation.

What would Audrey Hepburn do? I wondered.

*

Back in the café, the moment I took my seat Max scooted around to my side of the table to sit next to me while they set up.

'So, who's Andrew?' he asked immediately.

'My husband,' I said lightly. Why was I so reluctant to let Max know I was married?

'You never told me you were married!'

'I thought you knew. I thought Natalie would have told you.' It certainly sounded believable. I'd told Andrew all about Max. More or less.

'No, she never did. I'm shocked.' He sounded shocked too.

'Why?'

'You don't act married, that's why. Show me your hand.'

I held up my left hand and he turned it over, looking at my wedding ring and engagement ring very suspiciously. I waggled my fingers.

'See?'

'Well, I guess I never looked at your hands before.'

'What's all the fuss about anyway?' I said. 'You're practically married too.'

'Yeah.' He considered this for a second and a sneaky smile crossed his lips. 'So I guess that makes this all right then.'

My heart skipped a beat. 'Makes what all right?' I asked innocently.

'You know,' he said and gave me a playful shove with his shoulder.

If I thought my being married would somehow cramp Max's style, I was wrong. While they filmed the scene with Vicki trying desperately to hide her breasts from Toby, the silent conversation at our table was also breast obsessed. My lip-reading was getting so good by now, I could probably get a job with MI5.

'LET'S BE READY ON THIS, THEN! STANDBY TO SHOOT!'

'What do your nipples look like?' mimed Max.

I thought for a second. 'Raspberries.' To hell with it, I figured. I might as well play along. If anyone could read my lips, they'd think I was ordering dessert.

'Oooh.' He shivered and half closed his eyes. 'Are they chewy?'

'You'll never know,' I mimed back. I couldn't take my eyes off his mouth. I was like a rabbit caught in his headlights. His pupils were like pin-pricks under the bright studio lights.

'CUT!'

'It's hot in here under these lights, isn't it?' he said at last. 'Maybe we'd better stop this now. It's getting a little dangerous.'

'Yeah, you're right,' I said, meaning exactly the opposite. I didn't want to stop now, it was just getting interesting. The whole situation was totally, wonderfully surreal.

'Do you mind not eating the bread,' said the prop man, throwing some fresh slices of ciabatta into our basket. 'It's continuity.'

'AND ONCE AGAIN! FIRST POSITIONS!'

A few tables away Vicki and Toby wrestled over the menu. The waiter hovered.

'Would your breasts fit in both my hands?' mimed Max, holding out his palms. He didn't miss a trick.

When they repositioned the cameras so that Max's profile would be in shot, I thought he'd have to give his silent seduction a rest, but I was wrong.

'Would you like some cream on your raspberries?' he asked.

I wasn't paying much attention to the filming going on around me, but before long, they were on the final part of the scene where the waiter tries to take the bib from Natalie and she's still desperately trying to hang on to it.

'You know what?' I heard Natalie saying in her Vicki voice. 'This is such a cool bib I'd really like to buy it. Is that OK? Don't you think this is a cool bib, Toby? Everyone's wearing these in LA now. Gwyneth Paltrow – my very good friend

Gwyneth . . . Gwynnie . . . has got one just like this in calfskin.'

'If you don't want those raspberries, I'll lick them for you,' said Max.

'CUT!'

'CHECKING THE GATE!'

'THANK YOU ALL VERY MUCH, EVERYBODY. IF THE GATE'S GOOD WE'RE WRAPPED AT THIS LOCATION AND MOVING ON TO LOCATION 2 FOR SCENE 18.'

'GOOD GATE!'

There was a ragged splatter of applause and immediately everybody started packing up all the gear. They were moving straight on to Portobello Road for some quick montagey shots of Toby and Vicki just mooching about. They had different extras for that scene already waiting.

I stretched my arms above my head and yawned, then quickly lowered them again when I saw Max staring at the effect this had on my T-shirt.

'What happens now?' I asked him.

'Well,' he began, but Natalie was already beside him, one hand on his shoulder. 'Hi, darling!' he told her. 'You were great.'

'Thanks, hon. Are you coming with us to Portobello, Lindy? You can probably do some photos between takes. Ask Dan. I'm sure it will be OK.'

'Look, this probably isn't the right time to bring this up,' I explained, 'but *The Hoop* are really keen on an interview. If there's no interview, I'm not sure if they'll be able to use the pictures at all . . .' My voice trickled away with embarrassment. It was so awkward having to ask Natalie like this. It was such an enormous favour.

'Well, that would be OK, wouldn't it?' said Max. 'Lindy could interview you. I'm sure you two don't have any secrets.'

I absolutely resisted the temptation to look at him.

'I'm really sorry, Lindy but I just can't. It's nothing personal. You can understand why, can't you?'

'Yes, I do. Really. It's OK, honestly. I hope you don't mind me asking, though.'

'Why do they need an interview anyway?' she said. 'What's wrong with just pictures? It seems very ungrateful of them.'

It was almost a relief that she'd said no. I was feeling so guilty about the way Max was carrying on with me, Natalie didn't owe me anything. I'd do the photos and cover the costs somehow. Somebody else was sure to want them even without an interview. Probably.

'I'll just go ask Dan about coming to Portobello with you.' I got up to speak to the director and my legs were like jelly. I garbled some words at him which, to my surprise, he seemed to understand and he said yes, it was fine if I took photos as long as I kept quiet and out of the way and didn't shoot while they were rolling. And make sure you tell Wendy, who was the woman with the blonde quiff. I'd have to go home first and get my camera bag. Was it possible to somehow grab five minutes alone with Max? I wandered back to Natalie and Max to tell them I was going to pop home first and would meet them back here.

'Get Vince to drive you,' offered Max and he held my eye for just a second longer than he needed before turning away and walking off with Natalie like a good little boy.

I could barely manage one-word answers for Vince as he drove me home.

'It's very boring all this filming business, isn't it?' he said.

'Mmhmm.'

'All those people standing around all day. What do they all do? They must have fifty people there.'

'Yeah. Crazy.'

'What's he like, that director, then?'

'Seems nice enough.'

'Wouldn't mind his money! Ha ha!'

'Yeah. Ha ha.'

At home I grabbed my cameras, light meter and a dozen rolls of film: black and white, colour, 35mm, medium format. This stuff is expensive when you have to pay for it yourself. Somebody had better want these photos or I was going to be seriously broke.

Back at Portobello Road, Natalie was having her make-up reapplied under a large white umbrella. I went over to say hi and deliberately didn't catch Max's eye.

'Oh, hi,' she said. 'Are you going to capture me in all my glamour?'

'Do you mind?' I already had my camera out.

'No – but remember you promised you'd let me tear up any where I look really terrible.'

'I don't think it would be possible to take a photo of you looking terrible.'

'You'd be surprised!' she laughed bitterly. 'Can you rub my shoulders, honey?'

As Max gave Natalie a shoulder massage, she lay back and closed her eyes and he watched her adoringly. Isabella was brushing on her lipstick and her lips were gently parted. I snapped away. Portrait of the star being pampered. Isabella stepped aside and Natalie opened her eyes and gazed dreamily up at Max for a second. Snap snap of the happy couple in love. Then she closed her eyes again and Max looked straight into my lens. I tried to read his expression but I didn't know what he was trying to say. I had to close my eyes to stop my heart from thumping.

Snap.

Once they'd started shooting, Max went and sat with Dan behind the monitor, looking like butter wouldn't melt in his mouth, just glancing over in my direction ever so occasionally, so that no one watching him would suspect a thing.

The assistant director was having a hard time. 'Look, I don't have to tell you we've got A Lot To Get Through

Today!' he shouted. 'Will you all put away those fucking conkers and stop messing about!'

The sound recordist and his assistant sheepishly stopped their conker competition at the semi-final stage and went back to work. All over the set, conkers were quietly shoved back into pockets.

Were the photos I was taking any good? I didn't know. I went through the motions of checking my light readings, loading my cameras and composing the shots in a kind of daze: Natalie walking towards the camera with her face in sharp focus and the background stalls an impressionistic blur; Natalie resting under a tree, her face lit by dappled late-afternoon sunlight through the branches.

When they finally wrapped for the day, Natalie was by Max's side in an instant, holding his hand.

'I've had a great day,' I told her. 'Thanks so much for letting me come out here today.'

'It's been so nice having you here, hasn't it, Max?' she said.

'It's been wonderful,' he agreed.

'Well,' I said. 'I guess I'll see you soon.'

'Vince will give you a ride home,' said Natalie. 'Me and Max can get a lift back to the hotel with Dan.'

'Are you sure? That's really kind of you,' I said.

'I nearly forgot,' said Max. 'I've got the phone number for that American magazine you were interested in.'

'Oh, great. Thanks.' I had no idea what he was talking about but I instinctively played along.

'I left it in the car. I'll walk back over there with you. I've really had fun today,' said Max when we were out of ear shot.

'Yes,' I said, trying to sound stern. 'I know you have.'

'I've been thinking about your breasts all afternoon.'

The car was parked right by the camera truck and there were half a dozen technicians loading gear.

I wanted to kiss him so badly I thought I might explode but there were too many witnesses.

He kissed me on the cheek under the watchful eye of Vince

and two burly riggers. 'I'll see you soon,' he said, and I got into the back seat. He watched me drive off, with one hand raised to say goodbye.

When Andrew came home that night, I was waiting for him wearing just a silk Chinese dressing gown. The words 'gagging for it' didn't even begin to describe my state of mind.

'Hi, bunny, how did it go?' he was saying, but I grabbed him by the hand and dragged him upstairs.

'Hey!' he said, delighted. 'What's got into you?'

By way of an answer I threw him down onto the bed and began pulling off his shoes.

'You should do TV more often,' he said approvingly.

I unzipped his trousers and pulled them off as he started tugging off his shirt and tie.

'What have you got on under there?' he said, taking a peek under my dressing gown. 'Oooh. It's a naked bunny!'

I wished he'd just shut up and get on with it. I kissed him hard and untied the sash of my dressing gown, rubbing my breasts against his furry chest.

As he kissed me, I felt . . . absolutely nothing. It was like kissing a cheese sandwich. What on earth was wrong with me? I closed my eyes tight and tried to summon up some kind of passion, some sort of emotion for my husband. I tried to concentrate on Andrew but the only thought filling my mind was Max. Max. Max. Max. I saw his blue eyes. I saw his soft kissable lips. 'Can I lick them for you?' he was saying in my head.

'Do you think I have nice breasts?' I asked Andrew.

'Oh, yeah, bunny. They're fine. Don't worry about them. You don't need a boob job.'

'Who said anything about a boob job?'

'Isn't that what you meant?'

'Of course it's not,' I said furiously. 'Why on earth would I want a boob job? I have great breasts. You'd know that if you ever paid the slightest bit of attention to them.'

'Oh, bunny, I'm sorry,' he said and clamped an obedient cold hand on my chest. He might have been fumbling for a light switch.

'It's too late now,' I muttered but Andrew was well into his stride. As he jiggled away on top of me I lay back and thought of Max, reliving every second of our deliciously wicked afternoon. I imagined Andrew's lips were Max's lips, that Andrew's hands were Max's hands. But I hated doing it – it made me feel cheap and deceitful. This wasn't making love, this was telling lies. I just wanted it to be over with. Afterwards I lay beside my husband with a sick, guilty feeling at the betrayal I'd committed. But then a thought struck me that was even more disturbing. It wasn't Andrew I felt I was being unfaithful to, it was Max.

This wasn't good. This wasn't good at all.

fourteen

'Thanks so much for coming yesterday.' It was Natalie on the phone.

'Hey, I loved it.'

'I'm sorry we didn't get a chance to talk more but you know how it is. I barely get a moment to myself.'

'Yeah. You're working. I know. It's not a problem. I thought it went really well by the way. It was very funny.'

'Do you think so? It's really hard work doing it without an audience because there's no one laughing. You hear yourself saying these lines and you feel them going down like a lead balloon.'

'No, it was great, really.'

'Anyway, I thought we could do the photo shoot next Sunday. It's practically my only day off.'

'Oh, I can't then. We're going away for the weekend. To Italy. It's my birthday. What about the Sunday after?'

'Even better. And they will pay for Isabella to do my hair and make-up, won't they? I don't trust anyone else.'

'No problem.' I'd have to pay her myself and try and get the money back somehow. 'Are you sure you don't mind doing this on your day off? Don't you want to spend some time with Max?'

'No, he'll be fine. He can come along and hold your lights for you. Make himself useful. Have a good time in Italy.'

'I don't really feel like going now.'

'Is there anything special you'd like for your birthday?'

Just half an hour alone with your fiancé. 'No – nothing I can think of.'

'Well, see you when you get back.'

I drove to Sainsbury's to do the shopping but all the time I was wheeling my trolley through the aisles, I couldn't get Max out of my mind.

What was happening to me?

I thought of all the heart-breaking bastards I'd been out with before I met Andrew and how I'd been pathologically faithful to every single one of them – usually for months after we'd split up. All I'd ever wanted was someone who would love me as much as I loved them and I'd found that in Andrew. So what was I playing at now, fancying every man who came along?

I barely even know Max, I thought. The whole thing is ridiculous. A schoolgirl crush. Remember that time I thought I was in love with Mr Blunstone, my art teacher? This is just like that.

But I'm a married woman, I reminded myself. Married women aren't supposed to have crushes on people. And Mr Blunstone never once mentioned my breasts. Hell, I didn't even have breasts when I was fourteen. He didn't even know I was alive. The longest conversation I remember having with him was that day he said he liked the photos I'd taken on sports day and I should think about studying photography properly. If he'd told me to take up free-fall parachuting I would have done it, just to please him. So really, this is all his fault. If I hadn't taken up photography, I'd never have been trying to get work on *The Hoop* and I would never have dared contact Natalie again and I would never have met Max in the first place.

I'd just be perfectly happy being married to my lovely Andrew.

And I am perfectly happy, aren't I? We're OK, Andrew and me, aren't we? OK, we seem to be arguing a lot lately, but all married couples have rows. It's normal. And his friends get on my nerves but that's not the end of the world. And, OK, so we don't make love as much as we used to, but we're just in a bit of a low spot at the moment. That'll pick up again won't it?

But I couldn't shake off one disturbing thought. If Andrew and I were so perfectly happy, why was I so violently attracted to other men all of a sudden? What was that all about?

First it was Nick, now Max – in the space of just a few weeks. It was like my hormones had gone on a bender.

Maybe it was Nick's fault. He was the one who'd got me all stirred up in the first place. And he was the one who'd made me see my job at *The Ledger* for the pile of crap that it was and made me question whether I was really prepared to do it any more. In a weird, subconscious sort of way, I knew that I'd gone after the job at *The Hoop* hoping to impress him. Maybe one day he'd see my photo credit in there and think of me with renewed respect. As if he cared. So maybe this whole thing was Nick's fault.

The strange thing was, all my life, I'd despised people who had affairs. I thought they were disgusting. Why get married at all, if you're just going to cheat? Hadn't they ever heard of honesty? There were married guys at work, first at the local paper and then at *The Ledger* who I knew were screwing around and I could barely bring myself to speak to them. I had no respect for them whatsoever. I'd deliberately close the lift doors if I saw them coming. I especially hated that whole ball-and-chain concept they subscribed to. As if they'd be astronauts or England manager if it weren't for 'er indoors holding them back.

And now look at me. Barely married three years and I was as bad as any of them. I hadn't actually slept with anyone else – all I'd done was kiss one guy and let another one flirt with me but that was a mere technicality. I would have made love to Max without a second thought.

Really? Standing there in the supermarket that's when it hit me. I realised I was prepared to risk my marriage, my friendship with Natalie, her future marriage, everything. I would have thrown it all away for just one night with Max. If I thought I could get away with it, that is. Given half a chance, I was willing to ruin everyone's lives over some primal instinct that's as mundane as eating or going to the toilet. Sex is nothing special. Anyone can do it. So what's the big deal?

'£123.76, please.'

'Sorry?'

'£123.76.' The woman on the check-out looked well and truly fed up, imprisoned in her tight little cubicle all day. I handed over my credit card and my Reward card. I could hear the woman behind me tutting because she'd been forced to stand in line for an extra second. I knew I'd do exactly the same thing.

Christ, is that how much food costs? I was going to have to get a job sorted out pretty damn soon or we'd be in big trouble.

On the way out with my shopping, I checked the magazine racks to see if the new issue of *The Hoop* was out yet and scanned all the glossy covers to see if anything else leapt out at me that I could do some freelance work for.

Freelance. That's what I was, I told myself. Not unemployed – just freelance. A flash gun for hire. There were certainly plenty of options.

Fifty Beauty Lies Exposed

My Sister is My Mother!

Taboo Love! Dare You?

It's the pits! The stars who are hanging on to underarm hair!

Free Makeovers For 10 Lucky Readers!

Doctors Left THIS Inside Me For Nine Years!

Your Pony's First Gymkhana!

Oxygen – The New Beauty Must Have!

Daddy and Me – One Woman's True Story Of Abuse.

9 Pages of Blissful Bathrooms
Why Everyone's Talking About Tuna!
Relight His Fire! Put The Spark Back Into Your Marriage!

Hmmm. I picked the last title off the shelf and paid for it at the cigarette counter. Perhaps that was the answer. Perhaps all I needed was to put the spark back into our marriage. Maybe that would stop me going around lighting fires everywhere else I went like some kind of emotional arsonist.

As soon as I'd unpacked the shopping – £123 for washing powder and cat food . . . incredible – I sat down with a cup of tea and flicked open to the article.

The photo showed a tanned couple, coyly covered from the shoulders down by a red satin sheet smiling at each other and sipping champagne. The woman, young, blonde, too much lip gloss, was pouting at the bloke and he'd got one eyebrow raised as if to say 'careful or everybody will notice what your other hand is doing under the bedclothes'. They didn't look married. They looked like two porn stars who'd got five numbers on the lottery. I checked the photo credit. Picture posed by models, it said. That'd be right. Actually I recognised the bloke. He used to do a lot of our boxer-short photos at *The Ledger*. Philip somebody. Bent as a three-pound note. Oh well – you're not getting sex tips from him. Don't be so cynical.

I read on, wondering just how desperate you had to get to think you'd find any answers in a women's magazine.

The key to perfect tenderness is an acid-based marinade. Soak in pineapple juice and chill for 24 hours.

What? Oh, no – wait. That's *20 Tips for Blissful Barbecues*. Right – here we are.

1. *Impose a no sex rule for two weeks. Then set aside one night to massage and explore each other's bodies with scented oils* . . . Well the no-sex-for-two-weeks part would be easy. It was over two months now and apart from the other night our marriage was practically a bonk-free zone.

2. *Talk dirty to him . . .* Worth a try, I suppose, if I could manage to keep a straight face. But what would I say? 'Fuck me now, Andrew with your enormous cock!' No, perhaps not. He'd die of fright. Maybe I'd think of something better in the heat of the moment.

3. *Take a tip from strippers. Keep him on tenterhooks as you very slowly unpeel layer by layer, down to nothing but a sexy thong and peek-a-boo bra. Or swap your underwear for cling-film and let him unwrap you with his teeth.* Well, the clingfilm might help my cellulite, but would it really boost my sex-life to disguise myself as leftovers?

4. *Next time he'd rather watch the football than you, surprise him with a saucy lap-dance. Keep all your clothes on – if you can – and as you sway your hips just inches above him, remind him of the house rule: no touching allowed. We guarantee it won't be long before he's offside and you're both headed for an early bath.*

5. *Change the venue. Move sex out of the bedroom and try somewhere new – the bathroom, the garden, upstairs on the Number 88 bus.* No thanks. We tried doing it in the bath years ago and I had tap shaped bruises on my back for a week.

6. *Indulge in aphrodisiacs . . . oysters, asparagus, truffles, chillies, bananas, peaches, strawberries, celery . . .* Gosh – is there a fruit or vegetable that *hasn't* jumped on the aphrodisiac bandwagon? What about chips? *And you can forget the washing up, because you'll be eating these treats off each other's naked bodies.* That didn't sound bad, providing it didn't involve cooking. I still had post-traumatic stress from Delia's roast tomato soup. Champagne and coffee were meant to be aphrodisiacs too, according to this. That would explain a lot, but it's not much good if you can't point your hormones in the right direction. Mine were going off like a scatter gun all over the shop.

7. *Re-enact the love scenes from your favourite sexy movie. Whether it's 9½ Weeks or Betty Blue don't forget your video camera so you can watch your Oscar-winning performances*

later. Hmm. I knew Andrew got off on *Gladiator.* I wonder what he'd look like in a toga and sandals. We could dress Billy up as a tiger.

8. *Turn your bedroom into a passion zone. Chuck out the TV, the dog, the football posters, dim the lights – think Arabian Knights* . . . The bedroom could do with a tidy-up, I suppose. But Billy could still sleep on the bed if he wanted to – I'd known him twice as long as Andrew after all.

9. *Play the Postage Stamp game to discover erogenous zones you never knew you had. Take it in turns to tie each other's hands and feet to the bedposts – then very slowly lick each other all over to find those never-before-explored areas that will make you both moan with pleasure.*

10. *Become his sex slave and fulfill his most private fantasy. Ask him what he really wants and satisfy his every darkest desire. Then tomorrow night, it's your turn!* Hmm, I could just imagine that one. 'Darling, what I really, really want is a tumble drier, oh, and can you fix it for me to snog Max?' Yeah, I could just imagine the look on his face.

I suppose anything was worth a try to save my marriage and my sanity but it all seemed so pre-meditated. When Andrew and I first got together it wouldn't have mattered if I'd been wearing crotchless knickers or fireman's trousers. The only aphrodisiac we needed was each other. Night-time, morning, Tuesday tea-time, it was all the same to us. But then that all sort of dried up.

The first time we slept together without making love it had felt like the end of the world even though I knew it wasn't really such a big deal. But maybe I was right. Maybe it really had been the end of the world. The end of the beginning anyway. The end of the bit where you simply can't keep your hands off each other.

One night one of us – I can't even remember which one of us it was – had gone to bed and realised that we were more interested in sleeping than sex that particular night and the can't-get-enough-of-you-spell was broken. After that, every time we went to bed, sex wasn't automatic any more. Now we had options. We could have sex *or* go to sleep. We could have sex *or* read a book. We could have sex *or* stay up and watch a movie. We could have sex *or* not have sex. Bit by bit the arguments in favour of having sex became less and less overwhelming.

And sex had become a bit predictable. After all, it's not as if you don't know how it's going to turn out, is it? You could work your way through the *Kama Sutra* page by page but the end result is always pretty much the same. It's like driving – you can take the motorway or you can take the scenic route and stop for a picnic on the way, and still end up in Birmingham.

But, like I said before, it was worth a try and I made a start by tidying up the bedroom. Actually, there was a lot of clutter in here. All the books and magazines went back onto the shelves or in the bin. All the clothes lying around the place were folded up or hung back in the wardrobe. Odd bits of jewellery, stray cassette cases, free books of matches, a receipt for having the central heating boiler repaired, the spare buttons to Andrew's suit, a pair of Walkman headphones – all the stuff that didn't seem to have a natural home – I tossed into a shoe box and put under the bed to worry about later. Andrew's collection of action figures on the chest of drawers got hidden on the window sill behind the curtains.

I changed the light bulbs and hung a pink silk shawl over the bedside light and another one over the TV – it was too heavy to carry downstairs all on my own. I dug out a couple of scarves that seemed like they might come in handy for tying Andrew to the headboard. Then I made a special trip to Kensington High Street to get some jasmine-scented massage oil from the Body Shop and some asparagus from Sainsbury's. It didn't come with instructions, but I guessed you just boiled asparagus and put some butter on it. That couldn't be too difficult.

Lurking forgotten in my underwear drawer was a very expensive pistachio bra and knicker set. Pistachio is good, I thought. Not as obvious as black. Not as sluttish as red. Not as virginal as white. Kind of interesting.

I knew Andrew had got a thing about stockings and suspenders, but frankly that was his problem. I used to wear them for him when we first started going out but they made me feel like a trussed-up chicken. But I'd compromise and wear my snake-skin sandals with the ankle straps that I knew he thought were really hot. At seven-thirty I was trotting around the kitchen in my undies and sandals, steaming my asparagus. Upstairs, the jasmine massage oil was warming nicely in a cup of hot water by the bed. I wonder what Max would think if he could see me now? I thought. I'd been trying not to think about Max all day but it was like trying to make your mind go blank. The more I pushed thoughts of Max out of my head, the more they came flooding in.

The words of a song kept going around and around in my head: 'If you can't be with the one you love, love the one you're with . . . love the one you're with.'

But what did that mean exactly? Did it mean that if I couldn't be with Max I should love Andrew, or was it saying that if Andrew wasn't around, I had permission to love anyone who happened to be handy at the time? Like Max, for example?

When the phone rang, I ran to answer it, convinced it must be Max. I was thinking about him so much, I had made the phone ring. But it was Andrew.

'Hi, bunny. I'm going to be home late tonight. Maybe around ten. It's Russell's birthday. I'm meeting up with him and Robin for a drink. You haven't cooked anything yet, have you?'

'Cooked? No, not really – just a few vegetables.'

'Do you want to come and join us?'

'No, I'm home now, I can't be bothered getting dressed and going out again.'

'Oh, well. I'll see you at home later then. Love you.'

'I love you too. Don't work too hard.'

I put the asparagus in the fridge – the last thing in the world I needed right now was an aphrodisiac – and went to watch TV, anything to take my mind off Max. Come to think of it, why didn't he ring? Natalie was working. It wouldn't be too difficult for him to get my number.

When the phone rang again, I leapt on it, convinced that this time it must be Max. But it was Atlanta Parrish of all people.

'Hey. I'm just calling to see how it's going with Natalie Brown.'

'Good,' I said. 'The studio session is all booked.'

'That's brilliant. I don't suppose you're free tomorrow?'

'I could be – what's up?'

'Do you know Angus Rawle, the actor-painter-mad bloke?'

'Not personally but I know who he is.'

'We've got a shoot set up with him but Hervé's just rung to say he's got flu and can't do it. Do you want to do it for us?'

'Sure.' I tried to sound business-like and was glad we don't have video phones so that Atlanta couldn't see me sitting there in my pistachio undies with my legs thrown over the side of the sofa: Portrait of a Frustrated Housewife.

'It'll be at his studio in Hoxton. He's done an interview for us about his paintings so the pictures need to reflect that, rather than the actor side of him. Phone Justine on the picture desk in the morning and she'll give you the address.'

I was fast asleep in bed when Andrew finally came home.

'Why is it so dark in here?' he asked.

'The light bulb burned out,' I lied. 'We only had forty-watt ones left.'

'I'll buy some proper ones tomorrow. And what's that strange smell downstairs? Have you been cooking cabbage?'

'No, it's asparagus.'

'You and your funny diets,' he said, kissing me goodnight. In a second he was fast asleep.

Well, at least I hadn't wrapped myself in cling-film.

fifteen

I unloaded all the rented lights from the back of the car and struggled with them up the stairs to Angus Rawle's studio. I was a bit nervous about parking my car in the street in the middle of this industrial wasteland. There wasn't a soul in sight and it was the kind of setting where a horde of angry mutant zombies wouldn't look at all out of place; a limbo-land of warehouses that were no longer used for their original purpose of storing bananas and ladies' corsets but hadn't yet been converted into multi-million pound lofts.

What was a nice girl like Angus Rawle doing in a place like this?

I'd never actually seen any of his plays but I'd read some of the reviews. He wrote them himself – the plays that is, not the reviews – and they were apparently very physical, violent, shouty pieces with lots of fake blood and swearing. He had been known to physically attack audiences for coughing.

Off stage, here in his studio, he was a huge, terrifying bear of a man, with a thick grey beard and manic eyebrows. While I lumbered up his Art Deco stairwell, making trip after trip with all my gear, he ignored me, busily engrossed as he was in the task of making toast under the grill of an ancient Baby Belling stove.

As I struggled upstairs on my last trip he was delicately smearing butter on a piece of charred bread, the size of a paving slab. I watched entranced as he covered every milli-metre of the bread's surface. He smeared first vertically, then horizontally, with a patience that was a little unnerving, so that every crumb received exactly the same amount of butter – no more, no less – right up to the crust. It took him almost a minute just to butter one slice of toast and wipe the knife absolutely clean on the bread. It was fascinating, in a spooky kind of way, like watching a walrus sew on a button.

I'd expected to find his studio in the usual state of artist's disarray with beakers of paint scattered around, newspapers on the floor, bits of rag, half-used bottles of white spirit, mugs of coffee, canvases piled any which way in every corner and paint splatters on the lino. But it was almost supernaturally pristine and antiseptic. All his materials were stacked neatly and labelled in aluminium filing trays. Light streamed in through the enormous windows and there wasn't a trace of grime on any of them. No specks of dust to dance about in the sunbeams. Weird.

The only sign of chaos was on the solitary canvas on view: a rage of browns and reds and ochres violently depicting the naked body of a young man with his entrails hanging out; birds pecked at his brains; a rat gnawed on his penis. The paint looked as though it had been thrown on with a four-inch brush from Homebase.

'Do you like it?' said Angus Rawle. Precisely the question I had been dreading. The kind of question that had got me kicked out of art classes when I was fourteen.

'It's very powerful,' I replied truthfully, hoping I wouldn't be quizzed any further. 'What's it called?'

'Desire. Would you care for some toast?'

We sat munching toast and honey in a companionable silence. Angus seemed to have little inclination to make polite small talk and was intently cutting his toast into neat squares with a knife and fork. I had already decided that he was quite mad.

'And who else have you been photographing?' he asked.

'I'm about to do Natalie Brown,' I said, rather proudly.

'Never heard of her!' he snorted. 'Who else?'

Oh, blimey. I racked my brains. Who had I photographed? It had been ages since I'd done any regular work. I'd photographed the instructors at my gym for their notice board but I decided this was unlikely to cut any ice with Angus Rawle.

'Well, I just did some shoes – fashion stuff . . .' probably best not to add that they'd been modelled by a three year old '. . . and I did Nigel Napier a while ago.' How desperate was that? I think I got one shot of the outside of his house.

'Oh, yes. He's that newsreader. Got caught with his pants in the till. What's he doing now?'

'A pet show on TV,' I said.

'And who was that girl he was bothering? Hard-faced little thing?'

'Her name's Tania Vickery. She does a show called *Dial M For Money*. She's quite famous now.'

'Really? Actress is she?'

'Well it's not acting exactly, it's mostly just pointing at things and reading out a telephone number.'

'So how do you want me?' he said, when he'd finished his toast.

'Well, I'd like to do something that would represent you and your work – as an actor as well as an artist.'

'The only thing that represents me is me!' bellowed Angus, as though I'd insulted him in some way. Had I? What had I said?

'My body is my instrument!' he roared. And with that, he stood up unexpectedly and began unbuttoning his shirt. He folded it neatly on the chair beside him and then undid his trousers. As they dropped to the floor, I tried not to show my alarm when I realised he wasn't wearing any underpants.

I set up my darkroom equipment in our tiny bathroom, with my enlarger and trays of chemicals on a decorating trestle table and pinned my blackout curtain across the narrow window. The Angus Rawle negatives looked fine but I barely glanced at them because I had two rolls of black and white film that I'd taken on Exmoor. As soon as the negatives had developed I pegged them up over the bath and tried to get a glimpse of Max's face without getting any fluff on them.

Hurry up and dry!

Those native tribes who were afraid that cameras would steal their souls were probably onto something. That's what I felt those photos of Max were – a part of his soul that belonged only to me, too terrifying to look at with the naked eye. Like the Ark of the Covenant at the end of *Raiders of The Lost Ark*. Who knows what powers would be unleashed when those photos were developed?

I slid the negs very, very carefully into the contact sheet frame and exposed it for exactly eighteen seconds. Then I pushed it gently with my tongs backwards and forwards in the tray of developer, smiling fondly at all the little images of Max's face as they slowly appeared, smiling back at me. I whizzed it through the stop bath and the fixer then washed it for two minutes under the cold bath tap, gave it a quick squeegee before finally drying it with my hair drier. Hurry up! Hurry up! Then I rushed into the kitchen to examine it in daylight.

There he was. Oh, look at the way he's throwing back his head when he laughs! What was he laughing at? Look at his mouth and the lovely little creases around his eyes. Look at the way he's looking right into me. Thirty minutes ticked by while I studied every tiny image with a stupid grin on my face. I didn't pay nearly so much attention to the black and white roll I'd shot of Natalie at Portobello. That could wait and there was one shot on the end of the roll of Max giving Natalie a shoulder rub that I could hardly bear to look at.

I printed up just one 10 x 8 picture of Max to keep me going and then made myself buckle down to business and print up the Angus Rawle pictures. Every now and then I'd look over at Max's laughing face staring back at me from the string over the bath where he was pegged up to dry, and give him a little smile.

Andrew had flown to the Isle of Man for the day, just long enough for a meeting and to pick up some kippers, a jar of lemon curd and a bottle of malt whisky at the airport. His duty-free bounty.

'I've made some baked potatoes,' I said when he finally came home. All my Max photos were safely tidied away. 'Do you want one with a bit of tuna?' I was on a desperate low-fat diet, trying to lose weight before Natalie's photo shoot next week when I would see Max again.

'Have we got anything else?'

'I could grill you some chicken.'

'I might just order a pizza. Do you want some?' He'd already picked up the phone. Pizza Hut was on our Friends and Family list.

'Don't get pizza now,' I complained. 'We're going to Italy tomorrow. You can have real pizza when we get there.' There'd be no pizza for me of course. Or bread. Or pasta. Just green salad, grilled fish and mineral water. I had it all worked out. Maybe just one glass of wine on my birthday. It's meant to be good for the digestion. Besides, I couldn't be expected to deal with Robin and Russell completely sober, could I?

Andrew didn't answer because he was already ordering a Large Super Supreme, chicken wings and garlic bread.

'You'll be dead by the time you're fifty if you carry on at this rate,' I told him when he'd hung up. 'You really ought to start looking after yourself.'

'I do look after myself,' he said. He poured himself a large glass of whisky in one of the crystal glasses I'd bought for him on our anniversary. 'I'm very contented.'

'You're starting to look a bit too contented,' I said. 'A bit too Pooh Bear-ish.'

'Oh, but you like Pooh Bear,' he said in a babyish voice, trying to give me a cuddle.

'Yeah, but I wouldn't want to be married to him,' I said, pushing him gently away. 'Maybe if you didn't drink so much you'd lose some weight. Why don't you come to the gym with me once in a while? It wouldn't kill you.'

'I don't want to,' he whined. 'Don't make me. I'm too tired.' He flopped on the sofa and Billy immediately went and sat on his tummy. Traitor, I thought. I'm the one who feeds you.

'Are you all packed?' he said.

'Mmmhmm.'

'Did you pack all my shaving stuff?'

'No, it's still in the bathroom. You'll have to do that in the morning.'

'Did you find my swimming goggles?'

'Mmhmm. All packed.'

'You OK, bunny-bun? You seem sad.'

'You know. Just tired. I've been in the darkroom all afternoon. I think I'll get an early night. We have to be up at five tomorrow if we're going to check in at seven.' The thought of leaving London, where Max was, and flying to Italy, where he wasn't, was making me feel sick.

'What's on telly?'

I tossed the TV page over to him.

'*Don't Call Us* is on,' he said, flicking over to Channel 4.

How could I possibly forget that? It was torture watching Natalie on TV. She was so completely gorgeous and adorable, no wonder Max was crazy about her. I must be mad, I thought, to let my hormones get worked up over him.

'It's so strange to think that she's your friend,' said Andrew. 'The two of you seem so different.'

'Actually,' I told him, 'we've got more in common than you'd think.'

sixteen

We were both quiet on the drive to Gatwick the next morning, but you could maybe put that down to lack of sleep. Russell and Robin were already in the check-in line with their expertly packed rucksacks and wrap-around silver cycling goggles that seemed totally out of place under the airport's fluorescent lights. We went through to international departures and got a coffee while we waited for our flight. Robin was her usual unchatty self so I left the small talk to Andrew and Russell. I kept my nose buried in my Rough Guide to Italy, reading the same sentence over and over again about the horse race in Siena.

'You're very quiet this morning,' said Russell in that supercilious way of his. He was still wearing the stupid glasses, so I couldn't see his eyes. A small blessing.

'I've just got a bit of a headache,' I told him.

'Then you shouldn't be drinking coffee. That's the worst thing you can do for a headache.'

'Thanks for the tip,' I said drily and took another large sip.

Andrew took my hand on take off like he always did which I knew was his way of saying, if this plane crashes, we'll be holding hands at the end. It was doom-laden and touching all at once. I squeezed his hand back but didn't care much whether this particular plane burst into a fireball or not. At least our untimely demise would make the papers. At least then I would have fulfilled my part of the till-death-us-do-part bargain.

I left my airline breakfast untouched and just drank the

coffee. I wanted to lose at least ten pounds before I saw Max again so I might as well start now. I shut my eyes and thought of his face and landed at Pisa with a smile on my face.

We were herded into the baggage claim area but after forty minutes there was still no baggage to claim. Kids were crying and the voices around us were getting angrier and angrier as it gradually became apparent that there was no escape from the small airless room we were stuck in.

'This is completely out of order,' Russell kept saying. Andrew and I were sitting on the floor and Robin was perched unsteadily on her carry-on bag. There were several announcements in Italian which we couldn't understand. Then I heard somebody behind us saying they couldn't get the doors of the plane's baggage hold open.

'Well, that's just terrific!' fumed Russell, and went marching off looking for someone to complain to.

I had a rising sense of panic and frustration in my throat. It was like the feeling you get when you're stuck in a traffic jam and there's no place to turn off. If I tried to speak I knew I'd probably scream or burst into tears or both. Robin was fanning herself with a copy of *Marie Claire*. Andrew was wearing a tight little smile and trying to make the best of things. Russell had already staked out the angry, shouting option for himself which meant that Andrew had to be the calm one; you can't have two angry, shouting people – it just doesn't work.

It took us two and a half hours to finally get out of the airport with our luggage – longer than the flight itself had taken. Then Andrew and Russell had to join another fractious queue at the car rental place. We'd wanted to get to the villa while it was still light and it was already half past two with a three or four-hour drive ahead of us to the villa outside Orvieto.

'I'll drive,' said Russell and leapt into the front seat. We were all hot, bad-tempered, tired and angry.

'Are you OK, bunny-bun?' asked Andrew in his concerned

little voice. He was sitting up front with Russell and Robin and I sat in the back.

'I'm fine,' I assured him. 'I'm just going to close my eyes and have a nap.'

Russell ranted most of the way about the useless airline, the hopelessly archaic airport, the unhelpfulness of the Italians, their terrible driving and the pointlessness of any nation that didn't speak fluent English. He sat on 90mph, blaring his horn at anyone who blocked his way.

'You're driving like a complete fuck-wit,' I told him. 'I don't care what risks you take with your own life, but you might like to spare a thought for the rest of us.'

'It's perfectly safe for me to drive this fast because I've got excellent reflexes,' he explained self-importantly. 'I can respond to road conditions in a split second.'

'Well, I hope for our sake that all the other drivers on the road have got lightning reflexes too so they can jump out of the way when they see you coming,' I replied.

Robin just smiled at me nervously, terrified to say anything that would contradict her beloved Russell.

Actually, I half hoped he would crash – it would serve him damn well right.

We got lost of course. We were fine as far as Orvieto but then the road-signs petered out.

'It says here, turn left after two hundred metres,' said Andrew, reading the hand-written directions the man who owned the villa had faxed us. 'We can't be on the right road because we've gone more than a mile now and there's been no left turn at all – unless it was through that gate back there.'

'I have to go to the toilet,' piped up Robin.

Russell ignored her and threw the car around in a reckless U-turn. 'Right!' he screamed. 'We'll just go back to that T-junction and start again!'

I shut my eyes and tried to block out his self-righteous

anger. If I got through the holiday without him killing us or me killing him, it would be a miracle.

It was late afternoon when we finally reached the old stone villa and, as we switched the lights on inside, we saw it was filled with mis-matched furniture that looked about thirty years old. Piles of magazines were stacked against the walls. There was a small TV in the corner. A fine layer of dust had settled over everything.

'It looked nice in the brochure,' I said.

'It's lovely,' said Robin.

'It's a bloody rip-off,' said Russell. He was already on his way upstairs to check out the bedrooms.

'We're in here,' he said to me, when I'd dragged my bag upstairs. 'You and Andrew are down the hall.'

Russell had already bagged the largest of the three bedrooms but really there wasn't that much in it. The bed in our room had a hand-crocheted bedspread made from multicoloured scraps of wool and brown and yellow sheets with a daisy pattern. Austin Powers, eat your heart out.

'Is this going to be OK?' said Andrew nervously. Even he could tell this room was never going to make it into *Elle Decoration*.

'It's fine,' I said wearily. 'It'll do.'

'There's probably a great view out of this window,' he said, rolling up a pull-down blind and being rewarded with a faceful of dust as it clattered upwards.

'Yeah, probably,' I agreed. I didn't care much where I was. If I wasn't with Max, then paradise itself would be a poor substitute.

Towards sunset we drove down to the shop by the lake and I made the mistake of saying that the milky blues and swirly yellows made the sun look like a Turner painting. Russell just scoffed and said mockingly, 'Of course they do. This is the road where he painted them' as though this were common knowledge and he hadn't just read it in the guide book.

*

Robin made a green salad and plain spaghetti with olive oil. Russell opened his bottle of duty-free gin and poured large glasses for all of us. We found the porch light and went outside with our drinks to inspect the swimming pool. Russell was wearing his very brief red-and-black-striped Speedos.

'Smell that chlorine!' said Russell. 'They've used way too much.'

'Well, thank God you're here, Russell, to fix it,' I said sarcastically. 'You can probably sort out the Italian economy for them too in your spare time.'

'It's too cold to swim now, though, isn't it?' suggested Robin. She'd put on a jumper but was still shivering in the night air.

'For you, maybe,' he told her, just before he dived in. 'Not for me.'

With any luck he might drown.

There was a tyre hanging from the branches of a tree on the other side of the garden. The perfect place to drink my gin and tonic and daydream about Max. Andrew came up behind me and gave me a gentle nudge. Why didn't he just push off and leave me alone?

'Are you coming up to bed?' he asked.

'It's still early,' I told him. 'I'm not tired.'

'That's good,' he said with a happy smile. 'Neither am I.'

'Oh, Andrew, do you mind? I'm just not in the mood. Sorry.'

'Oh. OK.' He sounded hurt and disappointed. 'I just thought you might want to have a cuddle.'

'I'm just going to sit out here for a while if that's OK,' I said heartlessly.

'Can I sit here with you?'

'If you like.' I sucked on an ice-cube and listened to the clicking of the cicadas. Or were they grasshoppers?

'Don't you want to talk to me?' he asked.

'Sure,' I said, feigning enthusiasm. 'What do you want to talk about?'

164

'I don't know. Just talk.'

'Well, you start and I'll join in.' I could hear the impatience in my voice.

'Are you OK, bunny?'

'Yeah, I'm fine. Stop asking if I'm OK all the time. It's getting on my nerves.'

'You're not being very romantic,' he said. 'We're in Eee-taly.'

'I guess it hasn't quite sunk in yet.'

When I eventually went up to bed and slid in between the clammy daisy sheets, I could hear Andrew and Robin downstairs playing backgammon in the living room. Russell was doggedly watching a game show on TV under the delusion that he could understand Italian.

Andrew was so patient putting up with my moods. There was always another chance with Andrew. I was like the cat with nine lives where he was concerned. That was one of the things I liked about him. The fact that I could take him totally for granted. No matter how badly I behaved, whatever my faults, whether I needed to lose 10lb or not, Andrew didn't seem to care about any of it. I guess that's what being married was all about. Putting up with stuff. I was really going to have to learn how to do that. But in the meantime, all I could think of was Max.

I dreamed that night that the sun got broken. I was sitting with Jill, watching the sky, just enjoying the way the clouds kept blowing past so that the sun could come out. At least, that's what we assumed was happening. But then we kept watching and it gradually dawned on us that it wasn't the clouds that were moving but the sun. It started zig-zagging back and forth from left to right, then dipping up and down, swooping across the sky.

'That's funny,' said Jill. 'I thought the earth was meant to revolve around the sun. Shouldn't the sun be standing still?'

So we kept watching and then the sky became like a

whirlpool, as though someone had picked up a big spoon and stirred all the clouds and the blue sky in together. It was so beautiful we called out to Andrew to come and have a look. But as we watched, the sky began to disappear into a vortex, as if it were being sucked away by a giant Hoover, so all that was left was greyness and cold.

We shivered, a little afraid and waited to see what would happen next.

'Look!' I shouted. 'It's OK. There's the sun! It hasn't gone at all.' I pointed at a small golden orb shining in the distance and we all breathed a sigh of relief. It seemed to be coming closer – it was definitely coming closer – but it wasn't getting any bigger and then, when it got really close, I could make out a prop man carrying a round glass lampshade that he'd sprayed gold and covered in glitter. He came right up to us, put the sun down on a coffee table and then just walked away.

'Is that what the sun was all along?' I said. 'What a swizz.'

But then the sky started getting light again and the real sun began rising slowly right in front of us. The huge golden arc rose inch by inch. It was so close now we could almost touch it, but when it had fully appeared we could see that it had been in a terrible accident. It looked like a cracked egg with great jagged chunks taken out of the bottom. Where all the gold had been scraped off, there was blood and egg yolk oozing out.

Then, as we watched, the sun fell off of its hook, tipped forward and fell into the ocean and died. We watched it sink until there was nothing left to see except a few ripples on the surface.

'Well,' said Jill. 'That can't be good.'

seventeen

If I looked at one more fresco I was going to scream. And worse than having to put up with Robin and Russell today of all days was the fact that so far Andrew hadn't even wished me a happy birthday. When we woke up that morning I expected him to bring me breakfast in bed, a wild flower in a glass, and a present magically produced from under the bed. But he didn't.

As I cleaned my teeth and ran a bath I thought, any minute now he's going to remember it's my birthday and we'll both have a good laugh at how forgetful he is. By the time we'd finished breakfast and were getting ready to leave and he still hadn't said a word, I realised that he'd completely forgotten. I could still see the funny side, though. He was bound to remember by the time we got to Siena and we could order champagne in the restaurant and it would be fine. After all, I told myself, I'm not a kid any more. It's not like I'd been hoping to get a bike.

All the way in the car I'd told myself it didn't matter that my birthday had slipped his mind, even though that was the whole reason we were in Italy and the reason we were going to Siena today. Birthdays don't really matter once you're past twenty-five, do they? Just another year – and who needs to be reminded that they're getting older? Not me.

But now we were in the restaurant – the one I'd booked specially for my birthday lunch, which you'd think would have been a clue – and Andrew still hadn't even wished me happy birthday. Fair enough if he hadn't got me a present. I knew he'd been really busy before we came away. But would it have killed him to get me a card? Russell and Robin were in the kiosk next door buying postcards. Or maybe they were buying me a birthday card. Andrew must have told them it was my birthday. Mustn't he? He was busily studying the menu.

'Do you know what you're going to have?' he asked.

'I'll just have the salad,' I said. 'I'm not feeling very hungry.' I was trying not to show how upset I was feeling. Keeping my voice level. Perhaps the waiters would suddenly appear with a cake and everybody would sing to me in Italian. I'd look pretty silly then if I ruined the surprise.

'Don't be silly, you can't just have salad.'

'I told you. I'm not that hungry. It's too hot to eat.'

'Fine. Suit yourself,' said Andrew. 'I won't have anything either, then.'

'I'm not stopping you from eating,' I told him.

'Yes you are. It's not much fun going to a restaurant and having you just sit there and watch me eat.' The tone of his voice didn't sound like somebody who'd ordered a surprise birthday cake. It sounded more like someone who hadn't eaten for four hours and was getting cranky from low blood sugar.

'Oh, for goodness' sake,' I said. 'Why do I have to eat, just so you can pig out? Don't be so childish.'

'Look. You've been a complete misery ever since we got here. Not eating. Not talking. And try and be a little polite to Russell and Robin when they come in. It's their holiday too and it's not fair if you spoil it by having a go at Russell the whole time.'

Oh that's a good one. He didn't want me to spoil my birthday for him.

'Well, do you think it's polite of Russell to try and kill us all every time we get into the car with him?'

'Why do you always have to overreact to everything? You're so melodramatic.'

'No, I'm not. There are heroic ways to die but I'm afraid that being horribly mangled in a car crash isn't one of them.'

'You know, ever since you got your hair done you've been impossible. It's true what the say about redheads – they are bad-tempered!'

'This is dye, you idiot!' Sometimes Andrew was so stupid I wanted to strangle him. Russell and Robin walked in just then and Andrew and I pretended to be reading the menu.

They all ordered pasta and a meat course, and a bottle of house red.

I ate my tomato and lettuce slowly, not really tasting any of it. Perhaps I should have just had the melon. I expect Natalie would have had the melon. You don't get a figure like hers eating solid food.

Andrew is bound to remember by the time we finish eating, I told myself. He has to.

But he didn't. He just said, 'How was your salad?'

And I said, 'Fine.'

Birthdays are silly things anyway. Just a date. Meaningless. I bet there are millions of people who don't even know when their birthday is. Eskimos, for instance. The Punan tribe of Borneo. Orphans.

When we left the restaurant the sun had come out. The plan was to go and look at the Duomo but I couldn't put a brave face on the day any longer.

'Look, I can't face a cathedral today,' I told Andrew. 'I'm going to go find a café and read my Harry Potter in the sunshine.' It was my birthday and I'd rather spend it on my own than with people who'd forgotten all about it.

'You sure?' he asked. 'Do you want me to stay with you?'

'No. You go. Honest. I'll be right over there when you're ready to head back.'

'Well, you don't know what you're missing.'

'I know exactly what I'm missing,' I told him and practically ran over to the café on the other side of the piazza that still had the afternoon sun. If ever I'd needed a cappuccino, I certainly needed one now, so it was lucky that I was in the country where they'd invented the stuff.

It wasn't the fact that Andrew had forgotten my birthday that was upsetting me so much, but the principle of it. He said he loved me all the time, but you can't love somebody and then forget something like this. Can you? If you really loved somebody then you'd have to remember. It would be like forgetting your own name. Oh, God. What if Andrew doesn't really love me after all?

I was about to come over all indignant when I noticed that I had written the word 'Max' in the froth with my spoon.

Of course Andrew loved me. That was the one thing in the whole world I knew I could count on. Even if I didn't deserve to be loved the way I was carrying on. Would Max have remembered my birthday? What was he doing right now? Was he thinking about me? Was he missing me as much as I was missing him? The thought of that cheered me up for a second, but then it evaporated just as quickly. He probably wasn't even thinking about me at all.

The others didn't come back for two hours. I imagined Andrew suddenly remembering what day it was and rushing to the cathedral gift shop – or preferably the Siena branch of Prada – to buy me something wildly extravagant. I waited for him to appear, full of apologies, carrying enormous bunches of white lilies and then everything would be all right. But all he'd bought were some postcards.

'Who are you going to post those to?' I said. 'We fly home tomorrow.'

'They're just for me. Something to remember the day by. Have a look – they're beautiful.'

'No, thanks. I won't have any trouble remembering today. There's nothing wrong with *my* memory.'

It was five o'clock, too late now for him to remember. He had one last chance. If we got back to the villa and all my friends and family jumped out from behind the dusty sofas and shouted 'Surprise!' I would forgive him. But it seemed like a bit of a long shot.

It was a long drive back to Orvieto. Andrew drove but he was driving just as badly as Russell, either to show off to Russell or to annoy me, or both. He was deliberately going too fast and driving way too close to the car in front but I was past caring.

'Why are you so angry with me?' he asked as I stormed into the house without saying a word. 'I just want us to have a nice time together. I don't understand what I've done.'

What have you done? What have you done? I thought. You're not Max – that's what you've done. How dare you not be Max! But I couldn't say that.

'It's not anything you've done,' I said. My voice was shaky but I didn't know if it was anger or tears. Everything was too weird.

'Is it something I haven't done, then?' he said. 'Is there something I was supposed to do?'

I couldn't say anything. I just glared at him, too angry and confused to speak.

Then I saw realisation dawn on him.

'Oh no! Is it today? Oh bunny, bunny!' He walked towards me to hug me but I stepped away.

'Don't bunny me!' I screamed at him. 'I hate you!'

'I'm so, so sorry. Oh, bunny. I don't know what to say! I'm so stupid. I'm so sorry!'

'It's too late to be sorry!'

'What can I do to make it up to you! I didn't forget on purpose. I don't know how I forgot. I can't believe I forgot. Are you sure it's today?'

'Of course I'm sure – it's the same date it's been every year.'

'But it's not the twenty-second? It can't be.'

I couldn't believe what I was hearing. 'No,' I replied coldly. 'It's not the twenty-second. My birthday is August the twentieth. The same day it was last year and the year before that. The same day it's been all my life.'

I pushed past him into the corridor and saw Robin and Russell standing at the foot of the stairs watching me.

'Well, I knew it was an even number,' said Andrew desperately.

'Happy birthday, Lindy,' whispered Robin – the first thing she'd said all day.

'Oh, just shut the fuck up,' I shouted at her, and slammed the door behind me.

eighteen

I couldn't decide which was worse: being married to a man who forgets your birthday, or being married to a man who doesn't even know what day your birthday is.

Andrew was beside himself trying to make it up to me.

'This isn't your real present,' he said when I got home. 'But it was all I could get at the airport.' I looked at the plastic bag. It was the wrong shape for perfume or an expensive watch.

'It's Abba's Greatest Hits,' he said as I opened it.

Now I knew what was worse. Being married to a man who thinks I like Abba.

'What did you get me this for?' I said. 'You know I don't like Abba.'

'Yes you do.' Andrew was insistent. 'You love Abba.'

'Look – don't tell me who I like and who I don't like,' I told him. 'I can't stand Abba. You must be getting me confused with one of your other wives.'

I looked at Andrew's crestfallen little face and despite myself I started to laugh. He thought he'd done so well, poor thing. It was pretty funny really. Andrew was hopeless but his heart was in the right place. And even if he was a dunce, I knew he loved me.

I just hoped that if I ever became a very famous photographer and died, they would find someone who knew me a little better than Andrew to write my obituary.

'She loved pizza and Polish cinema, but most of all, she loved Abba,' is what Andrew would write if it was left up to him. 'And her birthday was definitely an even number – possibly in June.'

I put on my Abba CD and pretended to love it. Andrew and I danced in the kitchen to 'Gimme, Gimme, Gimme' and somehow, everything was sort of OK after that.

'These are brilliant!' said Atlanta as we studied the photos of Angus Rawle's knob. 'you must have made quite an impression on him!'

'I don't know what I did,' I said honestly. 'I didn't say anything. I was just sitting there eating my toast and he suddenly started taking his clothes off. Can you use them?'

'Of course we can use them! They're priceless.'

I hadn't given her any of the Max photos yet – they were still my personal property.

'This is my favourite,' I said, pointing to a black and white of Angus Rawle in all his hairy-arsed naked glory, holding a large gilt picture frame in front of him. 'I thought you could call it "Off The Wall". I took some head-and-shoulders shots as well, too, just in case.'

'Oh, his face.' Atlanta waved her hand dismissively. 'Who gives a toss what his face looks like? We can probably use this one life-size.' She stared through the magnifying glass at one of the close-ups I'd taken and it suddenly occurred to me that one day Atlanta would wake up and discover that she'd turned into Elaine.

'I bet it must hurt, though,' I said, 'having a huge bolt shoved through your willy like that, don't you think?'

Andrew was working at home on Wednesday getting ready for yet another trip to the dizzyingly exciting Isle of Man so when the phone rang, I let him get it because it was probably the office calling him.

'Who's calling?' I heard him say. Then, after a second, in a much higher voice: 'Oh! Hi! Hello! It's so great to talk to you! We watch you on TV all the time! We love the show! Really!

I'm a *huge* fan of yours. How are you enjoying London? Oh, but you're from London, aren't you?'

His voice was getting more excited and hysterical by the minute. I picked up the extension in the bedroom.

'Hi, Natalie. It's me.'

'Oh well, I'll let you girls chat. I'm sure you've got a lot to talk about. Bye!'

'Bye!' said Natalie. 'Hi!'

'Hi – sorry about Andrew,' I apologised. 'He's a little starstruck. He's probably going out to get an "I Heart Natalie" tattoo right now.'

'He sounded sweet.'

'He is. Incredibly sweet. He's so sweet he sets my teeth on edge sometimes. What's happening? Not working today?'

'Oh no, I am. That's why I'm calling. I wondered if you'd do me a favour. Well, it's not a favour actually, it's rather a nice thing.'

'Sure. What is it?'

'We've been invited to a movie premiere tonight but I just can't face it. I've got pages and pages of script to learn still and I have to be up at five again tomorrow morning. Max is moaning at me because he says if I don't go, he won't have anyone to go with. But I'd rather get a good night's sleep. These things are always so ghastly.'

'What's the movie?' I asked. As if I cared. A night out with Max? It was too good to be true.

'Oh, some rubbish. I can't even remember what it's called.'

'I don't mind. It'll be fun just to go,' I said. Fun to go with Max is what I meant.

'Good. Shall I tell them to pick you up? It starts at eight.'

'No, that's silly. Why don't I just meet Max at the hotel? Tell him I'll see him around seven-thirty. Oh, but what shall I wear? Is it a dressy-up thing?'

'Darling, it's a *premiere*. And there's a party afterwards as well if you're up to it. I'm sure Max will be. He's like the sodding Duracell Bunny. How was Italy, by the way? Did you have a lovely birthday?'

'Wonderful,' I lied.

As soon as I hung up, I went into a panic. I was going to go to a premiere with Max! I'd need at least two months to get ready – and I only had three hours! I'd covered so many of these film premieres for the paper but I'd never actually been a guest at one before. I knew that it was a mixture of stars dressed to kill in their borrowed designer frocks and then everybody else – anonymous film business types and complete nobodies who somehow ended up on guest lists. Well, I guess I knew which category I fitted into. It was a bit late in the day to strike up a friendship with Alexander McQueen, so I'd have to make do with one of the two little black dresses in my less-than-vast collection. Boring, boring, boring. Hang on, what was I thinking? I had the absolute perfect dress somewhere. A silver mini dress with a zip-up front that I'd bought in the Whistles sale two years ago. I'd bought it for a New Year's Eve party, but in the end it had been too cold to wear it. All those magazines who say throw out any clothes you haven't worn in two years – thank God I never listened to them.

'Where are you going?' asked Andrew, coming upstairs and seeing me laying out clothes on the bed.

'To the pictures,' I said, looking for my pistachio bra and knicker set. 'Natalie's got tickets to a film premiere tonight, but she doesn't want to go, so she's given her ticket to me.'

'Can I come?'

'No, I'm sorry, sweetie. There's only two tickets. I have to go with Natalie's fiancé.' I couldn't bring myself to say his name out loud. I had to call him Natalie's fiancé to emphasise the fact that he was engaged to Natalie, and therefore of no possible interest to me.

'She only had one spare ticket,' I added. 'You don't mind, do you?'

'No, you go. Have fun. Do you want a cup of tea?'

'Ooh. Lovely. I love you.'

'I love you, too.'

There was just enough time to put on a face pack, drink my tea, shower, wash my hair, shave my legs and underarms, apply Aloe Vera body lotion, search for some tights that didn't look completely naff, abandon the tights idea, slap on some instant fake tan from Boots, phone for a taxi, stick rolled-up tissue between my toes, apply bronze toe-nail polish, wipe bronze toe-nail polish off bathroom floor, clean my teeth again, hunt for dental floss, floss my teeth and resolve to do this *every day* and not just on special occasions, blow-dry my hair to make it curl under, then curl it the other way to make the ends flick up nicely – I was getting the hang of this now – curl my eyelashes, zip myself into my silver dress, try to apply eyeliner, realise that this would need an entire decade of practice to get right, wipe it all off, put on my usual make-up, plus two different colour eye-shadows that I got free from Clinique just for spending £40 on cleanser and moisturiser, and step into my snake-skin high-heeled sandals before it was time to go.

Being married, I was a little out of practice with the routine and it was ages since I'd had any sort of excuse to dress up, but it's like riding a bike. You never forget how.

'Wow, bunny. You look gorgeous,' said Andrew.

'Thanks,' I said casually, as though this was what I really looked like and the grey T-shirt, saggy tracksuit bottoms and yesterday's mascara that I usually wore were all just part of an elaborate disguise.

'How come you never dress up like that when you go out with me?' he asked.

'Because, darling,' I said, giving him a hasty kiss goodbye, 'you never take me to film premieres. I shouldn't be too late home.'

I tipped the driver £2 – too much – when he dropped me at the

Metropolitan, and strode confidently past the two chatting doormen and up to the front desk.

'Can you call up to Suite 910 please? I'm meeting Mr Ogilvy.'

'Certainly, Madam.' The reception chap dialled the room and almost immediately Max picked up the phone.

'Mr Ogilvy. I have a young lady in reception to see you . . . Certainly, sir.' He hung up. 'Mr Ogilvy will be right down. If you would like to take a seat.'

I wandered over and arranged myself neatly on one of the gorgeous cream leather armchairs. I was starting to get butterflies in my stomach. What if Max was disappointed to be going with me? Instead of turning up at this premiere with the fabulous Natalie Brown, he was stuck with me. The friend. It was like all those times in school whenever Natalie and I went out with boys together. They'd go all sulky and virtually ignore me if she so much as went to the loo for five minutes. They weren't interested in me. They were only interested in Natalie. It was the natural order of things.

'Hey, Red!' Max called out to me as soon as he stepped out of the lift. He was wearing his customary huge smile, plus a really sharp black suit with an orange shirt and matching orange tie. He kissed me enthusiastically on both cheeks.

'You look fantastic!' he said approvingly.

'Thanks,' I told him. 'So do you.'

He giggled. 'Really? Why, thank you.' He studied my dress and flipped the metal ring at the top of the zip front.

'Does that zipper go all the way down?' he asked wickedly.

'Pretty much,' I laughed.

'Oh, my, I'm not going to be able to concentrate on the film now.'

I blushed. 'Shall we get a taxi?' I suggested. It wasn't far but my flicky hair wouldn't last five minutes if there was so much as a drop of rain. Or humidity. Or wind. Or weather of any kind.

The doorman looked straight past me to Max, asking 'Taxi,

sir?' and no sooner had Max nodded than a taxi slid up to the kerb.

'Leicester Square please,' I told him. I climbed in and Max hovered, trying to unfold the back seats. 'Ooh, these are fun.' A kid with a new toy to play with.

I was as nervous as a kitten. This was practically a date. Apart from the fact that we were living with two other people, this looked exactly like a date. I could see Max giving my outfit the once-over and I felt suddenly very self-conscious of my knees. He was still studying my zip and, without asking permission, he reached forward and pulled it down three inches. So that my modest round-neck dress suddenly had a plunging V-neck.

'Max! What are you doing?' I said, trying to sound scandalised.

'That's how they used to wear them in the sixties,' he protested. 'Trust me. I was there.'

I flushed and looked down at my cleavage. Maybe he was right, I thought, but I hoiked the zip back up a quarter of an inch to show that I wasn't a total pushover. I was a respectable married woman.

Max wanted to walk of course so we got out at Piccadilly Circus and fought our way through the crush of tourists to get to the cinema. Italian students with Benetton sweaters tied around their shoulders stood around in large aimless flocks as though they'd been hired by Westminster Council specifically to block the footpath and watch somebody play the piano accordion. Vain blonde girls were having their pictures drawn by bored pavement artists while their boyfriends stood by, even more bored. Another man I'd never seen before in a white stetson was perched on an upturned milk crate preaching fire and brimstone. Terrific – evangelists! Just what Leicester Square needed!

'Do you know where you're going when you die?' he was calling out and his voice was amplified so you couldn't ignore him. 'I believe what the Bible tells us and the Bible says there's a place called Heaven and a place called Hell. Do you want to go to Hell when you die?'

Personally, I couldn't imagine how Hell could be any more unpleasant than Leicester Square, but he was suddenly looking right at me and I dropped Max's hand.

'Isn't this fantastic?' said Max, loving every ghastly inch of it.

'Brilliant,' I agreed through gritted teeth, stepping over the swarthy bloke squatting on the pavement who could make your name out of wire.

We could hear the crowds around the Odeon before we saw them.

'Oh, my God, there's thousands of people here,' I gasped. 'What's the movie?'

'*Snatch*,' said Max.

Ahead of us, the flash-guns were going crazy for Kelly Brook in pink sequins.

'Kelly!'

'Kelly!'

She turned and twirled and everyone screamed as she sauntered inside. It took ages to push our way through the crowds.

'Why didn't Natalie want to come?' I shouted at Max.

'She doesn't like British films,' he said. 'She says they make her hyperventilate.'

'Oh, right.' Maybe Brad Pitt would be here!

We managed to make it up to the crash barrier and a policeman in a reflective yellow vest escorted us through. A murmur went up among the crowd as we headed for the red carpet. I didn't have to hear them to know what they were saying:

'Are they anybody?'

'It must be somebody.'

'Nah, it's nobody.'

All the same, I felt really pleased to be arriving with Max. I couldn't help thinking that we must make a pretty cool-looking couple. So what if my dress only cost twenty quid? Max hooked his arm through mine in a protective kind of way. Even with my high-heeled sandals on, he towered above me.

Suddenly I heard a voice shout out: 'Lindy! Over here, Lindy!'

I turned in surprise, caught a blast of flash and then saw a half-familiar face surrounded by floppy dark hair standing at the front of the scrum, grinning at me. Oh my God. Nick.

What was he doing here? I froze for a second, flustered and red-faced at the memory of that night. What an idiot he must have thought I was.

'What's up?' said Max.

'Oh, it's just a friend,' I squeaked. 'From work.'

'Don't you want to go and say hello?' said Max.

I glanced over at Nick who was holding his camera and waiting for me to go over and speak to him. Perhaps I should just say hello. It would look odd otherwise. 'Can you excuse me just a second, Max?'

I walked over to Nick, praying that Max would have the good sense to disappear inside. Instead, I could see him hovering on the red carpet, checking out the new arrivals. He didn't want to miss a thing.

'Hi, Nick,' I said, hardly daring to look at him.

'God, I'm so sorry. I just shouted out without thinking. Have I dropped you in it with your husband?' He sounded really worried. His lovely face was screwed up with concern.

'My what?' I didn't know what he was talking about. 'Oh. I see what you mean.' I realised that Nick must think I was married to Max. How funny. 'Oh,' I laughed. 'He's not—' and then I looked over at Max standing by the door, watching everybody else arrive and I thought how wonderful he looked in his Issey Miyake suit, like a cross between Bruce Willis and Kevin Costner – except taller with glasses – and wondered how anyone could possibly mistake him for dear, dull old Andrew. As if I'd be lucky enough to be married to somebody as amazing as Max, who only dates actresses and models and maybe ballet dancers at a pinch. I mean, if I was married to Max, what would that make me? I was going to say, 'He's not my husband.' Really I was. And then I thought, well, if that's what Nick thinks, who am I to disappoint him? After all, there was no chance of him ever finding out the truth.

So what I said was this: 'Oh he's not going to suspect anything. Half the people I know are photographers.' And I smiled at Nick serenely, the way I'd seen Natalie smile a million times. 'So, how are you, Nick?'

'I'm OK. I nearly didn't recognise you. You look fantastic.' He looked me up and down with a mixture of surprise and admiration.

'Thanks – I think.' Still as serene as hell. Thank you, Max. So this is how it feels to have a trophy husband. 'How come you're covering this tonight?' I asked him. 'I thought you only did political stuff.'

'The diary guy broke his arm at a polo match.'

'Well, it's a very dangerous sport.'

'Not really. He tripped over a crate of champagne in the lunch tent. What about you? Not working tonight?'

'No. I left *The Ledger* a while ago. I've gone freelance.' I wasn't actually listening to our conversation any more because I was now totally absorbed by the tiny little bump on the bridge of Nick's otherwise perfect nose.

'Oh, yeah? Been busy?'

'Not yet, but it's starting to pick up.' He had three little hairs at the corner of his left eyebrow that were growing in a different direction to all the others. Funny I'd never noticed that before. I was seized by the impulse to reach up with my finger and smooth them down straight for him. I clenched my fists behind my back to make sure I didn't accidentally touch him. 'You know how it is,' I said.

Then, out of the corner of my eye, like a nightmare unfolding in slow motion, I saw Max walking over. With a sense of mounting panic, I could see his outstretched hand. I could see Nick moving his camera into his left hand. Reaching out with his right hand. Taking Max's hand. Shaking it. Firm.

'Hi. Max Ogilvy,' said Max briskly, giving Nick the once-over.

'Nick Weber,' said Nick. 'Pleased to meet you.' And I could practically see the cogs in his brain turning over thinking, Max Ogilvy, Max Ogilvy. Where do I know that name from?

'Do you and Lindy work together?' said Max.

'Um, well . . .'

'Oh, look,' I interrupted. 'There's Michael Portillo. You'd better get back to work, Nick.' I grabbed Max's arm and steered him quickly out of the danger zone.

'Maybe see you at the party,' Nick called after me, starting to click away.

'Maybe,' I called back with a mixture of dread and something that felt awfully like excitement.

'What's the big rush?' asked Max as I dragged him back up the red carpet.

'I just want to get a good seat.'

'I'm pretty sure these are numbered tickets.'

'Oh, are they? Never mind.'

'So who was that guy exactly?'

'I told you. A friend. From work.'

'Oh I get it,' said Max with a very knowing smirk. What is it with these guys? Do they have radar or something? 'You bad girl!'

Could he see me blushing? 'Don't be silly,' I said. 'Shall we go in?'

'I have to get popcorn first,' he said. 'I can't watch a movie without popcorn. Why don't you take your ticket and I'll come in and find you. Sweet or salty?'

'Surprise me. And a bottle of water.'

There were massive screams coming from outside and I guessed that Brad Pitt must have arrived. I sat in the dark watching all the celebs shuffle into their seats, wishing Max

183

would hurry up. I felt a little thrill of one-upmanship when I realised that Natalie had scored better seats than Mel from All Saints. I'd have to tell her that – it would make her day. And that looked like Sara Cox down there in a flowery top.

What exactly had I said to Nick? Why wasn't I paying more attention to what I was saying? Think, think. Had I actually said I was married to Max? In so many words? On a scale from one to ten, how stupid had I sounded exactly? I wondered how long it would take him to figure out who Max Ogilvy was. For a second I felt thrilled imagining how impressed he would be that I was married to such a world-famous architect. Then the next second I came crashing back to despair, knowing that the main thing Max was famous for was being engaged to Natalie Brown. But maybe Nick didn't know that. Maybe I could get away with it. Provided Nick hadn't watched television or read a newspaper in the last five years I'd be OK.

Oh, God, I was sunk. First a forgotten husband and now an imaginary husband. Nick would think I was unhinged. Where was Max anyway? Trust him to disappear.

Down in front I spotted Nigel Napier and his two daughters making their way awkwardly to the middle of a row, followed by a woman I assumed must be Mrs Napier. So they were still married, then. The lights were just going down as Max came struggling down the row with his Diet Coke, popcorn and my water.

I tried to forget about Nick and concentrate on the movie, but all I could think about was that I was sitting in the dark with Max. What had I done to deserve this? He offered me the bucket of popcorn, but I held up my hand to say, no thanks. I didn't feel like eating.

'I can't believe they let anyone call a movie *Snatch*,' Max whispered in my ear. He was giggling and his warm breath on my ear was unbearably delicious. The tips of his fingers brushed against my cheek for an instant and I thought I'd fall out of my seat.

If anyone ever asked me what *Snatch* was about I would never be able to tell them. Something about a dog? And a caravan? Brad Pitt was definitely in it anyway. Just concentrate on the movie. Concentrate.

My elbow was leaning on the armrest between us and I could actually feel Max's sleeve – even though it was more than an inch away and not in fact touching me.

Max held out a piece of popcorn to me on the palm of his hand, like he was offering a sugar lump to a horse. Well, maybe just one. I took it from his hand and popped it in my mouth. Salty. Naturally.

His arm moved a fraction closer and came to rest against mine. What should I do? Should I move my arm? Maybe I was just imagining it. Maybe it was just the tub of popcorn. I tried to move my arm away. I thought really hard about moving my arm away but it seemed to be clamped there with a mind of its own. It wouldn't budge. Honest.

Max reached up and held a white bubble of popcorn to my mouth.

In the dark I could see him watching me with curiosity and I thought suddenly of Communion. Oh, Christ! What would Audrey Hepburn do? I tried to take it as demurely as I could without letting my lips touch his fingers.

Max's leg sidled over to mine and came to rest lightly against my knee. The spot where they touched felt like molten gold. I was sure people in the cinema would be able to see it glowing in the dark.

I decided to conduct an experiment. I crossed my ankles so that my leg straightened out and waited to see what happened next. I counted to three and then Max stretched his legs out too, so the whole length of his leg was resting against mine. I didn't dare move or breathe.

Oh no, here comes more popcorn. Max held the fluffy white ball between his fingers and, as I opened my mouth a fraction of an inch, he placed it on my tongue. I was so startled to find his fingers inside my mouth I almost slid off my seat. Max seemed to find this a very satisfactory outcome and beamed at me approvingly.

He fed me popcorn one piece at a time until the tub was almost gone. One piece for him. One piece for me. One piece for him. One piece for me. He was treating me like a little girl and that's how I felt – as helpless as a kitten. Each time I took a piece of popcorn, I could taste the salt on his fingertips and wanted desperately to hold them on my tongue and suck them clean. My heart was thumping wildly and Max just sat there watching the movie, occasionally turning to me, laughing, his face a picture of innocence. Maybe it was just me. Maybe this is what everybody does when they go to the pictures.

When the movie finished, I sat all the way through the end credits, pretending to be fascinated by the names of the grips and Foley artists. When the lights went up, I stretched self-consciously. Now what? I knew I should go home to Andrew, even though he'd probably be asleep.

'So, shall we go to this party, then?' Max asked.

'Sure – if you like,' I agreed, trying to sound like I wasn't fussed, one way or the other. Well, I couldn't expect Max to go to the party on his own, could I? That would be very rude, I thought. I'll go for half an hour – but I won't enjoy it. I'll just drink Diet Coke. And I won't dance. But what would I do if Nick was there? I was too preoccupied to formulate a plan.

The party was at a club on the Embankment so Max decided to walk. He'd slipped his business face back on, the one that wouldn't dream of putting popcorn on a girl's tongue. Had I fallen asleep and somehow dreamed the whole thing?

But when we went to cross the road, he held out his hand. 'Give me your paw,' he ordered.

I stuck out my hand obediently and let him escort me safely across the road, expertly avoiding the solitary motorcycle that had no intention of coming anywhere near us. His fingers felt warm and solid as they cupped the back of my hand and I was acutely aware of the area of skin on the palm of my hand where it touched his. Our thumbs making a little X together.

'You know what I love about London?' said Max, swinging my arm. 'Just being able to walk around like this. Nobody walks anywhere in LA.'

'I'd walk with you in LA,' I told him. I'd walk over hot coals with you, I thought, just as long as you keep holding my hand like that.

'Oh, thanks, Red.' He linked his arm through mine and pulled me closer into him, playfully. I leaned in towards him and rested my head on his chest, just for a moment. I'd follow you anywhere, I thought. But where exactly was this heading?

Suddenly he dragged me across the pavement. 'God, just look at that!' he explained, pointing at a bare wall.

'What is it?'

'Just look at the effervescence on this brick! Oh, I wish I had my camera!'

All I could see was some white patches on a dirty brown wall and I couldn't understand what Max was getting so excited about.

'Look,' I said, 'that must be the place up there.' I could see taxis pulling up at a club further along the road and was able to tear Max away from his interesting bricks. Thankfully there was no sign of Nick outside. I didn't know whether I was disappointed or relieved. As soon as we stepped inside we were accosted by a dazzle of strobe lights, mirrored disco balls and loud music. Max grabbed a couple of glasses of wine and handed one to me as we pushed into the melee.

Well, I guess I'll have to drink it now.

'WHO ARE ALL THESE PEOPLE?' he shouted in my ear. 'ARE THEY ALL FAMOUS?'

'ARE THEY WHAT?'

'FA-MOUS!'

'SOME OF THEM.' I pointed out people in the crowd and shouted in Max's ear who they all were. He'd never heard of any of them but I loved the sensation of Max's lips brushing ever so lightly against my ear whenever he asked a question. I caught a brief glimpse of Tania Vickery in a scarlet gown that looked like it had been stuck together from glitter. So she was here and Nigel was here? That was very interesting. I wonder if he'd stashed the wife and kids after the movie and come to join her at the party. Max and I finished our first drink quickly and started in on the second.

'Do you want to dance?' Max asked.

'Do I what?' I'd heard him perfectly well the first time, I just wanted him to press his head against mine again.

'Do you want to dance?'

'OK!' One dance wouldn't hurt. While we were here. The champagne had gone straight to my head.

As we squeezed our way to the dance-floor, I thought I caught a glimpse of the back of Nick's head through the crowd and I panicked, but then I lost sight of him again. It probably wasn't him anyway. Photographers never get invited to the party, they just get to stand outside and watch.

At school Natalie and I had a theory that boys who were good dancers would be good kissers. Max greeted every new track with the words, 'Oh, I *love* this song!' and then started chucking himself about. I was dying to kiss him and find out whether our dancing theory was right. I was dancing right next to Sporty Spice, who had a new blonde bob, and over there was Lulu and – oh my God – there was Guy Ritchie and there was Brad Pitt himself in a greyish suit. I could have gone right up to him and touched him. I couldn't wait to tell Jill! I'd always wanted a little of Natalie's glamour to rub off on me and tonight was definitely my night. How cool was this? Just check me out, drinking champagne and dancing here with Max.

'Look,' Max yelled in my ear. 'Guy and Brad haven't brought their partners with them either! We must have started a trend!'

Sporty trod on my foot and she said, 'Sorry' and we both laughed. How cool was this! Max and I danced non-stop for about an hour until I could feel my hair starting to get flat and sweaty and I thought I'd better go to the loo and check it out. I deliberately walked right past Brad Pitt on my way to the ladies.

'Loved the film!' I told him, and he smiled very courteously and said, 'Thank you.'

Brad Pitt said thank you to me! Jill was never going to believe this.

When I opened the door of the ladies I nearly gagged on the cloud of hair-spray inside. I had to fight for mirror space with Jerry Hall, Vinnie Jones's wife and Kate Moss looking expensive and flawless. I took one look at my reflection in the cruel fluorescent light with my twenty quid dress and flat hair and felt like a short, fat, squashed bug. Who was I kidding? I was lucky they'd even let me into the party. I didn't belong with these people. Just who did I think I was marching up to Brad Pitt like that?

It suddenly hit me that Max would be horrified if he knew that I had a secret crush on him. So what if he was flirting with me? He probably flirted with everybody. It didn't mean a thing. All he did was share his popcorn with me. He was just being generous. I zipped the neck of my dress back up, wishing I could somehow wipe away this whole evening and start again. Max must think I was completely stupid. The terrible thing was – he was right.

I pushed back through the crowd of dancers and eventually found him standing in the doorway to a smaller side room on the corner of the dance floor, holding two glasses of champagne. 'I thought you'd got lost,' he said. 'I've found us somewhere to sit down and catch our breath.'

There were a couple of empty seats in the corner. I sat down, not wanting to even look at him.

'You're a great dancer,' I told him. 'I couldn't keep up with you. My feet are killing me.'

'Put your feet up here,' he told me, patting the side of his leather chair.

'No, it's OK,' I said hastily.

'Put your feet up here.' He was insistent. Reluctantly, I stretched out my legs and rested my feet beside him. I sipped my wine nervously. He undid the buckle on my sandal and stood it neatly on the floor beside him.

Resting my leg on his knee, he held my calf in one hand and began to stroke my foot. At the touch of his fingers, my mouth went dry and I could feel my heart start to thud against my ribs. We were surrounded by people but Max didn't seem to care and nobody paid us a blind bit of notice anyway. He carried on slowly and deliberately tracing his fingers along my instep, brushing the sole of my foot with the lightest feathery touch.

OK, I thought. So it's not just me. There is something happening here. He's stroking my foot. This is not just my imagination.

I closed my eyes and felt myself dissolve under his touch. My God, I thought, this is just my foot! Then he was taking off my other sandal and tracing the arch of my foot with delicate strokes. It was so delicious I could hardly bear it. When I opened my eyes, he was still watching me.

'The foot is a very erogenous zone,' he said, his voice sounding very husky all of a sudden.

'No kidding,' I croaked in a voice sounding not at all like my own. We were both more than a little drunk. He put his leg up on my chair beside me, and I rested my hand tentatively on his trouser cuff, rolling the fabric slowly between my fingers.

'This material's very soft,' I said idiotically.

'Feel inside,' he said. 'It's even softer.'

I was suddenly unaccountably shy. My hand was frozen, afraid to move. I was about to step on to somebody else's property. Trespassers will be shot.

'Go on,' urged Max. As my hand edged inside the fabric, he closed his eyes and I slid my thumb and forefinger experimentally along the front of his calf. I saw his chest rise, heard his breathing deepen. My mind was already racing ahead to the end of the night. We could get a taxi back to his hotel before Max went back to Natalie. There'd be a kiss goodnight and who knows what else?

Oblivious to the music and everyone around us, I couldn't decide which was more incredible and wonderful – me touching Max or Max touching me. I watched his lips part as I ran the length of my hand slowly up the back of his leg, felt myself go weak with desire as he drew a small circle on the inside of my knee. This is definitely not my imagination.

There was a fuss over at the bar because Brad Pitt had got behind there and started serving drinks. Amid the laughter and cheering I heard a voice I recognised but I couldn't place it. An American voice. A man. Camp. Where did I know that voice from? I wondered. Max's fingers doing something amazing on the front of my heel. He was somebody on TV. What show was it? Lazily, I opened my eyes and saw the face at the same time as the voice recognition software in my brain kicked in. Michael Knightley from *Don't Call Us*. The gay one. Keith. Natalie's co-star. Oh my God. Not six feet away from us and talking to another man. Had he seen us? Or rather, had he seen Max? He didn't know me from a bar of soap. But I bet he knew Max. I slid my hand out from inside Max's trousers and swung my legs down off his chair, making a dive for my shoes.

'Don't turn around,' I hissed at Max, then mouthed silently at him. 'Michael Knightley!'

'What?' said Max and did exactly what I'd told him not to, turning around to look at the bar, just as Michael Knightley glanced in his direction and waved. He was already coming over. I hastily slid my feet back into my shoes.

'Hey, Max! Did you catch the movie?'

Max introduced me to Michael and he shook my hand. I blurted out something about hoping he was enjoying London and studied his face looking for some clue as to whether or not he'd seen us. I don't think he had. But maybe he was a really, really good actor.

'Where's Natalie?' he asked.

'Back at the hotel, learning her lines like a good girl,' said Max. 'We were just thinking about leaving actually. I told her I wouldn't get home too late and wake her up.' Was this Max's way of sneaking the two of us out of here – alone? I hoped it was.

'Well, I'm going right now. Got to make that seven-thirty call. My car's parked right outside. I can give you a ride to the hotel.'

'That would be great. Thanks,' said Max. Had he been lying about leaving just to throw Michael off the scent? I wondered. Either way, his bluff had been called.

'Is that OK with you, Lindy?' asked Max.

'Sure,' I replied, my heart sinking. What could I say? I didn't have any rights in this at all, as far as I could see. Hell, I wasn't even invited. It was somebody else's ticket, somebody else's man, somebody else's car. What right did I have to complain? I followed Max and Michael out of the party which took a long time with people stopping to say hi to Michael.

I felt sick at the thought of how close I had come to being caught out. If Michael had seen me and Max and told Natalie, I don't know what I would have done. How could I have explained away the look of utter rapture on my face?

Over by the bar I suddenly spotted Tania Vickery chatting to another woman.

'Excuse me, Max,' I said. 'I'll be back in a minute.' I barged my way through the crowds until I got to Tania and planted myself in front of her. She probably thought I was after an autograph. 'Excuse me,' I shouted in her ear. 'You don't know me, but there's something I have to tell you. The tabloids have found out about you and Nigel Napier. They're staking out your house waiting to get a photo of the two of you together. They're probably outside in the street right now waiting for you. Be very, very careful if you don't want to get caught.'

She looked absolutely stunned, and I just turned and walked off before she could ask me how I knew.

Maybe it was a stupid thing to do, but it was only fair that I warned her. If I were Tania, I'd certainly want to keep my affair with a married man a secret. I'm sure Nigel's wife wouldn't want to find out about her husband's infidelity from *The Ledger* anyway. If their marriage was in trouble, let them at least have their trouble in private.

Max and Michael were already a little way down the street. Michael was behind the wheel of a charcoal-grey Porsche that he must have rented for his stay in London. Max was standing around, not sure whether I was coming with them or not. I looked at the Porsche's tiny back seat. There were black cabs passing in both directions with their lights on. I couldn't use the no-cab excuse.

'I live in the opposite direction,' I said. 'I might as well get a taxi from here.'

'Oh, OK.'

'Thanks for a terrific evening.'

'Thank you for coming.'

I was all too aware of Michael sitting in his car watching us. 'Well. Goodnight, then,' I said.

'Goodnight.'

I meant to shake his hand, but Max leaned forward and kissed me on the lips and instinctively my hand flew up to touch his cheek. It only lasted a moment, but then, as if to prove that it wasn't a mistake, he kissed me again.

'Goodnight,' I said again and, out of the corner of my eye, I saw Michael Knightley watching me with a newly awakened curiosity. Quickly, I turned away, not looking back as Max got in beside Michael. As I held out my arm to hail a taxi I heard the Porsche roar off down the road, taking Max away from me and safely back home to Natalie.

nineteen

There were a million things I was supposed to be doing but I didn't even bother to get out of bed. I just lay there all morning, remembering the touch of Max's hand on my leg, the way his fingers had stroked my foot, the way he had kissed me on the mouth, not once but twice, the way he had looked deep into my eyes as if he could not only read my mind but was writing the script. I wanted him so badly it was like a physical pain. Every time I thought of his hands on me, his lips on mine, the look in his eye, the sound of his voice, I felt a contraction deep inside as though he had reached in and squeezed. There were little fault lines running all through my body and Max was the earthquake ripping them apart.

If I didn't kiss him properly soon I was going to self-combust. I could hardly wait until Sunday when I would see him again.

Atlanta rang sounding in a complete panic. 'Are you free to do a photo-call for us this afternoon?'

'Sure. What is it?' God knows I needed the work.

'Half four. House of Commons.'

'No! I can't!' I could hear myself almost shrieking. Nick was almost certain to be there. He probably lived at the House of Commons. 'Sorry – Atlanta. I've just remembered. I've got a doctor's appointment.'

'Oh, bollocks.' She hung up without saying goodbye.

By now Nick would definitely have figured out I was lying about Max being my husband. I couldn't afford to turn down work like this, but I'd die of embarrassment if I saw him again.

When I got to the studio on Sunday, Adele the stylist was already there, sullenly hanging out rails of clothes all loaned from designers only too eager to have their clothes worn by Natalie Brown.

I unloaded all my cameras from the car and got a cappuccino from the canteen. I wished I had an assistant to send out and get coffees. I didn't really need one but it might impress Natalie and Adele. I bet Annie Liebowitz has an assistant.

I'd need lots of coffees today because I was incredibly nervous. Two kinds of nervous: nervous about the photo shoot because this was the most important assignment I'd ever done. If I blew this, there'd be no more work from *The Hoop*. You only get one crack at getting it right. But I was even more nervous about seeing Max. I was desperate to see him again. Ever since Wednesday night, I hadn't been able to get him out of my mind. But how was I going to act with the two of them together? Max wouldn't flirt with me in front of Natalie – he wasn't that stupid – but would I be able to stop myself from flirting with him? Would I be able to talk to him in a normal-sounding voice or would my eyes be shining just a little too brightly whenever I looked at him? Would it be blindingly obvious?

I checked my make-up in the mirror for the tenth time that morning. Would Natalie be able to tell that I lusted after Max so badly it hurt? I noticed Adele's Benson and Hedges lying on the counter. 'Can I steal a fag, Adele?'

'Sure. Help yourself.'

I hardly ever smoke but perhaps today would be a good day to start. I wondered if Adele had any Prozac. Today might be a good day to start that as well. It was probably best not to ask Adele, though. She looked like the sort of girl whose make-up bag would be packed with Class-A drugs. Nobody could be that thin without some kind of chemical assistance.

She was wearing black pedal-pushers and her legs didn't even touch the sides.

I took two drags on the cigarette and felt immediately light-headed and sick. Whatever else happened today, at the very least, I mustn't faint. I stubbed it out in the ashtray when Adele wasn't looking and finished my cappuccino to get rid of the taste. I tested all the studio's flash units to make sure they weren't going to give me any nasty surprises. Adele had also got in a gold chaise longue, a big saucer-shaped 70s chair and some bent-wood dining chairs I'd asked for – just like the ones in *Cabaret*. I thought of me and Natalie endlessly singing 'Goodbye Mein Herr' in terrible German accents with Natalie draped all over the kitchen chairs until even we got sick of it. I had the CD with me today.

Natalie arrived almost on the dot of ten with Vince and Isabella close behind her, Vince carrying four plastic suit hangers and Isabella dragging a large aluminium make-up box on wheels.

There was a flurry of kisses and hugging all round. Natalie wasn't wearing a scrap of make-up and yet looked stunning. But I was looking past her, unable to take my eye off the studio door. Where was Max – was he following on behind? Was he still in the car? Was he coming later? Did I dare ask?

I was too nervous to even say his name in case I gave myself away. Natalie knew me so well. Well, she used to. Perhaps Max had stopped at the canteen on the way to get some coffees. Perhaps he'd gone to the toilet. Perhaps he'd spotted an interesting drainage system.

'Can I get you all some coffee?' I asked.

'Black for me, please,' said Natalie. 'No sugar.'

'Same here,' said Isabella.

'I'll have a tea please, if I may,' said Vince. 'Milk and two sugars.'

'Vince can go and get them,' suggested Natalie.

'No, that's OK, I know where it is.' I was already walking towards the door. If Max was still on his way down the corridor it would give me a chance to steal a few seconds with him on his own. It had taken my brain less than a second to formulate this plan and carry it out.

I practically ran out of the studio and down the corridor to the canteen. No Max. I ran to the front door and checked the car park. Vince's car was parked there – empty. I even went and looked in the car, juts to make sure Max wasn't asleep on the back seat. I knew I was acting crazy but I was on auto-pilot. No Max.

I was shaky with disappointment. Maybe he's coming along later, I thought. There's still hope.

I walked back inside and ordered the coffees and two large bottles of still mineral water, putting them on the bill for Studio 7. If *The Hoop* didn't like these photos, the drinks bill alone was going to finish off my savings.

Maybe Max was already in the studio. Maybe I'd just passed him somehow. I pushed open the studio door with my bottom, taking care not to spill the tray of drinks and still praying I would see Max when I turned around. But there was just Natalie rifling through the clothes rail, choosing something to wear.

'I never wear red,' she said banishing a £3,000 dress to the end of the rail without a second glance. 'Or black – it just washes me out.' Another £600 pounds worth of shirt bit the dust. 'But I love this.' She held up a plain cream dress with a drawstring neck that looked to me like a lifeless piece of jersey. Without any kind of self-consciousness, she slipped off her Earl jeans and T-shirt and pulled the dress on over her head. I tried not to stare at her in her underwear, but I couldn't help surreptitiously checking out her thighs, which were still perfect. Not a trace of cellulite. Damn. Well, I guess that's what you get from a lifetime of ballet lessons.

She unhooked her bra and pulled it out through the neck of the dress in one deft movement. 'I'll need a strapless bra, but what do you think?'

It was amazing. What had looked like a bit of rag on the

hanger was suddenly transformed into the kind of dress that would stop traffic. Just add one star. How had Natalie known that? I wondered.

She was twisting the neckline around to read the label. 'Oh God, it's a size eight! That's so depressing. You wanna know the best thing about living in the States? The absolute most fabulous thing? I was a size six! Just like that!' She snapped her fingers. 'I got on at Heathrow, got off in LA and bam! I'd dropped a whole dress size right there in Business Class. Sometimes I'm even a size two!'

'That's amazing.'

She slipped out of the cream dress and into a white waffle cotton robe and started massaging her face with an electric vibrating thing she'd brought with her. She was staring at her reflection in the mirror, lifting her chin this way and that and I turned my back on her so she wouldn't see my face as I asked her my next question.

'So, how's Max?' I said casually.

'He's fine – I think. He had to fly back to LA the day before yesterday.'

Now I really was going to faint. I felt as though the floor had opened up beneath me and all the blood started draining from my head and into my feet. I grabbed hold of a chair and sat down unsteadily.

'He had to go back to sort out some crisis. Some . . . building.' Natalie waved her hand to show that bricks and mortar – or, in Max's case, glass and steel – were plainly beneath her. 'Something about the foundations not being deep enough or high enough or some boring detail like that. I told him there was no way he was going to be able to take a holiday for a whole month. It was crazy for him to think he could just get away like that.'

I put my head between my knees and tried to breathe. Max was gone and I was never going to see him again. I desperately wanted to cry and knowing that I couldn't only made it worse.

'Are you OK, Lindy?' Natalie was watching me in the mirror.

'Yeah. I'm fine.' I sat up and smiled, opening my eyes really wide to hold back the tears. 'I was just trying to visualise how we can do the first shot.' I took another deep breath and forced a smile. Somehow, I was going to have to get through this. 'Anybody want another coffee?' I suggested. Perhaps if I could just get out of here for a couple of minutes, I'd be OK.

'I'll go,' offered Adele but I was already out the door.

I ran down to the canteen, collapsed onto a chair and tried to take some deep breaths. Max was gone forever and I didn't even get to say goodbye! It was unbearable. How could he? After Wednesday night, how could he just leave like that?

The answer to that question was painfully clear. He obviously doesn't care about me one bit, does he? I realised. I was going to have to pull myself together. Put an end to this pathetic infatuation.

For God's sake, Lindy, I told myself. You're meant to be running a photo session here. You've got a stylist, a make-up artist and a big star in there who are all working on a Sunday just for you. If they can keep their minds on the job, you should be able to as well. Particularly since it's your career that's at stake here, not theirs.

I ordered some more coffees and, as I waited for the cappuccino to froth, I tried to get my professional head back on. The one that can concentrate on the job I'm supposed to be doing and not be distracted by the dirty postcards that my body kept sending to my brain.

You will not think about Max. You will not think about Max. You will not think about Max. You want to be a photographer? Well, get back in there and start taking photographs. I gritted my teeth and marched back into the studio. Isabella had started applying Natalie's make-up, but I knew this was going to take her at least an hour, so I went around the studio rearranging all my lights.

I Am A Camera, I told myself. I Am A Camera. It seemed to help.

I dragged the chaise longue into various positions just to give myself something to do. I already knew exactly how I was going to do the shot. Atlanta and I had decided on a blue-green background that would set off Natalie's eyes and positively leap out from the newsstands. That was the theory anyway.

I Am A Camera. I will not think about Max. I *Am* A Camera.

'How was the film the other night?' she asked.

'Great. You should have gone. It was fun.'

'Oh no – I can't stand British films. Why should I turn up to a premiere and get my photo in the paper just to promote somebody else's movie? I mean, what has Guy Ritchie ever done for me?'

'Brad Pitt was there' I said.

'Oh darling, Brad Pitt's everywhere.'

'Keep your head still,' said Isabella.

When Isabella had worked her magic, Natalie arranged herself on the chaise longue and gave me a cartoonishly sexy pout through the camera.

'How's this?' she said.

'Fine,' I said. 'Don't worry about posing for a minute. I just need to shoot off some Polaroids to get the lighting right.' I was trying desperately to concentrate on the job in hand. But my hands were shaking so much, I was having a job holding my light meter steady.

'Can you move that mirror so I can see how I look?' she asked. I wheeled the mirror around and Natalie tilted her head this way and that and started playing with her hair. 'I'm so impressed by all this,' she said, not taking her eyes off her reflection. 'You've really got this photography thing together.'

'Oh, well – you know,' I said, embarrassed by the praise and uncomfortable because it was so untrue. I didn't even have my head together. And as for my career, it was all riding on these photos with Natalie.

'I don't like this shadow under your eyes,' I said. 'Adele, would you mind holding this for me?' I unfolded my large silver reflector and Adele sat just out of shot tilting it up towards Natalie's face. Her cream dress had been a great success so she'd perked up. But I was still getting some weird shadows on the background so I shifted one of the lights and we tried again.

'Do you want me to smile?' asked Natalie.

'I'd rather you didn't,' I said. 'It makes it look as though you want people to like you. I think *The Hoop* don't care whether people like them or not.'

She leaned back on one hand and turned her head to the camera so that she was in three-quarter profile.

'Move your hand a little bit higher . . . no, not that one, the other one . . . OK. Can you lift your chin about half an inch? That's great.' I shot another Polaroid and sat down with Natalie to see what it looked like. Now that I was actually working, I felt a little bit better. I fanned myself with the Polaroid pretending that this was just to make it develop faster. 'What do you think?' I said, showing it to Natalie.

'I see what you mean about not smiling. It makes me look more mysterious. Like I'm thinking about something really important.'

I changed the back on my camera and offered up a silent prayer for luck. 'OK, everybody. I think we're in business.'

'Hang on,' said Natalie. She made a sort of huge quacking move with her lips, made her eyes go really wide like a startled goldfish, blinked four times and then screwed up her face and went, 'BRREEEEEEEE!'

'OK. Now I'm ready. You have to relax your face,' she explained.

I shot five rolls of film of Natalie in the cream dress on the gold chaise longue, some of her looking at the camera over her shoulder, some of her sitting up with her arms behind her, thrusting her chest forward towards me, some curled up on the chaise with her hands thrown up over her head. Every time I looked through camera, I was amazed at how beautiful Natalie was. It didn't matter what angle I shot her at, she was flawless.

Did I really think for one second that Max was going to choose me over her? Was I completely insane? Had any man in my whole life ever chosen me over Natalie? Only Richard – and look how that had turned out.

'You're very good at not smiling,' I told her.

'I bet you can't guess what I'm thinking about,' she said.

And I hope you can't guess what I'm thinking about, I thought, but I just said, 'No. What?'

'Remember that time in biology when we got sent out of the classroom because we wouldn't cut up that rat?'

'I'd forgotten all about that! You told Mr Harrison that we couldn't do it because we were vegetarian – and what did he call you? It was something really terrible.'

'He said I was an empty-headed princess.'

'That's right! He was so horrible to you. So this is your "I hate Mr Harrison face", is it?'

'Yeah. It's sort of self-righteous and highly principled and really, really wanting to kick someone in the balls.'

'It's brilliant. You look dead mean. I wonder what ever happened to Mr Harrison?'

'Perhaps we should go look him up. Shove a rat through his letter box.'

'Do you think he watches *Don't Call Us*?'

'Oh, God, I hope so. I hope he's still driving that crappy Austin Allegro and thinking of me in my lovely white chauffeur-driven BMW.'

'Are you still vegetarian?'

'Kind of. But I eat fish, so not really. And I only eat chicken without the skin. And lamb, very rarely. My acupuncturist told me I needed red meat. But I won't eat Polo mints because they've got gelatine in them. What about you?'

'I was until I started going out with Andrew and then I started eating chicken again because it was so much hassle having to cook two separate meals. It's really hard being married to a carnivore. The closest Andrew ever gets to a vegetable these days is an onion bhaji.'

Six rolls later I felt that we'd probably exhausted all the possibilities of that particular set-up.

'Now what?' said Natalie. 'I've brought a couple of outfits of my own as well. Do you want to see?' She unzipped her suit holders and brought out a pair of tiny bronze leather trousers and a matching lurex T-shirt. They looked too small for a human being to fit into.

'What, are they making clothes for cats now?' I asked.

'Oh, don't be silly!' she scoffed, stepping into them. 'They're actually quite stretchy. They've got Spandex in them or something.'

The effect wasn't so much poured into them as sprayed on and the lurex T-shirt was virtually transparent, so that her black satin bra was clearly visible under the sparkly fabric.

'Wow,' I said. For the first time that day I was grateful Max wasn't there. I don't think I would have been able to bear watching his reaction.

'I was wondering if I'd get the chance to wear this in London,' she admitted.

'No kidding,' I said. 'Can you actually move in those trousers?'

'Yeah, look.' She swung her leg out to the side so high that she was in danger of kicking herself in the head.

'Wow,' I said again. I seemed to be saying 'Wow' a lot. 'You're still as bendy as ever.'

'Oh, no! I'm nowhere near as flexible as I used to be,' she protested, grabbing her foot and pulling it up a bit closer to her ear. 'My hamstrings have really tightened up. Look.'

'You could have fooled me,' I said. I was already dragging out the *Cabaret* chairs.

'I can't believe you've got these!' she squealed. 'You remembered!'

'As if I could forget,' I told her.

She grabbed a chair from me and straddled it from behind with her legs bent at an angle of 180 degrees. She crossed one arm over the back of the chair and propped her chin up against her other fist. 'Is this the kind of thing you wanted?' she asked.

'That's perfect,' I told her. 'I've brought some music to get you in the mood.' I hit play on my boogie box and Liza Minnelli started singing 'Money makes the world go around'.

'Oh my God, fantastic! I wish I'd known, I would have brought a bowler hat.'

'Nah – too corny. It wouldn't go with your outfit anyway. But do you think Isabella should re-do your make-up? Something a bit more . . . obvious . . . muss up your hair a little?'

'What she means is, make me look like a slut, Isabella!' Natalie laughed.

Adele and I dragged the chaise out of the way and I repositioned the lights to create a spotlight effect on the floor. Not so flattering as the other lighting but more dramatic. I got us all another round of coffees and watched Isabella transform Natalie from TV sweetheart into snarling vamp. Without any prompting, Natalie ran through her Sally Bowles routine – draping herself over the seat of the chair, legs akimbo, high kicks, jazz hands, the works. Isabella was working up a sweat just powdering Natalie down between rolls.

I took the camera off the tripod to follow her and loaded a second camera so that I could shoot everything in black and white as well. With every frame, I had that wonderful rush of excitement where even as I was shooting I couldn't wait to get the film back from the lab. For her big finish, Natalie hit the splits on the floor and leaned forward on her elbows, looking up at the camera threateningly.

'This one wasn't in the movie,' she explained. 'I just wanted to make sure I could still do it.'

'How do you do that?' I marvelled. 'It hurts just to watch you.'

'You know Mummy can still put her ankles behind her head?'

'And on that bombshell,' I said, 'I think we should call it a day.'

Maybe it was just as well Max hadn't been here, I decided. Would I have been able to concentrate for even one second if he'd been in the room? No way. And maybe it was for the best that he had left. Now I wouldn't have to worry what to do about Max because there was nothing I could do. He was gone. It was out of my hands.

It didn't take long to pack away all the lights, roll up the backdrop and finish labelling all my film. Isabella wiped off Natalie's make-up and I helped Adele carefully load all the clothes and shoes back into her car.

'Thanks very much for all your help today,' I told her.

'It was really nice working with you,' she said and gave me her card. 'Call me any time.'

That's a good sign, I thought. Instead of me looking for work, somebody was asking to work with me. Maybe that meant things would start picking up.

'Will you come back to the hotel and keep me company?' asked Natalie. 'Mean old Max has left me all on my own.'

'What about the rest of the crew and all the cast? Don't you hang out with them?'

'Them!' Natalie rolled her eyes. 'Don't get me wrong, I love them all dearly. They're my very best friends – but I need a break. All they ever talk about is themselves. And their careers. You can't talk to them about anything real, like politics, or . . . or the environment . . . or art.'

'Gosh, I had no idea. I'll have to think of some good Tony Blair stories for you.'

'Oh, is he that guy that cuts the sheep in half? I think he's *so* interesting.'

'Er, no, he's the Prime Minister.'

'Oh, right, right! You know it's so hard to keep up in the States – it's all America this and America that. Tony Blair. I remember now. And what's he? Conservative?'

'Labour.'

'Of course, of course! You see, this is what's so great about you. You know all this *stuff*!'

Natalie's corner suite on the second-but-one floor of the hotel had massive windows overlooking the park. As she pushed open the big wooden door, I felt a sense of trepidation at stepping inside the room she had shared with Max. There was a vast sitting area with a sofa, a desk and a couple of armchairs. I looked through to the bedroom and the king-size bed. Max had slept there, I thought.

'This is gorgeous,' I said, admiring the view.

'It's OK. But you wouldn't believe how cheap the production are being on this trip. I asked for a StairMaster in my room and they said that I'd have to use the hotel gym. Have you ever heard of such a thing? Dan the director had the right idea. He's rented a huge fuck-off apartment in Holland Park. That's what I should have done.'

I walked around the room pretending to be examining the soft furnishings but really I was looking for some sign of Max's presence: a watch, a comb, a pair of shoes. Any little piece of him for me to latch onto.

Natalie kicked off her shoes and picked up the phone. 'I was going to order an egg-white omelette,' she said. 'Would you like one too?'

'That sounds great.'

'Oh, I almost forget! Happy birthday for last week!' She handed me a huge carrier bag from Prada. 'I meant to bring it to the studio, but I forgot.'

I unwrapped it, feeling excited and guilty. 'On wow, a

bowling bag! You shouldn't have. Really. This is too much.'

The card read 'With love from Natalie and Max' and there were two kisses. I kissed Natalie and tried not to wonder who'd actually written the card. Was one of those kisses really from Max?

'What did Andrew get you?' Natalie asked. 'Something wonderful?'

'Oh – loads of things,' I said. 'I can't even remember them all.'

'Look what Max bought me in Agent Provacateur,' Natalie said, holding up a sheer teddy. 'Isn't he sweet? He said he wanted to think of me sleeping in this while he wasn't here.'

'Why doesn't he just picture you naked?' I said, examining the almost non-existent material. 'It would amount to the same thing.'

'Oh, he's such a romantic. Whenever we're apart, we have the most amazing phone sex.'

'Phone sex?'

'God! Haven't you ever done that? He makes me say and do the most disgusting things. And I have to dress up for him. It's absolutely wild.'

'You don't say.' Please don't say. Please.

'You know, some men would be so jealous of me being this pin-up girl, but Max totally gets off on the idea. Which is so adorable, I think. It's because he has this terrific confidence. That's what I find so sexy about him. Because a lot of men, you know, are very intimidated by me and scared to approach me because of my looks, which is so boring. I mean, I'm just like any other normal girl. I can't help that I was born this way. Or else they always try to impress me with how much money they make, or what a big-shot they are, or how many staff they've got on their yacht. But Max just took one look at me and made up his mind to have me. And no girl can resist that, can she?'

'No, I guess not.'

'When he met me, I was already doing *Don't Call Us*, but it wasn't a hit. It didn't really take off until the second series so when we started going out there was no guarantee there would even *be* a second series. But he didn't care that I was just another struggling actress. He believed in me and he wanted to take care of me and he encouraged me. But I don't think that was because he wanted to have a girlfriend who was this famous actress. I truly think that if I'd wanted to work in a shoe shop he would have encouraged me in that as well. I mean, God forbid that I ever *would* have to work in a shoe shop, but you know what I mean. And then, of course, the first time I kissed him there was this amazing chemistry between us and that was it, really.'

'That's great.' I felt sick. How dare she kiss Max! Why is she always the one who gets what she wants?

'Don't you think he's just the sexiest man alive?' she asked.

'Yeah – he's really . . . nice.' I couldn't look her in the eye.

'My therapist says Max is like my father and my lover all rolled into one.'

'You see a therapist?'

'God, yes. All the time. Everybody does. It doesn't mean I'm crazy or anything.' She crossed her eyes and made circles with her finger at the side of her head. 'It's just so fantastic to have someone who'll just shut up and actually listen to you when you're talking. Everyone in LA is so shallow. Anyway, she helped me make sense of all that stuff with Richard and made me see that it wasn't my fault and then helped me deal with my sudden fame. People who aren't in the business can't imagine how stressful that is. Right now we're working on jealousy.'

'Jealousy? Of Max?' Surely she couldn't suspect!

'God, no – not Max. I trust him absolutely one hundred per cent and he trusts me. No, I just have this teensy weensy little problem with other actresses. Not all actresses. Just British ones. Actually – just British ones working in America. So you see,' she smiled, clasping her hands serenely in her lap, 'it's not really a very big problem. Because there aren't that many of them at all!'

'You mean, like Liz Hurley?'

'Exactly! Exactly!' She bounced up and down on the bed, pointing her finger. 'There I was thinking I'd done so well getting a TV series and that bitch has to go and get a sodding movie! I mean, when I got to LA, there were no British actresses there. None! I was the first! And now they're all over the damn place!'

'Yeah, like Minnie Driver.'

'God, don't get me started on Minnie Driver! Please! I'm much prettier than her, don't you think?'

'Oh absolutely. And far more talented. And you're doing so well. I mean, there's just you and Liz Hurley and Minnie Driver and that's it. Oh, and that girl from *Frasier*. What's her name?'

'Jane Leeves,' muttered Natalie through gritted teeth. 'Have you ever heard a more ridiculous Manchester accent?'

'Right, Jane Leeves. But that's it. Oh, and that one with the frizzy hair in *ER*. She used to be married to Ralph Fiennes.'

'Alex Kingston,' said Natalie darkly.

'Right, Alex Kingston. And that girl who was in *Sixth Sense*. Olivia Williams.'

'Do you see what I mean?' seethed Natalie. 'They're all over the fucking place. But me! I was the first! I was the trailblazer! And what thanks do I get? I was the one who had to go over there all by myself and kick down the door with my bare hands, so all that lot could waltz in after me. It's not fair!'

'But, Natalie, it's OK,' I said, trying to calm her down. 'None of them are as good as you. You're the original. I'd give anything to trade places with you.' I decided now was not the right time to mention Catherine Zeta Jones.

I went back into Wardour Street first thing on Monday morning to drop off all my colour film. On the tube on the way home, the man sitting next to me was reading the

Telegraph, making such a performance of folding and rustling the big broadsheet pages that reading over his shoulder was almost unavoidable. A tiny story caught my eye: PRESENTER AND WIFE TO SPLIT. *Former newsreader Nigel Napier confirmed yesterday that he and his wife had separated. Napier, 53, and his second wife Judith, 48, have been married for 14 years. They have two daughters, Hayley, 13 and Emily, 9. No other parties are believed to be involved.*

When I got home, I checked out the newsagents by the station to see what was in the rest of the papers about it. All the tabloids had the story, with photos of Judith Napier looking weary but determined in a navy-blue cardigan. All of them had regurgitated the details of Nigel's tacky departure from the newsroom. But not one of them mentioned a new romance with Tania Vickery. Not even *The Ledger*. I guess they just hadn't been able to get the proof they needed. Elaine and Debbie would be spitting blood, I thought cheerfully.

The photos of Natalie were gorgeous, of course. Atlanta would be impressed. But I couldn't take all the credit myself – it probably helped to be photographing one of the most photogenic women in the world.

I phoned Natalie on her mobile to tell her the photos were ready and she could have a look any time she wanted. I didn't expect her to have her phone turned on but to my surprise she answered straight away.

'Bring them over,' she said. 'We're shooting in Victoria Park. You can't miss us. We're the ones with the million trucks.'

I found them without any trouble, following the throngs of on-lookers clutching autograph books and instamatics. But Natalie hadn't bothered to tell anyone I was coming so the security people wouldn't let me through. They thought I was just another mad fan.

'No, really, I'm a friend of hers. She asked me to come,' I

promised, which is exactly the kind of thing a stalker would say.

Damn Natalie. I could actually see her off in the distance talking to Sean who played Toby. Quite oblivious to me, of course. Perhaps I should just go home. Then I spotted the woman with the blonde quiff I'd seen the other day at Portobello handing Natalie the publicity stills. Oh, God, what was her name again?

'Hello! Hello!' I waved my hand trying to get her attention. 'I've got photos for Natalie!' I shouted. 'Do you remember me?'

She looked over and made some motion to the security man so that he could let me through. 'You shouldn't really be here,' she said, 'but I can give you five minutes.'

They were shooting a scene for the second episode of the two-parter where Vicki and Toby go rollerblading. I watched Natalie for a while as she whizzed by again and again – not too steadily – with Sean holding on to her waist. When she had a break while they reset the camera, she came rolling over.

'Let me see! Let me see!' she squealed, holding out her hands to take my folder.

'I didn't think they were going to let me in to see you,' I told her. 'Now that you're such a big star.'

'Oh, but I'm not a big star, darling. Not yet. I'm just a medium-sized star.' She sat in the canvas chair with her name embroidered on the back and held the transparencies up to the sky.

'If there are any you don't like, just say and I'll take them out,' I promised.

'Hey, these are really good!' she said, sounding surprised. 'You've done a great job! Oh! Look at me in this one! What am I doing? And I don't like this one – I'm doing something funny with my mouth.'

I handed her a yellow chinagraph pencil to put crosses through any of the ones she didn't like. I saw her co-star

Michael Knightley walking over and tried to keep my head down.

'What are all these?' he asked.

'Photos of me for a magazine,' said Natalie. 'Do you want to have a look? Michael, this is Lindy, my best friend.'

'Hi,' I said and prayed he wouldn't say, 'Oh yeah, you were the girl I saw kissing Max the other night.'

But he just said, 'Hi' and barely glanced in my direction.

I breathed a sigh of relief. That was the good thing about famous people. Unless you were famous too, you simply didn't register with them. You might as well be invisible.

'These are all fabulous,' said Natalie when she eventually handed back the sheets. 'Just take out the ones I've marked and I'm really happy.' She'd put big yellow crosses through two thirds of them. 'And can I have a copy of this one?' she asked. She pointed to the black and white contact sheet and the photo of Max giving her a shoulder rub. The way they were gazing into each other's eyes was like a knife through my heart.

'Sure,' I said.

'Promise?'

'You know me, Natalie.'

'Good. Well, don't forget, because it will be a lovely present for Max.'

There was no way I was going to be able to print up that photo myself. I'd have to get it done at the lab. I left Natalie rollerblading around Victoria Park and traipsed back into town to get some copies made. By the time I got home I was fed up with all this to-ing and fro-ing. I threw the contact sheet with the shoulder-rub photo onto the kitchen table and it lay there taunting me, a tiny Max and Natalie frozen forever in a moment of mutual adoration.

Why wasn't my marriage like that? Why wasn't I still attracted to Andrew the way I used to be? Is that what happens with magnets? I wondered. If you keep two magnets in the same box for long enough, do they lose their magnetism for each other so that instead of attracting one another they start to repel each other? I remembered doing something with magnets at school – stroking them with a pin. If only I'd paid more attention. Maybe Andrew would know.

I made myself a cup of tea in my favourite mug – actually it was Andrew's sun mug that he'd got from the Science Museum. I liked it better than his moon mug or his Einstein mug, but I'd never really looked at it before.

Sun (sun) n. 1. Medium-sized star around which the solar system revolves.

A medium-sized star. That's exactly what Natalie had said. Not a big star. Just a medium-sized star – nothing special.

I had one of those cosmic flashes where the whole universe suddenly reveals itself to you in an instant and you realise what a tiny, insignificant speck you are in the great scheme of things. How many other suns there must be out there, how many other planets. How totally arbitrary civilisation is. How all the stuff we think is so important – like jobs and money and a nice house and glossy magazines and the right trainers – are all just stuff we've made up. They weren't in the original blueprint at all.

I stared at the mug and thought about all the organisation that must have gone into creating life on earth. I imagined the first planning meeting:

'Right, we're going to need a planet and a star.'

'How big a star, boss?'

'Not too big, not too small – one of those medium-sized stars ought to do it. And don't put it too close to the planet or all the people will fry.'

'Good thinking, boss. What say we make it cold at the top and hot in the middle? Then the "people" can decide where they like best. No pressure.'

'And they'll need stuff to eat so make some plants and animals as well. You'd better warn the animals. And water – lots of water. They're each going to need at least eight glasses a day – although most of them won't bother.'

'The designers have come up with some initial sketches for an eardrum if you've got time to look them over. They're more complicated than we were expecting, I'm afraid. But I could probably persuade them to leave out the middle ear if you think it's a bit OTT.'

'Leave them on my desk and I'll get back to you on that one.'

'How many people should we make, boss?'

'Oh, not many. Just a few to start with and then they can reproduce themselves.'

'How are they going to do that exactly?'

'I'm glad you asked. I had Marketing prepare a short film. Lights, please.'

Flicker flicker flicker.

'Well, gee, boss, I don't think you'll be able to persuade them to do that!'

'Ah, well, that's where the advertising boys have been so clever – they're going to make the people fall in love. They'll be falling over each other to do it.'

I expect they all clapped each other on the back after that and swanned off to a nice long boozy lunch, thinking that now they'd sorted out their little planet and their medium-sized star, all the people would just get on with the business of reproducing without a murmur.

As for all the other stuff we've thought of by ourselves, what would the creation boys make of that? Rollerblading, acid jazz, timber decking, *Ready, Steady, Cook* – they must be amazed at all the stuff we've dreamed up without them. I could just imagine them up there in the planning department tearing their hair out.

'No, no, no! What are you doing?' they'll be saying. 'You've got no time to learn to snowboard! You're supposed to be reproducing! Get busy! We need more of you! What if we run out!'

Fall in love, get married, have babies – it was a pretty simple plan, really. How had I managed to make such a mess of it?

But maybe, just maybe, the original plan was that we were only meant to fall in love just long enough to make a baby, teach it to stand up, learn a few basic phrases, then send it off to school. Maybe this love thing was designed to wear off. Like cars. According to Andrew, you're supposed to trade them in every five years so you don't lose your trade-in value. Maybe there's something a little freakish and fetishy about driving around in a vintage model.

But you're supposed to have your car serviced every year, aren't you? And if it breaks down, you take it to a mechanic. You don't just abandon it on the side of the road and steal the first car that happens to go past. Do you? It was all so confusing. If only I could talk to Jill. If only we could thrash this one out the way we used to. God, once upon a time I would have been able to talk to Natalie but that was absolutely out of the question. Then I remembered what Natalie had said about therapy. It didn't mean you were crazy. It was just someone to talk to.

My marriage might have broken down but that didn't mean it couldn't be fixed. Maybe all it needed was a bit of tinkering under the bonnet, an oil change and it would be right as rain. Like having your wheels aligned so they don't go veering off in opposite directions, like Andrew and I seemed to be doing.

I grabbed the phone book and looked under Therapy. The first place I rang turned out to be for colonic irrigation. But the situation wasn't quite as desperate as that. And then I found Relate. They could see me for an initial consultation on Thursday morning if I was interested, the woman said.

Was I interested? Why not? It wasn't like I had anything better to do.

'Will your husband be coming with you?' the woman asked.

'No,' I told her. Not bloody likely.

twenty

The Relate centre was a thirty-minute drive away in an unlovely north-western suburb. It was tucked in behind the Civic Centre, a building that might have been designed to drum up business for a depression clinic. Cheerless and unloved slabs of grey concrete slapped together in the seventies, it begrudgingly fulfilled all of the basic criteria for a building – walls, roof, floor, doors and windows – without in any way enticing you to step inside. Max would have had it condemned, I thought.

Two council workers in faded overalls were glumly scooping out slime from the empty fish ponds. Oh, the romance of it all. You'd have to be completely desperate to give this place a shot – and I was. Did I really expect to find an answer here? Or was I just going through the motions? Half of me wanted to turn back the clock to the days when I was in love with Andrew and no other man existed for me. The other half of me was afraid there was no going back. Maybe the situation was hopeless, but I had to at least try, didn't I? What kind of person doesn't even try?

The office was conveniently situated right next to the open door for the toilets. A notice, stuck on a glass window so that it covered the entire opening, said: 'Ring bell for attention'. I pushed the buzzer and immediately one of the windows slid back. The receptionist must have been hiding there all along.

'I've got an appointment for eleven-thirty with Annette Brennan,' I said.

'Go around,' said the woman, 'and I'll open the other door for you.'

There was a push-button combination lock on the door which she had to open from the inside. I wondered what all the security was for. Were people sneaking in perhaps and stealing marriage guidance when no one was looking?

I'd barely had time to flick through the copy of *OK!* magazine in the waiting room, when a woman in her mid-forties with greying hair and a kind, patient face, rather like a slightly harassed school teacher called out: 'Ms Usher? Come through, please.'

So this was the woman who was my last chance at saving my marriage. She wasn't what I was expecting. Secretly I'd been hoping for the Good Witch Galinda from *The Wizard of Oz* who would sprinkle me with fairy love dust and send me skipping merrily on my way.

'Everything we discuss in here will be completely confidential,' she said as she started filling in her forms. 'Are you married? How long? What do you do for a living? How old are you? How old is your husband? Is English your first language? Do you have any physical disabilities? Are you on income support?'

Yes, three years, photographer, twenty-eight, thirty, yes, no, no. File me under white and middle class with no real problems except the ones I've created for myself.

'How can we help you?' she said finally.

Where should I start? There was a blue-and-white-checked cushion propped up on the wall beside her chair and I studied the pattern as I tried to think of a way to explain what was going on inside my head. Perhaps I should just come right out with it and tell her I'd been possessed.

'Well, basically, I'm not sure if I love my husband any more,' I began.

I was afraid she might say, 'Well, you're just a dreadful person, aren't you! Get out of my office now!' But she just said, 'I see.'

'I really want to make it work between us. I really do. At least I think I do. Because I couldn't bear to hurt him. But it's like I've lost control over all my feelings. I'm doing things and feeling things that I know are wrong and I hate myself for it. But I can't stop. I need help.'

'I see. And what makes you think you don't love him any more?'

'Just lately I've started to get ratty with him over stupid things. But what's really bothering me, the thing that's made me come here today, is that I'm suddenly finding myself seriously attracted to other men. It's happened twice in the last couple of months and I don't know what I'm supposed to do about it.'

'Does your husband know you've come here today?'

'Oh, God, no! I wouldn't be able to talk about this in front of Andrew. He doesn't know about any of it. And I don't know if any of it has anything to do with Andrew or whether it's just me. What I mean is, Andrew hasn't done anything wrong at all. I can't sit here and say, I'm attracted to other men because my husband is so awful, because that's not true. I couldn't wish for a nicer husband and I don't know why I don't feel like I love him – because I really want to. It would make life a hell of a lot easier.'

'You say you couldn't wish for a nicer husband. Why is he so nice?'

'Well, he's very kind and caring, and he works really hard and everyone likes him. Everyone always says how lucky I am to have him and they're right. And he's never done anything to hurt me. He puts up with me and I trust him completely. I mean, he does stupid things like forget my birthday, but I know he really loves me.'

'But if he's so perfect, if he has everything, what does he want from you?'

That stumped me. 'I don't know,' I admitted. 'Company, I guess. What does anybody want from anybody?'

'Do you share a lot of things together?'

'Yeah, loads of things,' I said, trying to think of even one.

'What sort of things do you enjoy doing together?' she asked. 'Going for walks? Eating out?'

'Well, I like going for walks and he likes eating out,' I said. 'Andrew only likes Indian food and Chinese food and pizzas, you see. So we don't even eat the same things at home. But we watch TV together sometimes.' Talk about clutching at straws.

'And what about your sex life?'

'Er – that's a bit of a non-starter at the moment actually.'

'And how does Andrew feel about that?'

'I don't know.'

'Don't you ever talk about it?'

'Not really – only in a jokey way about how lazy we are.'

'Does he tell you he feels frustrated?'

'No. I mean sometimes he says he wishes we did it more, but it doesn't seem to be a big issue with him. I think he just accepts it. We both work really long hours. Well, I suppose I don't any more, but I used to. And Andrew still does. So we've kind of got used to the fact that we always seem to be too tired or too busy.'

'So you don't really know how he feels about this?'

'No – I guess I don't.' I felt pathetic admitting to this stranger that I didn't have the slightest idea what was going on in Andrew's head. She was wearing sensible brown sandals that somehow didn't show her toes and cotton trousers with an Indian print. I wondered what her sex life was like. I couldn't imagine her having sex with anybody ever.

'Are you able to talk to him about how you feel?' she asked.

'Not really,' I admitted. 'I get frustrated when I try to explain things like that to him because he never quite gets the point I'm trying to make. He gets it confused, somehow. He's supposed to have this super-analytical mind and he's got this fancy big-shot degree from Cambridge, but sometimes I think he's just an idiot.'

'And is he able to talk to you about how he feels?'

'Well, he's a very easy-going sort of person. He never seems to feel much about anything. I mean, if he's got a problem with people at work he'll tell me about that, but nothing else seems to bother him very much.'

'You say you get ratty with him. What sort of things do you argue about?'

'Oh, stupid things. Like what colour the vacuum cleaner is. Last week I threw a tea towel at him for ringing Directory Enquiries to get the number of a Thai restaurant instead of just looking it up in the phone book.' It sounded ridiculous even to me. Why on earth did Andrew put up with me?

'What happens then? Does he get angry with you?'

'Not really. He just gets annoyed with me. He'll just say "Why are you being so horrible to me?" because he knows he hasn't done anything to deserve it.'

'And can you tell him why you're acting that way?'

'No, because it's always over something so stupid that I can't even explain it myself. What usually happens is that we end up not talking to each other for a bit.'

'So you withdraw from each other?'

'Yeah, and then the next morning, I'll have cooled down again and we just pick up where we left off, until the next time.'

'So all the emotion seems to be coming from you? I'm trying to build up a picture here.'

'I suppose so.'

'It can be difficult if there's a lack of emotion there,' she said. 'If everything's soft, like cotton wool, there's nothing to grab hold of. There's no passion.'

'I think that's what the problem is. No passion. We're sort of bumping along happily enough but we're more like friends than lovers.'

'Well, sex is about the mental and the physical. If you're not able to share your emotions openly, the rest can be difficult.'

'Maybe. But at first, before I hardly knew him, the sex was fantastic. It was only later when we started getting closer that it went off the boil. In fact, the better I got to know him, the less often we had sex. Now I know him so well, it's got to the point where it would be like having sex with my brother. I just don't fancy him like that any more.'

'Does he know that?'

'No! How could I tell him that? That's a terrible thing to tell somebody. It would be like telling him he smelled funny.'

'But don't you think he must know that's how you feel if you don't want to have sex with him?'

'Maybe. But thinking about something and being told it out loud are two different things.'

'Do you think he still wants to have sex with you?'

'Yes, of course he does. I mean, I suppose so. But maybe he feels the same way as I do. I don't know.'

'So sex seems to be the main problem in your relationship?'

'Well, kind of. But not really. It's only a problem because it's the one thing that could split us up. Not the not-having-sex part – but if I had sex with someone else. I feel like I'm on the brink of having an affair and I know if that happens it would tear everything apart. Except it can't now because the other man has gone away.'

I hoped she'd ask me who that other man was. I was bored talking about Andrew and was dying to tell her all about how amazing Max was and how much I missed him but, infuriatingly, she kept on and on about me and Andrew.

'Perhaps you and Andrew both need to look at your relationship and decide what it is you each get out of it and whether that's good enough for you,' she said.

'What do you mean – good enough? How do you know if it's good enough?'

'It's not always possible for your partner to fulfil all of your needs and it's necessary to look outside the relationship to have those needs met. Socially perhaps, or some sort of intellectual stimulation or interest. For example, perhaps one partner doesn't dance and the other loves dancing – that's something they can safely look for outside of the marriage.'

'But I can't say to Andrew that I want us to stay together and everything in our marriage is great except the sex, so I'm going to be going somewhere else for that. It's not like saying they've run out of spring onions in Sainsbury's so I'm going to Tesco. How can I possibly say that to him?'

'No, I'm not suggesting you do that. I agree that would be dangerous. But it would be helpful if you were able to talk about this issue together.'

'But how can I even talk about it? If I tell Andrew I even fancy someone else, that could kill our marriage on the spot. I don't want to risk that. I'm scared to tell him what I'm feeling and what the problems are because I don't have any ideas yet about what we can do to solve them.'

'How do you think we can help you?' she asked.

'I don't know.' Fairy love dust was probably out of the question.

'What do you want to happen?'

I stared at the squares on the blue-and-white pillow again. Behind my head, the clock ticked loudly. 'Well, in an ideal world, I'd like someone to give me a pill that would make me fall in love with Andrew again. Or maybe an injection that would stop me fancying this other man. Or there's Option Three – only I'm not sure what Option Three is. Do you think it's possible to fall in love with your husband again? You see people all the time – have you ever heard of that happening?'

'Yes, it can happen,' she said cautiously. 'I'm not saying it will in your case, but it can happen, certainly.'

'So what happens now?'

'Well, even if you decide you don't want to continue with counselling, I think it would be helpful for you to think about the other relationships you've been in and try and understand how you can reach that balance between closeness and intimacy. If you do decide you want to continue with counselling, do you think you would like to see a counsellor with Andrew?'

'I don't know if he'd want to come. He's very resistant to anything like this. I can't even get him to take vitamins.'

'But he might be quite relieved to be asked. The two of you seem very lonely in your relationship, with this area that you're not talking about. He may not always show what he's feeling. He may have his own way of dealing with it, but he still has all those feelings locked inside.'

Time up.

I told her I would think about everything we'd discussed and went away feeling like a Grade One bitch. Poor Andrew with all those feelings locked away inside that I never let him talk about. I didn't deserve him. I was crap at relationships. I really would make it up to him. I'd call him as soon as I got home and cook him – us – a special dinner tonight. Get a bottle of wine. Just the two of us. We'd spend the evening just talking. And listening. Sharing. Doing all that intimacy stuff. I'd ask him what he wanted from me.

The answering machine was flashing when I got home. It was probably Andrew ringing to see how I was. He was so thoughtful like that.

At first I didn't recognise the American voice on the machine.

'Hey, Red! Natalie asked me to call to see if you and Andrew are free for dinner tomorrow night. I'm at the hotel – call me when you get this message. Bye bye!'

It was Max. He was back! I played the message again just to hear the sound of his voice and all my good resolutions flew straight out the window.

twenty-one

My heart was racing as I dialled the hotel number.

'Suite 910, please. Max Ogilvy.' I felt a thrill just saying his name out loud.

'Hello?'

'Max. Hi. It's Lindy.'

'Hey, how are you?' I loved the sound of his voice. The way I could tell he was smiling. The way he could make 'How are you?' sound indecent.

'I'm great. I thought you'd gone to LA.'

'I did but I came back. We're going to Spain to visit Natalie's mother. Why? Did you miss me?' He had this way of putting me on the spot, making me say things I didn't want to say.

'I didn't even notice you were gone,' I teased him.

'Now you've hurt my feelings.'

'Oh, well, you're a big boy. I expect you'll get over it.' I was curled up on the sofa with my eyes shut, imagining his face.

'So, are you coming out to play with us tomorrow?'

'You bet.'

'Does this mean I get to meet your husband finally?'

'Only if you promise to behave yourself.'

'Oh, you're no fun.'

'I'm serious.'

'Have you told him about me?'

'I've told him Natalie's engaged to this mad architect, if that's what you mean.'

'Did you tell him how good looking I am?' He was like a little boy fishing for compliments.

'No, I completely forgot. I must have left that bit out.'

'Did you tell him that you're crazy about me?' He was doing it again! There was no way I could answer that question.

'Who said I'm crazy about you?' I demanded.

'Well, aren't you?' His voice was dripping with wicked self-confidence. He barely knew me and yet he assumed – correctly, as it turned out – that there was nothing I could hide from him.

'Stop it!' I said. 'You're making me blush.'

'Oooh, I'd like to see that.'

'You'll have to wait till tomorrow, won't you? Where are we going anyway?'

'I've booked a table at downstairs at Nobu for eight o'clock. Natalie said I should invite Jill and her husband as well – do you have their number?'

'Sure. Or I can call them if you like.'

'OK. That would be good because you know them and I don't.'

'So, what are you up to?' Maybe there was a chance I could see him this afternoon.

'I'm up to my eyes in computer graphics. The animation company who are doing the presentation for me are over from Switzerland.'

'Oh, right.' I had no idea what he was talking about. I hoped I didn't sound too disappointed, even though I knew there wasn't much point trying to play it cool with Max. He already had my number on that score. 'I guess we'll see you tomorrow night then.'

'I'm looking forward to it,' he said.

'Me too. Bye, then.'

'Ta ta!'

I rang Jill and told her we'd been invited out to dinner, leaving out my conversation with Max even though I was dying to tell her every single detail.

'You'll be able to get a baby-sitter, won't you?'

'Yeah, no problem. Mum'll do it – but even if she can't, Simon would pay £100 an hour just so he could have dinner with the wonderful Natalie Brown. I can't wait to see her.'

Everyone was just dying to see Natalie which suited me fine. It would mean I had Max all to myself.

'Do I have to wear a suit?' said Andrew. I'd chosen what he was going to wear right down to the socks. It was the Paul Smith suit he'd bought for our wedding; the only thing he owned with a designer label, not counting his Adidas T-shirt. I'd picked it out myself to avoid the humiliation of him turning up at the register office with his pink-and-white-striped shirt and grey M&S suit.

The Relate woman had been right. I had absolutely no idea what was going on in Andrew's head. The thought processes alone involved in the way he selected clothes were an absolute mystery to me. Left to his own devices he might turn up at Nobu wearing a white belt and his sweatshirt tucked into his jeans.

'You want to make a good impression on Natalie, don't you?' I told him. But what I really meant was that I didn't want him showing me up. I didn't want Max to think I was married to a nerd. He might go off me.

'You look so handsome in this suit,' I told him. 'I'll have to keep an eye on you to make sure Natalie doesn't make a play for you herself.' That did the trick.

Marriage guidance would have to wait, I decided. Right now I was too busy using Andrew as a pawn in my master plan to distract Natalie so I could flirt with Max.

Obviously, I didn't own a single item of clothing that would do for Nobu, so I went to Joseph in Brompton Cross and spent £120 on a black jersey dress like the one Natalie had worn for the photo session. On me, it might not stop traffic exactly but it might make it drop down a couple of gears. I also booked a three-hour appointment at Clarins for a full leg wax, pedicure, body scrub and mud treatment that would, I was assured, leave my skin silky soft.

'Do you want me to do your bikini line as well?' the beautician asked. She had her little waxy cloth poised and ready to rip.

'Sure. Might as well,' I told her, gritting my teeth. As long as Max was in town there was still hope that I might get my money's worth out of a bikini wax.

I saw Jill and Simon in the bar as soon as we arrived. There was Natalie, sitting with them in a corner booth. But where was Max? Oh no. Don't do this to me, again. Please be here. I can't bear it.

'Hi! We made it,' I said. 'Andrew – Natalie. Natalie – Andrew.'

Natalie half stood up and kissed Andrew and I knew I'd get no more sense out of him for the rest of the night.

'It's really lovely to meet you at last,' she said. She looked absolutely stunning in an asymmetrical sparkly bronze dress that slid elegantly across her shoulders, and matching diamanté sandals.

'I'm such a huge fan of yours,' Andrew gushed. 'We always watch the show.'

'That's really sweet of you. Thank you. Would you like a drink? Max is just over at the bar.'

I turned my head almost in slow motion and felt my heart swell as I caught sight of him. He was standing at the bar, looking straight at me and smiling. I felt so happy just to see him again I thought I would burst.

'I'll go and help him, shall I?' I suggested. 'Leave you to get acquainted.' I knew Andrew would be so excited to be in the company of Natalie Brown that he wouldn't even notice I was gone.

'Have a champagne cocktail,' said Jill, waving her glass. 'They're lovely.'

I was going to have to be on my best behaviour tonight because Natalie was here. But I couldn't keep the smirk off my face as Max watched me every step of the way.

'You look good enough to eat,' said Max, looking me up and down.

'Thanks. So do you.' I told him. I kept a modest two feet between us because I dared not stand too close to him. He was wearing another perfect dark, dark, grey suit over an open-necked white shirt.

'Can I get you a drink?'

'I'll have a champagne cocktail please – and Andrew will have one of those Japanese beers.'

'So that's Andrew, is it?' he said, staring over at him very obviously. 'He's not a bit like I expected. I thought he'd have a beard.'

'A beard? Don't be silly,' I laughed. 'Do I look like the sort of person who'd marry a man with a beard?'

He passed me my glass.

'So how much longer will you be in town?' I asked him.

'We leave on Sunday. We're spending a few days visiting Natalie's mom in Spain, then going straight back to the States. It's a pity, because I'd hoped to see some more of Europe.'

'Stay in London with us,' I suggested, boldly.

'You mean, like a threesome? I don't think Andrew would be too pleased about that.'

'I wouldn't tell him,' I said quickly. I was surprised to realise I wasn't joking.

'Now you've made me blush,' he said.

'That's OK – it just looks like you've got a healthy tan.'

'It got a little dangerous the other night, didn't it?' he said. 'At the party.'

'Oh, was that dangerous?' I smiled. 'I thought it was pretty safe.' I was slightly surprised he'd brought it up. I thought it was the sort of thing he might not mention. I was enormously turned on by the fact that he did.

'But you know, we have to be very careful tonight because of Andrew and Natalie.'

'I know. I promise not to lay a finger on you.'

'But you'll be thinking about it, won't you?' He looked right into my eyes and I felt my legs turn to jelly.

'You know,' I confessed, 'I don't think I'm going to be able to stand here much longer and talk to you and pretend everything is normal. If we carry on like this, I'm going to end up in a little pool on the floor.' I couldn't take my eyes off him.

'Let's take these drinks and go back to the table and join our partners, shall we?'

I helped him carry the drinks over and everyone scooched around to make room for us to sit down.

'I don't believe you've met my husband, have you?' I said to Max mischievously. 'This is Andrew.'

'Pleased to meet you,' said Andrew.

'Me too,' said Max. 'I've heard so much about you.'

What a perfectly civilised lot we all were.

We went through to the restaurant; the waiter held out a chair for Natalie and Max immediately motioned for Andrew and Simon to take the seats on either side of her.

'Come on,' he chivvied them. 'Boy, girl, boy, girl.'

So I sat next to Simon, Jill sat next to Andrew and Max slipped in between Jill and me in the last available seat. It was like watching a very well-rehearsed card trick. Natalie and Jill were talking across the table about shoes. Andrew was asking Max if he knew the architect who had designed the restaurant. Simon was craning his neck, star-spotting madly.

'Look,' he whispered. 'Isn't that Boris Becker?'

The menu was full of Asian dishes I'd never heard of.

'What do you think Toro Toban Yaki is?' said Andrew, too loudly. But Max said he'd order for all of us.

'You all have to try the black cod,' he said. 'It's the best dish in London.' Under the table, he shifted his leg an inch so that the side of his knee rested lightly against my thigh. The spot where they touched glowed red hot. I hoped the service in this place was very, very slow.

Natalie was on top form with stories of LA and her real-life experiences of flat-sharing with wannabe actors and directors. Andrew and Simon were hanging on her every word.

'When I first moved to Hollywood I shared an apartment with another girl whose boyfriend turned out to be a coke dealer,' she was saying. 'I didn't know that when I moved in, or I would never have taken the place. I'm such a wimp about drugs. Anyway, this guy, Nathan, was actually quite sweet. Very well educated and he had a terrific job as an editor for a company that made pop videos. He said the drugs were just a sideline to make some big money really quickly to finance his movie. Like everyone else in LA. But anyway, the coke made him so paranoid he actually used to sleep with a baseball bat next to his pillow. And the guy he used to buy his stuff from was even worse. He'd say to Nathan, "Don't come to the house. Just drive down the road and when you pass me on the kerb, don't stop, just slow down. I'll get in the car while it's still moving so we don't attract attention."

'Their brains were so fried they actually thought that getting into a moving car was less suspicious than stopping to pick someone up. They couldn't see how dumb they were.

'Eventually, this guy, Nathan's dealer, really started getting on my nerves. He'd ring up and talk in this stupid code because he was convinced the lines were tapped. I answered the phone one time and he goes, "Has Nathan got the train set I sent him?" and I pretended I didn't know what he was talking about, just to wind him up.

'So I go, "Has Nathan got the what?" and he's like, "You know – the train set." And I go, "Oh, you mean the cocaine?" and he hung up the phone so fast! I was glad to get out of that place, I can tell you.'

'Uhh, cocaine is so *eighties*,' said Jill, not at all impressed by Natalie's little walk on the wild side.

But Andrew and Simon were hanging on her every word.

'That's very interesting because I can't do drugs either,' said Andrew, seizing his chance to leap into the conversation. 'Somebody gave me a muffin with hash in it when I was at Cambridge and it made me hallucinate. I thought I was going to jump out of the window. It was very scary.'

Oh, God, Andrew, shut up, I thought. He was trying to sound cool and impress Natalie with his hard-man druggie past but he wasn't fooling anybody. And did you notice the blatant plug that he slipped in there? Just once I'd like him to meet someone new without feeling compelled to tell them that he'd been to Cambridge within ten minutes of meeting them.

'So what did you do at Cambridge?' asked Max. He'd been making a point of talking to Andrew all evening. Anyone else would have thought he was merely being friendly, but I knew he was doing it deliberately to torment me.

'Engineering,' said Andrew with transparently false modesty.

'Oh, so you're an engineer? We're crying out for good engineers in the States at the moment.' Max knew damn well Andrew wasn't an engineer. He was just stirring.

'No – I'm an accountant.'

'What kind of thing do you do? A lot of number crunching is it?'

'Well, there's a bit of that,' smiled Andrew. 'My area is mostly liquidations and corporate takeovers. But there's a lot of people skills involved in that as well. It's not all just numbers.' Andrew had this touching notion that accountants were gregarious extroverts who spent all their time socially interacting with one another and only glanced at spreadsheets accidentally once in a blue moon. I don't know where he got this idea from but it seemed to make him happy.

'Does Lindy ever help you with your work? Natalie tells me she's got a mind like a steel trap.' He rubbed his knee up and down against my leg so that I was temporarily lost for words and could only smile stupidly.

'No, Lindy thinks what I do is really boring. She thinks accountants are all just dull men in grey suits.' Andrew smiled in a self-satisfied way as if to say, 'How wrong can you be?'

'Lindy! How can you say that!' Max pretended to be shocked. 'Some of my best friends are accountants.'

I don't know exactly what Max had ordered but waiters kept appearing with endless dishes of exotic slices of fish sprinkled with coriander. After six or seven courses, I excused myself to go to the ladies.

'I'll come with you,' said Jill, getting unsteadily to her feet. We'd both had too much to drink but it only hit me when I tried to stand up.

In the loo, we clattered into adjoining cubicles and I started laughing loudly at nothing in particular, in the way that you do when you've polished off three quarters of a bottle of sake.

I was nervous about leaving Max and Andrew on their own. Knowing Max, there was nothing to stop him persuading Andrew to put his knob on the table so he could measure it. My head was swimming a bit – was this whole evening completely absurd or was it just me?

'Natalie and Max make such a great couple, don't they?' I said to Jill as I flushed the loo.

'I suppose so,' she said. 'If you like beautiful, mega-rich, successful people.'

She stood beside me at the round frosted glass basins to wash her hands. 'Which one of these things is the tap do you think?' She tried pulling a few levers but all they did was pull the plug up and down. 'Natalie's just the same as she always was. Still as pleased with herself as ever.'

'What do you mean?'

'Well, all she's talked about all night is herself and how fantastic she is.'

'Really? I never noticed that.' I hadn't been paying much attention to Natalie at all.

'You're probably just used to her because you've known her all your life,' said Jill. 'She hasn't asked me one thing about what I've been doing. Or about the kids. I think she just invited me and Simon so that Max would think she has lots of friends.'

'He's such a funny guy, isn't he?' I persisted. I couldn't stop talking about him. 'He really makes me laugh.'

'Who does?'

'Max.'

'Oh yeah, right. Well, he seems very taken with you too.'

'What?' I squeaked. 'What do you mean?'

'The way he's been flirting with you all evening.'

'Really? I didn't notice. Do you think Andrew noticed?'

Jill snorted. 'I think Andrew's completely forgotten you're here. He hasn't taken his eyes off Natalie all night. Neither has Simon if it comes to that. It's quite, quite sad.'

Then she saw the stricken look on my face. 'Oh, babe, you know I'm only joking. Andrew hasn't really forgotten you.'

'Oh, Jill, it's no good I can't keep it up. It's killing me.'

'What is?'

'I'm obsessed with him. I'm crazy about him.'

'Isn't that sweet!' Natalie swung through the doors and paused to examine her reflection in the full-length mirror. 'Married all this time and you and Andrew are still like a couple of love-sick teenagers. I'm crazy about him, too. He's such a sweetie.'

Jill and I watched each other in the mirror, not saying anything as Natalie swung open the door of first one cubicle and then another to find a toilet she approved of. She tore off a long sheet of toilet paper – throwing away the first couple of squares that might have been touched by someone else's fingers – and then lay the rest of the white ribbon in a neat crescent shape on the toilet seat.

'What are you doing?' said Jill.

'Oh, darling, I haven't sat on a toilet seat since nineteen ninety-two.' Natalie shut the door smugly.

'*Max?*' mouthed Jill at me urgently and I nodded furiously.

'*Does Andrew know?*' She was shouting at me without making a sound.

I shook my head vigorously.

'*Does she know?*' Jill jerked her head towards Natalie's cubicle and I shook my head harder still.

'*Just you,*' I mouthed back.

'What are you two whispering about?' asked Natalie.

'We're not whispering,' said Jill calmly. 'We're just fixing our lipstick.'

We heard the toilet flush and Natalie came back out, pressing the tap button with her elbow to avoid germs.

'So that's where the water comes out,' said Jill.

'Just look at the three of us,' Natalie smiled, gazing at our reflections. 'Isn't this just like old times?'

'It sure is,' said Jill.

'You coming back out?' Natalie asked.

'We're just going to have a quick fag,' said Jill. 'Simon doesn't like me smoking.'

'Oooh! It'll give you wrinkles,' warned Natalie.

'That's OK. I'm giving up tomorrow,' lied Jill.

As soon as Natalie was out the door, Jill turned on me. 'Now, have I got this straight? You're talking about Max?'

I nodded. 'I think I'm in love with him.'

'Are you mad?' she demanded.

'Yes. Probably,' I admitted. 'I think I am.'

'How long has this been going on?'

'Since he got here practically.'

'And how does he feel about you? Does he know?'

'I'm not sure. I don't know what he feels. It's all very odd.'

'Odd in what way? Has anything happened? Have you done anything?'

'No. Not really. Nothing. Not much. I've been wanting to tell you for ages.' I took her cigarette from her and inhaled deeply. 'Oh, God – do you think I'm terrible?'

'No. Of course not. I'm just so surprised. You're the last person in the world I'd expect to be telling me this.'

'Am I? Why?'

'Well, because you and Andrew are so great together.'

'But that's just it. We're not.' I felt like a great weight was rolling off my shoulders. 'I know we should be but it feels like it's all coming unravelled between us. We just don't have anything in common any more. Not one thing.'

'Yes, you do.' Jill put her arm around my shoulder and stroked my back. 'You've just forgotten. It's like me and Simon. There are days when it feels like he's the last person on earth I want to be with – and I'm sure he must feel the same way about me. But that's not really how we feel. It's just like a cloud going over the sun. It passes. Maybe you should see a counsellor or something.'

'I already tried that. Just the other day.'

'You're kidding. Did it do any good?'

'I only went once. But love isn't something you can turn on and off like a tap just because you know you should. Do you ever fancy other people?'

'Of course I do. All the time. It's normal. But that's just make-believe. It doesn't mean you have to do anything about it.'

'Doesn't it?'

'Of course not. Not if you don't want to.'

'But I *do* want to. I can't think about anything else.'

'You don't mean that. You couldn't do that to Andrew.'

'It's not Andrew I want to do it to,' I joked weakly.

'Oh, but Lindy, you can't. Not with Max. Look, I can understand you want to get back at Natalie for what she did with Richard—'

'No, that's got nothing to do with it. I don't care about Richard any more. Honestly.'

'Well, why then?'

'It's just Max. He looks at me and I turn to jelly. There's something about him I can't resist. I can't explain it. It's like he's just pure *maleness*. You can practically smell it.'

'Look. They're leaving the day after tomorrow right?'

I nodded.

'So that'll be it then – won't it?'

'I guess so.' I couldn't bear to think that I'd never see Max again.

'You've got to promise me you won't sleep with him.'

'How could I?' I protested. 'Like you said, he's leaving the day after tomorrow.'

'Just promise me,' she insisted.

'OK. I promise,' I said. 'And you've got to swear on your life that you won't breathe a word of this to Simon.'

'Of course I won't,' she said. 'I'm not that silly. Are you going to be OK?'

I nodded.

'Come on, then,' she said. 'We'd better get back out there before our husbands drown in their own drool.'

Simon was using two little sake cups and a book of matches to explain English football to Max and Andrew was telling Natalie about off-shore accounts. Jill was scowling at me so I edged my chair six inches away from Max as I sat down and forced myself not to look at him.

A mountain of exotic fruit arrived covered in chocolate and Max started picking out un-chocolately bits for Natalie and putting them on a little plate.

'So, how did you two meet?' Max asked. To my horror, I realised he was talking to Andrew.

'Well,' said Andrew proudly, 'we were skiing and she threw herself down a mountain to get my attention.'

'That's so sweet,' said Natalie.

'Do you ski, Natalie?' I asked, trying to change the subject.

'Oh, no,' she said. 'I don't like the cold.'

'And was it love at first sight, then?' Max ploughed on.

'You'd have to ask Lindy that,' said Andrew modestly.

'Lindy?' said Max.

Everyone turned and looked at me.

'Absolutely!' I said. 'Who could resist him?'

Andrew beamed and Jill kicked me under the table.

Andrew and Simon made a big show of wanting to pay their share but Max insisted on putting it all on their room bill.

'You'll have to let us treat you next time,' Andrew said, but I was thinking, what next time? When will I see you again?

We headed back down the staircase and Max and Natalie came too, to say goodbye. My chest felt so tight I could scarcely breathe. 'So when will I see you again?' I asked Natalie. 'I guess you're busy tomorrow?'

'Yeah. I've booked myself into Agua at The Sanderson for a day of total pampering before we leave.'

'And I've got some last-minute shopping I need to do,' said Max, without being asked. 'My niece has told me I can't come home unless I bring her some Teletubbies. Do you know a good toy store in London?' He was looking straight at me.

'Yeah you should go to Hamley's – in Regent Street. It's very near the hotel.' My heart was thumping.

'And what time do they open?' He was still looking right at me.

'Ten o'clock, I should think,' I said as casually as I could. Jill was saying goodbye to Natalie. She didn't notice a thing.

'Well, I guess that's exactly where I'll go, then,' he said.

'You know, any time you guys feel like a trip to sunny California, you're more than welcome to come and stay with us,' said Natalie.

'We just might take you up on that,' said Simon.

'We'd love to,' said Jill.

'Bring the kids,' said Max. 'There's plenty of room.'

'We'd love to have you,' said Natalie.

There were lots of hugs and kisses all round. I kissed Natalie and we promised to keep in touch. 'I'll phone you every week,' she promised. Max shook hands warmly with Andrew, towering over him. Shook hands with Simon. They said how much they'd all enjoyed meeting each other. Simon told Max he'd bring his football to LA. Max promised to kick his ass. Natalie and Jill hugged each other for ages and Max kissed me politely on both cheeks while Andrew looked on, beaming approvingly. He'd kissed Natalie Brown. He was never going to wash his face again.

A couple of taxis crept over from the Hilton across the road and Natalie and Max waved us goodbye.

'What a major babe!' said Andrew, staring after them.

'Yeah, she can leave her nightie under my pillow any day,' agreed Simon.

'In your dreams, boys,' said Jill, dragging Simon into the waiting taxi. They dropped us off in Maida Vale and took the cab on to West Hampstead.

Jill gave me a big hug as I got out the taxi. 'Be good,' she told me.

'I'll try,' I told her. But when I got home I set the alarm for seven-thirty. Tomorrow was going to be a big day.

twenty-two

'Why are you getting up so early?' mumbled Andrew as I leapt out of bed. 'It's Saturday.'

'I've got an appointment with the dental hygienist. I told you – remember? It was the only time she could fit me in.' The adrenalin was already pumping and I was wide awake even though I'd barely slept a wink last night, tossing and turning until I heard the electric whirr of the milkman's van in the road.

But Andrew had already gone back to sleep.

I jumped into the shower to shampoo last night's smoky restaurant smell out of my hair and unfog my brain; worked up a lather with my Johnson's puff ball, letting the suds caress my skin; wrapped myself up in my fluffy white bath robe and wound a turban around my head; squeezed a generous slurp of honey-scented lotion into my hands and massaged it in all over my body; blow-dried my hair in the kitchen so the noise wouldn't disturb Andrew; made myself a cup of tea even though I was too sick with excitement to taste it.

What to wear? It was warm but overcast. I pulled on my pink camisole top and my grey silk skirt. Bare legs and sandals. Keep it casual. Like I haven't made an effort. I'd take the matching cardigan in case it got chilly. And brand new matching lilac satin undies – just in case you thought I was actually going to Hamley's to buy toys. Then I remembered the photo I'd promised to give Natalie. Damn. Of all the photos I'd taken that was the one I least wanted Natalie to have. But I'd promised. And I might as well take it with me and save the cost of postage anyway. Hmmph. The happy couple. It almost killed me to see the gleam in Max's eye as he looked at her. That's why Natalie like it so much, I realised. It was a photo of her being adored. Well, how lovely for her. I couldn't look at it. I just shoved it in a cardboard sleeve and tossed it into my Prada bowling bag.

I left the house at nine-thirty – plenty of time – and caught the Bakerloo Line to Oxford Circus. At the station I bought a paper and flicked through it on the train without taking in a single word.

The first jet-lagged tourists were already descending on Oxford Street waving street maps and arguing about which way was north as I headed down Regent Street. I got to Hamley's almost dead on ten and the store was practically empty. I darted up the escalators from floor to floor looking for Max, but I could sense in my gut that he wasn't there. I was ridiculously, unfashionably early.

Past the Buzz Lightyears and the PlayStations and the Barbies; no Max. My heart was racing and I felt light-headed and clammy. No need to panic, I told myself. That doesn't mean he's not coming.

Perhaps I should just go out and come back in again.

I went back downstairs and made a detour to Pret A Manger for a latte; got a nice caffeine buzz going and felt like I could conquer the world. I made myself sit down and drink it calmly, although inside I was terrified I might miss him. What if, while I was sitting here, he went into Hamley's, bought his toys and then left again? I'd never see him. This was a terrible plan of Max's. Why didn't I have his mobile number?

I left my latte half finished and almost ran back to Regent Street, past Liberty and Dickens & Jones, keeping my eyes peeled. I went through the front doors of Hamley's with a feeling of dread and anticipation. It was twenty past ten. I pretended to watch a boy demonstrating a bug that climbed up walls. I watched it crawl up and fall back down again half a dozen times but I was watching the front door all the time. The bug didn't know when to quit.

'Can I help you?' A Saturday girl trying to earn brownie points. Must be her first day.

'No. Thanks. Just looking.' I acted like I was fascinated by a little polystyrene plane that you could just throw into the air and it would fly. Then I looked back over my shoulder and there he was, just coming in through the front doors. He didn't see me and I suddenly felt a wave of panic. What if he's not expecting me to be here? What if Natalie's with him? What had he said last night exactly? Perhaps I should just hide.

Out of the corner of my eye, I could see him standing just inside the front doors by the giant water pistol stand, trying to figure out where to go. He was wearing chinos, a burnt-orange shirt that looked like it came from Gap and a brown sports jacket. A small leather rucksack. He looked like just another American tourist, smartly dressed in a slightly geeky kind of way, but when I looked at him I felt my heart well up as though I was going to cry. Was this what falling in love felt like?

I walked around the side of the store, so that I came up behind him.

'Hi there,' I said. I thought at first he hadn't heard me and then he turned around. What was that expression on his face? Surprise? Maybe he was a little too surprised. Didn't he know I'd come?

'Well, hi! Fancy bumping into you!' Max was definitely pleased to see me. 'I wasn't sure if you'd come.'

'Well – you know,' I said awkwardly. I picked up a purple gonk called Tickle Me Elmo just for something to do and started stroking it absent-mindedly. 'I thought I might find you here.' Tickle Me Elmo started chuckling and vibrating madly and I blushed and quickly put him down again.

'Do you have that effect on all men? Or is it just the furry ones?' asked Max, raising an eyebrow.

I smiled in what I hoped was an enigmatic way, feeling myself getting hot and flustered.

'Hey, nice bag,' he said, noticing my Prada kit. 'Do you like it?'

'I love it. It's beautiful,' I told him.

'Good,' he said. 'I thought you would. I chose it myself.'

Really! I couldn't speak.

'I had a great time last night,' he said. 'How about you?'

'Yeah, it was good fun,' I said. I hoped he didn't think I was stalking him.

'I especially enjoyed meeting your husband,' he said wickedly. 'What a nice guy!'

'Yes, isn't he?' I agreed. 'I'm a very lucky girl.'

'And he's a very lucky guy,' said Max, but I guess he had to say that.

'I know. We're just one terrific couple.'

'Is he here with you today?' he asked.

What – is he nuts? Did he really think I'd bring Andrew with me? 'No, he's at home,' I said. 'He's doing . . . stuff.'

'So what are your plans for the day? Are you free all morning?'

'Sure.' I shrugged.

'Well,' he carried on. 'I've got to get this thing for my niece. And then there are a couple of other errands I need to do. Is that OK with you?'

'Absolutely.' Errands? What errands? I thought. He's getting on a plane tomorrow morning. This is absolutely my last chance to spend time with him and he's doing errands? 'Sounds great,' I said. This wasn't going entirely the way I had expected. But then what had I expected?

I trailed around the store with Max while he collared an assistant to help him find the Teletubbies for his niece. I desperately wanted to get him on his own somewhere, but instead I waited patiently with a big indulgent smile on my face while he examined all the boxes to find a complete set that wasn't scuffed. Then he wanted them all gift-wrapped. Jesus Christ. They have toy shops in LA, don't they?

I could feel the morning slipping through my fingers. I was

standing close enough to Max to breathe in his warm smell: a mixture of wool and creamy soap and something else that was just Max. If I closed my eyes and buried my face in his chest would anybody notice? Do you think he'd mind?

'OK, now there's a book I'm trying to get hold of. Is there a good book store around here?'

'The best place is Charing Cross Road,' I said, snapping out of my daydream. 'We can walk there from here.' And then, I thought, I can get you someplace on your own.

When we came out of Hamley's it was starting to rain. Max took out a tiny umbrella from his rucksack and slid his arm around my waist. 'Stay close now,' he ordered. 'Which way?'

'We can cut through Soho and avoid the crowds,' I said, pointing down Beak Street. I didn't want to risk Carnaby Street. I had visions of Max going off on an Austin Powers trip and spending the whole morning trying on velvet bell-bottoms and go-go dancing with dolly birds. Better not risk it.

We squinched together under his umbrella but I didn't know what to do with my inside arm. I was too shy to put it around him – it seemed corny somehow – so I rested it awkwardly on his shoulder. It wasn't really raining that hard but I wasn't going to suggest he put his umbrella down. I was enjoying the closeness too much.

Down Beak Street, right into Lexington where he had to stop for ages and examine the green ceramic bricks on the side of a building, down Brewer Street, cut across into Old Compton Street and out into the Charing Cross Road.

Max was being mystifyingly distant. Physically we were practically joined at the hip, but there was a business-like tone in his voice I hadn't heard before. Instead of talking about us and whether we would ever see each other after today, he was chatting about nothing, looking in all the bars and shop windows, more interested in the detailing on the door handles than he was in me.

'What is it you're looking for anyway?' I asked him.

'It's a book called *Hot Couture*. I want to give it to Natalie's mother. And yes . . .' he smirked, '. . . it is called "Hot" – it's not just my accent.'

'I didn't say a word,' I protested. Jeez, why was he being so touchy?

On Charing Cross Road, we went into three book stores – and none of them had *Hot Couture* in stock. In bookshop number four, we went upstairs to where the fashion books lived. Max couldn't find it on the shelves and asked one of the sales assistants if they had it. While she went to look it up on the computer, Max browsed idly through the postcard racks. 'What do you think – for my niece?' he asked, holding up a card of a fat drag queen dressed as Madonna.

'Mmm.' I wasn't really paying attention because I'd suddenly noticed the in-store classical music. I listened to it for a minute or so without saying a word, while Max flicked through the postcards.

'Max?' I said eventually. 'Why are they playing "The Wedding March"?'

'To remind you that you're married,' he said solemnly and my heart sank.

'You know,' I told him, 'if we were in a film and they were playing that music, no one would believe it.'

The assistant came to find him. 'I'm sorry, it's out of stock at the moment. But we could order it for you.'

'No, that's no good. I'm leaving London tomorrow. Is there anywhere else around here that might have it?'

'Well, according to the computer, there're two copies in stock at our Hampstead branch.'

'Where's that?' Max asked me. 'Is that near here?'

'No,' I said, 'It's out of the West End. Do you know where Hampstead Heath is?'

'Oh, I've heard of that. It sounds great. Can we get tea and scones there?'

'More like cappuccino and an almond croissant.'

'Do you want to come with me?'

If Max had his heart set on going to Hampstead, I wasn't going to stay here. Besides it might be quite cosy.

'Sure.' What the hell.

By the time we got outside, the rain was chucking it down. Max marched out to the kerb with his tiny umbrella. All the black cabs had disappeared in that mysterious way they do the moment it starts raining, so we walked on a little way to a mini-cab office just off Old Compton Street.

Rain hammered down on the roof and fountains of muddy water flew above the windows as we hit puddles at speed. The driver's radio was tuned to an Indian station playing frenetic Hindi love songs and one of the front windows was wide open.

'Can you close the window?' I asked the driver.

'Sorry, no. Is broken,' he said cheerily.

'It's freezing in here,' said Max.

'Do you want to borrow my cardigan?' Brightly. Like a girl scout. Be prepared.

'Do you have a cardigan?' He sounded genuinely interested so I fished it out of my bag. I went to drape it over his knees but he stopped me.

'No, we can both wear it. You put one arm in and I'll put one arm in,' he said. I scooted a few millimetres closer towards him as he slid his outside arm through the pink lacy sleeve. I did the same with my arm so that the cardigan covered our laps. Without any further discussion our inside hands clasped around each other.

'We're not holding hands, we're just keeping warm,' he stated firmly.

'Absolutely,' I agreed.

The mad Indian music kept banging out of the speakers behind our heads. Let this drive never end.

'This is very romantic,' he conceded. 'Sitting in a taxi with all the rain outside.'

'Mmmm,' I murmured, not trusting myself to say anything

more. Instead, I uncurled my fingers from his and began to stroke his arm, ever so gently. Ever so lightly. Barely touching him really. Is this allowed? I wondered. Please let this be allowed.

Max turned his head and buried it in my neck. 'Dangerous,' he whispered with his lips brushing my ear. 'Dan-ger-ous.' But he didn't stop me or move his hand away.

'I'm just stroking your arm,' I pointed out, trying to sound innocent. Casual. I turned my head towards him, wanting nothing more than to look into his eyes, but instead I saw his mouth, lips parted coming towards mine. So slowly.

And then I was kissing him. Thank God, thank God, thank God, thank God. At last. It was actually happening. Finally! I felt like a marathon runner stumbling gratefully over the finish line. An astronaut splashing down on earth after a light year in hypersleep. I'd only known him a few weeks and my patience was already stretched to its limit. Now I wanted nothing more than for our lips to be joined forever.

'Put your tongue in my mouth.' Max's voice was husky, breathless. A shiver of pure pleasure shot through me. Turned on even more by his request, I didn't have to be asked twice. As my tongue slid around his lips and deeper into his mouth, he gave an involuntary little moan. 'Ohh' and my womb contracted like an accordion. My tongue curled around his tongue and fell in love.

'This is only for the taxi ride,' he whispered. 'We have to stop this as soon as we get out of the taxi.'

'Mmmhmm.' Whatever. Please don't let this journey end. Please let the traffic be really bad. Please make him go via Clapham. I was struggling my arm free out of the cardigan and stroking his face, his neck; kissing our way through the sodden streets, holding his face in my hands, my fingers curling into his hair. Blissful.

His hand moved confidently up my thigh, under my skirt, stroked the elastic on the edge of my knickers experimentally. Any moment now and he was going to find out how much I wanted him. If he thought it was raining outside, a London thunderstorm was nothing to the effect Max had on me.

'Put your tongue in my mouth again.' Are these the most fantastic words in the English language or what? I sucked slowly on his delicious tongue, aching for him. Please can we stay in this taxi forever?

What's that ringing sound?'

Max leapt away from me as though I had 1,000 volts running through me. We both stared at the noise coming from the rucksack on the floor.

'It's Natalie,' was all he said. His face was ashen. Ghastly. He didn't make a move to answer it.

I bunched up my cardigan, rolled it in my lap and hoiked my skirt back down. I didn't know what to say.

'I can't answer it.'

It stopped ringing.

Silence.

Max couldn't have looked more grey and guilt stricken if Natalie had suddenly bobbed up from the front seat and caught us red-handed.

'Oh, God, oh, God, oh, God. I can't do this,' he said.

'It's OK, it's OK,' I said, trying to soothe him as though he was an injured dog. Does this mean I can't kiss you anymore?

'I can't speak to her,' said Max.

The phone started ringing again. Bleep bleep. Bleep bleep. Still Max didn't answer it. Just sat in the corner of the taxi pole-axed, unable to move. Please hurry up and answer it and tell her some lie and let me go back to kissing you again. Please? Bleep bleep. Bleep bleep. We're wasting valuable kissing time here. We were already at Belsize Park.

'If I thought Natalie was out there somewhere doing this, it would kill me,' he said. He looked like he was about to cry.

Bleep bleep. Bleep bleep. Why doesn't he just turn it off? She can leave a message. The phone stopped again and we drove the rest of the way to Hampstead in silence.

'If she calls again, I'll have to speak to her,' said Max.

'Where on the High Street do you want?' asked the taxi driver.

'Just over there on the left,' I told him. 'Where that white car's pulling out.'

The driver pulled over and I climbed out of the cab crossly, handing him the fare. As soon as Max got out the car the phone started ringing again. I sheltered under an awning as he answered it.

'Oh hi, how's it going?' His voice didn't betray any sign of turmoil. I wanted to listen, but moved away to give him privacy. See how mature I am? I wanted to grab the phone from his hand and throw it under a passing bus but I watched him talking. He was smiling. Incredible. What are they talking about? You just saw her this morning, for God's sake.

'Love you.' I heard him say as he hung up – or rather pressed Yes to end the call. There should be a word for that but there isn't.

There should also be a word to describe how I was feeling right then as he walked over to me with a smile on his face. But there isn't. A cocktail of embarrassment, shame, guilt, lust, fear – but mostly lust. The English language comes up short again.

'It's OK. I feel better now,' he said.

Well, bully for you, I thought.

'Natalie's just leaving the hotel. She's going to Agua.'

Lucky old Natalie. We were at the doorway of the book-shop and I went in so I wouldn't have to think of anything else to say. I hung around by the paperbacks, quietly hyperventilating while Max asked one of the assistants for *Hot Couture*. I didn't know what to do any more. Max had been flirting with me outrageously ever since we met and now he was making me feel like I was the one who was chasing him. As if I was the one who'd started it. Had I got my wires crossed completely? Was that possible?

'Shall we get a coffee, then?' he said, looking guilty. The book was bought, paid for and in a carrier bag under his arm.

'OK.' I shrugged. 'There's a Café Rouge just up the road.'

The rain had almost stopped. Max put his umbrella up again, but I walked on my own a few steps ahead of him, with my arms folded across my chest to keep warm. We took a table by the window and ordered two cappuccinos. There was an awkward silence.

'Look,' I said. 'I'm really, really sorry if I made you do something you didn't want to.' No, I wasn't.

'It wasn't you. It was both of us,' he said. 'But I can't do this any more. I've been through this too many times.

'I've got three kids I never see all because I did stuff like this. I see my niece more often than I see my own daughters. I can't cheat on Natalie. I just can't go through all that again.'

'God, I'm sorry. I didn't know. I didn't realise.'

'You don't have to keep saying sorry,' he said. 'You didn't make me do anything I didn't want to.'

'Hey, we didn't do that much. Nothing happened.'

'It was enough. It was more than enough. I don't want to be that kind of husband again. Natalie and I have a terrific relationship. I don't want to wreck this one like I wrecked the others.'

'I know. I understand. It's OK. I don't want to break anybody up.'

'I'm just really nervous that she'll find out.'

'Look, relax,' I said. 'You're getting on a plane tomorrow and flying eight thousand miles away and I'm never going to see you again. I can promise you, you'll be safe from me. But I'm afraid I can't vouch for the rest of the female population.' I amazed myself by how cool and light-hearted I sounded because I was anything but.

The waitress brought our coffees and I remembered how it had all started, Max wiping the chocolate from my mouth and licking his finger.

I stared out at the people going past on the footpath; couples shopping together on a Saturday morning. How many of them were in love with other people?

'I guess we just met at the wrong time.' I was trying to sound grown-up and philosophical.

'No. It wasn't the wrong time,' he said. 'I'm glad we met.'

'Yeah, but I just wonder why this is happening now, the day before you leave the country.'

'To stop us ruining our lives,' he said. I don't think he meant it unkindly. But then, what did he mean exactly?

I suddenly remembered the photo I'd been carrying around all day and got the envelope out of my bag. 'Here,' I said. 'This is for Natalie. I promised I'd give her a copy.'

He opened the envelope and pulled out the photo of the two of them – Max with his arms around Natalie's shoulders, worshipping her, Natalie with one hand lightly on Max's arm, claiming him. He gave a kind of chuckle as though that day had completely slipped his mind. 'This is very good,' he said. 'Did you take this?'

'Yes, of course I did.' I was a little offended that he sounded so surprised. Did he think I'd torn it out of the *Radio Times* and was carrying it around all day just for the hell of it?

'Thanks,' he said. 'Natalie will appreciate that.' He put the envelope in his rucksack and we both stirred our coffees in an awkward silence. 'I ought to get back,' said Max. 'I've got a lot of packing to do this afternoon.'

I knew it was a lie. He'd just flown back from LA a couple of days ago. What was he going to pack?

'OK,' I said.

We got another taxi back to the hotel and Max put his umbrella on the seat between us. It made my leg wet but rather than put it on the floor, I moved further away and rested my forehead on the window thinking that this was really goodbye.

'Can I ask you something?' I ventured, still looking out the window.

'Sure. What?'

'Were you flirting with me right from the very beginning?'

He seemed surprised. 'Yes. Kind of. Why?'

'I was just wondering.'

He didn't say anything for a while and then he asked, 'Do you feel guilty about Andrew?'

I shook my head firmly. 'No. I don't.' What was the point now in pretending? 'If I didn't kiss you I was going to go nuts.'

He was surprised. Embarrassed. Inordinately pleased. I caught his eyes and gazed into his pupils until he blushed and looked down. 'When did you first think you might kiss me?' he asked. He was flirting again already. Fishing for more confessions.

'That Wednesday night.'

'When I was stroking your foot?'

'That was about the time, yeah.'

'We did kiss that night,' he said. 'Twice.' As if I needed reminding. 'Lip kisses,' he said. 'With Michael Knightley sitting in the car watching us.' He laughed. At what? The recklessness of it? I couldn't understand how Max could be so paranoid about kissing me in a taxi, and yet was quite happy to kiss me in front of Natalie's co-star and flirt with me on set under Natalie's nose while the cameras were running.

When the taxi pulled up outside the hotel, I jumped out before Max could suggest that I took it on to Maida Vale. I couldn't just say goodbye to him like this. The doorman leapt into action to open Max's door for him.

'Well,' I said. 'I guess this is goodbye then.' Did I sound brave? Did I sound like I didn't care?

'You can always call me,' he said. 'I'll give you my cell phone number. Have you got a pen?'

'No.' Which was the truth, by the way.

He opened his wallet searching for one of his business cards. 'Look,' he said. 'Come upstairs to my room. Just for a minute. I'll give you my number.'

Max and I stood at opposite sides of the lift, our reflections ricocheting endlessly down the canyon of mirrors. Neither of us said anything. I stared at the gold mosaic tiles on the floor, not daring to look at him. The doors opened at the ninth floor and Max led the way down the corridor, not saying anything even when we reached the door of their suite. He just took out his keycard, opened the door and walked straight through to the bedroom and opened the closet.

There were blueprints sticky-taped to all the walls in the sitting room, and a model made of layer upon layer of circular white paper inside a perspex case on the coffee table. The twin domes of Perth's new art gallery.

Should I follow him? I wanted to but I couldn't. I hadn't been invited – yet. He'd told me it had to stop. So I lurked in the sitting room, looking through at the huge white fluffy pillows on the bed, the neatly turned back grey cover. Their bed. I wouldn't go in there. I'd be good.

He handed me his card and our eyes met for the billionth time.

'This is very dangerous,' he said. 'We're in a hotel room so we can't do anything. You have to go.'

I nodded. 'Right. You're right.' I stared at the writing on his business card. Words. Numbers. Some of them in brackets; I stroked the card as if appraising the quality of the embossed lettering, didn't feel like leaving.

'Everything is OK,' he said, trying to reassure me.

'Yeah. I'm OK. You're OK.'

'And Andrew and Natalie are OK, too,' he said. 'She thinks the world of you, you know.'

That's right. She was my best friend. She'd never do something like this to me would she? Oh, but she would. And she had.

'I never expected any of this to happen, you know,' he said. 'But I feel a very strong connection to you.'

I looked into his blue eyes and felt that unmistakable current flowing straight from my soul to his soul. Neither of us blinked or looked away. 'I'm just finding it very hard to say goodbye to you,' I admitted.

'Kiss me,' he said suddenly. 'Lip kiss.'

I stood on tiptoe to reach him, pressing my mouth on his, my body against his. Melted against him. I prayed for a last-minute reprieve that would keep him in London pressed against me, just for a few more days. I could feel his penis pressing hard against my stomach and he uttered a little 'Ohh' as I stretched up some more so that our groins were locked. Alarmingly, shockingly, I could feel his penis pressing quite a long way down my thigh as well. Natalie wasn't kidding. What did he have down there? I wondered. A vacuum cleaner hose?

'We can't have sex,' he said, his voice so husky it was just a whisper, his lips grazing mine as he spoke.

'No,' I agreed.

'You're married. I'm as good as married. It's wrong.' He was still kissing me, holding my face in his hands.

'Mmm hmm.'

'We shouldn't do anything we wouldn't do in public.'

'That's right.'

'So kissing is all right.'

'That's right. I've kissed you in public. Kissing is allowed.'

'Give me your tongue,' he whispered, and I marvelled at how brilliant it was that lip kisses didn't count as adultery. We were being good and it felt like Heaven. 'We can't lie on the bed,' he breathed, and I shook my head to agree with him. 'But we could sit on the couch. There are couches in public.'

I couldn't speak because his tongue was licking the roof of my mouth. I just kind of nodded as he walked me over to the couch and sat us both down without moving his lips away from mine. For a few minutes we kissed on the couch – me kneeling, him sitting, with our arms by our sides. Eventually he said, 'What about taking our clothes off? If we keep our underwear on, it will be like being at the beach. Underwear is just like what you wear at the beach, isn't it?'

That was right. He was so clever to think of that. He shrugged off his jacket then reached down and slipped off my shoes, then his shoes and socks. 'See,' he said. 'No harm done.' Then he unzipped my skirt and lifted me so that I was standing up and my skirt fell around my ankles. Where his hands touched my hips it felt like someone had turned the sun on. I kneeled down again and unbuttoned his shirt; first the cuffs, kissing him again as my fingers fumbled for each button in turn. Sliding my hands over his shoulder and down his back as the shirt fell to the floor. He stood up then and stepped out of his chinos and I tried not to stare at the enormous bulge in his blue boxer shorts.

'See. Just a day at the beach,' he said, and gently pulled my camisole top over my head. My heart was pounding so hard, I was sure he would be able to see it. He sat down and kissed me again hard and deep and I thrilled to the touch of his skin against mine. My hands discovered the hard muscle under his skin, the softness of the curls of hair on his chest and shoulders and down his thighs. Just a day at the beach, I told myself. Just two people sitting on a couch in their swimming costumes kissing – that's all we're doing.

'What about touching your breasts?' he whispered. His breath was hot on my neck. 'What if it happened accidentally? Say, if I was reaching out to turn on the TV and I accidentally stroked your breast with my hand . . . like this . . . That could happen, couldn't it?'

'Uh, huh.' I could hardly get the words out.

'And what if, say, my thumb somehow got caught and it ended up inside your bra . . . like this . . . so that it was resting on your breast . . . like this . . . and I didn't know . . .'

'I suppose so,' I whispered. It was like fairy lights being switched on all over my body.

'And then, what if . . . my thumb accidentally brushed your nipple . . . and it couldn't help itself from stroking it very slowly around and around and around . . . like this . . .'

'That would be all right, too.'

'And then, say, I was to lean over towards you . . . like this . . . but somehow I tripped and my face landed on your bra . . . like this . . . and the only way I could save myself from falling was to wrap my tongue around your nipple . . . like this . . . How would that be?'

'That would be just fine!' I murmured, feeling myself start to float as though I was being swallowed up by the ocean.

'And what if, just supposing, this beach was on a desert island . . . and there was no food or water . . . and I thought your nipple was a raspberry . . . and I started to suck on it . . . like this . . . no one could blame me for that could they?'

I shook my head and sank back on the couch underneath him. It was like my hips had a mind of their own as they began to gently rock against him like waves lapping on the shore. I think I could feel the tide coming in.

I don't know how long we lay there, kissing and rocking and stroking and licking and sucking. Was it an hour? A minute? When the phone rang it was all over.

'Great,' I heard him say. 'I've just been taking a nap. I'll see you soon. That was Natalie,' he told me but I was already looking for my clothes. 'She's on her way.' He came over and took my hand and kissed me again as hungrily as he had the first time, pressing his body tight against mine and I tried to memorise that feeling of his skin against mine because I knew it would be all I had left.

'I won't see you again, will I?' he said.

'No, I guess not,' I said, trying to make my voice sound light.

'Will you come and visit?'

'I don't know. Maybe. Who knows? Maybe you'll come back to London.'

'Yeah, maybe.' He was stroking my hair. 'Are you going to be OK?'

'I'll be fine. I am fine.' I pulled on my top, not feeling fine at all. Max was still in his boxer shorts.

'Natalie will be here soon,' he said.

'I know. I have to go.'

255

'Give me your tongue one last time,' he urged huskily, and lifted me up so I didn't have to stand on tiptoe, holding my body close against him. I hugged him, stroking his back, feeling like my heart would break.

Saying goodbye with our tongues.

He followed me to the door and I stood with my hand on the door handle for a long time, not turning it, just watching him, trying to memorise his face: the lines around his mouth, the freckle above his eyebrow, the exact shade of his eyes, the way the light caught the tiny white hairs on the top of his ears. The single grey hair in the curl just above his belly-button.

'Goodbye, Max.'

'Goodbye. Call me.'

When I opened the door, the first thing I saw was a flash gun going off and then a photographer running down the hallway to the lift.

twenty-three

'What the fuck?' said Max.

'Do you know who that was?' I asked but even as I said it I could tell it was a pretty stupid question. My brain was having difficulty adjusting to this new information. For a split second I thought it was something to do with the hotel. Like those log flume rides at amusement parks. When you get off at the bottom, there's a little booth where you can go and buy a picture of yourself screaming 'Whoooargh!' and getting covered in pond bilge.

But why was someone taking a photo of me and Max standing in the doorway of his hotel room? Max wasn't even dressed for a photo – he was just wearing his boxer shorts.

'Oh Jesus!' I dropped my cardigan and ran down the corridor to the lift hoping to catch him. I had to catch him. Which newspaper was he from? Not *The Ledger* surely? Nobody I knew. A photographer with sandy gingery hair. Wearing a turquoise waterproof jacket. Dark trousers. I could give the police a fair description. Medium build. Looked early forties but he was probably younger. They don't age well, these chaps. Not sure about the shoes. Black leather? With a tassel? I'm not sure. It all happened so fast, officer.

Which way did he go? Down obviously. Only people in the movies make their getaway by sprinting across the rooftops. There was a young Japanese couple waiting by the lifts. They turned to me and smiled politely. No one else there. There were two lifts. He could have just gone down in the other one.

I had to get that film. Should I wait for the next lift or find the stairs? We're on the ninth floor. How many stairs would that be? How fast could I run down nine flights of stairs? The Japanese girl who had long socks and five-inch platforms smiled at me again. I turned left and ran around the corner to the fire exit, then heard the lift bing bong and ran back again, pushing through the doors just as they were closing and shoving the Japanese girl out of the way.

'So sorry,' she said, automatically like a wind-up doll.

God, was this lift never going to get going? How much were those photos worth? They couldn't be worth that much. Max wasn't famous – just one of the top ten architects in the world. He wasn't tabloid famous, not a celebrity. It's not like he'd made a movie or anything. And I'm nobody at all. No one. They're probably not worth that much at all. I'll just find the photographer, I thought, explain there's obviously been a mistake and ask him to give me the film. I'll pay him for them. I've got my cheque book with me. I wonder how much he wants. It's only because he's going out with Natalie that anybody would be interested in him. I've only got a £50 cheque guarantee card. Maybe he'll let me write two cheques. It's not as though we were doing anything wrong. I was just saying goodbye to him. In his underpants. Oh, God, oh, God, oh, God. Would he take a credit card?

Why is this lift stopping on the sixth floor?

If that photo turns up in the Sunday papers how am I going to explain it to Natalie? How am I going to explain it to Andrew?

Four grey Americans in head-to-toe Aquascutum got in very slowly examining their tube map. I pressed the ground button six times to make the door close. Will you lot get a bloody move-on!

'We have to get the blue line at Hyde Park Corner, then we change to the grey line at Green Park, and then we change to the red line at Notting Hill Gate.'

'Why don't we take the grey line to St James's Park?'

'Then we have to take the green line to Kensington High Street.'

'That's one, two, three, four, five, six . . . seven stops.'

'I thought we had to take the yellow line?'

'Can't we take the blue line to South Kensington and then take the green line?'

'I'm sure he said take the yellow line.'

'Can we change to the green line at St James?'

'We can get the yellow line at Baker Street.'

'Why don't you take a taxi?' I suggested, leaping out of the opening lift doors. 'It'll be much cheaper.' They'd get lost in the subways at Hyde Park Corner and never be seen again. Bloody Americans – what on earth was I thinking getting mixed up with one of them?

I scooted out to the street and looked up and down Park Lane. There was no sign of the photographer. I ran up to the doorman who was standing nearby. 'Excuse me – have you seen a man carrying a camera come out of here in the last few minutes?'

'Yes, Miss, there was a gentleman just a moment ago. I think he went back into the hotel to use the telephone.'

'Thank you. Thank you.' I rushed back into the hotel. 'Excuse me!' I shouted at the receptionist, who was checking someone in. 'Where are the telephones here?'

The girl pointed to the two payphones past the lift. There was a man using one of them. Thank God. I'd offer him money. I'd beg him. Perhaps I could just steal his camera. I could break his camera. I could knock him out with a copy of the *Yellow Pages*.

Oh no! It was just a tourist with a video camera around his neck. I looked about. There was no one else there. I ran back to the doorman.

'That wasn't him,' I gasped. 'The guy I'm looking for isn't a tourist, he's British.'

'I am sorry,' he said very sympathetically. 'So many of our guests have cameras it's hard to keep track of them all. I'm afraid I didn't see the gentleman you were referring to. I must have been looking the other way.' And he gave me an innocent smile that made me suspect that he'd not only seen him, he was probably the bastard who'd tipped him off in the first place. Just then the American group arrived and he walked off to call them a taxi.

Geoff. Geoff the lovely picture editor at *The Ledger* would know. He could help me. It was Saturday and he wouldn't be in the office, but maybe he'd have his mobile on. His number was still programmed into my phone. Please answer. Please answer.

'Hello.'

'Geoff! It's Lindy. How are you?'

'Lindy! I'm very well, thank you.' He sounded slightly drunk. 'Have you rung to enquire about my health or do you want your job back? Because you're too late. We've given it to someone else.'

'I know. That's fine.'

'His name's Martin. He's just out of college but he's very keen.'

'That's terrific. I'm sorry for calling you on a Saturday but I need to ask a favour.'

'Well, you haven't rung at a very good time. I've got thirty people in my garden for a barbecue. And I've done a honey-glazed ham stuffed with apricots. It's a Gary Rhodes' recipe.'

'Oh, lovely. Look. My friend Natalie Brown – you know, from that show *Don't Call Us*—'

'Nobody watches Channel 4.'

'Yes, I know. Well, a snapper's taken some photos of her bloke with another friend of theirs. A girl. It's all perfectly innocent but she'd really like to get them back. I wondered if there's any way you could find out who's got them? You know everybody, don't you?' That was it. Appeal to his vanity.

'Yes, I do. But I'm rather busy at the moment. I've got thirty red peppers to roast and they're buggers to peel.'

'Geoff. It's really, really important. Put them in a plastic bag – it makes it much easier. Please. I'd be so grateful. Natalie would be so grateful.'

'What are these photos of, exactly?'

'Just her fiancé – Max – he's an architect. He's not famous at all. And a friend of theirs.'

'What's so special about them? They don't sound very interesting.'

'Oh, they're not. Not at all. It's just that he's only wearing his boxer shorts and people might get the wrong idea.'

'And what's the right idea? Why's he wearing his boxer shorts?'

'I don't know exactly. Um, I think he spilled something on his trousers. And this friend happened to drop by and . . . or it might have been a fancy-dress party. I don't know really. Natalie didn't say.' What *was* Max doing in his boxer shorts? I was going to have to come up with a better alibi than that.

Geoff snorted. 'It all sounds very fishy to me. But leave it with me and I'll see what I can find out. It won't be till later on, mind you.'

'Oh, Geoff. Thank you. Thank you so much. You've still got my number, haven't you? Call me. It doesn't matter how late.' I hung up and ran across the road to the park looking for the snapper but he was long gone. Of course. He wasn't exactly going to hang around and wait for a bus. I could see the doorman watching me in a supercilious kind of way. Bastard. Isn't there some kind of law about taking photos of people in hotel doorways without their permission?

So what should I do now? I should go back up and see Max and figure out what we were going to do.

Just as I was about to walk back to the hotel, I saw Natalie's white BMW pull up. I hid behind a phone box so she wouldn't see me as out she stepped in a beige wrap-around dress slashed to the waist and impossibly pointy matching slingbacks.

I shivered and suddenly realised I had dropped my cardigan

when I ran from Max's room. I had to speak to Max before Natalie got there! Thank God for mobile phones. What on earth did we do before they were invented? I had to ring Directory Enquiries for the hotel number and asked them to put me right through. God, was there time?

'Hi – Suite 910 please.' Please let there be time, please let there be time.

'Hello?'

'Max, it's Lindy. I'm downstairs in the street. Natalie's on her way up – she didn't see me. I can't find the photographer. I don't know who he is but I'm absolutely certain he's a papparazzi. Papparazzo. Whatever. That photo could be in one of the Sunday papers tomorrow. You've got to think of something to tell Natalie to explain where it came from. And hide my cardigan! Are you there? Max?'

'Yes, this is Max Ogilvy. And can you send up a tuna sandwich and some fries to my room, please?'

'What are you talking about? Oh, I get it. Has Natalie just come in?'

'That's right. Room 910. Thank you very much.'

'I'm sorry, Max. I'm so sorry.'

Now what? I hung up, not having the faintest idea what I should do next. Go home I supposed. But how? I felt like I was going to be sick. I walked back down towards the tube station in a daze. Every time I blinked I would feel the lingering imprint of Max's kisses and a wave of euphoria would rush over me, blocking out every other thought. For a second, it would stop me in my tracks and I'd be back in his arms, quivering under his touch. And then I'd open my eyes and the realisation would hit me like a ton of bricks as if for the very first time that I was in deep, deep shit.

I sleepwalked all the way onto the tube, feeling like I was swimming against the current. My one over-riding impulse, mad as it sounds, was to march straight back to the hotel and just pick up where I had left off with Max, Natalie or no

Natalie. Desire was like a magnet pulling me back and sending weird electrical impulses through my brain that might make me do practically anything. I could still taste him. I could still smell him. I still wanted him.

Back at Maida Vale, as soon as I hit street level, my phone rang. It would be Geoff with news. He'd got the photos for me! I was saved.

'You have a new voice message . . . Hi Lindy. It's Natalie. You left your cardigan in our room. Do you want to come by and pick it up? Because we're going in the morning. Otherwise I can leave it at the front desk for you. Max has told me all about your little adventure – and I've got the photo – so thanks very much. See you later, maybe.'

I had to dial my message service and listen to it again. Her tone of voice was so calm. What did it mean? Natalie's got the photo? How? Did the photographer come back and just hand it over? What had Max told her?

I stood in the street clutching my mobile phone, wondering which way to turn. Home? Or back to the hotel? Was there some way I could phone Max without Natalie listening? I had to find out what had happened. What did he tell her? Had he confessed everything? Home? Or hotel? Andrew or Max? Safety or uncertainty? I started walking for home, got half way and then ran back to the tube station again and down the stairs.

Even if Natalie stabbed me to death with her pointy sandals, it was still an excuse to see Max – just one more time.

twenty-four

'Hi, Lindy. Come on in.'

Natalie answered the door. I'd been standing outside for five minutes staring at the lit-up number 910, plucking up the courage to knock. What if she had a gun? Americans have guns. Maybe she'd killed Max and then lured me here to pick up my cardigan so she could kill me too.

But she was smiling. She kissed me. 'Got time for a cup of tea? I've just made a pot of Earl Grey.'

'Great.' No sign of Max. The bedroom door was tightly closed. Was he already dead? Perhaps he was tied to a chair with masking tape, tapping out a message for help in morse code by banging his head on the bath-tub.

'Max is in the shower. He says sorry for giving you a fright. He thought you were me.'

'Oh, that's OK.' What is she talking about?

'Your cardigan's just there on the couch.'

'Thanks.' She was pottering around with the milk jug. 'How was Agua?'

'Gor-geous.' She handed me a china teacup and I sat down on the couch, surreptitiously stroking the fabric with one finger. This is where it happened. This is where we were. Me and Max . . .

'I wish we were staying at The Sanderson but Max says the rooms are tiny. I had a massage and a full body polish. And then I had an Indian head massage and a pedicure. I feel so incredibly relaxed right now like I could just float back to LA

264

without the plane. Completely at peace with the world. But I expect it won't last long.'

'No,' I agreed. 'Probably not.'

'Do you like my toenails?' She leaned over to study her bare feet – without bending her knees, of course, dancers never do – and flicked a toe dismissively with her little finger.

'They're great.'

'It's called Damson,' she said. 'You don't think it's a little dark, do you?'

'No. It's nice.'

'Hmm.' She wasn't interested in my opinion. 'I think it's a little dark. I specifically told the girl I didn't want anything in the purple end of the spectrum. But I really don't think she was listening. She just didn't get it. And I was so blissed out from the Indian Head Massage, I wasn't paying attention. I'm supposed to wear autumn colours. Not purples.' She was walking around the room now, examining her toenails in different lights. 'I guess I can put up with it for a day or two until we get to Spain. But it's going to really bug the hell out of me. Don't you just hate it when things aren't exactly perfect?'

'Yes, I do,' I agreed. Oh, my God, I was thinking. If she gets this worked up about the colour of her toenails, what's she going to be like when she finds me and Max in the Sunday papers together?

'You know, I just might have a lighter colour here I can use as a top coat – just as a stopgap measure.' She opened an aluminium flight case – the sort of thing the Rolling Stones might take on a world tour to carry their amplifiers – and started rummaging through the bottles and tubes.

I got up to have a peek. That's when I noticed the photo of Natalie and Max that I had brought for her lying on the coffee table. 'Oh,' I said with surprise. 'Max remembered to give you the photo then?' I'd forgotten all about it.

'Yes. Thanks for bringing it over.'

'Yes, that's right,' I said quickly. What a perfect excuse. I'd come here to bring her the photo. I had a look through all her beauty products feeling an immense sense of relief. Blimey, she had everything in here: eyelash conditioner, dry-skin remover, lip balm, instant tanning lotion, wash-off tanning lotion, hair serum, hair-shine spray, bronzing gel, the full range of Mac lipsticks, day cream, night cream, sunblock cream, under-eye cream, fine-line remover, skin revitaliser, peel-off masks, exfoliating masks, vitamin masks, scar-removing serum, scar-removing plasters, under-eye concealer, body lotion, hand cream, nail cream, cuticle conditioner and two dozen bottles of nail varnish in minutely different shades of beige and arranged in order of height in foam padding that had been specially cut to fit each bottle. She held up two possibles critically before selecting one and taking out her foam toe wedges.

'Oh, thank goodness. I wouldn't have been able to sleep tonight worrying about the state of my feet.'

There was silence suddenly as the noise of the shower in the other room stopped. Max was just behind that door, wet and naked, and I was here drinking Earl Grey watching Natalie nestle on the couch and paint her toenails Honey Glow. When the phone rang, she held her bottle of nail varnish aloft at me as if to say, 'Well, I can't possibly answer it.'

'I'll get it,' I said.

'Natalie?' said the woman's voice on the phone.

'No. It's a friend of hers,' I said. 'Natalie can't come to the phone right now.'

'Well, tell her it's Wendy and it's very urgent.'

I covered the mouthpiece and said to Natalie, 'Wendy? She says it's urgent.'

'Uurgh,' said Natalie, not getting off the couch. 'They better not have messed up our flights for tomorrow. Bring the phone over here.'

I trailed the cord around the furniture but it wouldn't reach far enough, so I stood in the middle of the room holding the phone and passed the receiver over to Natalie.

'Yes, Wendy,' said Natalie, in the voice she used to charm people she didn't particularly like. 'What's the problem?'

I couldn't hear the other end of the conversation but a nasty feeling in the pit of my stomach told me I knew exactly what the problem was.

'That's ridiculous. How did they get hold of the photo? Max told me a tourist in the hotel took it.' Natalie was looking at me now and shaking her head as if Pizza Hut had sent her the wrong order. She was still pretty calm. I went cold all over. 'Yes, I know all about the photo. It's not "some girl", as you put it. It's Lindy. She's my oldest friend.' She was waving her hand over her toenails to dry them. 'That was her who answered the phone.'

Just then the bedroom door opened and Max stood in the doorway behind Natalie, wearing a fluffy white robe and wiping the steam off his glasses with a towel. He put on his glasses and we stared at each other over the top of Natalie's head. I wanted to rush over and kiss him, to bury my head in his hot, damp chest hair but I was stuck there in the middle of the room – Natalie's phone servant. Neither of us said anything.

'I've known her since I was five . . . Ha ha. Really?' She covered up the phone. 'The *News of the World* says you look like a slapper,' she told me, as if this was the funniest news in the whole world.

I closed my eyes, wishing the floor would open up and swallow me. Why did I come back to the hotel? Why did Max have to be standing there, listening to this?

'Well, it's really very simple,' she went on. 'Lindy had dropped by to deliver a photo I'd asked for . . . well, because she's a photographer . . . yes, I suppose it is rather . . . But Max thought it was me at the door and that I'd forgotten my card key again . . . Yes. And that's why he was in his boxer shorts. Lindy's lucky it wasn't worse. She could have got a real eyeful . . . We don't know who took this photo. Max said he thought it was a tourist . . . He's standing right here, I'll ask him. Max – why did you think this guy was a tourist?'

'Well, he was just walking past when I opened the door, so I assumed he was somebody staying in the hotel.' Max's voice sounded incredibly calm. He'd had plenty of time to rehearse his lines in the shower. He even sounded like he believed it. 'I thought perhaps men in their underpants were considered amusing where he came from.'

'Did you hear that, Wendy? It was just some guy walking past when Max opened the door. He probably knew I was staying here and thought it would be me opening the door. So the poor chap would have been very disappointed to get Max. Except that wouldn't explain why he's given it to the *News of the World*. That is a mystery. I mean, who on earth would be interested in a photo of Max and Lindy?'

I could hear the murmur of Wendy going into a long explanation. Natalie had the phone under her neck and was absorbed in the task of applying her toenail varnish again, until she said, 'They're insinuating what? That they're having an affair?'

That was it. I was going to faint. I didn't dare look at Max. Perhaps I could just throw the phone out the window. Or myself out the window.

'Well, that's just ridiculous . . . Why? Just trust me, it is. It's completely ridiculous. I know Lindy and I know Max and that is never going to happen . . . They want a statement? OK. Here's my statement. Let them print their stupid photo and they'll hear from my lawyers . . . No, I know I haven't, but I could get some lawyers, couldn't I? . . . Honestly, the whole thing's just insane. Lindy's standing here right now. You can ask her if you don't believe me. Ask Max. Lindy is *so* not your type, isn't that right, darling?'

'Well, you know what they say,' he purred. 'Why go out for hamburger when you can have steak at home?'

I think if I'd had a gun at that moment I would have shot them both.

twenty-five

I slunk out of the hotel, crimson with shame, hoping never to see Natalie or Max again as long as I lived.

'God, you've been gone ages,' said Andrew when I finally staggered home. 'Your gums must have got a good polishing.'

'What!' I squeaked in panic. 'I don't know what you're talking about.' How had he found out? I would deny everything. He had no proof.

'At the dental hygienist. Give us a look, then.'

I bared my teeth desperately, thinking they were still the same old off-white gnashers I'd left the house with that morning.

'Ooh, very sparkly,' said Andrew, and I thanked the Lord yet again for unobservant men.

'I went shopping,' I lied, realising that it was now five o'clock and I had been out for eight hours.

'What did you buy? Anything nice?'

'No, I just tried on some things. I saw something I liked but they'd sold out. And I looked at some make-up.'

'That's nice.' Andrew wasn't listening.

I tossed and turned all night and at seven a.m. I couldn't stand it any longer. I got up and got dressed in my tracksuit and trainers quietly so as not to wake Andrew.

'What time is it?' he mumbled from under the covers.

'I'm going out for a run,' I whispered. 'Won't be long.' Then I ran downstairs, and jumped into the car. The roads were deserted and I got to Euston Station in fifteen minutes. I left the car on a double yellow line and raced over to the newsstand. I grabbed a copy of the *News of the World* and started flicking through the pages, scanning for that picture of me and Max. I checked twice. Nothing. It wasn't there. I was home free. Their big scandal that week was about a footballer's girlfriend who their investigative reporters had uncovered – in every sense of the word – as a secret lap dancer. The *News of the World* were apparently shocked by this. In fact, it outraged their sense of decency so much that they'd printed five very large photos of Candy in action.

That had to be better than a picture of a middle-aged man in his boxer shorts.

Thank you, Candy, and all lap-dancers everywhere.

'You going to buy that paper, love?'

'Oh, yes, sorry,' I took out my purse. 'And the *Sunday Times*, please.' Panic over, I could go back to bed, read the papers. Get some croissants, squeeze some oranges. It would be just like a building-society commercial. As I was handing over my money, the front page of the *Sunday Mirror* caught my eye. In the bottom corner there was a photo of a cute bald guy wearing a clingy white muscle T-shirt and tiny white hotpants with a heart shape cut out of the back to reveal his tight little arse. He reminded me of somebody. And the headline said: *Pages 4 and 5 – The Bare Facts About Why* Don't Call Us *Star Hung Up On Her Hubby*.

I looked at the guy's face again. I tried to ignore the shaved head . . . put my finger over the moustache . . .

Oh, my God – Richard!

I flung over another pound coin for the *Sunday Mirror* and didn't wait for change. I ran back to the car and started flicking through to find the story but immediately cars started hooting at me to get out of the way. So I had to drive on, trying to read the story out of the corner of my eye at the same time. Not dangerous at all.

In Regent's Park I pulled over and started reading.

It was all there. There was a copy of Richard and Natalie's

wedding certificate. Their wedding photo. And pictures of Richard and his partner Gregory – a much older, rather fat, lemon-lipped man.

All the quotes were from Gregory. How happy Richard had been since he had found his true soul mate in Gregory. Natalie and Richard's marriage was a sham, he said. Richard never came to terms with his sexuality. He never had the courage to admit he was gay until he met Gregory. The photo on the front had been taken last Thanksgiving at The White Party on South Beach in Miami.

And there was another photo too. A small one, but one I recognised. Richard must have been seventeen when it was taken. Aah, he looked so cute. He was at a party, dancing with his arm around a girl in a strappy pink top who looked very shiny and drunk and deliriously happy. Gosh. Had I really been that skinny?

According to Gregory, 'Richard never loved Natalie but she was the sort of girl he thought he should be seen with. He thought that getting married to such a beautiful girl might somehow "cure" him because he thought homosexuality was a disease. I blame his parents for that, especially his father.

'Richard said that Natalie was too vain and obsessed with herself to notice the pain he was going through, even though she must have known their relationship and their marriage wasn't working. Their sex life was non-existent. She used to beg him to make love to her and that was what finally convinced him he must be gay. If he wasn't even slightly aroused by a woman who he knew that other men found very desirable then that was proof he must be homosexual.

'He was finally able to admit it to Natalie and to himself, but he never found the courage to come out to his parents or his family.

'But Richard did tell me that he thought he had been in love with a girl once. She was his first girlfriend and they went out for almost two years. They had been at school together and her name was Lindy. She was Natalie's best friend and it was

Natalie who split them up when she deliberately seduced Richard. When Natalie saw something she wanted she wasn't afraid to go after it, no matter who got hurt.'

Well. I didn't know whether to laugh or cry. I read every word of the article over and over again until my hands were black from the newsprint. Natalie would go ballistic when she saw this. And what about Richard's parents? Maybe I should write to them. No. Somehow I got the feeling they might think the whole thing was all my fault.

I didn't have the heart to get croissants after that. I'd lost my appetite. Back home, Andrew was still in bed. It was just gone eight o'clock.

'Good run?' he mumbled.

'Not bad.' I made myself a coffee and sat in the kitchen pretending to read the *Sunday Times*. Every time I turned the page I half expected to find another story about myself. A picture of a man in shorts made me jump but it was just an ad for a Nordic Track exercise machine.

I knew it would only be a matter of time before I heard from Natalie.

Just an hour as it turned out. She rang from the airport.

'Have you seen it!' she shrieked, without even saying hello.

'Yes, I've just been out to get the papers. It's terrible.'

'The fucking hotel was besieged. They've followed me all the way to Heathrow. I expect they'll be waiting for me when I get to Palma. I've already phoned Mummy and told her not to open the door to anyone. God. What was he thinking of? The nerve of that bastard. I'm going to kill him. The photo he gave them of me is just horrible. My cheeks look so fat! I've been offered obscene amounts of money for an interview but they can all go to hell. Fucking vultures. I want you to do it.'

'Me?'

'Well, you said that magazine wanted an interview, didn't you? Let's face it, you're the only person in all of this I can trust to get the facts straight. Wendy says if I do one interview the other papers will back off and leave me alone.'

'But I can't,' I protested.

'Why not?' Natalie demanded.

Because after what happened I'm too embarrassed to ever face you or Max again, that's why not, I wanted to say. Because he called me a hamburger, that's why not. But what I actually said was, 'Because I'm not a journalist.'

'I know, thank God. So you'll write exactly what I tell you and not make stuff up, won't you?'

'Yes, I guess so.' How could I possibly get out of this? 'I'm not sure if my passport is up to date.'

'Oh, don't be so wet. You've just come back from Italy. We're going to be in Mallorca for a week. I'll tell Wendy to sort you out a flight in the next couple of days and you can stay at Mummy and Thomas's place with us.'

'OK.'

'Oh, that bastard. I swear I'll swing for him.'

'Who was that on the phone?' shouted Andrew.

'Just Natalie,' I shouted back. 'She wants me to go stay with her in Mallorca for a couple of days.'

'You're kidding! That's so great that you two are friends again.'

'Yes, isn't it wonderful.'

'Can I come too?'

'*No!* I mean – no. There's no room.'

'Oh, you're no fun.'

Wendy called a couple of hours later. She'd booked me on a BA flight the day after tomorrow coming back on Wednesday. Would that be long enough? She gave me the address of Natalie's mum's villa in Alcudia on the north of the island. I wrote it down but I wasn't really listening. All I could think about was the fact that I was going to have to sleep under the same roof as Max.

'The weather today in Palma is a cloudy seventy-four degrees.

But we expect it to brighten up later on this afternoon and we can look forward to more sunshine in the next couple of days. We hope you'll have a pleasant stay in Mallorca and that you've enjoyed flying with us today. On behalf of Captain Stuart and all his crew, we look forward to welcoming you on board again.'

The walk from the plane to the baggage carousel took almost as long as the flight, or was that just butterflies? Why, when I jumped into the taxi and handed the driver the piece of paper with Natalie's mum's address on it, did I feel like a lamb taking myself off to slaughter? Half of me couldn't wait to get there and the other half was so nervous about seeing Max again I wanted the drive to go on forever.

The villa was a couple of streets back from the beach itself with a view out over the bay. Any minute now I'm going to see Max. Any minute now. The door opened and Natalie's mum came down the step to greet me.

I recognised her at once as a slightly lived-in version of her chic younger self. The old girl was holding up pretty well, in fawn jeans, loafers and a cream blouse which displayed her considerable and only slightly leathery cleavage. Great legs, too. Her hair was still determinedly blonde and pushed back from her head by Gucci sunglasses. There was not a single line in her forehead and when she spoke you could practically hear the ice clinking in the bottom of a whisky glass.

'Hello, darling,' she said, giving me a kiss. 'Oh, you look wonderful. Look at your skin – it's all cleared up.'

'I should hope so,' I said. 'It's been over ten years.'

'Really? As long as that? Oh!' she moaned theatrically. 'You make me feel positively ancient!'

'It's a beautiful place you've got here,' I said, looking around for any other signs of life.

'Max and Natalie have gone out for a walk. They should be back soon. I'll show you your room. Do you need to use the facilities?'

'I'm sorry?'

'The loo?'

'No, I'm fine, thanks, Mrs Brown. I went on the plane.' Suddenly I was fourteen again, sleeping over at Natalie's house.

'Oh, God, you don't have to call me Mrs Brown. I haven't been Mrs Brown in a hundred years. I'm Mrs Mütter now and I was Mrs De Saumarez for a while before that, but you can call me Dawn.' She led the way down a corridor of white-painted walls and dark-oak woodwork. 'This is your room in here. Let me know if you need extra blankets, it can get very cold here in the evenings. Not like England, though. I don't understand why anybody still bothers to live there, quite honestly. Your bathroom's just across the hall. The pool's out there. It's heated all year round. Thomas and I are at the end so hopefully you won't be kept awake by his snoring, and Max and Natalie are next door. I put them in there because it's got the four poster.'

'What does your husband do?' I asked, to get her off the subject of Max and Natalie's sleeping arrangements.

'Oh, he owns things,' she said crossly, as though this were a particularly nasty hobby on a par with badger baiting. 'Property. Bloody Germans. They've taken over this island. I must have been out of my mind to marry one, but there you go. Would you like a café con leche? We can sit out on the terrace.'

The sun was starting to burn away the clouds and glistening off the turquoise ocean down below. I arranged myself as gracefully as I could on a teak steamer chair and watched the white sails bobbing about on the horizon. Deep breaths. Inhale and exhale. You're going to be fine. As long as the sun keeps shining you're going to be fine.

'So, you're going to interview Natalie?' said Dawn, putting a cup in front of me. 'Is that what you do now?'

'No. I'm a photographer.'

'Really? Fancy that! Actually, now you come to mention it, I remember you used to like taking photos, didn't you? I must show you my book from my modelling days. You'd find it very interesting.'

'Yes, I'd love to see it.'

'I modelled for Dior, you know. Mary Quant. I still do a bit now and then for various people. Just for a giggle, I'm past all that really, but it's nice to keep your hand in. To know you've still got it.'

'Mm. Lovely coffee.'

'Did you see the article in the paper about Richard?'

'Yes, I did.'

'Wasn't that shocking? Poor Natalie's beside herself. Luckily, none of the press have managed to track her down here. She was very clever. She checked into a hotel in Palma and they think she's still there. None of them have got the brains to work out she's staying with her poor mother.'

'That's good.'

'Of course, I always knew he was queer.'

I almost spat out my coffee. 'Really?'

'Oh, yes. Well, the modelling racket was full of his type. I could smell it a mile off.'

'I never suspected a thing,' I said.

'Oh, did you know him too?' Natalie's mum had conveniently forgotten the fact that her darling daughter had swiped him off me. 'Well, you were too young, probably. I told her it would all end in tears but she wouldn't listen. Just went ahead and married him anyway. She was determined to get that Green Card.'

'Hang on, do you mean she knew before she married him that he was gay?'

'Oh, God, yes. Of course. She's not completely stupid. She worked that out after about six months. I mean, a teenage boy doesn't refuse to sleep with a beautiful girl like Natalie unless there's something seriously wrong with him, does he?'

'No, I suppose not.'

'But they were still friends. Natalie liked having a gay male friend, she thought that was very trendy, especially such a nice-looking boy as Richard. And he hadn't come out to his family so Natalie was his way of proving to them he was normal. I bet his family still don't know he's gay. He's such a coward. And then when Natalie found out he had a job in California, she proposed to him and that was that. Would you like some more coffee?'

'Natalie proposed to him?'

'Yes. Didn't you know? I told you, she was desperate for that Green Card and it was no skin off Richard's nose, now, was it?'

I was shocked. Natalie had fed me a pack of lies. No wonder she didn't want the press knowing he was gay. It made her look like a fool, or a scheming, ambitious minx. Or both.

'And in a way, I think Natalie always half hoped she might change him,' her mum went on. 'That eventually he just wouldn't be able to resist her. He was quite a challenge for her. A complete waste of time, of course.'

I was hardly listening because inside I was fuming. All I could think about was how Natalie lied to me. All that rubbish about having an AIDS test. She'd just made it up to make me feel sorry for her. She'd even made me apologise to her!

'It's funny,' Dawn was saying, 'but it seems like every one of us has to go through life learning the same lessons as everyone else. I was the same when I got married the first time, to Natalie's father. My mother told me she wouldn't trust him a far as the end of the road but I was in love and thought I knew it all. So I had to learn the hard way as well. He cleared off before Natalie was even born. Came back afterwards for a few months pretending he was very sorry and saying he'd turned over a new leaf and all the rest of it and muggins here was only too happy to believe every word of it. Until he emptied my bank account and disappeared for good.'

'That must have been so hard for you,' I said, 'being left on your own like that.'

'Oh, well, you know,' she said, dusting imaginary crumbs from her tightly encased thighs. 'I wasn't on my own for long. There were lots more men where he came from. And most of them not worth the paper they were printed on, either. I think we should all get a rule book when we're born to save us all making the same silly mistakes on our own – don't you?'

'Like what?'

'Like, don't think you can change a man. Don't believe every man who says he loves you. Don't expect marriage to last forever. Any relationship you have to work at probably isn't worth the effort in the first place. Don't pluck your eyebrows because they'll never grow back. That sort of thing. But we all learn these things eventually, don't we? I mean, look at you – you've got a decent husband from what Natalie tells me.'

'And you've got Thomas,' I agreed.

'Yes, I've got Thomas,' she said, making it sound like she hoped science would soon discover a cure for this unpleasant affliction. 'And as for Natalie, well, I couldn't ask for a better son-in-law than lovely Maxie, could I?'

'No,' I said. 'He's a poppet all right.'

'Hey, you two!' I heard Max's drawl from inside and my heart lurched.

'Well, speak of the devil,' she smiled and sat up, automatically smoothing her hair.

He came out onto the terrace as if he didn't have a care in the world. 'Look at you two girls sunning yourselves!' he beamed approvingly. But he stood in the doorway and kept his distance.

'Hello, Max,' I said, hoping I sounded casual.

'Oh good, you're here.' Natalie was right behind him, incognito in Burberry headscarf, massive sunglasses, white jeans and a camisole top. She looked exactly like a TV star who doesn't want to be spotted. 'You have no idea what hell it's been. There were photographers all over the airport. I had to be bundled out through some side door, and then I pretended to check into a hotel in Palma – well actually, we did check in, we're still paying for the room – and then we had to sneak out here. I don't know if I can stand it.'

'Have you spoken to Richard?' I asked. 'Do you know why he did it?'

'Oh, it wasn't Richard. Richard would never have done anything like that. It was that shit Gregory. I rang the last number I had for them and actually spoke to him – Gregory, I mean. Richard isn't there any more. They've split up. That's why Gregory sold his story. Out of spite. The bitter old queen. He sold all the pictures to the *National Enquirer* and then the papers over here have picked it up. You know what he said? I can't believe it. He said, "Listen, sweetheart. Richard's not yours. He never was yours." As if I was actually jealous of him! I should have said, "Yeah, well, he's not yours either any more, is he, you big fat poof?" That's what I should have said. Why didn't I say that at the time?'

'Because you were upset,' cooed her mother, patting her hand.

'I can't believe he had the nerve to call me sweetheart. Who the fuck does he think he is to call *me* sweetheart? And he had that stupid lisp. You know? Uurgh!' She shivered. 'Well, I'm just not going to think about him any more,' she went on. 'I'm going to put him right out of my head – end of story.' She sat down on a sun lounger, stretched out in a yoga pose and closed her eyes. 'He is gone. Completely forgotten. Finito! Bastard!' After a second she opened her eyes again. 'Sweetie,' she pleaded in a little-girl voice to Max. 'Could you get me a glass of mineral water?'

'Sure, baby.'

'Not fizzy. And just one ice cube.'

'Sure, baby.'

She closed her eyes again.

'Oh, and Maxie?' said her mum.

'Yes, Dawn?'

'Bring a glass for Mother, too.' Natalie's mum reached up

and rested a perfectly manicured finger on Max's bare arm and smiled up at him for just a second longer than was absolutely necessary.

'Sure, Dawn.'

Dawn put her hands behind her head and closed her eyes with a satisfied smile, thrusting her bosoms to the sky.

Oh, great.

twenty-six

'So, how do we do this interview?'

'I don't know. You're the reporter.'

'No, I'm not. I told you I'm not.'

'Just turn on your tape recorder and ask me questions.'

'What about?'

'Oh, this is hopeless. I'll do it myself.'

We were sitting on the terrace while Dawn and Max prepared dinner. Natalie turned on the tape recorder I'd bought in duty free. It was just like the one Debbie at *The Ledger* used.

'I'll start by telling how I met Richard. OK?'

'OK.' I was trying to keep an eye on the kitchen window to see what Dawn and Max were up to. How close were they standing? What had he said to make her laugh like that?

'Richard and I were at school together,' Natalie began, her hands clasped in her lap as though she were reciting a bedtime story. 'Ever since the first time we saw each other, we had always had a secret attraction for each other. Little smiles when we passed in the corridor. Secret looks across the classroom—'

'Hey, hang on,' I interrupted. 'Since when? I never knew any of this.'

'Look. This is my story. OK? But,' she continued, 'Richard was going out with my dearest friend, Lindy – that's you – and so I knew that we could never be together. He used to wait for me after school in secret and ask me to go out with him but I told him it was out of the question. I would never dream of hurting Lindy like that. Our friendship was far too important to me.'

'But—'

'Lindy and Richard went out for a few months—'

'Almost two years!'

'A year,' she said firmly. 'And then one day they had a terrible fight. An awful fight. He had said some things about her that were so cruel she couldn't forgive him. Lindy came to me in tears and told me she'd broken up with Richard forever. She never wanted to see him again. I told her she should make it up with Richard, that what they had together was too good to just throw away, but Lindy had made up her mind. She said she hated him and it was completely over.'

There was absolutely nothing I could do. If I tried to protest, I knew I'd just be wasting my breath. Natalie had agreed to give an interview and this was the interview she was going to give, take it or leave it. She had one set of lies for me, one for herself and another for the rest of the world.

If I wanted to work for *The Hoop* – and I did – I was going to have to sit here and listen while Natalie stole Richard from me all over again. Maybe Jeremy Paxman would have got the truth out of her but Jeremy Paxman hadn't snogged her fiancé. Who was I to start insisting on honesty? I just sat there and listened and kept my guilty mouth shut, thinking it would serve her damn well right if I stole Max from under her perfect little nose.

'So anyway, a few months passed. Richard still kept pestering me to go out with him but I thought it would be too painful for Lindy and I always said no. Eventually, I think it was six months after they had broken up, Lindy started seeing another boy and I decided to tell her that Richard had asked me out. I had to admit that I was beginning to have feelings for him too. Lindy assured me that she had no objection to me going out with Richard and that I had her blessing because she was blissfully happy with her new love.

'I waited ten months before sleeping with Richard. I must

have put the poor boy through agony! Of course, I was a virgin when we first met so I wanted to make sure he was the right one. Every day Richard told me how much he loved me and I always knew he meant it. He was a very passionate and considerate lover. Because he was my first and I had no way of comparing, I never realised that he wasn't very well endowed – there, that'll show the bastard – but apart from that, we had a fantastic, absolutely normal sex life. It was only natural as far as I was concerned that we get married.'

I was only half listening to this barrage of lies she'd concocted out of thin air because I was still checking out the kitchen and Dawn seemed to have disappeared. Where had she gone? Max was in there on his own. 'Excuse me a second, Natalie, I'm just going to get a drink. Can I get you anything?'

'Still mineral water, one ice cube.'

'You just carry on while I'm gone.'

'Of course Lindy came to our wedding,' I heard her say as I headed inside. 'I seem to remember that she gave us a toaster.'

Whatever.

'Hey, Red,' Max sounded nervous. 'How's the interview going?'

'Oh fine. What are you making for dinner? Steak or hamburger?' Gosh – had I really said that out loud? I thought I was just thinking it.

'Hey. I'm sorry.' His voice dropped. It was soft and husky. 'You know I didn't mean that.'

'Do I?' I hoped my voice wasn't shaking.

'I had to say something, didn't I?' he whispered. 'I had to tell Natalie what she wanted to hear. I couldn't tell her the truth, could I?' He reached out and stroked my arm.

'And what would that be?' My heart was pounding.

'That I can't stop thinking about you.'

'What are you two cooking up?' Dawn came slinking loudly back into the kitchen.

'I'm just getting a glass of water for Natalie, Mrs B,' I said cheerily. 'It's getting rather hot out there.'

284

Natalie was in full flow. 'Richard and I desperately wanted children, of course. He would have made an excellent father. When we moved to California, one of the first things he did in our new house was to paint the room he called the nursery. We were just like any other happy young couple starting out.

'As far as I'm concerned, Richard is not gay. He is bisexual. No man could make love to me the way he did if he was not attracted to women. What do you think?' she concluded. 'Does that sound plausible to you?'

'Absolutely,' I said. 'I'm quite impressed.'

'Thank you.'

Let her have Richard, I thought. Let her have won him from me nobly and honourably. Let her have their blissful marriage. What difference did it make? It wasn't Richard I cared about now.

'Tell me about Max,' I prompted her. 'How did you two meet?'

'I've told you that story already,' she said.

'I know,' I said. 'But tell me again. For our readers.'

At dinner I made a point of not making eye-contact with Max.

Thomas was sitting at one end of the table, Dawn at the other, with Max in between Natalie and Dawn. I sat opposite Natalie and tried to avoid looking down Max's end of the table at all. You think I can't play it cool? Just watch this. Instead I studied the gigantic black and white framed photograph of Natalie's mum that dominated the end wall. She was wearing a leather mini dress and climbing out of the back seat of an MG with one endless leg perched on the back seat and the other slung over the car door with her toes resting on the ground. She was totally ignoring the man with the silk cravat who looked a bit like Imran Khan sitting in the driver's seat. And she had somehow managed to lean in towards the camera at the same time with a wide-eyed, slightly open-mouthed blank expression that seemed to say 'I'm completely in control. I'm beautiful and powerful. But come and save me anyway.' I don't know how she did it. The weight of the eyelashes alone would have made me topple over.

'You should stay for a week and enjoy the island,' Thomas told me. 'We have plenty of room. It is stupid to come for just one night.' Thomas was a very large, bald man wearing trousers the colour of Bird's custard, black leather slip-on shoes and a navy blue Lacoste polo shirt. I could only conclude that whatever it was he owned, he must own an awful lot of it for Natalie's mum to have married him.

'She has to fly back tomorrow, Thomas, it's all booked,' said Natalie.

'That's a pity,' said Dawn. 'We'd love to have you. And there's plenty of room. Maxie, could you be an angel and pass me the salad?'

'No, really. I have to get back to work,' I smiled.

'Yes, she has to write my interview so those other parasites will leave me alone,' said Natalie.

'You are very lucky to have a friend like this,' said Thomas.

'You know, Maxie, I think you've caught the sun already,' said Dawn.

'Oh, Mummy,' Natalie sighed. 'It's practically winter. There is no sun.'

'Well, let me see.' Dawn lifted up the sleeve of Max's white T-shirt to compare the colour of his skin. 'There, you see,' she said, giving it a gentle stroke. 'See how brown you are. Isn't Maxie looking brown, Thomas?'

'Yes, he is looking very well.'

After dinner Max announced he was going for a walk along the front and, before I could say a word, Dawn had jumped up to get her jacket.

'Anyone else?' said Max.

'Yes, I'll come,' said Natalie.

'What about you, Lindy?' said Max.

Hmm, let me see. A walk with Max and his future wife and

mother-in-law. No, thank you all the same, but I think I'll pass.

'No, I'm very tired. I think I'll just go to bed.' I faked a yawn.

'I will come,' said Thomas.

'No, Thomas,' said Dawn, sounding rather irritated. 'You have to stay here and keep Lindy company.' She made no pretence of even liking Thomas very much.

'No, really. I'm fine. I'm probably going to go straight to sleep.'

'Thomas, I wouldn't dream of you leaving a young girl alone in the house like that,' insisted Dawn.

'Mummy, this is Mallorca, not LA,' said Natalie.

'The Volkers had their Mercedes broken into just last week. It's not as safe as you think it is.'

'Oh, well, if you don't want me—' said Thomas, lifting his hands in a tired gestured of defeat.

'And use the phone if you like,' said Natalie to me.

I was confused. 'What for?' I asked.

'To phone Andrew. You haven't rung him since you arrived, he must be worried about you.'

'Yeah, of course.' I felt a guilty pang as I realised I'd quite forgotten that Andrew even existed.

'Hi, bunny. Why didn't you call me? I've been really worried about you,' said Andrew, just as Natalie had predicted.

'I'm sorry. I didn't get a chance. Natalie's stepfather has been waiting for an important business call.'

'How was your flight?'

'OK.'

'Are you coming home tomorrow?'

'Uh huh.'

'There's tons of messages for you on the answering machine.'

'Really? Who from?'

'I don't know, I think they're all from newspapers. Do you

want me to play them to you?' He put the phone by the answering machine and pressed play. Predictably, the very first call was from Debbie Gibb at *The Ledger*.

'Lindy! Hi, how are you?' She had her sympathetic, hospital-visiting voice on. 'I read about you and Natalie Brown in the paper and I thought it was so unfair that you didn't get a chance to tell your side of the story. *The Ledger* would love to give you the chance to put the record straight . . .'

Gosh, how very generous and sporting of *The Ledger*, I thought. What a fine bunch of humanitarians they are.

'. . . We'd pay £2,000 and if you've got any photos of Natalie from when you were at school together, I could bump that up a bit more. Anyway, I hope you're well.' She left her work number, her home number, her mobile number and her pager number. I didn't write any of them down. The rest of the calls were all the same old story. Every tabloid, women's magazine and TV talk show wanted my story and were all dangling different amounts of cash as bait. There was an invitation for a makeover and the promise of an overnight stay in one of Liverpool's finest hotels. One paper promised to pay me £5,000 and then there was a girl who sounded about eleven from a tatty TV listings magazine offering a measly £150. Even she didn't sound very optimistic. Several people I'd never heard of calling themselves agents were kindly offering to represent me and get me the best price for my story.

Then there was another call from Debbie offering £2,500 and then a call from Elaine, the editor herself, casually inviting me out to lunch, not mentioning the story at all and saying, 'It's ages since we had a chat.' Yeah, like never.

And then there was a call from Geoff saying he'd done a bit of detective work and the *News of the World* had got the photos I'd asked him about. Well done, Geoff, I thought. Only three days late.

'What photos are these?' said Andrew.

'Just more Natalie stuff,' I said hurriedly.

'So what are you going to do about all these calls?' said Andrew.

'I'm not going to do anything,' I said. 'If I just ignore them they'll all go away.'

'But they're just giving you the chance to tell your side of the story,' said Andrew. 'You could do it in *The Ledger*. You know them. They're like family, aren't they?'

'What are you – nuts?'

'Well, it seems like a lot of money.'

'Andrew, do you know anything about magnets?'

'Magnets? You mean, the fridge magnets? I never touched them. Why?'

'Oh – it doesn't matter.'

I sat out on the terrace with Thomas, watching him smoke an enormous cigar.

'I am not allowed to smoke these in the house,' he told me. 'My own house! And she tells me what I can't do.'

'Do you like living in Spain?'

'Oh, ya. The weather is good. The money is good. The sea is very beautiful. It is a good life.' But his voice sounded dejected as he puffed away in the dark in silence. How sad it must be to be married to a woman who couldn't stand the sight of you.

I went to bed, but I was wide awake.

Is it really possible for a couple of kisses to turn your whole world upside down? A couple of kisses and everything I thought I knew about relationships turned out to be wrong.

I'd thought I wanted to be married. Wasn't that what dating had been all about? A painful and messy exercise you had to go through to find the person you wanted to spend the rest of your life with? But maybe I'd missed the whole point. Maybe falling headlong in love with unsuitable people was actually the good bit. Whoever thought that I'd miss the excitement and anticipation that came with being single? When anything was still, theoretically, possible.

The uncertainty, the churning hormones, the helpless lust I felt for Max; the feeling of falling in love was in every way more exhilarating than being in love – that day-to-day state of contented coupledom that I thought I'd wanted.

When I married Andrew I really believed we could be happy ever after. But now, a couple of kisses from Max was all it took to make me realise that just being happy wasn't enough.

It was like skiing – you could spend your whole life cruising along on the easy greens and blues, or you could take the plunge and chuck yourself down a black run that scared you witless and made your heart soar with the giddy thrill of being alive.

Falling in love was an extreme sport. Maybe I'd got out of the game too early. But there was still time to get off the bench and back into the action.

About an hour later, I heard them come back home. Voices, laughter, glasses clinking. The fridge door opening and closing. Footsteps down the corridor. The bathroom door opening. A toilet flushing. More footsteps. Calls of goodnight. Then floorboards squeaking and a soft tap on my door. I'd left the light on and the door ajar just in case. Hoping against hope.

'Are you decent?'

I leapt up in bed, arranging the straps of my brand-new amethyst nightie on my shoulders. I'd got it on the way to Heathrow from La Perla and my Access card was still in shock. I wondered if they'd let me return it when I got back from Mallorca.

'Come in!'

Max's head appeared around the door with an unmistakable gleam in his eye. I couldn't believe that he'd take such a blatant risk – it was crazy – but I was so happy he had. I didn't say anything, just patted the sheets invitingly as he walked into my bedroom, with Natalie right behind him.

'God. I'm knackered,' she moaned, flopping down on the

bed beside me. 'I thought Mummy was going to walk all the way around the island.'

Max was standing behind her, just staring at the outline of my breasts through my nightdress, not saying a word. I tugged the sheet up around my neck self-consciously. It was like having an X-ray.

'What time's your plane tomorrow?' said Natalie.

'Ten, eleven – something like that.' My mind had gone blank.

'See you in the morning then.' She leaned over and kissed me on the cheek. 'Sleep tight.'

'Night,' said Max. I wondered if he was going to kiss me good night, but he didn't come any closer. He just stood there, gawping at my nightie.

'You should really take your make-up off before you go to sleep, you know,' said Natalie.

'Yeah. I know. I will.'

And the door closed behind them.

Oh, God. I sat there for ages, stroking the wall between us as I listened to Max and Natalie getting ready for bed. Then I heard Max's bedroom door open and footsteps coming down the corridor. The bathroom door opening and the sound of a tap running. Teeth cleaning. I hopped out of bed and crept into the corridor in my nightie, scratching lightly on the bathroom door before going in.

'Oh, sorry, Natalie,' I gulped, holding up my cleanser and cotton wool in explanation. 'I didn't know there was anyone in here.'

Natalie turned to face me with a string of dental floss between her fingers and I slunk back to my room.

Come and visit us in LA, Natalie had said. It was so simple. I'd pick a time when I knew Andrew couldn't get time off work and just turn up on my own. He wouldn't suspect a thing. I'd just be visiting my best friend and what could be more ordinary and respectable than that?

I could stay married to Andrew and just have an affair with Max. No one need ever know. I didn't want to break up his relationship. I didn't want to steal Max from Natalie – I just wanted to borrow him for a while. That was all. I didn't want to marry him. I was already married and, as I'd already proved beyond a shadow of a doubt, I was pretty crap at being married.

It might be months before I saw him again, but I'd learn to be patient. I could wait somehow. I closed my eyes and imagined myself stepping off the plane at LAX and into Max's waiting arms.

I heard a bedroom door open again and footsteps pause in the corridor before going into the bathroom. I waited, listening as the taps were turned on and the water gushed noisily into the bath tub. I picked up my bottle of cleanser again and my cotton wool balls and tip-toed into the corridor in my bare feet, being careful not to make a sound.

As I crept inside the bathroom, Max silently pushed the door closed behind me and without saying a word, he pushed me up against the tiled wall and pressed his hot mouth against mine. He was just wearing a white T-shirt and boxer shorts and his glasses were resting on the bathroom cabinet. He looked more like Kevin Costner than ever. His hands were up underneath my nightdress at once, his palms polishing my stomach as they slid upwards, not wasting a moment as he encircled a breast in each hand, kneading my nipples with his thumbs with a kind of feverish desperation.

'I love this nightgown,' he whispered in my ear. 'However much it cost you, it was worth it.'

I was terrified someone would walk in and find us. The door wasn't even locked. But I was more terrified that he would stop. His tongue was swollen inside my mouth as he reached down and thrust his right hand roughly inside my knickers and he moaned so quietly, I could only hear it like an echo inside my own head. 'Oh so wet, so wet,' he whispered. It was like we had a telepathic link. It didn't matter about any of the other women he'd had in his life, I realised. I was the only one who really understood him. Our souls were in love.

I tugged at his boxers and he stepped out of them without taking his lips off mine for so much as a second. I could feel him hard against me but the bath was overflowing and my feet were already getting damp. Anyone could come in and find us at any moment, but Max didn't seem to care. He was loving the danger.

And then he was lifting me up onto the vanity unit and tearing off my knickers with his teeth. I wanted to cry out but couldn't make a sound, and then he was kissing me again. Both his hands were kneading my breasts and then he was thrusting inside me, pushing me harder and harder up against the wall and still I was too afraid to make a sound. And, with his other hand, Max was pulling my hips into him harder and harder and the water was still pouring out – it was up to our necks now and I heard Max say we would have to learn to breathe underwater and – hang on a minute – with his other hand? What other hand?

I opened my eyes and Max had turned into Kevin Costner and, as I kissed his neck, I noticed he'd grown gills like in *Waterworld*. He was saying it was up to us to repopulate the earth and – oh, bugger!

I opened my eyes again and looked around my bedroom. It was already morning.

'Darling, I can't come with you to the airport,' said Natalie. She was sitting cross-legged in a wicker chair with her hair in a turban and sipping green tea. 'I dare not step out of the house. You understand.' She patted my arm. 'And Thomas is taking us out on his boat today. It's such a shame you can't come with us. I wish you didn't have to fly back to London.'

Considering that she was the one who'd told Wendy to book my tickets, I took this with a pinch of salt.

'Oh, well,' I said. 'Maybe another time. The next time I see you it will probably be in LA.'

'Yes, you must come out. It would be so lovely to have a chum.'

I was all packed. The taxi was coming in fifteen minutes. Just time to have a cup of coffee and say my goodbyes. I kissed them all in turn: Thomas, who held his arms out stiffly as he gripped mine; Dawn, who brushed my cheek with hers and smelled of Jean Paul Gaultier at nine a.m. in her immaculate ivory satin housecoat; Natalie, who clung to me theatrically and made me promise to phone her the moment I'd finished writing the interview so I could read it to her over the phone and she could check every word.

And then Max, who I saved till last so that it would look like I was only kissing him because I'd kissed everybody else and it would be rude not to. Gorgeous Max, who planted a chaste dry kiss on both my cheeks and secretly stroked the inside of my wrist with his finger right there in the kitchen in front of everybody, knowing it would throw me into blushing confusion and knowing he would not be caught.

'Bye, Max,' I said. 'See you in LA.'

I wondered if I should tell him about my dream. Maybe one day. I picked up my overnight bag and walked straight to the door before I said or did anything that was likely to get me into trouble.

I didn't look back, but already I was counting the days until it saw him again.

I phoned Atlanta the moment I got home and told her I had an exclusive interview with Natalie and pictures to go with it. Was she interested?

'Are you winding me up?' she said. 'The whole world's after that interview. Of course I want it. How did you get it?'

There was something about the way she said 'you' – implying that there was a very long list of people who might conceivably have obtained an interview with the fabulous

Natalie Brown, but my name wasn't on it – that really put my back up. I'd had just about enough of Atlanta sodding Parrish, I decided.

'Jesus Christ, Atlanta,' I snapped. 'Don't you read the papers? Didn't you see my photo in the *Sunday Mirror*? Don't you know who I am? I'm the only woman her first husband ever loved, that's who I am.' And her second husband-to-be is pretty fond of me as well, I nearly added. 'I can sell this interview to practically any magazine or newspaper in the English-speaking world for a lot more money than you would ever be able to pay,' I told her. 'But I'm offering it to you because I came to you with the idea first which is pretty damn generous of me, don't you think? So stop being so bloody condescending and tell me how much you're going to pay me.'

This was the way to deal with Atlanta Parrish I decided.

'I'll have to speak to the editor and call you back,' she said meekly.

'Fine,' I said. 'Do that. And you're not to change a single word. I want that in the contract.' I hung up and wondered what other demands I could make. Perhaps I could get her to come round and do my ironing for me. I was going to enjoy being bossy.

I must say it was a very laborious job typing out the interview. I'm not sure I'd want to be a journalist. The nice thing about being a photographer is that you take your photos, drop them in at the lab and then you pick them up when they're done. Job over. Three days later I was still tapping out Natalie's bogus life story, word by imaginary word. My fingers ached and my jaw hurt from grinding my teeth in fury as each outrageous lie about her and Richard appeared on my computer screen.

On Sunday, Jill rang to tell me I was famous again and sent me scurrying down to the corner shop to buy a copy of the *News of the World*.

Thanks to Wendy's assurances that Natalie knew all about their silly little photograph of me and Max, they'd managed to work out that the girl in the photo was the same best friend from the *Sunday Mirror* story about Richard and they ran it on page eleven under the heading *No Hard Feelings*. 'This is the girl who had her heart broken by Natalie Brown more than ten years ago. Natalie married Lindy Usher's childhood sweetheart Richard Howarth, but last week the marriage was revealed to be a sham when his former lover outed him as a homosexual. But Natalie, who was recently in the UK shooting episodes for her TV series *Don't Call Us*, is still pals with Lindy. In fact the girls still share everything – including Natalie's soon-to-be husband Number 2, architect Max Ogilvy. Max and Lindy are seen here sharing a joke in his London hotel room.'

I suppose the way we were both staring open-mouthed at the photographer did sort of look like we were laughing.

'So. Is there anything you want to tell me?' said Jill.

'No,' I mumbled.

'Don't you want to explain to me why Max isn't wearing any trousers in this photo?'

'Not really.'

'You promised you weren't going to sleep with him.'

'I didn't sleep with him. Not exactly. I'll tell you all about it some time. I promise. But not right now.'

There was a much bigger photo beside it of Natalie looking stunning which had been taken on set and the caption said: 'It's easy to see what would make even a gay man prefer Natalie to Lindy.'

Those evil bastards. And the awful thing was that every single word was true. Natalie wouldn't even be able to sue them. And nor could I. And the even more awful thing – if that was possible – was that Nick would now have proof in black and white that Max wasn't my husband at all. Perhaps I should just take out a full page ad in the *Standard* saying

'Lindy Usher is a big fat liar'. I would absolutely die of humiliation if I ever saw him again.

It was over a week before I could ring Max. It almost killed me but I cheered myself up by imagining him missing me too. He'd be back in LA on Monday. I thought I'd play it cool and phone him on the Wednesday but Andrew came home early and I had to wait until Thursday which nearly drove me crazy.

Andrew was going to the launch of the new website Robin was working on. She'd obviously given in to Russell's nagging and left the BBC for cyberspace. I said I'd love to go – which was a lie – but couldn't because I was too busy – which was true. I was still working on Natalie's sodding article.

At six o'clock, I took out Max's business card and two of the photos I'd taken of him that day in Exmoor. The intent expression in Max's eyes as he looked straight through the camera at me made me quiver. I missed him so much. I kissed his picture and propped the photos on the cushion beside me while I dialled the number: o o 1 3 1 0 3 6 9 . . . Suddenly I realised my mistake and slammed the phone down in panic. The number would show up on our itemised phone bill! What on earth was I thinking? How was I going to explain that to Andrew? I waited until my heart had stopped racing and dialled the number again – on my mobile, this time.

'Good morning, Ogilvy Associates. How may I help you?'

I was caught completely off-guard. For some reason I hadn't been expecting a switchboard operator. I had expected Max to pick up the phone himself, which I now realised was totally ridiculous. He was the head of a major corporation, he didn't answer his own phone.

'Is Max Ogilvy there, please?' I tried to sound official.

'One moment, please.'

I heard a machine message click on. 'Your call is being answered by AUDIX. Marcia Coffman is not available. To leave a message wait for the tone. Record at the tone. Beep.'

Who the hell is Marcia Coffman? I hung up and dialled again.

'Good morning, Ogilvy Associates. How may I help you?'

'Yes, I rang just a moment ago to speak to Max Ogilvy and was put through to somebody called Marcia Coffman, but she's got her voicemail on. Is it possible to be put through to Ma— Mr Ogilvy directly?'

'Ms Coffman is Mr Ogilvy's personal assistant. I'll see if her secretary is available.'

The line rang again. 'Claire Mancinelli!'

'Oh, hi. Um. I was trying to get through to Marcia Coffman's secretary.'

'This is she.' Why do all Americans have that strange singsong voice on the phone? They don't talk like that in the movies.

'I'm actually trying to get hold of Max Ogilvy.'

'I'm not sure if he's in the office right now. Who may I say is calling?'

Oh bugger, what should I say? What if this Claire Mancinelli person knows Natalie and just happens to mention that a British woman named Lindy Usher called asking for Max? Would Max want people in the office knowing that I'd called?

'Hello, ma'am? Who may I say is calling?'

What if Claire Mancinelli was also in love with Max? Knowing Max, this wasn't beyond the realms of possibility. What should I say?

'Hello?'

'I'm so sorry,' I said. 'I'm calling from Hamley's in London.' That should do the trick. At least he'd take the call, even if he thought they were just calling to ask him if his niece liked her presents.

'I'll try his line for you.'

The line went dead for thirty seconds while I practised what I would say. Hi, Max, it's Lindy. Hi, it's me – Lindy. Hello, Max, can you guess who this is?

'I'm sorry, ma'am. He's not in his office at the moment. May I take a message?'

'No, that's OK. I'll try him later.' I hung up and tried his cell-phone number.

'Hi. This is Max Ogilvy. Please leave a message and I'll call you back.'

I chickened out of leaving a message; what if Natalie used his phone? But I dialled the number twice more just to listen to the sound of his voice. I picked up one of the photos and kissed it again, stroking his face with my finger.

Oh, Max, where are you?

If he was out of the office, why wasn't he on his cell phone? Maybe he was actually in the office, but hadn't wanted to take my call? I imagined him telling his assistant's secretary, 'Tell her I'm not in!' Or did he not realise it was me? Had he forgotten about Hamley's? Damn. He'd given me his number, so he must have wanted me to call.

I hid the photos and the business card and decided to try again in an hour.

Meanwhile I had even more of Natalie's interview on tape to transcribe: the childhood sob story about how she never knew her father and how brave her mother had been bringing her up all alone, and then, of course, there were pages and pages about Max. How he'd flown her to Paradise Island in the Bahamas as a surprise for the anniversary of the day they met and they didn't leave the hotel room for two days. Huh. I bet Max never forgot her birthday.

His photo was on the cushion beside me again as I picked up my mobile phone. This time I'd skip the office and try his cell phone straight away.

When I heard his voice say, 'Hello', I was shocked. I'd expected to get his message service again. I felt completely unprepared to speak to him. What if he didn't want to hear from me? What if he was in the middle of an important meeting?

'Hi, Max, it's Lindy. In London.'

'Oh, hi.' He didn't seem surprised or even particularly interested. That was odd.

'How are you?' I asked.

Then suddenly his whole tone changed to great excitement. '*Oh hi*! I'm so sorry! I just realised who this is!'

'Why? How many Lindies in London do you know?' I asked, a little put out that he hadn't recognised my name straight away.

'I don't know, I didn't hear what you said properly. I thought you were a haulage company.'

I laughed. 'Well, thanks, that's just about the nicest thing anyone's said to me all day!'

'It's so great to hear from you. How are you?'

'I'm good. I'm fine. Can you talk? Are you at work?'

'No, I'm eating a Danish and drinking a coffee in a restaurant around the corner from the office. Your timing is fantastic! I'm just heading back to the office now for a meeting. In fact, I'm running late.'

'Oh. Shall I call back later?' I was so prepared to back off and not bother him that I was ready to hang up immediately.

'No, no, no! Just let me pay the bill and then I can talk to you as I drive back to the office.'

I hung on and listened to the LA café buzz around him. It sounded sunny, which was pure fantasy on my part. I could hear coins clattering on plates, a cash till being rung up. Max's eyes in the photo burned a hole straight through to my heart.

'OK, I'm back,' he said. 'I'm walking out of the restaurant . . .' I heard a bell chime as the door opened and closed again behind him '. . . and now I'm getting in my car.' He giggled. 'This is like a little slice of my life.'

'How was Spain?' I said. 'Did you have a good time?'

'We had a fantastic time. Natalie's mom spoiled me rotten.' He was shouting now to be heard over the traffic.

Yeah, I bet she did, I thought. 'Hey – it's not weird if I phone you, is it?' I asked.

'Weird? Why would it be weird?'

'I don't know. I'm just not sure what's the right thing to do. I haven't been in a situation like this before.'

'No, it's not weird. I'm really glad you called. How's London?'

'Oh, fine.'

'And how's Andrew?'

'He's fine. Well. To tell you the truth, Andrew and I haven't been getting on so well lately.'

He was genuinely surprised. 'Why's that? Is it because he knows that you kissed me?'

Just hearing him say the word 'kissed' was unbearably wonderful. He hadn't forgotten. I hadn't just imagined it.

'No, he doesn't know.'

'You didn't tell him about me, did you?'

'What? Are you kidding? No, to tell you the truth we weren't getting on all that well even before that.'

'I'm really sorry to hear that. Does Andrew know you're speaking to me now? Is he there listening?'

'Stop being so paranoid! He's not even home. He's gone to an internet launch party.'

'That sounds very exciting,' he teased, meaning the exact opposite. 'Why aren't you there?'

'I'd rather shoot myself,' I said.

'You don't have a gun, do you?' he asked.

'Don't be silly. We don't carry guns in England. This is a *civilised* country,' I teased him back.

'Natalie has a gun,' said Max. 'A little silver one.'

'Oh, terrific. Thanks for the warning. I'll have to wear a bullet-proof vest when I come to visit you.'

'No, don't do that,' he said. 'I much prefer that little T-shirt you were wearing that day in Portobello Road.'

I blushed.

'How are your nipples doing?' he asked.

'They're fine, thank you,' I laughed. 'They're exceptionally perky today as a matter of fact.'

'Oh, God,' he said in a strangled sort of voice. 'Hold on. I have to pull over.' There were some traffic noises for half a minute and then he came back on the phone. What on earth was he up to? 'Are you still there?' he asked.

'Yeah – where are you now?'

'I'm in a gas station. I haven't got long left on my battery. You shouldn't have said that about your nipples.'

'Well, you brought them up,' I said. 'So to speak.'

'I was thinking – how would it be if I dragged my tongue across them, very, very slowly?'

'That would be lovely,' I gulped. My God, it didn't take much to start his motor running.

'Will you touch them for me?'

'I'm sorry?'

'Touch them for me.' he breathed. 'Touch yourself.'

'Oh. OK.' I tentatively stroked my T-shirt, feeling very daft.

'Now rub them on the phone.'

'What? Don't be so silly.'

'Rub them on the phone. Go on.'

'Oh all right.' I decided to humour him, thinking that men were really quite strange. While I rubbed, I flicked through *Heat* magazine to see if there was anything on TV later. Ooh. Double *ER*. 'How was that?' I asked him.

His breathing was noticeably heavier. 'What are you wearing?' he said.

'A grey T-shirt.'

'Is it tight?'

'Very tight,' I lied.

'Roll it up,' he said. 'So I can see your bra.'

'OK,' I said, putting the phone down once more. This is ridiculous. I could be wearing the living room curtains for all he knew.

'Can you feel my hands on your breasts?' he asked.

'Uh huh,' I said in my best porn-star voice, trying not to laugh. Then something stirred inside me and I closed my eyes and tried to imagine that he wasn't five thousand miles away but right there beside me on the sofa.

'Can you feel my tongue?'

'Uh huh.'

'I'm rolling your nipple around on my tongue. Can you feel my lips?'

'Uh huh.' The sound of his voice was almost hypnotic.

'I'm sucking your right nipple really slowly and I'm rubbing your left nipple between my fingers. Does that feel good?'

'Oh yeah,' I murmured. Amazingly, it did.

'Now, move your hand lower. Between your legs. Can you feel me now?'

'Uh huh,' I whispered. Oh God, Max and I could do this all the time and it wouldn't be cheating!

'Do you know how hard you make me?'

'Uh huh.'

'Oh, you are such a bad girl – Oh Christ!' There was a short burst of crackle and then silence.

'Max? Max? Are you still there?' I sat alone on the sofa staring idiotically at the phone like an astronaut watching his space capsule bob away without him.

I pressed 'End' and wondered if Max would call me back. I must have sat there for fifteen minutes in suspended animation just staring at the phone before I recovered my senses enough to get off the sofa and make a cup of tea.

I saw Max's photo watching me and felt incredibly embarrassed, as though it had been a witness. Still, I cheered myself up, Max had been pleased to hear from me. I could call him again next week. Already I started looking forward to it.

When Andrew finally came home just before midnight, I was in bed still fantasising about Max, replaying every word of his phone foreplay in my head. Reliving every imaginary caress.

'How was the party?' I asked.

'Good. Good.'

'How are Russell and Robin?' Like I cared.

'Russell didn't turn up. He's not well.'

'Nothing fatal, I hope?'

'No, just a cold, I think.'

He switched off the bedside light. 'Good night,' he said, and rolled over to sleep while I lay in the dark dreaming about Max.

'You are such a bad girl,' I heard him say.

You don't know the half of it, I thought.

twenty-seven

Andrew was away in the Isle of Man for the whole week at the start of October, gone to liquidate some poor unfortunate company. It was so nice to have the flat to myself for a few days; wonderful to have a little space to think and daydream without him hovering around me asking, 'Are you all right?' every five seconds and filling the house with the smell of pizzas or take-away curries and getting on my nerves by saying, 'Are you sure you don't want some?'

Next time he phoned, I'd have to tell him not to get any lemon curd this time – it was too fattening, and too tempting to just leave lying around in the cupboard. I'd lost three more pounds on my low-fat-get-slim-for-when-I-see-Max-again diet and I was starting to feel strangely euphoric and light-hearted, as though it was actually my mind that was losing weight and not my hips. Max would be very pleasantly surprised when he saw me again.

It had been weeks since I'd spoken to him, but just knowing he was there made it bearable. I was making myself play it very cool. If I rang and couldn't get through to him on the first try, I'd make myself wait two days before trying again. Otherwise, I was afraid that he'd check his phone messages and see that somebody had been calling him every five minutes for the past eight hours. The idea of Max picking up his phone and being told, 'You have 72 missed calls' was a bit of a worry. I'd been saving up my next phone call like a treat to myself.

I had finally – finally – finished Natalie's interview and I'd phoned Natalie and read every word to her just like I'd promised. Annoyingly, she didn't mention Max once.

Then I went to the hairdressers to get my roots done and have a blow-dry. I wanted my hair to look its absolute flicky best as I swished up the glass-bubble lifts and in to Atlanta's office to deliver my words and pictures in a blaze of glory.

'She's on a long lunch,' said her secretary, barely looking up. 'Just leave them with me. I'll make sure she gets them.'

'But—!'

I swished out again rather crossly. All dressed up and no place to go, I thought, as I waited for the glass bubble to arrive. Perhaps tonight I'd try calling Max again. While Andrew was away I could call Max whenever I liked. A shame he wouldn't be able to see how nice my hair looked. Maybe I could describe it to him. There was no one else in the lift and I turned my head this way and that, trying to see in the reflection of the glass what my hair looked like from the back. The lift stopped at the fourth floor to let someone else on and, as the glass bubble hovered in mid-air, another bubble pulled alongside on its way up, paused to let someone out and I found myself staring straight at Nick.

Now, the one design flaw in glass bubble lifts which I hadn't previously spotted is that there's no place to hide. Not one. I shrank back against the lift buttons trying to melt into the wall, but Nick had already seen me. He was smiling. No, he was laughing. He was definitely laughing! I could see his teeth.

I lifted up my left hand an inch or two. It was meant to be a wave but it felt more like a surrender.

How dare he laugh at me! What's he doing here anyway? This is my building! Not his building! He waved back, as cool as you like, and then disappeared upwards, still smiling – or laughing – as he glass bubble glided up and mine sank to the ground floor.

I was so rattled I bought a bar of Cadbury's Whole Nut from the machine at the tube station, ate the whole thing in less than a minute and then bought another one before my train came. Damn Nick for making me eat chocolate. The cheek of him just turning up like that. At least my hair looked nice.

Atlanta rang an hour after I got home. 'This stuff is brilliant!' she gushed. 'I've just been in with the editor singing your praises and we're pulling the January cover and running Natalie instead.'

'Oh, that's nice,' I said in my very calmest voice as I jumped up and down and waved my arms in the air, silently screaming *yippee!*

'So anyway, how would you feel about doing one of our summer fashion spreads for us? Hervé's homesick for his boyfriend in Brazil and we think he might be deserting us. There'll be a staff job going if you're interested.'

Summer? I couldn't wait six months for work!

'It's set up for January. Somewhere in Colorado. Up a mountain. Lots of snow. You can ski, can't you?'

I leaped around the flat, hugging Billy and shouting, 'I'm going to Colorado! I'm going to Colorado!' I expect Annie Liebowitz jumps around her living room squealing all the time. I couldn't wait to phone Max and tell him how brilliant I was. It was already morning in LA – I could call him straight away.

His mobile was on voicemail so I boldly called his office. I was invincible today.

Switchboard operators didn't scare me.

'I'm very sorry, ma'am, Mr Ogilvy will be in meetings all day. If it's urgent, I can try to get a message to him for you.'

'No. That's all right.'

Good news can wait. Everything was going so brilliantly – what difference would one day make?

When the phone woke me up the next morning, I recognised Natalie's voice immediately. 'Oh gosh, Natalie. Hi!'

'Have I woken you up?'

'No, no, not at all, I was just getting up.' Why does nobody ever say, 'Yes you did wake me up, now sod off and call back in an hour's time'? I wonder. 'How are you?'

'Wonderful. We're both great. We miss you. We miss London.'

'Liar! I bet you're sitting in the sunshine looking at the beach right now.' It was amazing the way I could swap small-talk with her while at the same time obsessing on her use of the word 'we'. Was Max there with her? Did he know she was speaking to me? I felt faint.

'Actually, we're not, it's thunder and lightning here.'

'I'm sorry to hear that.' She'd said 'we' again. 'So what are you guys up to?'

'Well, I'm just calling to say hi, and to let you know there are a couple of changes I'd like you to make in that interview we did.'

'Oh, right. I spoke to the editor last night and they're using it on the cover of the January issue. Isn't that fantastic!'

'What was the name of the magazine again?'

'*The Hoop*. Hang on a second, I'll just get a pen.' I might have known she'd be calling to talk about work. She'd probably dreamed up some wildly flattering compliment Richard had once paid her, or some resolutely heterosexual activity he'd once engaged in that she wanted me to add. I found an old envelope to scribble on. 'OK. Fire away,' I said. 'But talk slowly because I can't do shorthand.'

'Right.' She sounded like she was about to laugh. 'Well, I just wanted you to put in a bit about me and Max.'

I swallowed hard. Had she found out about us? Surely he hadn't told her? 'Really?'

'Yeah, can you say that we're really, really happy?'

'Really . . . really . . . happy.' I repeated the words as I painstakingly wrote them down.

'Because we're going to have a baby.'

I stopped writing and shut my eyes. 'Oh, my God, that's fantastic,' I said, but inside my heart was breaking. I could feel the tears welling up in my throat. 'Congratulations! I'm so happy for you! When's it due?'

'The end of May. It seems like a hundred years away.'

'But that's just a few months . . . you must be . . . I mean, you didn't show—'

'I know. I've got just the weeniest bump. Mummy said she was the same. We told her in Spain but she was sworn to secrecy until the three months were up.'

'Three months?' I was doing frantic calculations in my head, but I could barely put two and two together. 'So you must have been pregnant when you were here?'

'Of course. You know, all these women who go on about morning sickness must be imagining it. I was only the tiniest bit sick once and I was never late on set.'

'What a trouper,' I said. I was counting back on my fingers. 'So that means you were pregnant before you even got to London.' Suddenly, I felt quite nauseous myself.

'Yeah – I've worked out exactly the night I must have conceived. It was July the fourth. Max certainly did his patriotic duty that night.' She gave a very dirty laugh. 'So is there time for you to put that in the article?'

'I think so. I'll phone the magazine.' So the whole time Max was messing about with me, he must have known. All that bollocks about never seeing his children – what was that all about? 'I'm so happy for you both,' I said. 'Max must be over the moon. Tell him congratulations from me.'

'He's right here, you can tell him yourself!' I could hear the receiver being passed across the room.

'Lindy?'

'Hi – congratulations. I'm really happy for you.' I could hear the ice in my voice.

'We're both so excited!' he gushed. 'I'm going to be a daddy!'

'I'm sure you'll be a terrific dad,' I told him.

'Thanks. I'm going to try.'

'And a terrific husband, too,' I added.

'I'd better pass you back to Natalie,' he said. 'She's dancing around here beside me.'

'Goodbye, Max. Good luck.'

'Lindy? You there?' said Natalie. 'So what are you going to put in the article? All the papers here think I can't have children. Actually we've been trying for a baby for ages. I thought I might have put a jinx on myself by telling lies. You better say it's a miracle or they'll think I've had IVF. Put it down to the magical properties of London tap water. Oh no, I know – you can say I got pregnant from sitting on a warm bus seat!' She laughed and dropped the phone. 'Sorry,' she said. 'Max is beating me up! Honestly, you have no idea what I have to put up with from this man!'

'No,' I told her. 'You poor thing. I don't know how you stand it.'

'Me neither! Beating a poor defenceless pregnant woman! He says he wants you to put in the article that it was his super sperm that did it.'

'I'll certainly see what I can do.'

'When are you coming to see us?'

'I don't know. I'm pretty busy at the moment. Maybe after Christmas. How would that be?'

'It'd be fantastic. I might even have a proper bump by then! But you'll have to come out for the wedding too. We're thinking July. That gives me nearly two months to get my figure back. Max! Stop it! You could have someone's eye out with that cushion!'

'I should let you go now,' I said. 'It sounds like you two have got a lot to talk about.'

'OK, but I'll call you again in a couple of weeks. Have a great Christmas, Lindy!'

'Thanks, you too. And congratulations again. I'm so happy for you! This is absolutely the best news.'

I hung up the phone and buried my head in my hands, sobbing like my heart would break. It was over. It was really over.

What on earth had I been thinking? I must have been insane. It was as if I was waking up from a trance. But unlike people who are hypnotised and told they're chickens or Elvis, I could remember absolutely everything I had done and went cold with shame.

How dare Max have done this? How could he have been such a bastard? Not to me, but to Natalie. He knew she was pregnant. They'd been trying for a baby for ages, Natalie said. He wanted this baby. He wanted to be a good father this time. Well, I wasn't going to stand in the way of that.

The video player in my head was on fast forward whizzing through my scenes with Max – holding my hand, rubbing my foot, flirting with me without saying a word, kissing me in the back of the taxi, undressing me in his hotel room . . . that phone call. Urgh! That phone call! I was suddenly so humiliated I wrapped the pillow around my head to try and block out the memory.

What had I been thinking? I thought I was in love with Max but I was simply out of my mind. What did I imagine? That he'd eventually get tired of his beautiful, TV star lover, pin-up of millions, and come and live with me in a one-bedroom upstairs flat in Maida Vale? Did I really think I could compete with Natalie? The Natalie Browns of this world win without even trying. How many times would she have to beat me before it finally sunk in to my thick head?

Aaarrgh! I squeezed the pillow tighter, thinking it would serve me right if I accidentally suffocated myself. Never again. Never again. Never again. How could one person have been so stupid?

So what are you left with now, I thought. A marriage to a man who loves you to distraction. That's not exactly a booby prize, is it? You should just be grateful for what you've got instead of chasing after something you'll never get. I dried my eyes and looked at the photo on the mantelpiece of the two of us signing our wedding register, Andrew looking like the cat who'd got the cream and me grinning like a radiant maniac.

I had promised to love Andrew and care for him and remain true to him for the rest of our lives together. I wrote those vows myself. They didn't say anything about 'Be fond of and tolerate until something more exciting comes along'.

I'll make it up to him, somehow, I decided. I'll hang on to him. He's a good man and he deserves better than I've been giving him. The fact that he has the memory span of a goldfish is probably for the best. It'll make it easier for him to forget how weird I've been acting.

I'd promised to love him, and I always keep my promises, so that's exactly what I'm going to do. Before it's too late.

twenty-eight

Andrew was coming home the day after tomorrow. I cleaned the house from top to bottom in preparation for his arrival. No more grumbling about the housework. I emptied out his chest of drawers and laid out all his boxer shorts and socks in neat piles, instead of chucking them in angrily like I usually did. I would learn to love magnolia walls and brown kitchen tiles and toasters with patterns of wheat on them. I drove to the supermarket to fill the fridge with beer and all the high-fat foods he loved. I found a recipe for Chicken Korma and bought all the ingredients so that I could cook it for him myself. The recipe called for yoghurt, but I'd use double cream instead – just for him. I bought the oldest, smelliest cheeses I could find, the porkiest pork pies, sausages the size of bananas.

I didn't know what flight he was on and hoped he'd call so I could go to the airport and meet him. He'd left his car in the car park, but I could get the tube to Heathrow so we could drive back together. It would be a nice surprise for him.

But when he phoned on Friday evening, he was already in the car driving home.

'Hi, darling! Did you have a good trip?' I said. 'I've missed you so much!'

'Really?' Well, I couldn't blame him for sounding surprised. 'Look, I'd like to take you out to dinner tonight, if that's OK. You don't have to eat anything fattening if you don't want to.'

I laughed. 'Oh, but I want to! I'm so bored with baked potatoes. Where do you want to go?'

'You choose.'

'Do you want to go to that place in Portobello Road?'

'Wherever you like.'

'Gee, you surprise me. Do you really think you can manage to go without Indian food for one night?' I was only teasing him. I hoped it didn't sound like I was having a go.

'I'll try. I should be home in an hour, so book it for eight.'

'OK. Thanks, hon. That's very sweet of you.'

'See you in a bit.'

An evening with Andrew was exactly what I needed to jump-start our marriage again. I hadn't seen him for a whole five days and before he'd gone away, he'd been working crazy hours, hardly ever getting home before nine or ten, going into the office on weekends. He deserved a luxurious night out with his loving wife.

Tonight would be a turning point for both of us.

If you can't be with the one you love, love the one you're with, I reminded myself. And in this case, the one I was with was Andrew.

I was doing the right thing. My mid-life crisis had come a decade or so early but now I was over it and prepared to commit myself wholeheartedly to my husband. That would be my New Year's resolution. To love Andrew. If I acted like I loved him, then eventually I really would be in love with him, just like we used to be.

I booked the table for eight then had a shower and washed and blow-dried my hair. I hadn't been to this restaurant before but it seemed like the sort of place you could make a bit of an effort for. I'd wear my new plum-coloured velvet dress to show off my new flat tummy and narrow hips.

I admired my new slimline reflection in the mirror, thinking that it was a long time since I'd dressed up for Andrew's benefit.

When I heard his key in the lock, I ran to meet him and gave him a big kiss. 'Hello, darling!'

'Hello!' He looked shocked. 'What's got into you all of a sudden?'

'Nothing. I'm just pleased to see you. What do you think of my dress?' I did a bit of a twirl in the hallway.

'It's gorgeous. You look terrific.'

'Thank you.' I took his suitcase and briefcase and realised I'd forgotten to tell him not to buy the lemon curd. 'Where's the duty-free bag?' I asked him. 'I'll put the lemon curd in the fridge.'

'I didn't get any this time,' he said.

'What, no whisky either?' I was stunned. 'No kippers?'

He shook his head. 'I was late for the plane. There wasn't time.' In the past I knew Andrew would have missed a whole fleet of planes just to save a few quid on his favourite brand of whisky. So maybe all my nagging about the amount he drank was finally paying off. I gave him another peck on the cheek. 'What's that for?' he asked.

'For finally listening to me about eating more healthily,' I beamed. 'I'm just going to put on a bit of slap and then we should go. Are you going to change?'

He was wearing his nerdiest grey suit and a blue-and-white-striped shirt. 'Do I need to?' he asked.

'No,' I told him. 'You've lovely just as you are,' and I kissed him again.

He gave me a very strange look and I smiled to think how confused he must be to suddenly have his old, happy wife back.

The restaurant was a baroque fantasy of opulent red velvet. Every plain surface had been gilded to within an inch of its life and the mirrors lining the walls reflected the hot glow of the candlelight all the way to infinity.

'Gosh, it's so romantic,' I whispered to Andrew as we were shown to our table.

We ordered a bottle of Chardonnay and with the first mouthful I felt immediately light-headed. I'd hardly eaten all day and hadn't touched a drop of alcohol in weeks. I was so glad I'd chosen this restaurant. The plush boudoir setting absolutely suited my mood.

'I know exactly what I'm going to have,' I told Andrew. 'I'm going to have the onion tart, and the salmon fishcakes and the Chocolate St Emilion for dessert. I don't know what that is, but it's got the word chocolate in it which has to be a good thing.'

While we waited for them to bring our starters, I checked out our reflections in the mirror and was pleased to note how pretty I was looking this evening. Lucky old Andrew to have me as a wife. I'd been perfectly horrible to him but now I was going to make it up to him. We'd been through a rough patch – wasn't that the expression? I imagined myself telling people, 'Yes, we've been through a bit of a rough patch, Andrew and I, but we're back on course now. We've had our ups and downs but we've come through them together and now we're stronger than ever.'

'This onion tart is delicious,' I said. 'How are your prawns?'

'They're very good.'

'Don't you want that one?'

'No.'

'Can I have it then?'

'OK.'

I peeled his last tiger prawn, rather expertly I thought – Andrew never gets the last bit of prawn out of the tail, which I think is a terrible waste – and popped it happily into my mouth.

The waiter took our plates away and refilled our glasses. My wine glass was already empty but Andrew had scarcely touched his. When the waiter had gone, Andrew folded his hands on the table in front of him and drummed his thumbs together.

'You look very handsome in this light,' I told him, laying my hand on top of his. 'You should have a couple of men follow you around with candles all the time.'

'There's something I want to tell you,' he said.

'Fire away.' I took another mouthful of Chardonnay. It was deliciously buttery.

'I've met someone.'

Buttery and oaky. Australian, of course. I'd have to write down the name of it so I could see if they had it in Sainsbury's. I'm terrible with wine. I never remember the names of the ones I like.

'Oh, yes? Who's that then?'

I wonder what those red velvet curtains would look like at our place? A bit too much probably. When we move to a garden flat we could get some then. I could maybe get the velvet in John Lewis. Why was Andrew looking so serious?

'Sorry, darling, I wasn't really listening,' I said. 'What are you talking about?'

'I think we should split up.'

For a moment I thought I'd gone deaf because all the sound in the restaurant seemed to drain away as though I'd fallen down a very deep well. 'Split up? You mean, like a divorce?' It's OK, I thought. He's only joking.

'I don't know if I mean divorce, but I don't want us to live together any more. I can't put up with it any more. I've had enough.' He was staring at his fingers and couldn't look up at me.

An icy hand curled inside my chest and squeezed hard. Oh no, I'm having a heart attack. 'You're not serious,' I said desperately. 'You don't mean that.'

'I do mean it. I've thought about it for ages. Ever since we came back from Italy.'

'That's not ages – that's no time at all!'

'I know, but things haven't been right between us for a long time.'

'Haven't they? What was the matter?' I was starting to sober up horribly quickly. Like a diver coming to the surface too rapidly, I felt dizzy as though my blood were full of bubbles.

'All your moods, the way you argue with me all the time over absolutely nothing – I've just had enough. You never show me any affection. I had so much love for you but you just kept throwing it back in my face. That's not the kind of marriage I want any more.'

'I'm sorry. I'm sorry.' I could feel the tears pricking the back of my eyes. 'I know I've been horrible to you lately, but that's over now. I promise. We can work this out.'

'I don't think I want to work it out,' he said.

'But I love you! I thought you loved me!'

'I do love you. It's just . . .' I could see him searching for the right words. 'It's just that I'm not in love with you any more. I don't think I have been for a long time.'

I felt like I'd been physically punched. 'No. We can't split up. We've just got married! We were going to move to a garden flat and have babies! We were going to get a tumble-dryer!'

'I know. I feel absolutely terrible about this. Believe me. I don't want to hurt you but I can't go on like this. Deceiving you. I feel like I'm living a lie.' He looked like he was about to say something else but then he stopped and I remembered what he'd said before.

'You've met someone else, haven't you? That's what you said.'

He nodded.

'And you've in love with her, is that it?'

He nodded again.

The waiter appeared with our main courses. 'Fish cakes?'

'For me, please. He's the steak.' My voice sounded horribly normal. I drained my wine glass while the waiter arranged our plates and the bowls of vegetables. Spinach for me. Shoe-string fries for Andrew.

'Enjoy your meal,' he said with a smile.

'Thank you.' It wasn't the waiter's fault my marriage was falling to pieces in his restaurant. 'So,' I said when we were alone again. 'Who is she? How did you meet her?'

'I've known her for years,' he said quietly.

'For years?' I demanded. 'So how long has this been going on exactly?'

'Not long. It's very new. But I know it's what I want.'

'Well, who is it? Is it someone you work with? What's her name?'

He still wouldn't look at me. 'It's Robin.'

'Robin who?' I said, trying to imagine who this paragon of beauty and intelligence must be.

'Robin,' he said again and then it hit me.

'No! I don't believe you! This has got to be a wind-up.' It couldn't possibly be *that* Robin.

'It's true,' he said.

'But she's engaged to your best friend!' I protested. Even as the words were leaving my mouth I realised how ridiculous they sounded.

'I know. I'm not proud of myself. But I wasn't going to do anything until she left Russell. She broke up with him after her launch party.'

The launch party. Russell had a cold. It was all starting to fall into place.

'Well, that must have been very cosy for the two of you,' I said sarcastically.

'I'm sorry,' he said. 'I don't expect you to forgive me. I know you must think I'm a complete bastard . . .' Something about the way his voice trailed away, something about the way he wouldn't look me in the eye made a missing piece of the puzzle finally click into place. That's what had been bugging me all evening.

'You haven't been in the Isle of Man at all, have you?' I said.

He wouldn't even look up, didn't even have the guts to deny it. The cheek of the man! The blatant bare-faced cheek of the man, shacking up secretly with Robin for a whole week while I waited at home, playing the dutiful wife and worried about how hard he was working! I was so angry I thought I might throw up.

'So let me get this straight,' I said. 'You're leaving me?'

'I didn't want to put it as bluntly as that, but yes.'

Then, for some reason I couldn't explain, I started to laugh. I looked at Andrew sitting there in his stupid grey suit with his stupid haircut confessing to an affair with a girl who had the personality of a car bonnet and I started to laugh.

'*You're* leaving *me*?' I said it again just to make sure.

'What's so funny?' he asked.

I thought of the emotional knots I had been tying myself in for the last few months. The guilt I had gone through over the hurt I was causing Andrew for not loving him enough. My misguided lust for Max. The trip to marriage guidance trying to super-glue my marriage back into place. The promise I had made to make it up to Andrew. My New Year's resolution. My plan to force myself to fall back in love with him if it killed me. The fact that I had lost 10lb and looked better than I had ever done since before I'd even met Andrew and it still didn't make a blind bit of difference.

'*You're* leaving *me* for *Robin*?' I was laughing so hard I thought I might choke.

'I still don't see what's so funny,' said Andrew crossly.

'Oh, Andrew,' I said, wiping my eyes on my serviette. 'You should be sitting where I'm sitting.'

twenty-nine

'But this can't be true,' said Jill. 'I don't believe it! You're the perfect couple!'

'Well you'd better believe it,' I told her. 'He's moving out on the weekend.'

'Is it because of Max? Did he find out? Oh, I warned you. It's because of Max, isn't it?'

'No, surprisingly enough, it's nothing to do with Max. Turns out it's all to do with me.'

In the cold light of day my marriage break-up didn't seem quite so hilarious but I was surprised to discover that I wasn't going to pieces either. I'd even loaned Andrew my big suitcase to pack some of his stuff in that morning.

'He's moving in with Robin. She's already left Russell and she's got a six-month lease on a flat in Elephant and Castle.'

'That sounds idyllic,' said Jill.

'Yes, doesn't it? I can't help thinking they make a lovely couple.'

'I expect Russell's devastated,' Jill added.

I gasped. 'I hadn't even thought of that! Oh, you are brilliant! Russell will be gutted! That's the best news I've had in weeks.'

'I must say, you're taking it very well.'

'Yeah, I am, aren't I?' I agreed.

'I think I'm more upset about it than you are,' said Jill. 'He'll come to his senses, surely. He'll come back. I'm positive he will. You mustn't give up hope.'

'Well,' I said, 'perhaps it's for the best. Andrew and I have been going through a bit of a rough patch recently. We've had our ups and downs and . . . well, let's just say we haven't exactly come through it together. But I'm fine.'

'What are you going to do? Where are you going to live?'

'Andrew is putting this place on the market, but he says I can stay here until it's sold and he'll still pay his half. And I'm not sure after that. Maybe I'll buy it off him, if I can persuade anyone to give me a mortgage.'

'I thought you hated this place.'

'Not really,' I said, looking around me at the big windows, the plane trees that lined the street outside, the polished wood floors and seeing them all suddenly in a new light. 'I just always wanted to redecorate but Andrew didn't want to spend any money on the place because he was always planning to sell up and move to this mythical garden flat that never quite materialised. I might stay. I really like the area.'

It was delayed shock, that's probably what it was. Every morning I expected to wake up and be overcome by a wave of misery but it never happened. I'd wake up all alone after a good night's sleep with the duvet miraculously still on my side of the bed and think, 'This is what being separated feels like, is it?' And I'd have a momentary panic where I'd think, 'If I'm not Andrew's wife any more, then who am I?'

Then Billy would hear me stirring and climb up onto my chest to rub his little wet nose under my neck and squeak at me, demanding his breakfast. And I'd rub his fluffy tummy and he'd roll on his back and look at me upside down and make me laugh. So then I'd give him a kiss and the two of us would get up and go to the kitchen where I'd give him his Whiskas and make myself a cup of tea.

I have to be strong and carry on, I'd tell myself sternly, for the sake of the puss. And I'd start to laugh, and wonder if perhaps this was the onset of bag-lady craziness – laughing at your own stupid jokes because there's no one else around to laugh at them.

It was hysteria probably. I was hysterical with grief, that must be it. I should be figuring out a plan to get Andrew back, that's what I should be doing. That's what a normal person would do. I could lose weight and change my hairstyle, except I'd already done that. Perhaps I should be cutting up all his suits to get my revenge – all those terribly valuable seven-year-old Marks and Spencer suits. But that just made me laugh even more. Sorry, darling, I was going to wreck your wardrobe but it looks like someone beat me to it.

I had to admit it had been a very strange few months. I'd chucked in my job, and then my husband had chucked me in. According to those scales of stressful behaviour, they run in the newspaper every now and then, I should have collected enough points by now to earn myself a triple-bypass. It would hit me any day now, I expect. But at least I didn't have to move house; unemployment and divorce I could deal with, just don't anybody ask me to put my things in cardboard boxes.

I had Robin to thank for that. She'd told Andrew she didn't want to live in the home we'd shared together because she didn't want to be constantly surrounded by reminders of me. Perhaps Robin was smarter than I'd given her credit for. She wasn't going to spend four years in a magnolia shoe-box – she was going to get the garden flat straight off. Clever girl.

Every so often, a wave of self-pity would wash over me and I'd let myself have a little cry. I'm going to die all on my own, I'd wail dramatically even though I knew this was absolute nonsense. And even while I was crying, I knew it wasn't Andrew I was shedding those tears for at all, it was Max. If I needed any further diagnosis of the state of my marriage, then that was surely it.

When Andrew came around on Saturday with his rented van,

I think he was a little disappointed to discover that I wasn't exactly kneeling on the kitchen floor with my head in the oven.

'Hi,' I said. 'Kettle's on. Want a cup of tea?'

'Sure. How are you feeling?' He was using the compassionate tone of voice they always use on *ER* when the patient has got ninety-eight per cent burns and will be dead before the commercial break.

'I'm fine,' I told him. 'How are you?'

'A little strange,' he admitted.

'So, no change there then,' I smiled. I handed him a mug of tea. 'Is Robin not with you?'

'No, she didn't think it was a very good idea.'

'That's a shame. Big strong girl like Robin could help you carry stuff. Well, I've sorted out all your records and CDs for you already.'

'Oh. Thanks.' He sounded surprised. 'You didn't have to go to all that trouble.'

'No, I wanted to,' I assured him. 'It was pretty easy. Anything released after 1990 was mine. Will you have room to take everything in one trip, do you think?' I hoped he would. I wanted to paint the living room tomorrow.

'What about the furniture? How are we going to split that?' he asked.

'Take it. It was all here before I moved in anyway, so technically it's yours. Just leave me the sofa until I can get a new one. And the TV is mine. Do you want the bed?'

'No, Robin's got a bed.'

'That's handy. One less thing to carry. Call me if you need any help. I'm just watching Ant and Dec.' Billy and I curled up on the sofa together while Andrew went out to the van to get his horde of empty boxes.

I watched him carry one load after another out into the street and it was like watching a stranger. Was I really married to this man? I hadn't seen him for three days and already he'd turned into somebody else. Somebody decent and dull in a bottle-green sweatshirt and white trainers. The kind of man you see on a Saturday morning pushing his trolley through Sainsbury's with a little boy in the front basket. The kind of man you walk past and don't give a second glance to. It was like those paintings that have been painted one on top of the other. The Andrew I thought I'd been married to had been wiped away and the real Andrew that had been hidden underneath was finally showing through. Funny to think that he'd been there all the time.

I lifted my feet so that he could move the coffee table, an ash-black monstrosity from the days before Ikea got fashionable that screamed Bachelor Pad.

'Do you want this?' he asked.

'God, no. Take it. Take it. Here, let me give you a hand.'

I helped him load the coffee table into the van, which was already full of boxes, plastic tubs and carrier bags.

'This is cute, isn't it?' I said. 'Just the two of us?' A week ago loading a coffee table onto a van would have ended in a huge argument over whether it should be stacked horizontally or vertically. I would have made Andrew wrap it in bubble-wrap and Sellotape so it wouldn't get scratched. There would have been screaming and shouting and slamming doors. Now I just chucked it into the back of the van without a second thought. If it fell out in the middle of the road and got squashed by a Number 12 bus, I couldn't have cared less.

'I think that's everything,' he said, dusting off his hands.

'No, it's not!' I told him. 'What about all your books? You can't leave them.'

'I've run out of boxes,' he said.

'That's OK. I'll drive down to the High Road and buy you some more plastic tubs. Give me some money.'

'You don't have to do this,' he said.

'No, I want to help. It's the least I can do. You get all your books off the shelves and I'll be back in a minute.' I ran back into the flat to get my keys and pull on a jacket, then drove to

Kilburn to a shop that sold plastic storage boxes for £2.39. I bought five of them, then sped back home.

'Look,' I said, feeling pleased with my purchases. 'I got you green ones, your favourite colour. If I help you pack, we can get this done in no time.'

'Doesn't it look empty?' said Andrew sadly when the shelves had been emptied and most of the furniture and junk had been piled into the truck.

'Yes, doesn't it,' I agreed. I was already getting the Hoover out to have a quick whizz round. Billy leapt out of the way as he heard the motor start up and went to hide in the kitchen.

'So I guess this is it, then,' said Andrew, shouting above the vacuum cleaner.

'Yeah, I guess so. Are you off then?'

'I'll wait till you've finished that.'

'OK. Mind your feet.' I carried on hoovering until every piece of fluff and fleck of cardboard had been picked up. Andrew lurked in the doorway, shuffling uncomfortably. I switched off the Hoover and pressed the button that made the cord disappear. I loved the way it did that. It was my favourite bit.

'Are you going to be OK?' said Andrew. 'I feel terrible just leaving you like this.'

'I'll be fine,' I promised him. He looked hurt so I added, 'Terribly upset, obviously, but fine.'

He handed me a yellow Post-It note. 'Here's the number of the new flat. You know you can call me any time, don't you?'

'What for?' I asked.

'You know, if you need anything. If you want to talk. We can still be friends, can't we?'

'Sure. If that's what you want. I'd like that. And don't worry about the flat. I'll take good care of it until it's sold. I might even buy it myself.'

'Really?'

'Yeah. I'll call you in a week or two when I've sorted myself out and we can talk about it. How's that?'

He kissed me goodbye on the cheek and for a moment or two I felt incredibly sad. Once upon a time we had loved each other. We'd had such high hopes for our lives together. But we'd been wrong, and that was terribly sad. No two ways about it.

'Goodbye, Lindy,' he said.

'Goodbye,' I said. 'You didn't call me Bunny.'

He just smiled and cast his eyes down, then let himself out of the flat. But moments after he'd gone, I rushed downstairs and out into the street after him in a mad panic. Thank God he was still there. I ran around to the driver's side and he unrolled the window.

'Here,' I said, handing him a brown wooden box. 'You nearly forgot the backgammon set.'

After he had gone, I walked around the flat thinking how bare it looked with most of the traces of Andrew removed. He'd taken the toaster. Oh, well. C'est la vie. The bathroom shelf looked strangely tidy. The shaving cream was gone and the razor. Just one lonely toothbrush standing in the mug. There was so much dust on the shelves where all his books and records had been. In the bedroom his chest of drawers was gone. His ridiculous collection of action figures had vanished. One side of the built-in wardrobe was practically empty, apart from a few black bin-liners of old clothes I could take to Oxfam. It all looked very different. It even smelt differently.

What was this strange feeling I was experiencing? I wondered. Was it depression? Was it fear? Was it heartbreak? It was a weird feeling of lightness I couldn't quite put my finger on? Was I getting the flu? Was I hungry? Perhaps I was anaemic.

I pulled back the curtains and opened the windows to let in some fresh air. The wind was cold but the sun had come out and there were patches of blue sky snuggled in amongst the clouds.

I closed my eyes and took a deep breath, turning my face up to the sun. Now I knew what this feeling was – it was freedom.

thirty

Telling Mum and Dad was the hardest part. I knew they'd take it badly. Mum burst into tears at once.

'But why? I don't understand,' she kept wailing. 'You two were so perfect for each other. He was such a nice man.'

'He is a nice man,' I said. 'You don't have to talk about him in the past tense like that. He's not dead.' I shouldn't have said that because that just set her off even more.

Dad pursed his lips and nodded his head sagely as if to say he'd seen it all before – he was a man of the world. This was patently untrue, of course. If there was one thing my dad could never be accused of it was being a man of the world. He'd sold insurance all his life, had only ever had sex with one woman – my mother – to the best of anybody's knowledge, and had never been further afield than the Algarve. But he watched *EastEnders* so he thought he knew all about wayward husbands.

'He'll come to his senses, you'll see,' he promised. 'Give him a couple of weeks and he'll come running back to you, just begging you to take him back.'

'I'm not sure I want him back,' I told them, helping myself to another slice of fruit cake.

'You say that now, but that's just because you're upset. You'll feel differently in a week or two, you'll see. This will all blow over before you know it.'

Mum was getting out our wedding album as if to prove that we couldn't possibly be splitting up because – look! – here was photographic evidence of the two of us together.

'Look how pretty you were!' she sobbed. 'If only you'd never cut your hair!'

'I don't think that's the reason, Mum,' I said.

'It'll work out, you'll see,' said Dad. 'Everything will be back to normal in no time.'

'Phone him now,' Mum was begging. 'Tell him to come here for Christmas. Please. Do it for me. I was going to do goose this year – just for him.'

'I don't think that's a very good idea, Mum. He'll be with Robin.' I wondered how Andrew and Robin would be spending their Christmas. I imagined the two of them huddled over the *Radio Times* with a highlighter pen to make sure they didn't miss any of their favourite programmes. Andrew would be entering them all into a spread-sheet on his computer and Robin would be calculating their average viewing time per day.

I remembered my initial gut reaction to Andrew the first time we'd met. I was convinced he just wasn't my type and the funny thing was, I was right. So why had I married him? For the same reason I'd gone out with him in the first place I guess. I just couldn't think of a good enough reason not to.

In the middle of December, *The Hoop*'s January issue came out with my photos of Natalie on the cover, my interview inside and four more pages of photos. Atlanta had written an intro herself about how this interview was written by the one person in the world who knew Natalie better than anyone else, then run my Q&A without changing a single word (apart from the typing errors) and given me the most enormous by-line I'd ever seen saying *World Exclusive by Lindy Usher*. Debbie Gibb would do her nut.

Two days before it hit the newsstands, *The Hoop*'s syndication department rang to say they'd had calls from a couple of other papers wanting to buy my story and pictures. Apparently, *The Hoop* had only bought first rights which meant that I was entitled to sell them to anyone else I wanted and could I sort it out?

The Ledger wanted it, the *Independent* wanted it, magazines in Australia, Spain and South Africa wanted it. I had more than thirty phone calls from newspapers and magazines in the States, so I rang Natalie and let her choose a couple she liked. She was delighted because having said her bit, she reckoned she could now disappear and not do any more interviews for another five years. And I was happy to sell it to anyone who wanted it – except *The Ledger*, of course. I had to politely turn them down, but they went ahead and ran huge chunks of the interview anyway without paying me a penny. What a surprise.

By the time I'd invoiced everybody, I realised that from that one job alone, I would have enough for a tiny deposit on the flat. I would have to buy Natalie something really nice for the baby.

In the end, I spent Christmas with Jill, Simon and the kids. Holly and Matthew loved the Teletubbies outfits I'd bought them. They refused to wear anything else, although there was a punching match which Holly won over who was going to be Laa-Laa and who was going to be Dipsy. Other people's kids are so cute, aren't they?

'You're being so brave,' Jill kept saying to me, as we peeled the carrots and wrapped chipolata sausages up in bacon.

'Well, if I can get through Christmas, I reckon I can get through anything,' I said.

'That's exactly how I feel every year,' said Jill.

I'd bought Jill a Tiffany heart pendant and a football video for Simon. Jill had also bought me a Tiffany heart which Simon thought was the most amazing coincidence until we explained that we'd both decided we wanted one months ago, but it was a bit sad buying jewellery for yourself.

'It's weird not getting a present for Andrew,' I said. 'Or getting a present from Andrew.'

'What did he get you last year?'

I tried to think, but my mind had gone completely blank. 'I

don't know,' I confessed. 'I honestly can't remember. But he must have bought me something. Oh, God, now I remember! It was a Bruce Springsteen CD box set.'

'I didn't know you liked Bruce Springsteen,' said Jill.

'I don't,' I laughed. 'But try telling Andrew that.' I laughed some more, feeling slightly hysterical.

I must have had too many mince pies because that night I had the strangest dream. In my dream a man I couldn't see kept trying to give me some kind of information. 'No, no, I don't need it,' I kept telling him. 'Fax it to me, whatever it is. Send me an e-mail. I'm too busy to see you.' He was trapped inside in a tall crate and the last time I turned around to walk away from him he stepped out of the crate and stood in the middle of a large field where I could see him. The first thing I noticed about him was that he was stark naked. He was tall with dark hair and pale skin and the moment I saw him I fell immediately in love with him. Even though I knew he was only a dream.

'Why haven't you got any clothes on?' I asked him.

'I wanted to make sure that I got your attention this time,' he replied.

In my dream I felt for the first time what it was like to be in love with somebody and for them to love you back and to want to be with that person forever. I wanted to spend every waking moment with this man. I didn't want to be separated from him for even one second. The feeling of being in love was more real than anything I had ever experienced in real life. It was extraordinary. When I woke up, I tried desperately to go back to sleep again and get back into the dream. I wanted to see who this man was. I didn't want to let him go.

But I could hear Holly and Matthew shrieking that they wanted to unwrap some more presents and every second I was awake he slipped further and further away from me and the feeling of being in love went with him.

thirty-one

So I survived Christmas. I even survived New Year – three days with Jill and Simon and the kids in a cottage in Devon, wishing the wind would die down so we could go to the beach.

January was gloomy, but *The Hoop* kept me busy and I read in the papers that Nigel Napier had been signed up to present a new show that was being billed as a cross between *Gladiators* and *Surprise Surprise*. Bitter enemies would be tricked into coming onto the show and forced to settle long-standing grudges by taking part in a series of one-on-one contests.

'It might be anything from mud-wrestling to abseiling,' Nigel promised. And in a masterstroke of publicity for the show – entitled *Bury The Hatchet* – his co-presenter was announced as none other than his arch nemesis Tania Vickery.

It's strange watching Natalie on TV these days. I keep trying to spot which bits are Natalie and which bits are her character Vicki. When she smiles, she smiles like Natalie but when she laughs, she's Vicki. The way she falls in love every couple of episodes is definitely Vicki – Natalie would never do that. The make-up is Vicki, the voice is Vicki and she walks differently to Natalie, too. She's more self conscious, because Vicki's acting too, all the time. She's always trying to impress people, talking up her meagre achievements and yet riddled with insecurities. I used to think that her tantrums when some other actress got a part she was up for were all Vicki. Now I know that's pure Natalie too.

She phoned every week, just like she said she would, filling me in on the bump's progress. She was shocked to hear that Andrew and I had split up. Full of sympathy. Just one of those things, I told her, not wanting to get drawn into details. People grow apart. Sometimes she'd say, 'Do you want to say hi to Max? He's right here' and I'd say, 'No, you say hi to him for me.'

I had lunch with Atlanta who was bending over backwards these days to be nice to me and offering me the nicest jobs.

The fashion shoot was all set up for the end of the month in Crested Butte, Colorado: two models, plus a stylist and hair and make-up, plus an assistant for me. She brought me an invitation that had been sent to me care of *The Hoop* office. The opening of Angus Rawle's new play next week at the Almeida. That was sweet of them to think of me.

It was a good excuse to go shopping too. I still didn't have any first-night clothes. I hadn't been shopping in ages but the first freelance cheques were coming in and my budget would just about stretch to a trip to the King's Road on Saturday.

I flicked through all the rails in Kookai on the off-chance that I'd find something that hadn't been designed for an eight-year-old nymphomaniac and accidentally bumped elbows with the girl next to me.

'Sorry,' I said and, as I looked up and clocked the stringy black hair and bad posture, I immediately froze.

It was Robin. Oh, for goodness' sake, what was she doing here? In all the time I'd known Robin, I had never, ever just bumped into her – so why now? I could tell by her horrified expression that I was the last person in the world she wanted to bump into too, but there was no use in pretending we hadn't seen each other. She was standing right next to me, for crying out loud.

'Hi,' I said. 'How are you?'

'Oh, good. How are you?'

'Good.' I nodded at the sparkly blue T-shirt she was holding. 'Going somewhere nice?' A flute recital probably, I figured. Perhaps a festival of Czech cinema if they were going to go really mad.

'Ministry of Sound,' she murmured.

What?

'Really? Who are you going with?' I asked.

'Well . . . Andrew,' she whispered. 'Sorry – I didn't mean to sound . . .'

'No, no, you're fine, don't worry about it,' I told her, but what I was really thinking was Ministry Of Sound? Andrew? Since when? 'How is he?' I asked, trying not to look as stunned as I felt. 'Working hard?'

'Oh, very hard,' she assured me. 'They've just told him he's being made partner from the first of next month.'

Well. Didn't that just take the cake? What would he be making as partner? Eighty grand? A hundred grand? 'That's terrific news,' I said. 'Tell him I said congratulations.'

'Thanks,' she whispered. 'I will.'

'Well, gotta go. Have a good time at Ministry of Sound. I'm sure you will.' I stumbled out of the store, feeling absolutely furious with myself for my crap timing. I'd always wondered what it must feel like to accidentally throw away a winning lottery ticket – well now I knew. The thought of those two having all that money was so unfair! They shouldn't let stupid boring people have money! They would only spend it on stupid boring things! They'd buy a big stupid house in Kent and fill it with magnolia wallpaper and millions of brown and cream kitchen tiles and an expensive, sensible car for Robin in the driveway. Andrew would take up golf and make lots of wise long-term investments. Just picturing all the horrible furniture they would buy made me feel much better. I went and had a tall caramel macchiato in Starbucks and by the time I'd licked all the foam off the top and stopped hyperventilating I was back to my old self again. Now that I thought about it, I'd had a very narrow escape.

But I still hadn't found anything to wear and the thought of bumping into Robin again had put me right off shopping so I just went home. I'd just have to wear the silver dress I'd worn to the premiere. That was perfectly OK. And I'd lost weight since then, so it would look ever better now.

If I'd known that splitting up from Andrew would make me lose 10lb without even trying, I would have done it years ago. Perhaps that was the real reason Liz Taylor got divorced so often – it probably worked out cheaper than a health farm.

Jill was meant to be coming with me, but she rang up in the afternoon to say she had a terrible cold and didn't feel much like going out. Sorry. I knew she hadn't been that enthusiastic in the first place. Rawle's play – *Weeping Sores* – didn't exactly sound like a barrel of laughs. So I thought I'd ask Atlanta – it was just the kind of pretentious clap-trap I knew she'd love.

While I was in the shower, the phone rang. I had to run to answer it.

'Hey, Red, how you doing? It's me.'

'Max! What are you doing? Why are you calling me?'

'I miss you.'

'What time is it there? It must be the middle of the night?'

'It's seven in the evening. I'm in Cape Town for a site meeting. All on my own.' He sang the last few words like an advertising jingle.

'What do you want?'

'I want to talk to you. Don't you want to talk to me?'

'I'm busy right now, Max. I'm getting ready to go out.'

'What are you wearing?' he breathed.

'Max, is this an obscene phone call?'

'May-be.'

'Well, cut it out.'

'Are you wearing those lilac panties?'

'Max, I'm serious. Cut it out. You can't do this any more.'

Not so long ago, the sound of his voice would have melted me like butter on a hot spoon. But now I was immunised. He was just another heavy breather.

'Don't you want to know what I'm wearing?' he said.

'You're wearing my patience very thin, Max. Is this your definition of being faithful? Phone sex?'

'Are you angry with me?'

'No, Max, I'm not angry with you, but we can't do this. It's not funny any more. Everything's changed.'

'I haven't changed.'

'So I see. But Natalie's going to have a baby and if you want to be around to see this one grow up, you'd better get your act together.'

'What's got into you all of a sudden?'

'Look, if you want to go ahead and wreck this marriage before it's even started that's your business, but you'd better find some other girl to do it with, because I'm not going to be a part of it. I don't want you to call me any more.'

'Lindy?'

'Goodbye, Max.' I put down the receiver and sat quietly on the bed. Why, when you do the right thing, I wonder, does it always feel like the absolutely wrong thing?

While I waited for Atlanta outside the theatre, I was stunned to see Nigel Napier's photo displayed on the wall outside. It hadn't even occurred to me to find out who was in this thing but I bought a programme and there was Nigel – the star of the show. And there was Tania. Since when were these two actors?

Atlanta turned up late in a complete state on a micro scooter and clutching an envelope. 'Have you seen a letter box around here?' she was demanding. 'I can't believe it. My flatmate gave this to me to post this morning. Me! I can't believe it. Doesn't she know I'm the most stressed woman in London? How dare she give me a fucking letter to post!'

I would have to think twice about that staff job.

Weeping Sores was a bit like a Greek tragedy with a chorus of tall, identically beautiful brunettes dressed, inexplicably, as American football cheerleaders. Nigel's character was a powerful Scottish clansman tricked into arranging his own assassination by the wiles of a blonde female temptress – Tania. Tania was also a lesbian (at least, I think that's what that scene was about) and, in a bloodthirsty final act, she cut off Nigel's penis and paraded around with it on the end of a pole. Then quite unexpectedly, Tania was attacked by a swarm of killer bees and fell down dead beside Nigel's dismembered body. The end. Curtain, as the sound of angry buzzing filled the auditorium.

Atlanta loved it.

The party afterwards was like luvvie central. Atlanta disappeared immediately, leaving me in the lurch while she went dashing off to schmooze with a young gay actor who she seemed to know extremely well. Just about the only person I knew there was Angus himself, so I went over to say hello. I'd framed one of the photos I'd taken that day to bring him as a gift.

'Hi,' I said. 'I loved your play. Congratulations.'

He looked at me without recognition. Just a couple of months ago, he'd dropped his trousers for me and now he didn't have the faintest idea who I was. Well, wasn't that just like a man?

'I'm Lindy Usher. I don't know if you remember me. I photographed you recently.'

'Oh yes?' I could tell he still didn't have a clue who I was. But then he ripped open the wrapping paper and saw his portrait and his expression changed. 'Oh, it's you! You look so different, I didn't even recognise you! I love this photo! Darling!' He kissed me on both cheeks and then on the left cheek again. Was this a new kissing trend? I would have to make a note of it.

'Do you know Alexander?' he asked, introducing me to a silver-haired man in a dark blue suit. I shook hands with

Alexander and we both said, 'Pleased to meet you' to each other, without having the slightest idea who it was we were meeting.

'I didn't catch your name,' said Alexander in an accent so sharp I could have used it to slice tomatoes with.

'Lindy Usher. I'm a photographer. For *The Hoop*.'

'*The Hoooop*,' he boomed. 'Is that some sort of secret society?'

'No, it's a magazine,' I said politely. 'And what do you do?'

'I'm Angus's dealer,' he said and walked off to talk to someone more interesting – i.e. male – so I never found out whether he meant art dealer or drug dealer. Perhaps he was a second-hand car dealer. I'd never know. Now I was left standing on my own in the middle of the room. God, I hate these things. I shouldn't have come.

'Terribly brave of Angus always using amateurs,' a tall man with a shock of white hair and a stutter was saying behind me. 'Personally, I found it added an e-e-e-extra t-t-textual dimension.'

Angus was walking back over to me with Tania Vickery on his arm. 'This is the girl I told you about,' he said, pointing to me. 'The one who told me what a fine actress you were!'

I was so confused I didn't know what to say. I hadn't said anything of the kind. Tania was just as bemused as I was. We shook hands warily.

'Sorry, do I know you?' she asked.

'My name's Lindy.' I felt incredibly awkward. 'We haven't really met before.'

She was looking at me very strangely and then she noticed my silver dress. 'You were the girl at the film party last year, weren't you?' she said. 'Why did you say that to me about Nigel?'

'Oh, I'd just heard things,' I said vaguely. 'On the grapevine. Like you do.'

'Well, thank you.' She was incredibly sincere about this. 'And thank you for recommending me to Angus. This is such a tremendous opportunity for me. I don't know what made you do it.'

'I didn't really do anything,' I told her.

And that was certainly the truth. If I'd told Angus I'd taken a photo of my cat, he probably would have given him a starring role in his new play as well. Billy would be furious if he ever found out how I'd held back his West End career.

Tania had turned away to talk to somebody else and I slipped away to the bar to get another drink. Atlanta was deep in conversation with a man wearing yellow-tinted glasses and a kilt. I didn't know anybody here. I'd just say goodbye to Atlanta then slip out quietly.

'Are you having a good time?' I heard someone say and whirled around to see Nick standing behind me.

'Oh, God!' I squealed. 'What are you doing here! Nick!' I looked around desperately. There was no place to hide. I wanted the ground to open up and swallow me. 'I was just leaving.'

'Well,' he laughed. 'Pleased to see you too. Why did you ignore me when I saw you in the lift that time?'

'I didn't ignore you,' I said indignantly. 'I waved. Why were you laughing at me?'

'I wasn't laughing at you. Why would I have been laughing at you?'

'I don't know. No reason.'

'I saw your by-line in the *Independent* the other week,' he said.

'Yeah, they bought the piece I did for *The Hoop* on Natalie Brown.'

'Is that who you're working for now? What are they like?'

'Pretty good. I'm off to Crested Butte next month to do a fashion shoot for them. It's going really well.' And it's all thanks to you, I realised. For making me see I was chucking my life away at *The Ledger*.

'They were nice photos.'

'Thanks very much.'

'Yeah, I especially liked the one of her and her fiancé.' His green eyes were sparkling at me. 'It's funny, though – he looked just like your husband.'

'Look—' I could feel my cheeks burning bright red. 'I never actually said he was my husband.'

'I know you didn't.'

'So there's no need to go on about it.'

'I'm not.'

'Fine.'

'Fine.'

'Are you laughing at me again?' I demanded.

'Why would I be laughing at you?'

Actually, now that I looked at him properly he wasn't laughing at all. He was just smiling at me. I didn't know what to do so I smiled back.

'What did you think of the play?' he said.

'I thought it was very interesting,' I said politely.

'Did you? I thought it was the biggest load of bollocks I've ever seen.'

'Well,' I laughed. 'I'd have to agree with you on that. But the killer bees were good. I liked them.' Maybe it wasn't so bad seeing him again. 'Your hair's grown,' I told him.

'Yeah.' He ran his hand despairingly through his thick dark-brown locks. 'I've got to get it cut.'

'No, don't,' I told him. 'It suits you.'

'And your hair's shorter,' he said. 'Every time I see you, you just look better and better.'

'Oh, gosh, what a lovely thing to say. Thank you.' I suddenly felt rather tongue-tied.

'So where's your husband tonight?'

'I have no idea. We're separated actually.'

'I didn't know. I'm sorry.' But he didn't sound very sorry.

'Don't be. It's OK. It's just one of those things. I think it's probably for the best.' In fact, bumping into Nick was turning out to be rather a pleasant surprise. I marvelled all over again at his haunting green eyes. His creamy skin. I hadn't forgotten how good looking he was – I'd just filed the information away somewhere and now it was all flooding back to me. He did look nice in those Levis.

'Not working tonight?' he asked.

'No. Angus invited me. I photographed him for *The Hoop* a few months ago. What about you? Where's your camera?'

'This is just a social thing. A friend of mine's in the play.'

I glanced jealously over to see who he was looking at. He didn't fool me with that 'friend' routine. Whenever men say 'friend' they always mean girl. Which of the scantily clad cheerleaders in the chorus was he referring to? Which one of them was his new girlfriend? Tania Vickery caught his eye and gave him a little smile.

'Oh,' I said. 'I didn't realise you were a friend of Tania Vickery.'

'Yeah. We've been mates since college. Since before she was famous. She's beside herself about being in this play. She's always wanted to act, but no one would ever take her seriously before. You'd understand why if you ever met her. God knows what made Angus Rawle think of her – it was a pretty mad idea, casting her and Nigel in this together.' He leaned forward and whispered in my ear, 'He's her new bloke, but don't tell anyone.'

I felt giddy with shock. I needed something to calm my nerves. 'I don't suppose I could steal a cigarette, could I?' I asked.

Nick clapped his pockets and shrugged. 'Sorry,' he said. 'I gave up. New Year's resolution. Two weeks now without a fag.'

'Good for you,' I said. 'Perhaps I'll just have another glass of champagne, then.'

Nick picked up a glass from the bar behind us, and took a sip. 'You be careful now,' he said seriously as he handed me the glass. 'I remember what happened the last time we shared a glass of champagne.' There was just the flicker of a smile in his green eyes as they met mine.

'I'll be careful,' I said and held his gaze. Just for a second. Just long enough. I remembered the first time I had looked at him like this. It was only a few months but it seemed like a lifetime ago. And then just a heart-beat ago.

'I was kissing you and then you ran off into the night back to your husband,' he reminded me.

'I remember,' I said.

'So, you'll have to promise me you won't do that again.' He reached up and ever so softly pushed back a strand of hair that had fallen onto my cheek.

'I won't,' I promised.

And I'm a girl who always keeps her promises.